Taming Tessa

"I appreciate you seeing me on such short notice," he began, then stopped abruptly. Instead of the country squire he'd expected, he found himself facing a vision of loveliness with shoulder-length curls the color of honey and a trim figure shown off to advantage in a pale yellow day dress.

"I'm sorry, my lord, but my father is unable to receive visitors," she said as she reached the ground floor. "I have sent for Mr. Emery so that you may discuss your business with him."

He blinked. This was none other than the young woman in breeches who had come to his rescue the night before, for all she looked quite different properly clad in a gown. The sudden shock in her brown eyes showed that she had recognized him at the same moment, though she quickly tried to conceal it.

Suddenly, this had become a most interesting visit.

BRENDA HIATT

TAMING TESSA

AVON BOOKS

An Imprint of HarperCollinsPublishers

AVON BOOKS
An Imprint of HarperCollins*Publishers*
10 East 53rd Street
New York, New York 10022-5299

For Bethany and Dawn,
who used to tame unicorns for me.

Chapter 1

Leicestershire, England
October 1816

"Easy, fellow, it's only an owl's shadow," Lord Anthony Northrup said as the horse he was leading along the deserted road shied yet again.

Already he was beginning to regret the favor he'd done young Ballard by purchasing this skittish hunter from him, but he was careful to keep his irritation from his voice so as not to upset the beast further. Justifiably famous for his skill in handling difficult horses, Anthony had been sure he could handle this chestnut better than the inexperienced Mr. Ballard.

Perhaps leading him back tonight hadn't been the best plan, however. His own mount was a placid, well-trained beast, unlikely to react to the nervousness of the new horse, but he'd underestimated the chestnut's spookiness. He'd be glad when he finally reached his hunting lodge with both animals.

For several minutes he continued without incident, riding Cinder, his gray gelding, at a slow trot through the gathering dusk with the new chestnut following on the lead. The road from Melton-Mowbray was mercifully empty at the moment, but Anthony knew that was unlikely to last with so many men arriving in the Shires for the start of foxhunting season.

Sure enough, a moment later he heard hooves approaching from behind at a quick trot. He glanced back and saw horse and rider silhouetted against the rolling fields that were fading from green to gray in the twilight. Slowing Cinder to a walk, he maneuvered both horses closer to the verge to give the other rider ample room to pass, in hopes of avoiding an incident with the skittish chestnut.

His hopes were dashed when a rabbit suddenly erupted from the hedge bordering the road, right under the chestnut's nose. Predictably, the horse spooked and reared, then lunged forward, dragging the lead rein across Cinder's neck. Anthony's gelding shied away from the sudden contact, dancing sideways even as the chestnut reared again, nearly pulling Anthony from the saddle.

One of the chestnut's descending forelegs caught on the lead rein, wrenching it from Anthony's grasp. Cursing, he vaulted to the ground to make a grab for the lead before the horse could bolt, but he was too late. The chestnut swung away from him, then galloped away up the road, the lead whipping behind.

With another curse, Anthony turned back to Cinder, but before he could remount to give chase, the other rider swept past him at a gallop, already in pursuit of the chestnut. Vaulting into the saddle, Anthony followed. He hadn't seen the fellow's face, but assumed it must be someone he knew, to spring so quickly to his assistance.

He and Cinder galloped only a furlong or so before reaching their quarry, for the chestnut had somehow managed to tangle his reins in the thick hedge that lined the road. Unfortunately, the horse was in full panic, bucking and kicking at the hedge, tangling the reins even more tightly as he whinnied with rising hysteria.

The other rider dismounted and took a couple of cautious steps toward the frightened beast. Judging by his stature, Anthony realized he could be no more than a lad.

"You'd best stay clear," Anthony said, dismounting as well. "He's in the devil's own temper and could do you an injury."

"Nonsense," came the reply.

Anthony stared, for the voice was undeniably feminine, despite the fact that the rider had been riding astride and wore breeches. Before he could process this remarkable anomaly, she took another step toward the panicked chestnut, leaving her roan mare standing quietly.

"Come then," she said soothingly, "what seems to be the trouble?"

To Anthony's amazement, the horse instantly stopped kicking and stood, trembling, with his ears pitched forward.

The woman continued to approach the still jittery chestnut. "There, now. It's not so bad, is it? Look at what you've done to yourself," she said to the horse in a singsong lilt that seemed to hold the beast's complete attention.

A moment later she had the lead in one hand and with the other deftly untangled the reins from the hedge. When she laid one small hand on the horse's neck, he gave a great shudder, then stopped trembling. Ducking his head, he turned to nuzzle her ear.

Smiling, she patted the chestnut's nose, and Anthony just caught her whisper, "I miss you, too, Zephyr." Then she turned and said aloud, "I don't think he'll give you any more trouble, sir," and handed him the lead.

Anthony had been watching in amazement, but now he thought he understood why the horse had responded to her. "Thank you. You seem to have—"

He paused, for the rising moon gave him his first good look at her face—and a lovely face it was, framed by a few honey-brown curls that had escaped her riding cap. The breeches outlined a fine pair of legs, causing his thoughts to veer down a totally different path.

"Horses like me," she said simply, clearly not realizing he'd heard her whispered comment to the chestnut.

Her dark eyes met his, and a spark of sympathy, of connection, passed between them. Anthony felt something deep inside him stir in response. Lust, of course. He was long familiar with that feeling. Anything beyond that was doubtless only the result of the moonlit setting and the unusual events just past.

"So it would appear," he finally replied. Shaking off his bemusement, Anthony managed a grin. "And I can't say that I blame them, Miss—?"

To his disappointment, she did not supply a name. "I'll be on my way, then," was all she said. With a fluid motion, she was back in her saddle and a moment later was cantering away down the road at a pace he had no hope of matching with two horses to manage.

He watched her appreciatively until she was too far away to see clearly, then turned to remount Cinder and continue his brief journey, still bemused by the mystery of the beauty in breeches. Her accent had not been that of some local farmer's daughter. Was she perhaps the pampered mistress of some gent here for the hunting season?

Anthony received a generous allowance from his father, the Duke of Marland, as well as a quarterly stipend from the army, where he'd attained the rank of major during the recent wars. Maybe the breech-clad beauty could be lured away from her protector. But no—if she was familiar with the horse, it was more likely she lived somewhere in the area. Besides, her manner hadn't been at all flirtatious—nothing like that of a Cyprian.

Busy with such thoughts, he didn't realize until he reached his hunting box that she'd been right about the chestnut. He'd given no further trouble. What had she called him? Zephyr? Ballard hadn't mentioned the horse's name, but he had no doubt that was it. He'd ask Ballard about it tomorrow.

Handing both horses over to a waiting groom, he warned him about the new gelding's skittishness. The man looked skeptical, given the chestnut's current placidity.

Anthony just shrugged, then turned to the house, one of the larger hunting boxes in the area, boasting six large bedrooms and a generous dining room. The half-timbered house had been left him by his great-uncle, an avid sportsman who had taught Anthony most of what he knew about hunting. Great-uncle Alden would be pleased, Anthony thought, to know his former hunting box now housed the Odd Sock Hunt Club, second in consequence in the Shires only to Melton's Old Club.

"About time you returned," he was greeted by Sir Charles Storm, better known as Stormy, upon entering the parlor. "Rush insisted on holding dinner for you, and I'm famished."

Anthony turned to Ryan Dean, Earl of Rushford, with a grin. "Good of you, Rush, but not really necessary. I'd no idea Ballard's beast would be so much trouble. That's what delayed me." He threw himself into an overstuffed armchair near the fire.

"Horse was a bad deal, then?" massive Grant Turpin, lounging opposite him, asked sympathetically. "That's what comes of doing favors for striplings. Warned you against that."

Anthony grinned, knowing his imposing friend would have done the same, for Thor, as he was known to his intimates, was a notoriously soft touch. "Yes, you did, but I knew I could handle the brute better than young Ballard. He's a damnably skittish thing, though. Starts at his own shadow. Or did, until—" He broke off, suddenly reluctant to mention the girl who'd come to his rescue.

"Doesn't sound like much of a hunter, though you'll set him right if anyone can," Thor said with gratifying confidence. "Is it temperament or training, do you think?"

"Too soon to know," Anthony replied with a shrug. "Could be a combination—"

"I say," Stormy broke in, "can't we discuss it over dinner?"

With a chuckle, the four men adjourned to the dining room, where they were joined by two or three other members of the Odd Sock Club. It was a jovial group, for among the requirements for inclusion were a lack of pretension and general amiability. Just now, everyone was in high spirits in anticipation of the first real hunt of the season four days hence.

Not until the roast beef was served did the conversation return to Anthony's new purchase.

"Where did Ballard buy that horse, anyway?" asked William Verge, Viscount Killerby. "There haven't been any auctions yet, have there?"

"Not that I know of," Anthony responded to the little bouncing ball of a man affectionately known as Killer. "He bought it from a local squire, a fellow by the name of Seaton."

"Seaton?" echoed Stormy from the opposite end of the table, where he'd been working his way steadily through the courses. "Of Wheatstone? Someone else had a bad mount off him last year— horse refused the jumps. Now, who was it?" He frowned and took a sip of claret in an apparent effort to jog loose the memory.

"Porrington, wasn't it?" offered Rush. "I remember him landing in a ditch when that new bay of his balked last year. Thought the dunking did him good, personally."

There were nods of agreement, Anthony's included, for Porrington was notoriously high in the instep. In fact, he suspected it had been Porrington who had blackballed Killer from the Old Club several years earlier, the event that had ultimately resulted in the formation of the rival Odd Sock Club.

"Perhaps I'll pay this Seaton a visit." If the young woman he'd met knew the horse, she might well be found somewhere at Wheatstone. "See if the fellow is making a practice of selling half-trained horses."

He remembered how easily the girl had calmed

the horse. Perhaps he hadn't made such a bad bargain after all . . .

"Good idea," Thor agreed. "We can act as though we're interested in buying and look into Seaton's setup. Could be Porrington and Ballard were isolated incidents, or it could be a pattern. I'd hate to see any other striplings like Ballard taken in, if so."

"It's not as though we've anything else to do, with the first hunt still days away," Stormy added.

Anthony had intended to go alone, but now he nodded. "Very well. In the morning I'll have another word with Ballard, then we can give Seaton's stables a look."

This suggestion was met with general approval, and the conversation turned back to the hunt and a spirited discussion of the season's prospects for good sport.

On her return to Wheatstone, Tessa Seaton was careful to ride the strawberry roan mare in a wide circle around to the back of the stables, well out of sight of the main house, before dismounting. If she was quick, she could return Cinnamon to her stall and get back before her father noticed she'd been away.

"How did she go, then?"

Tessa whirled, startled, to see her cousin Harold leaning against the corner of the main stable block. As usual, his hat was pulled low over his forehead, a piece of straw dangling negligently from his lips.

"Fine. She went fine," Tessa replied with a shrug. "I told you she would." Regret tugged at her, for she'd already become rather fond of Cinnamon. It was foolish, since the horse had been bought for resale.

Her cousin nodded. "With those lines, I'm betting we can get a monkey for her once the hunt begins."

Tessa frowned. "I doubt she's worth five hundred pounds, though she is better-tempered than most of our beasts." She refrained from pointing out that the pervasive temperament problems were a direct result of Harold's inept training.

"She jumps well," she continued, "but she's not as fast as most huntsmen would prefer. Perhaps with another season's conditioning—"

"What the devil difference does it make?" Harold interrupted. "She's worth whatever someone will pay. Nimbus is flashier, though, so we should show him in the first hunt. He'll fetch even more, I'd wager."

"Nimbus? He's not ready. We've only had him since August, and he's not shed most of his bad habits yet. He bit two stable lads last week, and kicked Rambler the week before that."

"The stable lads won't be riding him. You will."

"Me?" she echoed in amazement. "In the hunt, do you mean? Papa will never allow it." Sir George Seaton had very definite views on what constituted proper behavior for his daughter, and riding to hunt—or too much riding at all, for that matter—was not a part of it.

"Leave that to my father," Harold said with a smirk. "Your mother used to ride in the hunt, you know, and Sir George with her. He never objected to that."

Tessa shook her head. "That was different. If Papa could ride with me, perhaps—" But her father hadn't been able to sit a horse for six years, not since the hunting accident that had permanently crippled him.

"Father will be riding with you," Harold said. "He'll have to be there anyway, to negotiate the sale afterward."

Harold's father, Mercer Emery, brother to Tessa's late mother, had taken over management of Wheatstone shortly after Sir George's accident. Tessa had been sixteen at the time, and in no position to object, particularly as her father had remained bedridden for several months.

When Sir George recovered enough to take an interest in the estate again, Uncle Mercer confided to Tessa that Sir George's heart had been affected by his accident, making any sort of upset or exertion dangerous for him. He also informed Tessa that Wheatstone's finances were in far worse shape than her father had known, and that discovering the truth might be enough of a shock to kill him.

Tessa often regretted the decision she'd made then to help her uncle conceal the true state of Wheatstone from her father. The estate had continued to deteriorate over the years, until now they were living month to month, forced to buy and resell horses to supplement the meager rents from their tenants. It seemed clear that her uncle was no better an estate manager than his son was a horse trainer, but after six years, there was little she could do about it.

"Even if we can convince Papa to let me ride, Nimbus isn't trained for the hunt," she argued now. "His manners around other horses are atrocious."

Harold's mouth twisted for a moment with something that might have been bitterness, but then he smiled and put a hand on Tessa's arm. "He's gentle enough under you, just as they all are."

What he said was true enough, for Tessa had a special way with horses, just as her mother used to. A gift, she supposed. Though he fancied himself a horse trainer, it was a gift Harold, unfortunately, did not possess.

Nor did his father. That had been painfully clear last year when Uncle Mercer had ridden in the hunt. The horses had performed creditably only because Tessa had calmed them immediately before the runs. She didn't doubt that they would perform far better with her actually riding them. Still, did she dare agree?

"Uncle Mercer got Nimbus for a song because he was barely broken," she said, stepping away from Harold's touch. "Even if we invest another year in his training, he'll make a tidy profit when sold. There are drawbacks to selling too early. Remember Zephyr, that skittish chestnut we sold to Mr. Ballard a few weeks ago? Apparently he's already sold him to someone else."

She paused, remembering how handsome that someone else had been—easily the handsomest man she'd ever seen.

"What's that to us?" her cousin said. "We made a nice bit off that sale, enough to fix that leaning chimney you've been fretting about. Oh, that reminds me—Father mentioned today that the west wing roof is beginning to leak."

Tessa stifled an unladylike curse. Roof repairs would not only be expensive, they'd be as difficult to hide from her father as the chimney repairs would be. There was no denying the estate needed money, however she might dislike the means of getting it.

"If we get a reputation for selling half-broken horses, it could harm future sales," she felt obliged to point out.

"All the more reason to sell as many horses as quickly as we can," Harold retorted. "We've enough beasts to unload this season to lay some money by against the future."

When she still hesitated, Harold added, "I'm thinking you'd rather I not let anything slip to Sir George about these evening rides—and what you wear for them." He nodded significantly at her breeches. "No knowing what it might do to that bad heart of his."

"But it was you who—never mind." Tessa turned away before her temper got the better of her, handing Cinnamon's reins to a too-interested stable lad. "I must get back to the house."

Her cousin had suggested that she do some riding astride, so that the horses wouldn't be solely used to a sidesaddle. It would be just like him to use it against her, however, with no regard for what it might do to her father's health.

Without another glance at her cousin, she strode toward the back of the manor house. Entering by the kitchens, she could reach her own chamber without her father seeing her, for he could not negotiate the stairs in his chair. It was how she always escaped his notice, but tonight she felt guiltier about it, for some reason.

Perhaps it was because of her encounter with that gentleman leading Zephyr, she mused as she nodded to the kitchen staff, who were well used to seeing her arrive in breeches just before dinnertime. It had been foolish of her to come to his aid dressed like this, but when she had recognized Zephyr, she had felt an obligation, both to the man and to the horse.

Hurrying up the back stairs, she shook her head fiercely. Obligation or no, it had been stupid. Should the gentleman find out who she was, and word somehow get back to Papa, it would upset him far worse than anything Harold might say.

Sir George set great store on Tessa being accepted by the surrounding gentry in a way her mother, the daughter of his own father's horse trainer, had never been. Tessa cared little for the opinions of their neighbors, but as it was so important to Papa, she tried to at least pretend, for his sake. If the Leicestershire gentry whispered about "odd Miss Seaton," her father would never know—any more than he would know about the leaking roof of Wheatstone's west wing. Tessa would make certain of that.

What would he say if he knew that her lifelong dream was to take over management of the stables, where she could use her gift to train and breed the horses with which she felt such a deep connection? Not that she could ever suggest such a thing to her father, of course. Though undeniably proud of her skill as a rider, he discouraged her from even visiting the stables, preferring that her mounts be brought to the door.

To spend more time with her beloved horses and to give them a break from Harold's "training," she was forced to deceive her father. Her cousin, no doubt aware that her work with the horses mitigated his own ineptitude, was willing to keep her secret, with the help of his father.

She'd convinced herself that any sale was a good thing, not only for the money, but to remove another horse from Harold's cruel and clumsy methods. Now, though, she couldn't help questioning the wisdom of selling horses before they were ready. But what alternative was there?

With a sigh, she signaled Sally, her maid, to help her out of her male attire and into a demure blue gown suitable for dinner with her father.

*   *   *

"Were you able to find out anything more from Ballard?" Rush asked Anthony as they and a couple of others cantered along the road leading to Sir George Seaton's estate the next afternoon.

"Not as much as I'd hoped," Anthony confessed. "He seemed disinclined to talk about the circumstances of his buying the horse. Only said that the chestnut 'showed well,' and he'd been mistaken about its temperament. I couldn't tell whether there'd been deliberate deception or if he's simply a wretched judge of horseflesh." He had discovered that the horse's name was indeed Zephyr, but saw no point in mentioning that now.

"I can't imagine how anything short of deception could have made that horse show well," said Stormy from behind him. "He's a nervous wreck, ruined by bad training or treatment, at a guess."

The others agreed, for they had all paid a visit to the stable that morning. The calming influence of the mysterious breech-clad beauty had not lasted the night, unfortunately.

"There's Porrington, too, don't forget," added Thor.

"At any rate, we'll know more soon," Rush said. "Here's Wheatstone now."

The four men slowed to a trot as they reached the long sweep of gravel leading to a fair-sized manor house that looked to have been built in Elizabethan times. The house stood on a small rise, surrounded by wide lawns, still green, and dotted with occasional trees. Beyond the house they could glimpse paddocks and buildings that must be Seaton's stables.

"Fellow appears to be doing well enough," Thor commented as they headed up the drive.

As they drew closer, however, Anthony wasn't so sure. One chimney leaned slightly, and the roof of the ivy-covered western wing betrayed a noticeable sag. The main, central block of the house appeared solid enough, however, and as they drew up to the front steps, a groom appeared from around a corner, and a butler opened the oak and wrought-iron front door.

"What might your business be, gentlemen?" the retainer asked with an admirable blend of haughtiness and respect.

As they'd agreed earlier, only Anthony dismounted and stepped forward. "I am Lord Anthony Northrup, come to speak to Sir George Seaton," he said. "I may be interested in purchasing a horse from him."

"And we'll just nip down and take a look at the stables," Rush added, he and the others turning their horses' heads in that direction.

The butler looked alarmed. "Gentlemen, please! If you'll just—" But Anthony's friends had already kicked their mounts to a trot and a moment later disappeared around the corner of the house.

Anthony turned to the distressed butler with a smile. "Don't worry, my good fellow. They know their way around a stable and won't alarm the horses. And now, if you'll announce me to your master?"

He still appeared upset, lending weight to Anthony's suspicions about the stables. "I'm sorry, my lord, but Sir George is rarely at home to visitors. His man of business, Mr. Emery, handles all transactions."

"Nevertheless, I should like to speak with Sir George himself, if that is at all possible." Why should the baronet leave such matters to his steward? That was rather unusual. In any event, if this Mr. Emery was selling inferior horseflesh, Sir George needed to be made aware of it.

Something in his tone apparently convinced the butler that further argument was pointless. "Very well, my lord. If you will step inside, I shall discover whether Sir George is able to receive you today."

He left Anthony to wait in the parqueted entry hall, where he amused himself by examining his surroundings. These presented a curious mixture of shabbiness and elegance, as though taste outstripped the money necessary to fully implement it. Faded draperies were artistically looped above the long side windows which illuminated two lovely Grecian urns in shallow alcoves. Closer inspection, however, revealed that one of those urns had been cracked and carefully repaired.

Before Anthony could form a hypothesis to account for these anomalies, he heard quick footsteps coming down the staircase. He turned.

"I appreciate you seeing me on such short notice," he began, then stopped abruptly. Instead of the country squire he'd expected, he found himself facing a vision of loveliness with shoulder-length curls the color of honey and a trim figure shown off to advantage in a pale yellow day dress.

"I'm sorry, my lord, but my father is unable to receive visitors," she said as she reached the ground floor. "I have sent for Mr. Emery so that you may discuss your business with him."

He blinked. This was none other than the young woman in breeches who had come to his rescue the night before, for all she looked quite different properly clad in a gown. The sudden shock in her brown eyes showed that she had recognized him at the same moment, though she quickly tried to conceal it.

Suddenly, this had become a most interesting visit.

Chapter 2

"I hear voices. Is someone here?" came a voice from upstairs.

With an obvious effort, the young lady pulled her gaze away from Anthony's and moved toward the stairs. "It's just someone here on business, Papa," she called back. "You need not trouble yourself about it."

"Nonsense. I've nothing better to do just now. Show him up," came her father's reply.

She bit her lip, clearly hesitant, then turned back to Anthony. "Follow me. But pray, say nothing about—"

He responded with a half smile that made her eyes widen. "I have no idea to what you refer, Miss . . . Seaton?"

With a curt nod, she turned her back on him and preceded him up the stairs and into a cluttered study. Papers and books were piled on tables and the floor, though a wide path had been left from the door to the window, and along the low bookshelves lining the room.

"Papa, this is Lord Anthony Northrup," said Miss Seaton. "He has expressed an interest in purchasing a horse from us." She shot Anthony one last warning glance before stepping back.

"Thank you for seeing me, Sir George," Anthony greeted the man seated in an armchair on the far side of the room. "With the hunt to begin in only a few days, I fear I gambled on my reception rather than make an appointment, as I should have done." He stepped forward as he spoke, his hand extended.

"You will forgive me, I know, for not rising," his host said mildly, with a glance downward.

Following the glance, Anthony saw with a start that the armchair had large wheels attached, with smaller wheels fitted to those, within reach of the chair's occupant. Though he had never before seen one, Anthony had heard descriptions of the Merlin Chair, a new invention that allowed invalids to propel themselves rather than depending on a servant to push them.

It appeared Sir George Seaton was unable to walk or stand.

Swallowing, Anthony strove to conceal this second surprise in the space of five minutes with a smile. "Of course, sir. If I may?" He gestured toward a nearby chair.

"Please. You wished to ask about horses I have for sale?" Sir George prompted when Anthony did not immediately pursue his ostensible reason for visiting.

Before he could respond, however, Miss Seaton

stepped forward. "Pray do not tire yourself, Papa. Mr. Emery will be here shortly, and you can safely leave such business dealings to him."

She then turned to Anthony. "I should warn you that your friends who rode down to the stables are probably being sent to the rightabout even as we speak. Our trainer doesn't care for strangers watching him work. He can be quite testy about it."

Anthony raised a brow. "Surely that's rather—unusual?"

"He does an excellent job," said Sir George, "so we're willing to humor his quirks. He prefers to show the horses in the field rather than the paddock—says it gives buyers a better idea of their capabilities. Now, what did you have in mind? A hunter or a covert hack?" His eyes, rather listless when Anthony had first entered, brightened as he spoke.

Miss Seaton retreated, though with obvious reluctance.

"A hunter. I already have an excellent hack. I have a fine hunter, as well, but thought that I might attend more meets if I had another, so that I could alternate them." That had been his justification for buying that nervous chestnut from Ballard, to avoid wounding the young man's pride.

Sir George nodded. "A wise plan. I've seen too many horses ridden to ruin in the hunt."

"You—" Anthony stopped himself before he could ask the obvious question, but Sir George seemed to sense it anyway.

"Yes, I used to ride the hunt every season—was as mad for it as any of you young bloods, I assure you. In fact, that's what put me in this chair. It's not a safe sport, you know." There was more resignation than bitterness in his tone.

Anthony was impressed by his apparent lack of resentment. "Yes, I know. But many would say that the risk only adds to the thrill." He regretted the words as soon as he said them, but his host did not take offense.

"I thought the same once. Still do, I suppose. Believe me, I'd be riding the hunt still, if I could. But I forget my manners. Will you have some refreshment?"

"I, er, thank you, sir." Apparently he was not going to be given the opportunity to see the stables. He hoped his friends had managed a look before the trainer could intervene.

Sir George tugged the bellpull by the fireplace, hung low enough for him to reach from his chair, and a moment later a maidservant appeared, bearing a tea tray.

"You will pour out for us, will you not, my dear?" Sir George prompted his daughter, as the maid set down the tea tray.

Tessa moved forward obediently, wishing she could think of a way to send this Lord Anthony on his way without upsetting her father. What was he really doing here? Had he come looking for her? But how, when she had never given him her name?

"Have you discussed any particular horses with him?" her father asked her then.

"Not yet," she said, striving for a normal tone of voice when her every sense was focused on their visitor. Grasping at the one subject that gave her confidence, she asked him, "What qualities are you looking for in a hunter, Lord Anthony? Speed? Endurance? Or beauty?"

One of his eyebrows rose, and she instantly regretted that last word. She had been thinking that

Lord Anthony was the epitome of male beauty—a fine animal, in the physical sense—and it had just popped out.

"I hope I'm not so superficial as to buy a horse for mere beauty, Miss Seaton, though I'll admit it's a nice bonus in an otherwise exceptional . . . creature."

She felt her cheeks warming, but she refused to drop her gaze. "Speed and endurance, then?"

"I've always been partial to endurance over speed," he replied with a smile she could only call intimate. "It makes for more satisfaction in the long run, wouldn't you say?"

Innocent she might be, but it was clear he was talking about more than horses. Confused, she averted her eyes so that they could not reveal her unsettled feelings at this turn in the conversation.

"I suppose that might be true, for a long day's hunting," she said primly. "There is a certain cachet in being among the first in the field, however, is there not?"

There was a hint of laughter in his voice as he replied, "Oh, I always contrive to be among the first in any field, I assure you, Miss Seaton."

Shocked by such shameless flirting in front of her father, she retreated to business. "We have hunters with excellent stamina as well as speed. All are at least three-quarters bred, but with good depth behind the knees, which makes for excellent jumpers."

"Now, now, my dear," her father interrupted. "You know I don't care to have you discussing such things in company. We'll leave that sort of talk to Mercer, shall we?"

"Of course, Papa." She well knew that Sir George sought to shield her from any taint of trade, but Lord Anthony's impudent double entendres had clouded her wits. Harold had said Uncle Mercer was hoping to sell Nimbus after the first hunt, she mused. It might be amusing to see the handsome, polished Lord Anthony attempt to handle him.

But no. He had already apparently purchased Zephyr from Mr. Ballard. She wouldn't wish two difficult horses on the same man, even one who unsettled her as much as Lord Anthony did.

A commotion in the hall interrupted her musings, and a moment later old Griffith announced Lord Rushford, Sir Charles Storm, and Mr. Turpin, handsome, fashionable gentlemen, all—though Lord Anthony was easily the most handsome of the lot. They were accompanied by a visibly irritated Harold Emery, Mercer Emery entering just behind them.

Tessa's concern about Lord Anthony's motives quickly gave way to concern for her father. So much excitement could not be good for his heart. "Gentlemen, please—" she began as greetings were exchanged, but Cousin Harold interrupted her.

"These gentlemen have expressed an interest in your horses," Harold said to Sir George. "I could wish, sir, that you had warned me before sending them down to the stables. Such disruption is not good for the animals."

Lord Anthony spoke before Sir George could answer. "It's my fault, I'm afraid. I sent them down when I came inside. I'd no idea it would upset you, of course."

Harold's smile was more a grimace. "I'm not the least upset, my lord. It's simply not how we do things here, that is all."

"Then I must apologize," Lord Anthony replied, one brow raised. He seemed to be taking Harold's measure. Tessa wasn't sure whether that was a good thing or not.

Turning back to Sir George, he continued, "In truth, I did have another reason for my visit, sir. A friend of mine recently purchased one of your hunters and has had some difficulties."

A light broke upon Tessa, and she suddenly felt stupid for not seeing it sooner. Of course—Mr. Ballard must have told him where he had bought Zephyr. Lord Anthony's visit had nothing to do with her at all. She trusted he would honor his vague promise that he would say nothing of their meeting last night.

"Difficulties?" Her father glanced at Uncle Mercer. "Mr. Emery handles all sales for me, and his son, my trainer, is the one most familiar with the horses."

Uncle Mercer stepped forward, though he looked wary. "What animal did your friend buy, and when? Perhaps I can clear up any misunderstanding."

"It was a remarkably skittish chestnut, sold some weeks ago to a young man—a very young man—by the name of Ballard. He found himself unable to handle the beast, so I took it off his hands, as he was willing to give me rather a bargain price."

Folding his arms across his chest, Harold jutted out his chin. "I can't imagine what your young friend did to ruin a perfectly good horse in such a short time. There was nothing wrong with his temperament when we sold him, as Mr. Ballard himself surely must have told you."

Lord Anthony's eyes narrowed as they swiveled back to Harold. "Yes, he told me the horse showed well. But then, an animal will often respond favorably to a familiar . . . touch."

He glanced at Tessa, and her throat tightened with alarm. Surely he was not going to—

"A properly trained hunter cannot be dependent upon that for good behavior, however, or he will be useless in the field," he continued, turning back to Uncle Mercer, and then to her father, seeking their agreement.

"Are you implying that my training isn't all it should be, my lord?" her cousin demanded.

"Now, now, Harold," Sir George said soothingly. "He said no such thing." Then, to Lord Anthony, "I will stand behind any horse we've sold, my lord. If you feel your friend was somehow misled, then of course we will buy the animal back."

Tessa bit her lip. They couldn't afford to do that, but her father didn't know it. Before she could give way to panic, Lord Anthony responded, allaying her fears.

"That won't be necessary. My groom believes that in time the horse can be made useful, and as I said, I got him at a good price. But I thank you, Sir George," Lord Anthony said with a bow. "Now, we will impose upon you no longer. I'll be in touch about a hunter for myself."

Tessa relaxed. He was leaving, and had neither demanded money nor said anything about last night. But then he turned to her.

"It was an honor to meet you, Miss Seaton. Perhaps our paths may cross again sometime. You seem quite . . . knowledgeable about horses."

She dipped a curtsy, as much to hide her face as for propriety's sake. "Thank you, my lord. The honor was mine."

The moment the four gentlemen had gone, Uncle Mercer said, "Sir George, may Miss Seaton accompany Harold and myself to the stables? There is something we would like to show her."

Her father frowned, then nodded. "I suppose so, as long as she doesn't stay long. But wait until those young men are out of sight. It won't do to have any of them see her down there. It might not be perceived as quite proper, you know."

Then, turning to Tessa, "Well, this was quite a morning, my dear. So many eligible young men under our roof, even if they did not precisely come to call on you."

"I don't believe any of them knew of my existence before today, Papa," she replied, smiling in spite of herself.

"Ah, but they do now. You never would allow me to send you to London for your Season, but now, perhaps, you'll get your chance after all. I've never felt it right that a lovely girl like you should spend her life shut away in the country with her invalid father, you know."

Tessa dropped a kiss on his forehead. "I know, Papa, but I've felt it no sacrifice, I promise you. The whirl of Society has never appealed to me in the least." That was quite true, aside from the fact that they had no money to pay for such a thing. "I'm happy here with you, and with the horses."

He patted her hand. "You're a good girl, Tessa."

"I hope those gentlemen did not tire you too much, Papa."

"No, no, I quite enjoyed it," he said. "We should have callers more often."

Tessa smiled, but did not agree. "Now, I'm sure you'd like to return to your memoirs," she suggested.

"Oh. Of course. Of course." Turning to the nearest stack of papers, he began to rummage through them, his eyes already reverting to their usual vagueness.

* * *

"Sir George seems an upright enough fellow, for all he can't stand upright," Sir Charles said as they rode away from the Seaton estate.

"You should be smacked for that remark, Stormy," Thor declared with a shake of his head. "Still, I have to agree. Seaton himself seems an honest sort. That trainer of his, however . . ."

Anthony nodded. "I thought the same. Young Mr. Emery seemed overly defensive. So, what did you three discover at the stables?"

"Not a great deal," Rush admitted, "for the moment the fellow spotted us, he insisted we accompany him up to the house. When we reached the paddock, he was exercising a big bay—a pretty beast, I must say—while a few lads looked on. I'd wager that horse will fetch a pretty penny once it's properly broken."

"Yes, they do have some exceptional animals there, from what I could see," Thor agreed. "Of course, the Seaton stables used to be famous, so it's likely they still have some of the original bloodlines."

Anthony recalled that his Great-uncle Alden had mentioned the Seaton stock once, before Anthony had gone into the army. He'd completely forgotten it until now. "I wonder why we've heard so little about them in recent years?"

Thor shrugged. "I think the old trainer died a few years back. My guess is this new fellow isn't up to the same standard. Takes more than breeding to make a great hunter, after all."

They all murmured agreement.

"Well, it appears our little mystery is solved, then," Rush said. "I doubt, after today, that the Emerys will attempt to impose on any other greenlings—if, indeed, that's what they did. What say you all to dinner at the Swan tonight?"

"What did you tell that lordling that brought him running with his high-and-mighty friends and their accusations?" Mercer Emery demanded the moment they were out of the house.

Tessa stared at her uncle. "I didn't tell him a thing. Why should you assume I did?"

"Harold said you mentioned seeing him with Zephyr."

She hadn't exactly told her cousin that, but as it was true, she didn't deny it. "I merely helped him last night when Zephyr bolted. I didn't so much as give him my name, as I was in breeches at the time. Thank goodness he didn't see fit to mention that to Papa just now."

Harold snorted. "You must have said something, else why would he have come here the very next day?"

"Obviously, he asked Mr. Ballard where he bought the horse," she replied calmly. "I told you it was a bad idea to sell horses before they're properly trained."

"You know nothing of it. The gentlemen at those clubs auction off their mounts to the highest bidder after every hunt, and no one worries whether that day's ride was typical of the horse or not. Right, Father?"

Uncle Mercer nodded. "Your own father will say the same."

Tessa frowned. "That seems remarkably foolish. Most are educated gentlemen, are they not? Hunting is scarcely a poor man's sport."

Uncle Mercer gave a bark of laughter. "A rich man

can be as foolish as a poor one when he's drunk enough. These young bloods have the money to spare, don't you worry. Look how your Lord Anthony bought Zephyr off Mr. Ballard simply as a favor to a friend."

It suddenly struck Tessa that perhaps that was rather noble of Lord Anthony—or at least kind—but she knew better than to say so. Her uncle and cousin had always regarded anything that went against one's own self-interest as foolish. She'd argued that viewpoint with them in the past, to no avail.

"Speaking of those fine gentlemen," her uncle continued now, "I believe they will be our answer to convincing your father to let you ride Nimbus on Monday. It's clear from what he said just now that he'd like to bring you to their notice, and what better way than at the hunt?"

"But I thought—" Harold began, but his father silenced him with a quick shake of his head.

Though her heart skittered with excitement at the thought, Tessa said, "Really, Uncle, it just isn't done these days. Proper ladies never ride to the hunt."

"Ah, but Sir George lives in the past, and in the days of his youth it was not so uncommon. It's how he came to notice your mother, you know."

Tessa nodded, for she'd heard her father tell the story many times. "I can't imagine he'll let me do the same—though I do think it would be splendid if we could somehow revive the custom of women riding to the hunt."

They reached the stables then, and Harold signaled one of the stablehands to bring Nimbus out. Tessa thought the man looked nervous, and with reason, for when he reappeared a few minutes later, it was clear the horse was in even worse temper than usual.

"Having them strangers and their horses down here a bit ago has set him in a rare fury, sir," he told them as he and another man led Nimbus into the paddock.

His words were superfluous, for the horse was bucking against the lead, his ears laid flat against his skull and his lips pulled back to reveal enormous teeth. As they watched, Nimbus swung his head down and around to snap at the man on the right, who danced out of the way only just in time. The horse gave a half scream of frustration and tried to rear, but was prevented by the curb bit in his mouth and the martingale, which kept his head down.

With a sigh, Tessa stepped forward. "Here, give me the lead," she told the first man.

"Are you sure, miss? Even you may have trouble with him today. I've never seen him in such a temper."

"I'll be careful," she said, reaching out her hand for the lead. The man relinquished it and quickly stepped out of reach of Nimbus's hooves. Harold and Uncle Mercer, she noted cynically, stayed well back, on the other side of the gate. Just as well, since the two men tended to bring out the worst in the horses. Amazing that they shared her mother's blood.

"Now then, Nimbus, what seems to be the trouble today?" Tessa asked in the soothing lilt she reserved for problem horses.

As Zephyr had done the night before, Nimbus calmed noticeably. His sides still heaved and his eyes rolled, but he no longer bared his teeth or tried to kick. Tessa moved forward to place her palm against his neck. At the contact he gave a long shudder, then a sigh. Gradually his breathing slowed and his eyes returned to normal, the whites no longer showing.

Though she'd been able to do this for nearly as long as she could remember, Tessa never took her gift for granted, realizing anew each time that this was a sort of miracle she'd been equipped to perform. She was glad of it now, for clearly Nimbus was much happier than he'd been two minutes earlier.

"Would you like to use some of that pent-up energy in a ride?" she asked the horse then. "Billy, bring my sidesaddle, won't you?"

The younger man complied, but still looked visibly nervous as he approached the beast that had been so furious just a few minutes before.

"Don't worry. He won't hurt you," Tessa assured him.

Nor did he. Tessa continued to stroke Nimbus's neck, and Billy was able to put pad and saddle on the horse and even get beneath him to tighten the girth. Nimbus sidestepped a bit in protest but did not try to bite or kick.

"Thank you, Billy," she said when he was finished. "Now, Nimbus." She led the horse to the mounting block and jumped lightly into the saddle. Taking a moment to arrange her feet and skirts, she gave the lightest flick with the reins, and Nimbus obediently began walking. Another flick and he broke into a trot, then a smooth canter.

Tilting her face up to the wind, Tessa laughed, feeling herself coming fully alive, as she always did when she rode. Away from the horses, it seemed she lived but a shadow existence.

"Let's try a little jump, shall we?" she suggested to the bay, turning him toward the smallest set of rails in the paddock. Without hesitation, Nimbus sailed over the jump, so she set him at the next, which he again cleared without protest. After three more successively higher jumps, she cantered him twice more around the paddock, then gradually slowed him before returning to the gate.

Her uncle and cousin seemed to be arguing as she approached. "—ain't natural," Harold was saying. "I'm still willing, but—" His father jerked his head Tessa's way and he broke off.

"Looks to me like you won't have any trouble at all with him on Monday," her uncle said when she reached them.

"Perhaps," she said, "but you saw what he was like before. At a meet, there will be dozens of strange horses as well as men to set him off. Suppose he hurts someone?"

Harold spat. "He just needs a firm hand. Don't you, Nimbus?" He reached for the horse's bridle. Nimbus's ears started to go back, but at Tessa's reassuring whisper, they righted themselves, and he allowed the trainer to approach.

"Gentleness will do more good than your version of firmness, Harold," Tessa said as she dismounted. Nimbus was bound to behave better away from Harold's inept methods. Her thoughts went back to last night and Zephyr's near-catastrophe on the road. But he'd calmed quickly enough, she reminded herself, and hadn't actually hurt himself or Lord Anthony. She pushed the memory aside.

"Who's the trainer, then, me or you?" Harold asked, as he so often did when she offered advice. "Don't forget that my grandfather was one of the best horse trainers ever."

That much was true. Tessa refrained from mentioning that Staunton Emery had been her grandfather as well. "Yes, Harold, I know," she said placatingly.

Long experience told her that to antagonize her cousin was to risk his complaining to Papa—which too often meant a further curtailing of her time with the horses. She had far less of that already than she'd like, a mere hour or two a day.

"I'd better get back to the house." Already she felt the shadows closing in as she turned away from the stables, away from her one real source of happiness. She paused and looked back. "Uncle Mercer, I will ride in the hunt, if we can convince Papa."

Her uncle nodded, a gleam in his eyes, and Tessa continued up the hill, pushing away her misgivings. If nothing else, such a plan would give her far more time with the horses—and that was worth almost anything.

"Come along, Stormy," Anthony called from atop Cinder, his covert hack. "The meet begins in half an hour, and none of us want to bring up the rear, you know."

Sir Charles emerged from the stable on his own bay hack. "Sorry, sorry. Stirrups needed adjusting. First meet of the season and all that."

"Never mind your excuses," Rush said. "Let's head out. We've at least a ten-minute ride ahead of us."

A dozen members of the Odd Sock Club set their mounts at a brisk trot toward Quorndon Hall, spirits high in the brisk early November air. Anthony was almost bursting with eagerness to hunt again. Cub hunting and aimless gallops through the countryside weren't the same. *This* was what life was all about, in his view.

That his comrades shared his enthusiasm was clear from the rapid-fire chatter and bursts of song along the way. Soon they could hear the assembling Quorn: the babel of male voices, the whinnying of excited horses, and, over all, the high-pitched whines and yips of the hounds, as eager as the huntsmen to begin the chase. As they rounded the corner into the yard, the familiar throng of red coats and top hats greeted them.

"What ho, Smith," Anthony greeted the master of the Quorn. "How look the hounds this year?"

Thomas Assheton Smith, in his eleventh season as master, grinned. "Better than ever, Lord Anthony. They'll give us a good run, whatever the fox does. And we've three good coverts marked."

Thor and Rush rode up to discuss some of the finer points with Smith and one of his whippers-in. Thor, in particular, was keen on breeding hounds himself and always wanted to be up on the latest pairings and the pups they'd produced.

Anthony listened for a few minutes, then rode over to check on his hunter, Faro, which he'd mount once they reached the first covert. It was an unnecessary complication, he thought, for a good hunter like Faro wasn't likely to be tired by the short ride to the stand of trees or brush where a fox was likely to be found. However, it had become the custom in recent years to ride one horse to covert and another in the hunt itself. Cinder and Faro were both exceptional beasts, so Anthony had no real quibble with the practice.

Faro was just as he'd been when they'd left the lodge, so Anthony soon turned his attention to the crowd, renewing the few acquaintances he hadn't seen since his arrival in Melton several weeks ago.

Old Thripton, he noticed, was fatter than ever, and had a new, heavier hunter to bear him.

A flash of pink caught his eye and he turned to see that Lord Gryfton had a new mistress this year, mounted for the hunt, as usual. As Anthony himself had done in years past, the viscount made a point of keeping women who could ride, though some were better horsewomen than others. Last year's bit of muslin had been worse than most, refusing to even attempt any of the jumps, Anthony recalled. No wonder she'd been replaced.

Sight of the pretty blond in her habit recalled Miss Seaton, who'd never been far from his mind these past few days, if truth be told. Now there was a woman he'd pay money to see in the hunt, he thought. Not that it could happen, of course, since these days no women but the occasional mistress ever actually rode to the hounds.

Pity.

He'd seen only a small sample of Miss Seaton's riding, of course, and that in breeches, but there had been something about her fluid grace, something about the way she sat her mare, that made him certain she'd be a treat to watch flying across the fields, even in a sidesaddle.

Smiling at the mental image, he turned back to his friends—and blinked. There, at the edge of the yard, on one of the most beautiful bays he'd ever seen, sat Miss Seaton herself in an elegant purple habit. She was talking to Mercer Emery, her father's man of business, who was mounted on the same roan mare Miss Seaton had been riding the night Anthony had first met her.

Mr. Emery was dressed for the hunt, though his red coat appeared rather loose across the shoulders, as though made for someone else. He must have brought Miss Seaton to watch the Quorn start off, as ladies occasionally did.

Without realizing he'd done so, Anthony headed Cinder in their direction. He was only a few yards away when Miss Seaton saw him. Her deep brown eyes widened, and her color rose perceptibly as their eyes met.

"I'm delighted that you have come to see us off, Miss Seaton," he greeted her. "I hope you will be able to find a vantage point from which to watch some of the hunt itself, so that I can show off for you." He winked, mostly to see her reaction.

To his delight, her cheeks pinkened further, and she dropped her gaze charmingly—but only for a moment. Taking a visibly deep breath that made him notice how well-fitted her bodice was, she lifted her chin and met his eyes again.

"I expect to have an excellent view of the hunt, Lord Anthony," she said, "for I will be riding in it myself."

Chapter 3

Tessa could not help but feel some amusement at the shock on Lord Anthony's face. It helped to mitigate the nervousness she felt at being among more people at once than she'd ever seen in her life. She hadn't fully realized before how ill-equipped she was for socializing on this scale after living such a retired existence.

"You're riding with the Quorn?" Lord Anthony echoed disbelievingly.

"My father never allowed his subscription to lapse," she told him. That had been a welcome surprise, though it was money the estate could ill afford. "The master was willing to allow me on those grounds."

In fact, it had taken Uncle Mercer two days to convince Mr. Assheton Smith to allow her to ride, even equipped with a letter from her father. Only after calling upon Sir George Seaton himself had Mr. Assheton Smith grudgingly relented.

"How very forward-thinking of him," Lord Anthony said. "Or, perhaps, backward-thinking. Either way, I must say I approve."

Now it was Tessa's turn to be surprised, for every other gentleman who had learned of her intent had conveyed shocked disapproval. "Thank you, Lord Anthony. I hope that Nimbus and I will acquit ourselves well." She patted the bay's neck, striving to keep her own nervousness from infecting the horse.

"I've no doubt you will, if I'm any judge of horse-flesh," he replied, casting an appreciative eye over her mount. "What a handsome animal that is."

"Thank you, my lord," she said again. "We think so."

"And he'll be up for auction this evening," Uncle Mercer chimed in, speaking for the first time since Lord Anthony had approached. "Feel free to spread the word."

He nodded. "I'll certainly do so. Ah, there's the signal. I'll see you on the field, Miss Seaton." Touching the brim of his hat to her, he expertly wheeled his gray and headed for a knot of mounted gentlemen on the far side of the yard.

"I hope none of them gents will queer the deal for us," Uncle Mercer muttered as Tessa prodded Nimbus forward to join the field.

She paused. "What do you mean?"

"Three of them was down at the stables last week, remember? Nimbus wasn't exactly at his best just then."

Tessa frowned, her earlier misgivings nagging at her again. Remembering the leaking roof, she pushed them aside. "Then I'll just have to convince them they were mistaken, won't I?" Touching her heels to the bay's side, she directed him to a place at the rear of the others, alert for any sign of hostility he might show toward the other horses or their riders.

She still wasn't sure how her uncle had changed her father's mind. When she had first asked him if she might ride to hunt, her father had firmly refused, though there had been a certain wistfulness in his eyes. After an hour closeted with Uncle Mercer, however, he had all but insisted she ride, as though he had been in favor of it all along. Not for the first time, she felt vaguely disturbed at her uncle's influence over her father, even though in this case it had worked to her advantage.

Her performance today would determine whether she would ever ride with the Quorn again—or with any other hunt, for the masters of the Belvoir and Cottesmore hunts were also here for the opening of the season. She was therefore determined to make a good showing, her mount's temperament problems notwithstanding.

"What is Miss Seaton doing here?" Stormy asked as Anthony rejoined his friends. "Never say she means to ride to the hunt?"

Glancing back, Anthony saw that she and Emery were moving into position, ready with the rest to follow the master and his whippers-in to the covert. "So she tells me."

Rush and Thor followed his gaze, then both turned back to him in consternation. "That's the very bay we told you about last week," Thor said. "The one we saw in the paddock at Seaton's. I'd swear he wasn't even broken."

"Completely wild," Rush agreed. He looked

again. "Yes, it's definitely the same animal, for I noticed his left rear sock was shorter than the other three."

Stormy, after another long stare, concurred. "I didn't even notice the horse at first, what with the novelty of seeing Miss Seaton herself here, but they're right. He looks docile enough now, however, so perhaps we simply caught him on a bad day."

"Perhaps," said Anthony thoughtfully, remembering how she had calmed Zephyr on the road last week. "It will be interesting to see how they do in the hunt together."

"Aye, I'm thinking she'll be a treat to watch—if she isn't thrown," said Rush with a grin. "Maybe I won't ride so far forward today."

Anthony bit back a totally uncalled-for response. Why should he mind if his friends admired Miss Seaton? Kindred spirit though she seemed to be, she was really nothing more to him than an enigma. A very attractive enigma.

"Perhaps I'll join you," he managed to say lightly.

Mr. Smith set the hounds in motion then. Flanked by his two whippers-in, they guided the pack uphill, to the covert, just over a mile away. The hunting field followed at a distance, most riding covert hacks, with lightweight grooms mounted on their hot-blooded hunters. A very few rode their hunters to the covert, including Miss Seaton. Because no one else could safely ride him? Anthony wondered.

He and Rush allowed most of the field to pass them as they went, so that they could better observe Miss Seaton and her bay. The horse moved beautifully, without the slightest sign of skittishness. If he didn't trust his friends implicitly, Anthony would never have believed what they'd told him of that bay.

"Maybe Stormy's right," Rush commented as they approached the covert. "I can't find any fault with that horse today—nor his rider." He flashed Anthony a grin that made his hackles rise.

He longed to tell Rush to keep his eyes on the horse, but knew better than to open himself to the ribbing that would follow. "Their true test is yet to come," was all he said.

While those on hacks changed horses, the huntsman gathered the hounds and sent them out to draw the covert, a two- or three-acre stand of trees and thick underbrush. Anticipation rose to its height as all the assembled waited to see whether the hounds would find and flush a fox, or whether they'd have to change horses again to try another covert.

Long minutes passed, and Anthony couldn't help stealing quick glances at Miss Seaton, a short distance away. She looked tense, but that was not to be wondered at for her first hunt. Still, he might be able to—

The bell-like sound of the hounds giving tongue distracted him. They'd scented a fox! Excitement rippled through the fifty or sixty gathered horsemen. Then "Tally-ho!" came the cry of one of the whippers-in as the fox was spotted breaking cover.

It was bad form to override the hounds, so all held back until the pack was free of the covert and well in pursuit of the fleeing quarry. Then, with shouts of "Yoicks!" and "Hark!" by the younger, more excitable sportsmen, the field leaped into action.

Anthony felt the familiar thrill sweep through him. Oh, how he missed this, when hunting wasn't in season! He set Faro's head toward the center of the pack; those hounds had their heads down and were clearly hot on the scent, and would stick once the fox disappeared from sight.

So swept up in the hunt was he that for a moment he forgot to keep an eye on Miss Seaton as he instinctively moved closer to the front of the field. They neared the first hedge, still tall and shaggy this early in the season, as the field hands had not had time since harvest to layer it properly.

He thought to glance back then, and saw that Miss Seaton had passed most of the others as well, though Mr. Emery had fallen back. Eyes alight, face into the wind, she was flying along with the best of them. She was magnificent, as he'd known she'd be.

Angling toward her, he was able to watch her clear the hedge just ahead of him and she did so superbly, with none of the hesitation that might be expected of a lady riding sidesaddle. It was as though she and her mount were one.

The hounds grew quieter, and glancing ahead he saw that the fox had disappeared into the stubble of a harvested wheat field. The huntsman and whippers-in cast the hounds, and soon a clear baying told them that the scent had been recovered. Leaping a ditch and a low stone wall, the mounted sportsmen galloped in pursuit.

Anthony spared a quick look over his shoulder to see Mr. Emery's mount refuse the wall. Backing off, he set the mare at the wall again, and this time she cleared it, though now Emery was among the stragglers bringing up the rear of the field.

The wheat stubble gave way to a rougher fallow field, the transition marked by a three-railed fence. The hounds went under, as the fox had presumably done, and the master and whips over. The rest of the field spread out, some to jump the fence and others, less intrepid, to find a gate. Anthony set Faro at the fence as he always did, and saw that Miss Seaton was doing the same.

He couldn't deny a knot of alarm in his chest as he watched her charge the fence at full speed, but his concern was needless. The bay cleared the three rails as easily as he'd done hedge and wall, continuing on at a gallop on the other side.

Partway through the fallow field, the hounds lost the scent, allowing the rest of the hunting field to catch up to the leaders while they paused, as the hounds cast about to find it again. Anthony took the opportunity to ride close to Miss Seaton.

"First check," he said cheerfully. "What think you of your first hunt so far?"

Her shining eyes and brilliant smile answered him before her words did. "It's exhilarating." He couldn't help thinking the word applied equally to her. "What a shame that more ladies don't get to experience this."

"Perhaps you will start a trend," he suggested, admiring the color the wind had put into her cheeks, and the honey-colored curls that had escaped her tall, jaunty hat.

"That is certainly my hope. I fear most gentlemen do not share it, however." She glanced over at a small knot of older sportsmen who were glaring in her direction.

Anthony chuckled. "Their pride is pricked, that is all. They don't like to feel that they can be bested on the field by a lady. Those more secure in their own abilities will not feel so threatened."

As though to support his statement, Rush, Stormy, and Killer rode up just then. "My compliments, ma'am. Excellent run so far, eh?" Stormy said.

"Aye," Killer agreed, "even if this nag did refuse that last fence. That's a splendid beast you have there—Miss Seaton, is it?"

She inclined her head—regally, Anthony thought. "Yes. And thank you. Nimbus will be up for auction tonight, should you be interested. My uncle will be handling the transaction." She nodded toward Mr. Emery, who was only now joining the rest of the field.

Anthony raised a brow, for this was the first he'd known of the relationship. It explained much, he thought, recalling his original opinion of the younger Mr. Emery as well as the elder.

"Will he indeed?" Killer said enthusiastically. "I've had an eye out for a new hunter, as it happens. I believe I'll go have a word with your uncle now." He turned his horse in that direction.

"Don't do anything rash," Anthony called after him, mindful of what the others had said about the bay. Killer was a capital fellow, but not the best rider in the world.

Turning back, he found Miss Seaton frowning at him. "Do you mean to dissuade your friend from bidding on Nimbus?" she asked.

He shrugged, feeling slightly uncomfortable under her curious brown gaze. "I've never been in favor of buying a horse simply because it shows well at a single meet. I'll simply caution him to examine Nimbus for himself before committing any large sum of money to his purchase." He glanced at the others for support.

Rush cleared his throat. "Thing is, Miss Seaton, we happened to see this horse in your father's paddock last week. He seemed a bit . . . ill-tempered at the time."

"As I told them, though, we could have simply caught him on a bad day," Stormy put in. "Most horses have 'em."

"They do," she agreed with a smile that Anthony thought looked a tiny bit strained. "Surely none of you gentlemen think you would have trouble managing a horse that a mere female like myself can handle?"

They all laughed, but Anthony couldn't help feeling her line had a rehearsed sound to it. Before he could comment further, however, the hounds gave tongue and the huntsman blew several sharp notes on his horn, signaling the resumption of the hunt.

Everyone wheeled his horse around, and a moment later they were off again, flying across the fallow field and into the next. With the start the fox must now have, they were all but guaranteed a long, excellent run for the rest of the day.

Skimming across the countryside on Nimbus again, Tessa couldn't help feeling the hounds had found the scent in the nick of time. She'd been able to tell from Lord Anthony's expression that he saw right through her "mere female" ruse, and she feared he meant to call her to account for it.

Nor could she blame him, not really. Nimbus had improved remarkably over the past few days, as she'd spent more time with him in the company of other horses and people, but she was by no means confident that he'd behave himself without any influence from her whatsoever. Still, what choice did she have?

Father's readiness, even eagerness, to allow her to ride in the hunt, once Uncle Mercer convinced him, showed her how desperately he needed to believe that the Seaton family still held a position of importance in Leicestershire. To rebuild that position—or even a credible illusion of that position—they needed funds well beyond the rents, which seemed to cover fewer and fewer expenses every year.

At the next check, she was careful to keep her distance from Lord Anthony. She owed him no explanations, of course, but she feared that if he pressed she might say more than she intended. There was something about him that drew her, that tempted her to an openness that was unfamiliar to her after so many years of keeping her own counsel.

The third check was longer, as the fox had crossed a stream before heading into a rockier area that apparently held little scent for the hounds. While the hunstman and whippers-in sent the hounds here and there, Uncle Mercer approached Tessa, where she sat a bit apart from the others.

"This was a clever scheme, if I say so myself," he said. "Already three different gentlemen have expressed an interest in that horse. The bidding will be brisk tonight, unless I miss my guess."

When Tessa did not reply, he frowned. "What? I thought you'd be pleased, much as Wheatstone needs the money."

She managed a slight smile. "Oh, I am, of course. I'm, er, merely realizing that I'm likely to be sore tomorrow. It's been almost a year since I've ridden so much in a single day."

He grunted. "A hot bath and some liniment will cure it. If this goes as well as I think it will, you'll want to be ready to ride to hunt again in a few days, so we can sell this one as well." He gestured to Cinnamon, beneath him.

Tessa nodded, trying to shake off her lingering

misgivings. "I'm sure I'll be fine," she assured him, but then she saw Lord Anthony headed her way and wondered if she'd spoken too soon.

Her uncle wheeled away to speak to another knot of gentlemen, offering her no reason to ignore Lord Anthony's greeting.

"You seem to be holding up well, Miss Seaton," he said with a smile that made her hope she'd imagined his suspicion earlier. "I must say I admire your stamina."

She was abruptly reminded of that two-edged conversation in her father's study last week. "Thank you, my lord, though I was just telling my uncle that I expect I'll feel the effects tomorrow. I've not been used to such hard riding."

"It certainly doesn't show." His gaze was frankly admiring, bringing warmth to her cheeks. "Pray don't feel you must finish out the day if you are tired, however. Probably half of the men who started with us won't, you know."

She'd noticed that the only other woman in the hunt had gone back at the second check—not that she'd taken a single jump that Tessa had seen. She longed to ask who that woman was, but suspected from something her uncle had said that she was not quite . . . proper.

"Oh, I believe I'm good for another few miles, at least," she said, oddly anxious that he not think her faint-hearted. "And Nimbus here is barely winded." As soon as she said that, she wished she hadn't.

"So I see. He *is* a fine animal, however unpredictable his temper might be."

"His temper has improved," she felt obliged to say, hoping it was true. "We've not had him long—only a few months—but he responds far better than he did at first." That much was definitely true; he'd been difficult even for her to handle when Uncle Mercer first brought him home.

"Then you've had a hand in his training?"

Tessa stared at him, trapped. Her father was adamant that no one outside the family know that she visited the stables, nor would Uncle Mercer or Cousin Harold appreciate her confessing her assistance to this gentleman.

"I, ah, have ridden him quite a few times," she finally said. "That has allowed me to mark his progress."

He smiled, though his hazel eyes were again too perceptive. "Then I am even more impressed with how you are performing on him today. I would never have expected such riding from someone who wasn't intimately acquainted with his—or her—mount."

"Thank you," she said stiffly, refusing to acknowledge his implication. "I have spent more time with him these past few days, knowing I'd be riding him today." Papa had agreed to that, once Uncle Mercer had convinced him to let her ride with the Quorn. So much extra time with the horses was enough to make this enterprise worthwhile to her, apart from the money.

"Of course." His expression was knowing—perhaps even amused.

She met his gaze squarely, refusing to be intimidated or mocked, and sensed a subtle change in him as he returned the look. It was as though something, some sort of understanding or awareness, passed between them. Tessa felt her cheeks warming again but didn't look away, afraid that might reveal even more about her unsettled response to his nearness, his intensity.

The huntsman's horn recalled her to her surroundings. "The scent," she said unnecessarily.
"They've found it."

For an instant she thought she saw something like
surprise in his face, but she couldn't be sure, for they
both turned their horses at once to rejoin the field for
the next run. Tessa's heart was pounding, but not
from anticipation for the chase this time. No, she did
feel a sense of anticipation. It must be the hunt, therefore, for what else did she have to look forward to?

As the day wore on, Anthony found himself staying close to Miss Seaton. He told himself it was so
that he could more accurately evaluate her mount,
but he knew there was more to it than that. It bothered him, for he felt an attraction that went beyond
anything he'd ever experienced before.

"Infatuation," he muttered to himself as he
watched her clear a hedge that three quarters of the
field had elected to go around. He'd felt it before, to
a particularly alluring actress or even a fresh and
beautiful debutante. But it never lasted past a few
minutes' conversation, which invariably revealed an
empty head.

True, he'd had two—no, three—conversations
with Miss Seaton now, but it did not signify. He still
knew little about her except that she was a remarkable horsewoman.

And that her head was decidedly not empty.

A vague sense of self-preservation kept him from
approaching her at the next check, but it did little
good since Killer used the pause to discuss her
mount—and her.

"Amazing animal. Simply amazing. I must have
him," his diminutive friend was saying. "Gaston

and Bancroft are both interested as well, but I should be able to outbid either of them. Miss Seaton seems to like me, as well, which may count for something."

"Oh?" Anthony strove to conceal his amusement. "What makes you say so?"

"Every time I smile at her she smiles back. Not all women require height and broad shoulders in their men, you know," Killer replied, preening a bit.

"Not if he's got enough in his pockets," Stormy agreed, riding up to join them just then. "Since you're well padded there, that should give you a fighting chance with the fair maiden, eh?"

Killer frowned. Anthony felt like doing the same but restrained himself. "Miss Seaton ain't like that," Killer protested. "She's a real lady—anyone can see that."

He said it a bit too loudly, for Lord Porrington sidled over on his lanky dun gelding. "Where would a 'real lady' learn to ride like that?" he asked with an unpleasant chuckle.

Anthony had never cared for Porrington, but just now he found him more irritating than usual. "I suppose the same could be said for a real gentleman," he said casually. "Though that wouldn't explain you, now, would it?"

It took a moment for his import to sink in, but then Porrington scowled. "As for Miss Seaton, I've heard her grandfather was a horse trainer," he said with a sneer. "That makes her little better than the other females I've seen in the hunt, however much better she might ride." He headed off before any of them could respond.

"Guess he still hasn't got over that dunking he took last year," Rush commented. "Obnoxious fellow, isn't he?"

The others agreed, to Anthony's relief. He'd prefer not to be put in the position of defending Miss Seaton to his friends. "Killer, be sure you spend some time with that bay before bidding on him," he said then, as much to change the subject as anything.

"I suppose I can try," replied the plump viscount with a shrug. "But if a lady"—he emphasized the word with a glare at Porrington's retreating back—"can handle him so well, I can't imagine I'll have any trouble."

Anthony couldn't think of any other caution he might make that wouldn't prick his friend's pride, so he merely nodded and determined to take a look at the horse himself that evening, when Miss Seaton would presumably have gone home.

The hunt ended an hour or so later, one of the best opening hunts Anthony could remember. Against his better judgment, he rode over to Miss Seaton, who had indeed finished out the day. Not surprisingly, he supposed, she showed no desire to be in at the kill.

"It's all part of the hunt," he said, drawing Faro up next to her, for she was looking distressed.

She gave a strained little laugh. "I know. And I know foxes are pests, killing poultry and such, but this will never be my favorite part of the hunt, I fear. A noble beast that gives us such sport would seem to deserve a better reward."

"I've never thought of it like that," Anthony confessed. "If it's any comfort, I've been to many a meet where the fox has escaped in the end. No one seemed to mind, as long as we had a good run out of it."

"Thank you," she said, and her smile now seemed genuine. "It does help to know that the fox has a sporting chance."

Anthony was struck again by the beauty of her wide brown eyes, the smoothness of her skin, and the rich honey color of her hair, peeping beneath her hat and veil. "You have an affinity with more than just horses, I see."

She blinked, as though uncertain how to take his words. "I suppose so, though horses are what I've always been closest to. My mother—" She broke off and glanced away.

Remembering Porrington's ill-natured remark, he changed the subject. "My friend Lord Killerby seems determined to buy your hunter."

"Several others have expressed interest as well, according to my uncle. The final price may be high." Was she trying to give him ammunition to discourage Killer?

"He can afford it," Anthony said, trying to gauge her expression, "but I hope he won't be sorry."

She met his gaze for an instant, then looked away again. "Nimbus is an excellent hunter, as you've seen yourself today."

"With you mounted on him, at least." Was that a flash of alarm in her half-averted eyes? "Should he get a bad deal, I'd probably encourage him to speak to your father," he warned her.

He'd expected a reaction, but not the mixture of fear and anger in the face she now turned toward him. "I beg you will do no such thing! A gentleman stands by his bargains, my lord. But if there *is* any sort of a problem, I would ask that your friend come to my uncle, or to me. My father's health is poor, and I'll not have him bothered by such things."

"My pardon," he murmured, realizing he'd somehow hit a sensitive spot. "Sir George did not seem so feeble to me, for all he is crippled."

"No. No, I suppose not," she said, visibly reining in her anger. "It is his heart, you see. The doctor says it is not strong, so we strive to shield him from unnecessary upsets." Her lower lip trembled.

Anthony felt an overwhelming urge to reassure her, to offer her his help in some way, though he had no idea how. That lip looked so vulnerable, so . . . delectable. Firmly he checked that train of thought and wondered what else they might be shielding Sir George from. The sagging roof, perhaps?

His intense curiosity about her situation sounded another warning in him. "My apologies, Miss Seaton. I will direct Lord Killerby to speak to your uncle if he has any questions. And now, I see Mr. Emery coming this way, so I will take my leave of you. Dare I hope I will see you at another meet this season?"

She glanced quickly toward her uncle with an expression he couldn't read. "I hope so," she said, "though that will be up to the hunt masters. Good day, Lord Anthony."

With that, she wheeled the magnificent bay and went to meet Mr. Emery, who would presumably be taking Nimbus with him into Melton tonight, where any auctions and sales would take place. Anthony watched her go with mingled regret and relief, fully aware that he was beginning to enjoy Miss Seaton's company rather too much.

Chapter 4

"How are you, my dear, and how was the meet?" Sir George greeted Tessa upon her return. "Come, have a seat and tell me all about it. I've already rung for tea, as dinner is still more than an hour off. No doubt you are famished, as I always was after a good day's run."

Though she was already stiffening alarmingly, Tessa could not help smiling at her father's eagerness. "Will a brief summary do for now? I very much need to wash and change before dinner, as you can no doubt see—and smell."

He waved that concern away with one hand. "I never mind the scent of horses. It brings back some of the happiest times of my life. I assume from the hour that it was a good run today?"

"It was." She proceeded to give him the high points of the day—the various jumps, who refused them and who acquitted themselves particularly well, the terrain, the horses and the hounds. She did not, of course, mention the criticism she'd received from some of the sportsmen for her very presence.

"How I wish I'd been there," Sir George sighed when she finished. "I'm sure you were magnificent, my dear, just as your mother was the first time I saw her. Why, she could clear fences some of the boldest men feared to attempt."

Before he could wander into further reminiscences—all of which Tessa had heard before—she stood. "Now, Papa, I pray you'll excuse me until dinner. You may not mind the smell of horses and sweat mingling with your meal, but I'd prefer to have Cook's excellent dishes unadulterated."

The dreaminess left his expression as he focused on her. "And you're a bit sore, I see. Yes, a hot bath will do you good. I will see you at table, Tessa—and thank you."

She did not need to ask what his thanks were for. While listening to her account of the meet, he'd seemed more animated than she'd seen him in months—perhaps years. She'd wondered why he had capitulated so quickly when she and Uncle Mercer had proposed that she ride to the hunt, but now she understood. Through her, he could vicariously live again the glories of his youth and forget for a while the infirmity that prevented his ever hunting again.

Going up the stairs, eager for that bath, she could almost feel her bones creaking. Still, she would not trade the day she'd had for anything. Foxhunting had been more exciting than she'd imagined—the thrill of sailing over fence, ditch, and hedge, the gallops across the fields with other horses thundering alongside.

The frank admiration in Lord Anthony's eyes.

No! She mustn't dwell on that part, for that way lay folly and heartbreak. His practiced flirting made it clear he was experienced at the game. He no doubt found her an amusing novelty, a diversion for his brief time in the Shires, but he would forget her once he returned to London Society—which he would do as soon as hunting season ended. They all did.

Her bath was ready when she reached her chamber. Smiling with anticipation, she allowed Sally to help her strip off her mother's old habit, then her underthings, then sank into the blissfully hot water with a sigh.

Of course, Papa had been pestering her for years to spend a Season in London. But even if they could afford it, she would not follow Lord Anthony to Town like some lovesick puppy. She wasn't sure she even liked the man, for all he was devastatingly handsome. Besides, her lack of money made the whole matter moot.

Letting that brief, silly fantasy dissipate, Tessa picked up a cloth and began scrubbing herself clean of the day's dirt.

When Anthony and his friends arrived at the George for the first hunt dinner of the season, he was scarcely surprised to find that one of the main topics of conversation was Miss Tessa Seaton. Other than the occasional mistress, she was the first woman in a decade to ride with the Quorn, and that she had ridden so well was a matter of both wonder and resentment among those present.

"You'd think these fellows had never seen a

woman on horseback before," Thor commented to the others as they moved into the common room, which was thronged with men in the evening hunt uniform of scarlet lined with white. "Do none of their sisters ride?"

"Even your sister can't hold a candle to Miss Seaton on horseback, Thor, and you know it," Killer said to his much larger friend. "Though I'll grant you Miss Turpin is a fine rider."

Anthony nodded along with the rest, remembering when Thor's sister had petitioned to ride to the hunt last year—and been refused by both brother and father, in no uncertain terms.

"I can't help wondering why Sir George allowed his daughter to ride today," commented Rush, echoing Anthony's thoughts—and probably those of half the room. "That uncle of hers I can more easily understand, for he doubtless sees profit in it." He nodded to the group by the fireplace, where Mercer Emery was talking with a dozen or so gentlemen.

Partly for Killer's benefit, Anthony said, "Yes, he knows he'll get twice as much for that hunter because she was riding it today. I doubt he himself could have handled that beast at all, much less shown him to advantage in the hunt."

Thor glanced down at Killer, who was frowning suspiciously at Anthony. "I'll not bid on that horse myself tonight, even if he is one of the few fast hunters who can bear me. I prefer to know a bit more about a beast first—and did you note how Miss Seaton kept her distance during the checks? Did anyone else so much as touch her hunter?"

"I did, if you must know," Killer said testily. "Just after the meet, when Miss Seaton was turning him

over to Mr. Emery before she left. She didn't seem at
all nervous about letting me near him, for all you lot
want to read something nefarious into her motives
in riding him."

"I spoke with Miss Seaton more than once during
the hunt myself," Anthony felt obliged to confess.
"Her mount showed spirit, but no ill-temper that I
noticed, even when Faro was only an arm's length
away. Still, a horse may be different with every rider.
I'd insist on sitting him myself, were I interested in
buying."

"I'm minded to ask about the hunter Emery was
riding today," Stormy said then, gesturing to the
group by the fireplace. "That mare had pretty lines,
and might do well with a more skilled rider. She may
go cheaply after today's showing, too." He grinned,
and the others chuckled, for Stormy was well known
to have an eye for a bargain.

He led the way across the room, and the others
followed. As they neared the fireplace, they heard
Emery saying, "—not until after dinner, of course,
when everyone is here and has a chance to bid. I'll be
available for questions until then, however."

Several of those near him drifted away, allowing
Anthony and his friends to approach. "You've not
forgotten I'm interested, have you, Mr. Emery?"
Killer asked by way of greeting.

Mr. Emery, only an inch or two taller than the little
viscount, smiled. "Of course not, my lord. But, as I
was telling those others, you'll have to take your
chance in the bidding after dinner, along with the
rest."

"I have a question or two about that hunter, if you
don't mind," Anthony said then.

Mr. Emery's smile was almost too pleasant. "Of course, my lord. What do you wish to know?"

"Was he bred at the Seaton stables?" he asked, already knowing the answer from his conversation with Miss Seaton earlier. When Emery shook his head, Anthony continued, "How long has Sir George owned him? And from where was he purchased?"

"Nimbus is one of our more recent acquisitions," Mr. Emery replied, his smile now a bit stiff. "His sire was Equity and his dam Thundress, of the Preston and Littlebottom stables."

"*The* Equity, who won all those races a decade ago?" asked Killer, visibly impressed.

Emery nodded. "The very one. Nimbus is five years old, so should just be coming into his own as a superb hunter."

Though somewhat reassured, Anthony noticed that the man hadn't exactly answered his second question. "Then you purchased him from Littlebottom?" he asked. "Why so quick a turnaround? I'd have thought you'd have wanted to breed him."

"He was already gelded," Emery began, then looked off to the left. "Ah, it appears supper is being served. I'll speak with you gentlemen later."

Anthony didn't think it was his imagination that Emery seemed eager to escape his questioning. "It seems odd that a horse with such bloodlines would be gelded so young. It could indicate a temperament problem after all, wouldn't you say?" he asked his friends.

"Aye," Thor agreed. "I've known more than one valuable stallion that was gelded because he was too vicious to breed."

"Nimbus didn't show any sign of viciousness today," Killer pointed out defensively. "If that's why he was gelded, I'd say it worked."

"Perhaps so," Anthony said with a shrug.

"Let's go in to dinner, shall we?" Stormy urged. "We can continue this discussion while we eat."

As they were all hungry, this suggestion met with no resistance.

"—still say it's dashed odd," Sir Brian Olney was saying as Anthony took his seat next to the man at one of the long tables in the dining room. "Why is it no one had ever heard of her before today?"

"Porrington claims her mother was daughter to old Seaton's horse trainer," said John Bingle from across the table. "Word is, when his son, the current baronet, married her, the old man cast them off—then died a year later. Seaton's kept the girl close on the estate all her life."

"Can't think why," Sir Brian said, shaking his head. "Nothing to hide there, from what I could see. Quite a tempting morsel, in fact, even apart from her riding."

Anthony deliberately took a large helping of roast beef before speaking. "Bear in mind that the lady's uncle is here in this room. You wouldn't want to provoke any sort of . . . incident . . . by speaking too freely about his niece."

The thought of Mercer Emery challenging a Meltonian over Miss Seaton's honor was laughable, but Anthony's goal was to stop such talk before it went too far. Miss Seaton wasn't his responsibility, of course, but he couldn't help admiring her pluck. He had no desire to see her suffer for it by having her name dragged through the Melton gutters by men like Porrington.

"No, no, of course not," Sir Brian said, glancing

about with mild alarm. He was almost as unlikely a duelist as Emery. "Just curious, you know, as we all are."

Rush followed Anthony's lead. "Pretty and intriguing as Miss Seaton is, I confess myself more interested in the hunter she rode today. Mr. Emery tells us his sire was Equity."

That successfully diverted the conversation to horseflesh, and discussions of bloodlines and past hunts and races lasted for the rest of the meal.

After dinner, as the wine was passed around again, attention turned to business—specifically, the sale of horses ridden that day. The tables were cleared away, and the men moved about to question each other on the various points of their mounts. Killer, of course, made a beeline for Emery, with the rest of the Odd Sock Club behind him.

As before dinner, several gentlemen were asking about Nimbus and receiving the same answers Anthony had earlier. The bidding floor was established at five hundred pounds, but it was clear that the horse would go for far more than that.

After listening for a few minutes, Stormy spoke up. "What about the roan mare you rode today, Mr. Emery? Surely you'll start her bidding a deal lower than that?"

Mr. Emery glanced sharply at him, then smiled. "She's not up for sale tonight," he said, "though she'll be available soon, perhaps even by the end of the week."

Stormy looked disappointed. "Not for any price?"

"That depends," Emery said with a raised brow. "What are you prepared to offer?"

"I didn't see her take any fences, so I was thinking something on the order of two hundred pounds."

A few nods indicated that others thought this a fair offer.

"I'm sorry," Emery replied. "As I said, I'm not authorized to sell her tonight, though of course I'll mention your offer to Sir George. Yes, sir, you had a question about Nimbus?" he said, turning to someone else.

Anthony pretended to listen, but his thoughts had taken another path. "By the end of the week," Emery had said. He'd be willing to lay odds that Tessa Seaton would be riding that roan mare in an upcoming meet—after which Emery would be able to ask far more than two hundred pounds.

"Twelve hundred pounds?" Tessa echoed in disbelief. Uncle Mercer had announced the sale of Nimbus the moment he joined her and Sir George at breakfast the next morning. "But that's more than four times—"

"Well done, Mercer," her father broke in, just as her uncle sent her a warning look. "And well done, Tessa, for I've no doubt your riding helped Mercer to get top dollar for the horse. That should put paid to any questions about the quality of horseflesh at the Seaton stables."

Tessa, however, wasn't sure of that at all. By now, her calming influence over Nimbus had likely worn off. She only prayed that he wouldn't revert entirely to the unmanageable beast he'd been when they'd first bought him. Surely the time she'd spent with him the past few days would have *some* lingering effect.

"I hope you don't mind, Sir George, but I used some of the money to buy a covert hack that I thought could be increased in value with proper training," Uncle Mercer said then. "Harold already has it in hand."

Tessa's father nodded. "That was wise. We don't wish to deplete our stock by selling faster than we can acquire, after all. At least Nimbus wasn't of our bloodlines, so we're still fine there. How are the mares in foal doing?"

Uncle Mercer promised to send Cousin Harold up to the house later to give Sir George a full report on all the horses. Tessa supposed it was a good sign that Papa was showing so much interest, after leaving everything in Uncle Mercer's hands for so long, but she hoped he wouldn't tire himself. She also couldn't help fearing it might lead to his discovering too much about their financial straits. As for last night's sale . . .

"Who purchased Nimbus?" she asked, interrupting her uncle's self-serving monologue on how well he'd managed the auction.

"I was getting to that," he said. "Lord Killerby was the high bidder—a friend of those young men who visited the house last week," he added to Sir George.

Tessa's heart sank. After seeing Lord Killerby's performance in yesterday's hunt, she had no illusions that he'd be able to handle Nimbus. Surely, though, he'd have his own trainer work with the horse before attempting to hunt with him.

"Oh, that reminds me," her father said then. "I sent a message round inviting those young men to dinner after the Pytchley meet on Thursday. They seemed gentlemanly enough, and I realized last night how much I've missed hearing about the hunt."

"What?" Tessa stared at her father. "Papa, you know you haven't the energy for entertaining.

Think of the time away from your studies, your memoirs—"

Uncle Mercer nodded. "She's right, sir. As well, I must say I'm not certain you should encourage such intimacy, after the way those gentlemen questioned Harold's training—and the honor of this family."

"Balderdash," Sir George exclaimed with surprising spirit. "They quite understandably wished to discover more about a horse one of them had just bought. No doubt the man you sold him to was unable to give them as much information as they wanted."

"But Papa—" Tessa began, sure that such exertion would not be good for her father.

"It's done," he said. "Who knows? I may find I am able to entertain after all, which will open up all manner of possibilities—for you as well as for me, my dear."

She could think of nothing to say that wouldn't provoke further argument, but she remained convinced that this was a most unwise idea. When Papa found himself exhausted by the end of Thursday's dinner, he would realize that she was right.

"Are you willing yet to admit I was right about that hunter you bought?" Anthony asked Lord Killerby as they prepared to leave for the Pytchley meet.

Killer laughed. "Not a bit of it. Carter is making good progress with him already. Why, he didn't bite at all yesterday, and only kicked one other horse. I've no doubt I'll be riding him in the hunt by the end of next week."

The others chuckled, but Anthony only shook his head. The gelding had begun by biting Killer's groom, and had been trouble ever since. No other horse could be brought near him, nor was it safe for the grooms or anyone else to do more than feed him. True, Killer's groom, Carter, had managed to get a lead on him and longe him around the paddock yesterday without injury, but it had been touch and go.

Anthony glanced toward Nimbus's stall as they passed it, but the horse was quiet at the moment. He and his friends all mounted their hacks and headed off at a trot toward the meet, their grooms following with their hunters. Killer, of course, would still be riding his usual hunter, Firebolt.

"I'd recommend you stay well away from Nimbus until Carter pronounces him safe," Anthony finally said, in as neutral a tone as possible, so as not to ruffle his friend's pride.

Thor nodded. "Anthony's right. Remember, I'm willing to take a stab at his training myself. I might even buy him off you if he learns some manners."

"There's no need of that." Killer's chin jutted out pugnaciously—a comical sight, but his friends managed not to laugh. "I'll manage him well enough, you'll see. You'll all see."

Thor opened his mouth to argue, but Anthony intercepted him with a quick shake of his head, and the bigger man subsided with a nod acknowledging that Anthony was right. Killer had a decided stubborn streak, not to mention more pride than stature. More argument might prompt him to do something foolish in an attempt to prove himself to his friends.

"What think you of that invitation we received to Sir George Seaton's for tonight?" Stormy asked then, mainly to change the subject, Anthony suspected. "Frightfully decent of the old chap, I have to say."

"I'm surprised his daughter allowed it," Rush

said. "Did you notice how protective she was of her father when we were there last week?"

Anthony had thought the same thing, but only said, "I'd say Sir George is capable of making his own decisions. He seemed to quite enjoy our talk of the hunt when we were there before. Surely he must miss it, as avid a sportsman as he was before his injury."

The others nodded and rode on for a while in silence, clearly subdued by the thought of how it would feel never to be able to hunt—or even ride—again. Anthony, however, was wondering just how Miss Seaton figured into this invitation. Had she been behind it, or had it been sent over her protests—or even without her knowledge? Perhaps he'd be able to tell, once he saw her.

She hadn't been far from his thoughts since Monday's meet, even though he had not seen her since. He'd rather hoped she might appear at the Belvoir hunt yesterday, but she had not. He hoped she was not still sore from Monday . . .

They caught up with another knot of sportsmen on their way to the Pytchley, and he dragged his thoughts back to the present. What was the matter with him? He had no business mooning over Miss Seaton like some lovesick schoolboy. If anything, he should be angry at her for the role she'd played in encouraging Killer to part with such an exorbitant sum for that unmanageable hunter, Nimbus. He would say so, too, when next he saw her—tonight at her father's house, if not before.

"Ah, perhaps now we'll see what that roan mare is really capable of," Stormy exclaimed.

Anthony followed his glance and there she was, arriving at the meet just as he and his friends did, from the opposite side of the field. As before, she was accompanied by her uncle, Mercer Emery, and, as Anthony had predicted on Monday, she was mounted on the very mare Emery had ridden that day. Emery himself was riding a rangy brown gelding.

Though his every instinct urged him to ride over to her at once, Anthony resisted, determined to first bring under control the sudden acceleration of his heart and the inexplicable lift of his spirits. That she should have such an effect on him, and from such a distance, struck him as distinctly dangerous.

His hesitation, however, allowed several other gentlemen—including Stormy—to approach her first, and in a moment she was surrounded. Clearly, he was not the only one attracted by her unusual blend of spirit, competence, and beauty. Abruptly irritated, though precisely at what he could not say, Anthony kicked Cinder in her direction.

"—delighted to have you ride with us again," young William Jennison was saying as he approached. "I can't describe the pleasure you gave me on Monday, with your superb performance." There was a chorus of agreement from several others.

Miss Seaton blushed and lowered her eyes in obvious confusion. "I, ah, thank you, gentlemen," she murmured.

"Aye," Stormy agreed. "I must say, I'm looking forward to seeing you put this mare through her paces. I quite admire her lines, as I said on Monday." That last comment was directed at Mr. Emery, who was looking rather pleased with himself, Anthony thought.

"I also am delighted that you are joining us again, Miss Seaton," he said, rather more loudly than he'd intended.

Her startled glance met his, and her color deepened further. "Lord Anthony! I didn't—that is—thank you, my lord." With a barely perceptible shifting of her weight, she moved her mare forward, through the opening the others hastily created. Her uncle followed, now looking less pleased.

"I'd like to speak with you—with both of you," Anthony said before they could pass him, as they clearly intended to do.

"About what?" Emery asked with a certain belligerance.

Anthony coolly looked him up and down before answering. "About the horse you sold to my friend Monday night. It appears his temperament is not quite what we were all led to believe." His glance slid to Miss Seaton, who looked away.

"That auction was conducted fair and square." Emery was as defensive as his son had been last week about the chestnut Zephyr. "Are you suggesting otherwise, my lord?"

"No, really, Anthony," Stormy began, but Anthony silenced him with a glance. Stormy frowned, then shrugged and took himself off.

"I've no quibble with the auction itself," Anthony replied once he had gone, refusing to rise to Emery's baiting. "But I can't help feeling the horse was, ah, misrepresented beforehand." Miss Seaton still refused to meet his gaze, rather to his frustration.

"We did nothing illegal," Emery was quick to point out. "It's up to those interested in purchasing to do their own research and draw their own conclusions, after all."

Anthony raised a brow. "I implied no illegality. Ethics and the law are not always in accord, however." Then, turning deliberately to the silent girl, "I will be interested to see how that mare performs under you today, Miss Seaton."

Now she did meet his glance. "I've no doubt Cinnamon will do well, as she has a wonderful disposition—no matter who is riding her." There was a certain defiance about the angle of her chin.

"Indeed. I would not presume to doubt your word, of course."

"Would you not?" she retorted. "It sounds very much to me as though that is exactly what you are doing. How, pray, can you claim that we misrepresented Nimbus on Monday, simply because I rode him well? Surely you are not suggesting that any gentleman who calls himself a sportsman cannot handle a horse as well as a lady on her very first hunt?"

Anthony frowned, for that was exactly what he'd meant to suggest, though put into words it did sound rather absurd. "My apologies, Miss Seaton," he said shortly, then turned his horse and headed back to the rest of the Odd Sock Club.

Tessa stared after him, frowning—and seething. How dare he accuse her of deliberately deceiving everyone on Monday? She had simply ridden her best and left the rest to chance—and Uncle Mercer. And that money had already gone toward the absolutely necessary repairs on the west wing roof. Clearly, anyone who could afford to pay twelve hundred pounds for a horse had never faced such a choice.

It was all rationalization, though, and she knew it. "I warned you, didn't I?" she said to Uncle Mercer as her temper cooled, to be replaced by a degree of shame.

He shrugged. "Lord Killerby looks happy enough," he said, gesturing toward the little man. "I notice he hasn't said anything about being disappointed with his purchase."

Tessa tried to console herself with that, but she still felt uncomfortable—and guilty—both for her part in what really could be called a deception, and for reacting so angrily when Lord Anthony had called her on it.

With an effort, she thrust all such concerns from her mind, for she had a different job to do today. She had no qualms whatsoever about Cinnamon's temperament, so felt perfectly justified in making sure she appeared to best advantage and therefore sold for the highest possible price.

Termites had been discovered in the chimneypiece of the ground floor drawing room, and she feared more such unpleasant discoveries would follow as repairs progressed. And three fields needed draining before frost set in, or there would be no planting them next spring. She'd already discussed their entire stud with Uncle Mercer—and, reluctantly, with her father—with an eye to selling a few more horses this season to help make ends meet.

As Papa had pointed out, they could not afford to deplete their bloodlines, but she knew of no other way to raise the necessary funds for estate repairs and maintenance. She wished there was some way to hire a better estate manager than Uncle Mercer, but she refused to worry her father by bringing up such a difficult and potentially upsetting subject.

The signal to head out for the first covert came as a distinct relief from her troubling thoughts. Unfortunately, Cinnamon was so easy to manage that handling her gave Tessa no distraction from her worries.

Surely, though, the fences and ditches would do so, once the hunt began in earnest.

Alas, the first covert was dry, so the whole field had to follow the huntsman for a mile and more at no more than a trot to the next covert. While waiting there for the hounds to sniff out a fox, Lord Anthony moved within a few paces of Tessa, though he did not attempt to engage her in conversation.

After struggling with her conscience for a minute or two, she finally nudged Cinnamon his way and cleared her throat. "I, ah, wish to apologize for my outburst earlier," she said, softly enough that no one else could hear her.

Turning, he held her eyes for a long moment, causing an alarming flutter to commence in her midsection. "And I, for what I now realize was a foolish allegation. Perhaps—" he began, but just then the hounds gave tongue that they'd scented a fox.

Chapter 5

With a stab of disappointment he'd never before felt at the start of a hunt, Anthony turned away from what had promised to be a most interesting conversation to watch the progress of the hounds and huntsman. No doubt he would have ample opportunity to speak with Miss Seaton at dinner tonight, he reminded himself.

A few tense moments later, the fox broke cover, the hounds were rounded up and set on its scent, and the field leaped into action behind them. By the time they reached the first hedge, Miss Seaton had already moved near the front of the field, though the mare she rode now could not be as powerful as the gelding she'd ridden on Monday. Clearly, however, Cinnamon was far faster than Mr. Emery's riding in the Quorn had revealed her to be.

As before, Anthony noticed that Mercer Emery

stayed near the rear of the field, where his indifferent riding would be less noticeable. They were heading into rougher country now, country that would pose challenges to any who were not expert riders. Almost without thought, he worked his way closer to Miss Seaton. Proficient she might be, but she couldn't have much experience with this sort of riding.

The hounds wormed their way through the next hedge, which the lead riders discovered to be a "double"—a hedge with a ditch on the other side. Warnings were shouted back as the leaders recovered from their inevitable falls, and the field spread out, most looking for another way around.

Miss Seaton, however, checked only for a moment before setting her mare's head at the hedge. Anthony could only watch, fear rising in his throat. He had successfully jumped this barrier in the past, but—

The mare lifted, as if on wings, and sailed over the hedge, landing lightly on the far side of the ditch and continuing on without breaking stride. Gasps from the field were followed by cheers. Several of those who'd begun looking for a gap or gate set their horses at the hedge instead, unwilling to be outdone by a woman.

Anthony was the first to follow Miss Seaton. Though Faro landed heavily, he did not lose his footing or unseat his rider. Glancing back, Anthony saw half a dozen others clearing the hedge, all but one of whom ended up on the ground as their mounts stumbled.

He paused to be certain no horses or riders were injured, then urged Faro back into a canter behind Miss Seaton and her roan mare. Drawing level with her a few moments later, he called out, "My compliments. I could wish you hadn't given me—us—such a scare, however."

She grinned across at him, her veil flying in the wind. "Cinnamon can jump amazing distances, farther than most horses I've known. I see your Faro had no difficulty, either."

"We've had practice," he shouted back, above the thundering of their horses' hooves. Though it was tempting to take as much credit as possible in hopes of impressing her, honesty compelled him to add, "I've been riding this country for years, and have faced that double before. I didn't do so well my first time, I must confess."

She merely laughed—a wild, beautiful sound—and continued across the countryside. The two of them were now leading the field, and it was all too easy to imagine that they were alone, with the hounds and huntsman well ahead and the rest of the field well behind.

"Where did you learn to ride like this?" Anthony shouted after several minutes with no sound but the rushing of the wind, the thudding of hooves, and the squeaking of leather. He'd heard Porrington's explanation, but suddenly wanted Miss Seaton's own.

Her face was tilted into the wind, but at that she looked over at him. "Both of my parents loved horses and were excellent riders, so encouraged me to ride from an early age. My father claims I was riding almost before I could walk."

He found himself grinning. "My Great-uncle Alden used to say the same about me. He's the one who sparked my interest in hunting, when I was but a lad."

Their conversation was interrupted by a three-rail

fence, which both cleared without trouble, then came the hounds' first check of the hunt.

"So you've been hunting since you were young?" Miss Seaton asked before the rest of the field caught up. "Did you ever ride in a hunt with my father—or my mother?"

Anthony blinked. "Do you know, I think I did, though I wasn't acquainted with them at the time. I'd forgotten, as it was years ago, well before the war. Is your mother fairer than you are?" He dimly recalled his uncle pointing out a strikingly beautiful woman in a purple habit much like the one Miss Seaton now wore.

"She hasn't ridden in quite a long time, has she?" he continued when she nodded. "If she is the one I remember, I saw her only once, at one of my very first meets. I could not have been more than fourteen years old at the time."

"She died almost ten years ago," Miss Seaton replied, her brown eyes shadowed, "and had not ridden in the hunt for several years before that. I believe she only hunted once or twice after I was born, for it was becoming less and less common for ladies to do so by then. She contented herself with riding on the estate—and with teaching me."

Anthony nodded. "I seem to remember—"

"Miss Seaton!" Stormy's voice interrupted him. "I certainly understand now why Mr. Emery was unwilling to sell that mare on Monday. Alas, I fear that after today, with you showing her to such advantage, she will be beyond my means to purchase."

Sir Brian Olney sidled over on his chestnut. "I plan to take part in the bidding for her myself," he volunteered. "Emery does mean to offer her for sale, doesn't he?" he asked Miss Seaton.

"Yes," she replied. "Probably after the Cottesmore on Saturday." That would be the next gathering of the majority of the sportsmen in Melton-Mowbray.

"Has your father owned her for long?" Stormy asked then.

Anthony thought she hesitated before answering. "Only a few months, though I confess I have already grown fond of her."

"Then why—?" Sir Brian began.

Noticing the distress in Miss Seaton's expression, Anthony cut him off. "Sadly, business often leaves little room for sentimentality," he said. "Did any of you see Porrington after the tumble he took on that double? He was mud from the waist down."

The others chuckled and began discussing the advantages of knowing how to fall properly during a hunt. Anthony glanced at Miss Seaton and found her smiling at him with what could only be gratitude for his changing the subject. He smiled back, shaken again by the effect she had on him.

To his relief, the hounds gave tongue again before he was forced to analyze his feelings further. Glancing back, he saw that Emery was still more than a furlong behind, along with one or two other stragglers. The fellow really wasn't much of a sportsman.

Anthony couldn't help wondering if he was as inept at managing the Seaton estate as he was at riding to hunt. Perhaps at dinner tonight Anthony would have an opportunity to find out, with some discreet questioning.

It wasn't until the next check that it occurred to him that it was neither his business nor his responsibility.

The hunt ended only an hour after noon, when the hounds lost the scent entirely and were unable to find it again, despite repeated casting by the huntsman. Tessa was just as glad—not only because the fox had escaped, but because she'd be less sore while playing hostess for tonight's dinner.

It also meant she'd have more time to prepare. She almost hadn't ridden today, there was so much to do at home for their first dinner party in many years, but her father had insisted that the servants could handle everything. Tessa wasn't so sure, but when Uncle Mercer reminded her of how badly they needed the money from Cinnamon's sale, she had finally agreed.

As she turned her mount's head toward the road, Lord Anthony rode over to her. "I imagine you are in a hurry to return home, what with all of us descending upon you tonight," he said, echoing her thoughts, "but I wanted to compliment you again on your riding today. I hope we will see you at many more meets this season."

She smiled at him, startled to realize that she was almost looking forward to tonight's dinner party— though not to its effect on her father. "Thank you, my lord, but that will be up to my father. I confess I quite enjoy it, however, so I hope that he will agree to it."

"Perhaps we can encourage him to do so over dinner tonight," he said with a grin, as Lord Rushford and Sir Charles Storm approached, followed by Mr. Turpin and little Lord Killerby.

She debated cautioning him and his friends against tiring her father tonight, but decided she would wait to see how the evening played out. Lord Anthony seemed quite perceptive, so no doubt he would realize that Sir George's strength was limited. If not, she would simply ask them all to leave.

"Until tonight, then, gentlemen," she said, nodding to each in turn. As a man, they all bowed from the saddle, expressing their eagerness for the visit, and then she turned and rode back to where Uncle Mercer waited on old brown Thunder.

"Mind you don't get too chummy with the gentlemen," he cautioned her when she reached him. "Your father wouldn't like it. Most are only on the lookout for their next mistress, you know."

Stung by the reproach when she'd expected praise for her riding, she responded sharply, "My father invited those very gentlemen to dinner tonight, so I don't think it is for you to pass judgment on my socializing with them. I've neither said nor done anything improper."

She was not so certain she could vouch for her thoughts, however. More than once during today's hunt, she had admired Lord Anthony's physique as well as his riding, and even allowed her imagination to wander along paths that were far from proper.

"No need to snap at me, missy," her uncle said now. "I only mention it for your own good. Sir George did charge me with your protection, remember."

Tessa had to suppress a smile at the thought of Uncle Mercer trying to protect her from the athletic Lord Anthony—or any of the others, for that matter. "None of the gentlemen has said or done anything improper, either," she assured him.

Not entirely to her surprise, he looked relieved. "Glad to hear it—and your father will be, too. You rode well today, by the way. We should get five hundred easy—perhaps even more."

Though such a sum still seemed excessive, she nodded. "Good. We'll need it, for the workmen keep finding more that needs repairing in the west wing."

On reaching Wheatstone, Tessa went first to the

kitchen to be certain dinner preparations had begun, then hurried upstairs to see her father. He was in his study, as usual, a decanter of wine at his elbow and his notes spread out on a table before him. He appeared to be dozing.

"Papa?" she said softly, not wishing to wake him if he was deeply asleep.

He stirred at once. "Tessa, is that you? Back already, eh? It must have been a short run." Though he smiled, his eyes were bleary, either from sleep or wine.

"Yes, the fox eluded the hounds, but not before giving us a good race across the countryside. How are you feeling today? You look tired." She settled a mantle across his shoulders, tucking it in around the back of his chair.

"A bit tired, I suppose. I fear I didn't sleep particularly well last night. I so want this dinner to come off well, for your sake as well as mine."

"Pray do not worry, Papa. Everything will be fine, I'm certain, as long as you do not tire yourself unduly. I won't allow the gentlemen to stay late."

Sir George frowned. "It would be rude to ask them to leave before they are ready, Tessa, and I won't have that. You will be gracious, however late they stay."

"Of course, of course," she quickly reassured him. "I will be everything that is proper, just as you would wish."

He relaxed. "Of course you will, my dear. I never doubted it. And now you'd best go up and start getting yourself ready, hadn't you? Have a bath, put on your nicest gown, and have your maid do up your hair the way I like it. They'll be here in just a few hours, and, as I recall, it takes ladies some time to dress for a special evening." He was smiling now.

She'd had no intention of primping for Lord Anthony—or the others—but she would not upset her father. "I'll do that. Why don't you rest for a bit, so you will be fresh for the evening."

Dropping a kiss on his brow, she went to confer with the housekeeper and their few other servants. Uncle Mercer had gradually dismissed more than half the staff they'd had at the time of her father's accident, saying that they could not afford their salaries. As a result, they were now reduced to Mrs. Bealls, who did double duty as housekeeper and cook, two maids, one of whom acted as Tessa's abigail when not doing housework, one lad who filled the post of footman and general servant, and old Griffith, her father's personal manservant, who also served as their butler when necessary.

Tessa set them all to various duties, mainly in the kitchen, in preparation for the evening ahead before finally heading up to her chamber to ready herself for the coming ordeal.

After debating among themselves whether to wear London evening dress or formal hunt attire, Anthony and his friends decided on the latter. "Sir George made it clear he wanted to discuss hunting, so this will better set the mood," Anthony had reasoned, and the others had agreed.

The invitation had been for six, so the early November darkness had already fallen as they rode up the long drive to Wheatstone. Light glowed brightly from the windows of the lower stories, at least in the central block of the house. Fewer candles appeared to be kindled on the upper floors, and the two wings were nearly dark.

As the group neared the house, two grooms appeared to take their horses, though Anthony suspected from their youth that they were stable lads pressed into temporary service.

"Thankee, m'lord!" exclaimed the boy who took Cinder's reins when Anthony handed him a shilling. His enthusiasm implied that he was not accustomed to receiving vails for service.

The old butler, more polite this time, showed them into the house and up the stairway, into a sumptuously appointed parlor on the right. Sir George propelled his chair forward to greet them.

"Welcome, gentlemen, welcome indeed!" he exclaimed, his speech very slightly slurred. "We have quite looked forward to your visit, and hope we will make an enjoyable evening for you. Come in, do, and seat yourselves. We have time for a drink and some conversation before dinner."

As they all filled glasses from the decanters on the sideboard and disposed themselves about the room, Anthony took note of their surroundings, wondering if he'd been mistaken about the estate's lack of money. Nothing in this room, at least, looked faded, worn, or repaired.

"Will Miss Seaton be dining with us?" Killer asked as he sat near the crackling fire, saving Anthony from voicing the question.

"Indeed, she should be joining us at any moment," Sir George replied, beaming. "Made an impression on you, has my Tessa? Quite the rider, my daughter—much like her mother before her."

They all voiced agreement, and Rush said, "Yes, she's the admiration of the Quorn, sir, and now the Pytchley as well."

Sir George's smile dimmed slightly. "She's not

drawing too much attention to herself, is she? Improper attention, I mean." He drained his wineglass and held it out for the hovering butler to refill.

"She's done nothing the least improper," Anthony hastened to assure him. "It's simply natural that a woman riding to hunt would attract notice, rare as that is these days. Particularly when the woman is as accomplished at the art as your daughter. She takes fences better than nine-tenths of the men riding, from what I've observed. You have every reason to be proud of her."

He was glad to see the worry leave Sir George's face, which then brightened even further. "Ah, there you are, my dear. Join us, do. You all know Tessa—or, I should say, Miss Seaton?"

Anthony and his friends jumped to their feet as she entered, Anthony wondering how much of his praise she had overheard. Most of it, judging by her heightened color.

She was most becomingly dressed in a low-cut evening gown of rose silk cinched below her breasts by a wide ribbon of deeper rose. Though her face was perhaps not as white as fashion preferred—not surprising after two days riding outdoors—her shoulders and chest were as creamy as any London debutante's. It was all Anthony could do to keep to his place when every sense was urging him to go to her, to touch her smooth cheek, the silkiness of her upswept hair, the curve of—

"My compliments, Miss Seaton," he said aloud before his errant thoughts could progress any further. The others echoed his words as she advanced into the room.

Her blush extended down her front, to her cleavage, Anthony noted with interest. How much farther—?

"Thank you," she murmured, clearly nonplussed at so much blatant admiration. Not meeting Anthony's eyes—or anyone else's—she moved to her father's side. "Are you warm enough, Papa?" she asked, smoothing a fold of his cravat. "Would you like a lap rug?"

"I'm fine, I'm fine," he said, waving her away. "Don't fuss, Tessa. Have a seat, and we can all talk of the hunt until dinner is ready. I understand the fox won today?" He smiled around as Miss Seaton retreated with obvious reluctance to take the chair closest to her father.

Anthony obliged his host by beginning a blow-by-blow account of the morning's ride, supplemented by comments from his friends. Sir George became animated, his expression more alert than Anthony had yet seen it as he asked questions and offered his opinion on some of the older sportsmen he had ridden with in years past.

Miss Seaton, Anthony noticed, said not a word, casting frequent, worried glances at her father, though Anthony saw no particular cause for her concern. If anything, the color in Sir George's cheeks had improved, and the bleariness faded from his eyes as his refilled glass went untouched.

Dinner was announced a short time later, and they repaired to the dining room across the hall, Miss Seaton accompanying her father despite his looks and nods that were clearly meant to encourage her to take one of their guests' arms instead. At the table, however, she was obliged to take her place at the opposite end from her father, while the five guests and Mr. Emery, who joined them at the last moment, filled in along the sides.

Anthony was not the only one who moved to sit

by Miss Seaton, but after some subtle jockeying for position, he managed to take the chair on her right, while Killer sat opposite him on her left. Rush and Thor sat by Sir George, with Stormy between Killer and Rush, and Mr. Emery between Anthony and Thor. This suited Anthony quite well, as he hoped to discover a bit more about Mr. Emery this evening.

Accordingly, as the soup was served, he turned to the older man and said, "It must take most of your time to manage an estate the size of Wheatstone, and the stables as well. It is good of you to take time away from such duties to chaperone Miss Seaton on the hunting field, and to dine with us tonight."

Mr. Emery's glance slid around the table, then back to Anthony before he answered. "I am able to delegate some of my responsibilities, of course, my lord, as any good manager must do. I try not to neglect the demands of family—or society—for the sake of business."

"Speaking of the estate, Mercer, did I hear some sort of work going on in the west wing earlier today?" Sir George asked from the other end of the table. "What—?

"Some painting, Papa, that is all," Miss Seaton said before her uncle could respond. "It was my suggestion that we have it done."

Sir George nodded. "I suppose it is due, as were the chimneys you mentioned having cleaned. You will take admirable care of a house of your own someday, Tessa." He winked, then smiled around at the gentlemen.

Remembering the sagging roof on the west end of the house and the leaning chimney he had noticed on his first visit, Anthony raised his brows but asked no questions, instead changing the subject to alleviate Miss Seaton's obvious embarrassment at her father's comment.

"Sir George, did you perhaps know my great-uncle, Alden Trowbridge? He was a deal older than you, of course, but he was quite the avid foxhunter in his day."

"Trowbridge? Why yes, I remember old Trowbridge well," Sir George exclaimed. "Never saw him refuse a fence, even in his sixties. He was your uncle?"

Anthony nodded. "On my mother's side. He left Ivy Lodge to me, and it now houses the Odd Sock Club."

"So you are all members of the Odd Sock? I recall when it formed, a year or two before my accident, and the furor it caused at the Old Club. They needed the shakeup, in my opinion—and the competition. Some of them were far too full of themselves, too sure that their way was the only way. No flexibility."

"Exactly," Stormy said. "We didn't care for the way they did things at the Old Club, so we started our own. In fact we five are the founding members."

Stormy tactfully did not mention the specific incident that had led to the formation of the Odd Sock, to Anthony's relief. Killer was already feeling put-upon about his purchase of that bay. On that thought, while Stormy and Rush gave Sir George a few more details about their hunt club, Anthony turned again to Mr. Emery, though his question was really for Miss Seaton.

"That horse Lord Killerby bought, Nimbus—have you any tips on how to get the best out of him? He seems a bit, ah, resistant to the change of ownership."

"I, er—" Mr. Emery began, glancing across Anthony at Miss Seaton, who responded, as Anthony had hoped she might. She'd been silent far too long, in his opinion.

"Nimbus was gelded quite late," she said, "so he still thinks like a stallion in many ways. That's why he dislikes being near other horses, particularly males. I'd recommend stabling him next to a mare, if possible, and keeping him away from other horses until he's had time to get well used to his new surroundings."

Again, Anthony was struck by her intelligence, her insight about horses—and her beauty. "Anything else?" he asked, holding her gaze for a long moment and enjoying the way her cheeks pinkened. He felt an answering response stir within him, but then she glanced away.

"He's a big horse, so you'd think it would take exceptional strength to control him, but that's not necessarily the case," she said. "I've observed that gentleness and confidence generally get better results than brute force." She sent a significant look toward her uncle.

Anthony wondered if her words were aimed at Mr. Emery himself or at his absent son, the trainer. He wondered why the prickly younger Mr. Emery had not joined them for dinner, as he was also family, but before he could think of a discreet way to ask, Killer joined the conversation.

"Thank you, Miss Seaton," he said warmly. "That's just what I've been telling these fellows. Clearly you were able to handle Nimbus, and you're even smaller than I. But, tall chaps that they are, they insist on seeing my lack of inches as a handicap."

When she smiled at Killer, Anthony felt the first twinge of jealousy he'd ever felt toward the man. "Most men see being female as a far more severe handicap, I assure you, Lord Killerby. But we all have our own strengths and talents. We need only discover them and make our best use of them."

Glancing down the table at Sir George, who was still in animated conversation with the others, Anthony leaned toward her. "And when one talent is taken away, others should be developed, should they not? Your father has a keen mind."

She frowned at him, clearly startled. "Of course he does. He uses it to study, and to write his memoirs. The bits I've read are remarkably good."

"But is that all he does? What of the estate? The stables? Surely—"

Now she glanced down the table, alarm evident in her expression. "I'll not have him worried by such matters," she said in a lowered tone. "His heart—"

"—seems equal to mental exertion, if not physical." He kept his voice low, as well. "I fear you do Sir George no favors by coddling him, Miss Seaton."

Her cheeks pinkened again, but this time with anger. "I believe you forget yourself, my lord. This is surely none of your concern."

"Perhaps not," he replied with a shrug, "but I like Sir George and would see him happy—as he seems to be this evening. What say you, sir?" he asked then, turning to Mr. Emery, who had been listening but rather obviously pretending not to. "Would you like to see Sir George take more of a hand in the estate? It would lighten your load, I should think."

Mr. Emery blinked, then frowned. "I fear Miss Seaton is right, my lord, that Sir George is not up to the task. His heart is not strong. He is easily wearied, and often falls into melancholy, reminiscing about the past." His voice sank to a whisper. "I'm afraid his mind is not always as sharp as it appears tonight."

Anthony suspected much of that could be attributed to boredom—and, perhaps, to drink—but did not say so, sensing that he had antagonized Miss Seaton enough already.

"So the entire management of the estate is in your hands?" he asked, to clarify things. "Sir George has no input at all?"

"I occasionally consult with Miss Seaton, who has an interest in the estate, and who can be trusted to have her father's best interests at heart," Emery replied stiffly.

"Of course she does," Killer chimed in from across the table, though Anthony was sure he could not have heard everything they'd said. "You've no need to mollycoddle Sir George the way you try to do me, Anthony. Leave that to Miss Seaton."

Chapter 6

Tessa swallowed, glancing quickly at her father's animated face at the other end of the table. No, clearly he had not heard Lord Killerby's comment. Not that it was true, of course. She did not *mollycoddle* her father! She simply took care of him, which was surely her responsibility as his only daughter.

For six years, she'd never doubted for a moment that she was doing the right thing by allowing her father to live in the past, free from the worries that might sap his strength. Papa seemed perfectly content to putter about his study, secure in the belief that the estate was as rich as it used to be, that the stables were still the envy of all the Shires. How could it be better to dispel those illusions?

She rose. "If you gentlemen will excuse me, I will retire to the parlor so that you may have your cigars, or brandy, or whatever it is gentlemen do when they are alone at the end of a meal."

Every man but her father scrambled to his feet, clearly caught off-guard. Not surprising, as the sweetmeats had not even been served yet, but she felt a distinct need to get away from Lord Anthony's unsettling presence. Dropping a half curtsy, she turned and left the dining room.

What was it about that man that made her rethink every aspect of her life? It was most uncomfortable, she decided, and she didn't care for it at all. Or for him. She was tempted to go upstairs to bed, but knew her father would be disappointed if she did so. With a sigh, she entered the parlor instead.

"Finished entertaining all them swells Uncle George invited to court you?" Cousin Harold greeted her unpleasantly, making her instantly regret her decision.

"They're not courting, they're talking horses and hunting," she replied tartly, taking a seat as far from Harold as possible. "I only hope they do not tire him too much."

Her cousin snorted. "So them fine gents haven't been throwing pretty compliments your way? Maybe I should have come to dinner, whether I had the clothes for it or not, to make sure none of 'em said anything they shouldn't to you."

Tessa had noticed Harold becoming increasingly possessive toward her over the past month or two, if no more pleasant. Now seemed as good a time as any to put a stop to it. "You may trust my father to protect me from any unwanted advances, Harold. For that matter, I can protect myself. It is in no way *your* responsibility to do so, in any event."

"It could become my responsibility." He got up

and moved across the room to stand next to her, one hand brushing her bare shoulder. "You used to follow me about like a puppy, Tessa. You idolized me. Did you think I didn't know?"

She shifted in her chair so that his hand fell from her shoulder. "I was a child then. I didn't know any better. Now I do."

His thick lips twisted in a sudden sneer. "Oh, think you're too good for me, do you, now that all these fine gentlemen and lordlings are dancing attendance on you? If they knew you were granddaughter to a horse trainer, their intentions wouldn't be honorable ones, you know."

"As I told you, they came to see Papa, not me. And I've made no secret of who I am, so don't think to hold that over my head."

"So they know, do they?" He gave a knowing nod. "Now I get it. Word is, your precious Lord Anthony has a new mistress every year—usually gifts her with a horse, in fact. You'd like that, wouldn't you?"

Tessa glared at his leering face. "You have a nice job here, Harold, training my father's horses. I doubt you want to jeopardize that."

He laughed at her. "Who do you think you're fooling? Uncle George does whatever Father tells him to, and my own father's not about to turn me off. Especially now that we're getting such good prices for some of the horses I've trained."

"*You've*—" she began, torn between outrage and amusement. Did he really think his training had anything to do with it? Yes, he probably did. "I have influence with my father as well, Harold—rather more than Uncle Mercer does, I imagine."

He leaned over her, and she realized uncomfortably that he could probably see right down her low bodice. "We're all family, Tessa. No need to wrangle over influence—or for you to be missish. I never said I meant to tell anyone about Grandfather, now, did I? Let's be friends, as we used."

Again he put his hand on her shoulder, then slid it lower, beneath her collarbone. She twisted away from him and stood up. "Stop it, Harold. We are cousins, nothing more, and that's all we will ever be." It was almost a relief to finally have it out in the open.

He blinked, clearly surprised, though she couldn't imagine why, as it had been a decade or more since she'd shown him anything but distant politeness. In fact, she thought she'd made it fairly clear of late that she didn't even *like* him. Remembering the snippet of conversation she'd overheard out at the stables last week, she wondered what Uncle Mercer had been telling him.

"I'm sorry, Harold, but—"

Abruptly, his face took on the bullying expression he wore so often when "training" the horses, and he moved close to her again. "Oh, you'll be sorry, that's certain. I'll—"

"Is there a problem, Miss Seaton?" came Lord Anthony's voice from the parlor door.

Stepping away from Harold, she turned with a distinct sense of relief—and embarrassment at being seen in so awkward a position. "No, my lord. My cousin and I were simply arguing our different views on horse training."

As he'd done during his first visit to the house, Lord Anthony looked Harold up and down, consideringly. "I see," he said, in a tone that implied he saw far more than she'd explained. Then, to Harold, "Having observed Miss Seaton's excellent horsemanship, I'd recommend you heed whatever advice she might deign to give you, Emery."

Harold scowled, clearly ready to argue, but just then a commotion in the hallway heralded the arrival of the others. Tessa took the opportunity to put more distance between Harold and herself, though she was careful not to move too near Lord Anthony, either.

Why had she felt such relief at his entrance? she wondered as she took a seat near the fire. Harold would never have harmed her, for all he'd tried to bully her with words. She should instead have been annoyed that she had not been able to finish her confrontation with her cousin on the spot, for now they would doubtless end up having this conversation again.

Sir George and the rest of his guests entered the parlor, deep in a discussion of famous foxhunts of the past. Tessa looked searchingly at her father as he wheeled himself in, alert for any sign of fatigue, but at the moment he seemed animated and happy—though of course that could be a mere facade. Even if it wasn't, she was certain that once their guests were gone, he would realize how much the evening had tired him.

"Papa," she said when he paused in his recounting of one hunt he recalled, "come join me by the fire, do. You'll be more comfortable here, I'm sure."

For a moment his face lost its eagerness and she thought he would do as she asked, but then he shook his head. "Nonsense. This whole room is quite warm. In fact, I was just going to suggest some whist, as we have enough for two tables. It's been ages since we've played, and you know how I enjoy it."

He glanced around the room, clearly counting those present. "Ah, Harold, I see you've decided to join us at last. Gentlemen, most of you have met my nephew, Harold Emery, who does such a splendid job with the horses."

Tessa waited until greetings were exchanged before saying, "I'm sure these gentlemen have other things to do than to play whist with us, Papa." If once they sat down to cards, they might be here till midnight!

"Not at all, Miss Seaton," Sir Charles protested. "I think I speak for all of us when I say we'd be glad to oblige Sir George in a rubber or two."

The others gave a chorus of agreement, and Tessa's heart sank. It was true that her father used to enjoy the game. During the first year or so after his accident, Harold and Uncle Mercer had frequently been pressed into service to make up a table, though neither of them particularly excelled at whist. In recent years, however, Sir George had been too tired and withdrawn in the evenings to suggest it.

"We have nine, so we can take turns at one table, or two can play as one," Lord Rushford suggested.

But Uncle Mercer headed for the door, saying, "No need, for I can't stay. I have several matters to attend to after taking most of the evening for pleasure. No, Harold, you stay and play," he added when his son made as if to join him.

"We have just eight, then, which is perfect," Sir George exclaimed, motioning for Griffith and young Jonas, who was playing footman tonight, to set up the tables. A few minutes later, they all settled down to play.

Sir George had insisted that he and Tessa play at different tables, much to her frustration, as that would prevent her keeping as close an eye on her father as she'd have liked. Even worse, she was now trapped in close proximity with both Lord Anthony and her cousin Harold, the imposing Mr. Turpin making up their fourth.

Anthony, however, was perfectly content with the grouping, as it would give him an opportunity to learn more about this rather intriguing family.

"How long have you worked as trainer for Sir George?" he asked young Mr. Emery as the first hand was dealt.

The fellow shot him a suspicious glance before answering, reinforcing his opinion that the man bore watching. "Just over two years," he said. "I took over when my—when the old trainer died." He glanced quickly at Miss Seaton, then away.

Anthony remembered what Porrington had claimed, so was able to divine what Harold Emery had almost said. "I take it your father oversees your efforts?" he asked then, not wishing to pursue a topic that might make Miss Seaton uneasy.

The other man shrugged. "He oversees the whole estate, but he lets me handle the horses as I see fit."

"Will you be riding in the hunt this season, Mr. Emery?" Thor asked, arranging the cards in his hand.

Emery shook his head. "I haven't time for such nonsense. That is—I'm very busy with the stables." Anthony thought he looked distinctly uncomfortable, but whether from his rude slip or because he wished to avoid the topic of the hunt, Anthony couldn't say.

They settled down to play then, but once a few tricks had been played, Anthony tried another tack. "Much as he enjoyed the hunt, and clearly still enjoys hearing about it, I'm surprised Sir George hasn't found a way to watch it occasionally," he said to Miss Seaton.

Frowning, she missed her turn, realized it, apologized, then said, "Pray do not put such an idea into my father's head, my lord. I fear an evening such as this will be tiring enough for him."

"Do you mean to say he never leaves the house at all?" Anthony asked in surprise.

She shook her head. "Never since his accident. How would he, after all? Stairs alone are a barrier to him, as you can see."

A barrier she had learned to make use of, Anthony suspected, remembering the evidences of financial hardship he had seen on the ground floor that were lacking on this one. "The wings of the house—do they require navigating stairs for access from this floor?" he asked to test his theory.

"Well, yes," she replied with evident surprise. "There is a half flight up to the west wing and a half flight down to the east. Why?"

He sent her what he hoped was a disarming smile as he shrugged. "I merely wondered how limited Sir George's world had become since the accident. It must be hard for a man who was once so active to be confined to but one section of one floor."

"Oh, he's a great reader, is Sir George," Harold Emery put in cheerfully when Miss Seaton did not at once respond. "He seems happy enough puttering about with his books and papers, don't he, Tessa?"

Anthony thought her smile seemed forced. "Yes. Yes, he does. I fear they have bested us this hand, Mr. Turpin," she said, gathering up the cards as the next deal was hers. "I will strive to pay better attention to the next."

"That is our rubber," she said an hour later. She

had indeed paid more attention to the cards—helped, no doubt, by Anthony staying clear of topics that flustered her—and had played much better as a result.

For himself, Anthony wasn't sure any level of play on his part could have compensated for Harold Emery's inferior understanding of the game. As they were playing for points rather than pounds, he'd stifled his frustration with his partner by watching the delectable Miss Seaton at her play and by listening carefully to what little conversation went forth.

There was a tension between Miss Seaton and her cousin that he was certain went beyond different theories on horse training—but then, he'd surmised as much when he'd interrupted them just after dinner. Young Emery had been threatening her in some way, he was almost sure of it.

And he was determined to discover exactly how.

The other table ended their rubber a moment later, and though Sir George at once suggested another, Anthony could detect a trace of weariness in his voice.

"You are most kind, sir, but I believe we have imposed upon your hospitality long enough." When his host would have protested, he added, "Remember, your daughter was up early today for the hunt, and rode hard for several hours this morning. I'm certain she would not thank us for keeping her longer from her bed."

The grateful glance Miss Seaton sent him was almost worth the sacrifice of leaving her side so early.

"Why, I had quite forgotten that," Sir George said, looking at his daughter. "How thoughtless of me, Tessa, dear. Are you so tired, then?"

She rather elaborately stifled a yawn. "I confess I am beginning to flag a bit, Papa, after such a long, full day."

That settled the matter, and the gentlemen rose to take their leave, with many exclamations of gratitude for the enjoyable evening.

"Perhaps the Odd Sock Club may return the favor and have you to dinner at Ivy Lodge, Sir George," Stormy suggested, oblivious to the sudden alarm on Miss Seaton's face.

Anthony saw Thor nudge Stormy, but Sir George was looking thoughtful. "Perhaps that might be pleasant, if it can somehow be contrived." He glanced impatiently down at his chair. "It may be easier to have you all here again soon, however."

"I'm betting these fellows can get you in and out of a carriage, should you wish to come," Killer volunteered. "We'd love a chance to show you about the place, wouldn't we, Anthony?"

Caught between the urge to help Sir George and his reluctance to distress Miss Seaton, Anthony nodded cautiously. "I'm sure it can be managed, should you wish to come—and should Miss Seaton think it wise. I would invite you as well, Miss Seaton, but Ivy Lodge is a bachelor establishment, I fear."

"I quite understand," she said stiffly, her anxious eyes on her father. "Now, do allow me to see you all to the door."

Clearly, she was hoping that once they were gone, Sir George would forget the idea of leaving the house, but Anthony was not at all certain that he would—or that he should. He waited until his friends had all said their good-byes so that he could be the last to take leave of Miss Seaton.

"I'm sorry if you feel our visit was a strain on your

father," he murmured as he bent over her hand. "I believe you will find that he benefited from it on the whole, however."

She gazed up at him, her eyes wide and troubled. "Would that you were right, my lord, but I fear he may have overestimated his strength. It has been many years since he has attempted anything like this evening."

Retaining his light grasp on her hand, Anthony held her gaze with his own for a long moment, willing her to understand that he wished only good for her and her father. Her eyes widened slightly and he felt her fingers tremble in his before she hastily withdrew them.

"Pray don't underestimate your father, Miss Seaton," he said when she would have turned away. "He is capable of more than you give him credit for, and it would do him good if he could believe that as well."

She took a step back, her brown eyes now flashing. "I believe I know my father better than you can after a mere evening in his company, my lord. In all likelihood, he will be unable to rise from his bed tomorrow, after tonight's exertions—and the task of nursing him will fall to me. I must ask that you and your friends not visit again, especially if you are to put ambitions in his head that can only upset him when he realizes they are beyond his ability to realize."

With that, she turned and went up the stairs, leaving Anthony no option but to follow his friends out the door to their waiting horses. He was certain, however, despite the finality of that dismissal, that he had by no means seen the last of Miss Seaton.

* * *

Tessa heard the front door close with profound relief, though her anger at Lord Anthony's parting words still simmered. Who did he think he was, to imply that she was harming her father with her care of him? He had never seen Papa when he was unable to do anything but stare out the window, which happened all too frequently of late. He did not know how great an exertion tonight had been for Sir George after years of seclusion.

"They are gone, then, my dear?" her father greeted her when she reached the top of the stairs. Was that regret in his voice, or only weariness?

"Yes, Papa, they're gone at last. Let me call Griffith, for it is well past your bedtime. Where is Harold?"

"Gone to talk to Mercer, I believe," he said dismissively. "So, Tessa, what think you of those gentlemen? Fine young men, I should say, and they all seemed to admire you—and to have a good time. All in all, I'm quite pleased with how our first dinner party went, aren't you?"

"First?" Surely he didn't mean—

"Why, yes. Now that we've proved we are perfectly capable of entertaining, I expect this will be only the first party of many. Who knows? After a bit of practice, perhaps we will even hold a ball and invite the neighborhood. You never have had a proper come-out, after all."

Tessa stared, for it was not at all like her retiring father to suggest such a thing. "A ball? I can't imagine—that is—we haven't the servants for such a thing. And the ballroom hasn't been used in—"

"In more than ten years," he said. "Not since your mother died. I know. I've been very selfish, Tessa, and you've been deprived as a result, but now I'm determined to make it up to you."

"Oh, Papa, no! You haven't been selfish, you've been ill. It's not at all the same thing. And I haven't felt deprived in the least."

She *must* dissuade him from this notion. Not only would he tax his strength beyond endurance, but the ballroom, which was in the west wing, could not be made presentable without far more money than they had any hopes of. Its ceiling had been damaged by the leaking roof, and half the crystal from the chandelier had somehow gone missing. Then there was the sadly dilapidated giltwork, the motheaten wall hangings . . .

"Truly, Papa, I haven't the least desire for a ball," she said firmly. "I doubt I even remember how to dance."

He waved that objection away. "It will come back to you. You were a delightful dancer as a child, I recall, and we can always hire a master to give you a refresher lesson or two."

Griffith, Sir George's manservant, appeared, and Tessa beckoned to him. "We'll discuss it in the morning, Papa. Right now, you need to get to bed. Good night." She kissed his brow, and he held her close for a moment.

"Good night, Tessa, and thank you for being such a perfect hostess tonight. It meant more to me than you can know." He released her with a smile and allowed Griffith to wheel him to his bedchamber at the rear of the floor.

Tessa listened for a moment as he regaled Griffith with highlights of the evening just past, then headed upstairs to her own chamber with a sigh. It would be a miracle if her father was able to function at all tomorrow, after so much excitement today, and she needed her rest if she was to be able to care for him.

*   *   *

"You're sure you don't want to join the Quorn today?" Anthony asked Killer one last time before mounting Cinder. "There may yet be a hunter available for hire. We can ask when we get there."

The viscount shook his head. "I plan to use Firebolt's sore hock as an excuse to see how Carter is getting on with Nimbus. I haven't had a chance to watch him in action since purchasing him."

"Mind you don't get too close," Stormy cautioned, glancing in the direction of Nimbus's stall as he pulled on his riding gloves. "He's a terror, that one is. Anthony here could probably handle him, but—"

"But not little Killer, is that what you're saying?" their friend demanded, his pride clearly stung. "Size is no measure of horsemanship, you know. Look at Miss Seaton."

"No, no, of course not," Stormy said hastily, glancing at Anthony for support. "I didn't mean—"

"That's all right, never mind," Killer said, recovering some of his habitual buoyancy. "I know you mean well, both of you. Not to worry, however. Even if he threw me, I'd doubtless bounce." He patted his rounded stomach with a grin.

Anthony chuckled, then frowned in sudden concern. "But you're not—"

Killer interrupted him, saying, "Go on, go on, you're going to be late for the meet. I'll want to hear all about the hunt when you get back—particularly if Miss Seaton rides again."

Though still worried about what Killer might attempt in their absence, Anthony knew that to say anything else might be to prod his friend into taking a foolish risk.

"And we'll want a report on that bay's progress on

our return, too," was all he said, silencing Stormy with a look. They both mounted and headed out, cantering to catch up with Rush and Thor, who'd left two or three minutes earlier.

"You don't think he'll really try it, do you?" Stormy asked worriedly as they rode. "Not yet?"

"Not ever, I hope, unless that horse is capable of more improvement than I believe is possible," Anthony replied. "You know Killer, though, with his eternal optimism. I hope we stopped needling him in time."

Stormy nodded. "I think we did. Glad you shut me up when you did, though. Have a tendency to run on at times, don't I?"

"At times," Anthony agreed with a grin. "Look, there they are, taking that next turn. Let's gallop."

The four founders of the Odd Sock Club arrived at the Quorn meet together, and as one they searched the assembled riders for the purple flash of a habit.

"Don't think she's here," Thor said after a moment.

Anthony wasn't surprised, as she'd said nothing last night about hunting today. He only hoped her absence didn't mean that she'd been right about Sir George. Surely they hadn't tired the man as much as she seemed to think. If anything, the opposite had seemed to be the case.

Mr. Assheton Smith raised his horn to signal the hounds to the covert. Anthony resigned himself to not enjoying Miss Seaton's company that day, then wondered why he should feel so disappointed when he hadn't expected it anyway. Soon, however, his attention was given wholly to the chase, though still he found himself wondering at odd moments how Miss Seaton would have taken a particular jump, or what comment she might have made on some sportsman's blunder.

As the day wore on, he found himself very much hoping that she might turn out for the Cottesmore tomorrow, for hunting somehow seemed more enjoyable with her along for the ride.

The afternoon was growing cool and damp when Tessa returned from a long ride on the promising new gelding that Uncle Mercer had bought Monday. Her uncle had been right that with a bit of training, the hack could become a perfectly good hunter. She only hoped she'd be given enough time to work with him.

She was heading up the stairs to change out of her old brown habit before dinner when she was startled from her thoughts by a loud knocking at the door. Had she been wrong? Had the horse created some sort of problem once she was off his back? It hadn't seemed—

"Is Miss Seaton here?" came Lord Anthony's agitated voice the instant Griffith opened the door.

Turning, she hurried back down the stairs to interrupt the manservant's stammering excuse that she was not prepared to receive visitors at the moment.

"It's all right, Griffith," she said, dismissing him. "Lord Anthony, I did not look to see you here today. Is something the matter?"

He was still dressed in hunting attire, which surprised her, as the hunt must have concluded hours ago. At her appearance, he swept off his hat and bowed, though there was no mistaking the tension in his expression.

"I hope I find you well, Miss Seaton . . . and your father. Did we tire him unduly last night?"

"No," she was forced to admit. "He has seemed perfectly well today, somewhat to my surprise." She saw no point in confessing that her father was in fact more alert than she could recall seeing him since his accident six years ago—and more cheerful than he'd been since her mother had died, four years before that.

Some of the tension went out of Lord Anthony's face, but not all of it. "Good, good. If he will be all right on his own for a bit, perhaps I might ask a favor of you?"

"A favor?" she echoed, confused.

He slapped his hat against his thigh a few times, as though trying to choose his words before speaking them aloud. "It's Killer," he finally said. "That is, Lord Killerby. While we were at the Quorn today, he went out riding on Nimbus—alone."

Tessa's hand went to her throat. "Is . . . is he all right?" she asked, trying not to let her fear show in her voice, as that would be to admit the horse was unsafe.

"We don't know," he replied. "Neither he nor the horse has returned."

Chapter 7

All color drained from Miss Seaton's face, and Anthony stepped forward to put a hand on her shoulder, lest she collapse. "I'm sorry—I didn't mean to frighten you," he said. "But I was hoping, as you seem to know the horse better than anyone, that you might be willing to help me find them."

She took a deep breath, then nodded. "Yes. Yes, of course. I just need"—She put a hand to her head for a moment—"I need to let my father know I'm going out. Wait here."

With another steadying breath, she squared her shoulders, then headed up the stairs. Anthony watched her go, his appreciation for her well-shaped backside muted by his concern for his friend. He never should have left Killer that morning. He should have picked up on the clues in Killer's manner, should have—

But self-recrimination would get him no closer to finding Killer now than it had over the past two hours. Besides, if he was going to throw blame around, surely Miss Seaton deserved a fair share of it. That thought had driven him here, a desire to see her acknowledge her wrongdoing. Only when he reached the house had he realized that in fact it made perfect sense to ask for her help.

He was still trying to sort through his conflicting feelings when she returned, tripping lightly down the stairs, her brows still knit in a frown of concern.

"Let's go," she said. "I sent to the stables to have Cinnamon brought round, as Nimbus always seemed more comfortable with her than with any of our other horses."

"Cinnamon. The roan you rode yesterday?" Anthony asked.

She nodded, and Anthony realized that must be why Mr. Mercer had ridden that particular horse in the first hunt, on Monday. The mare, as well as Miss Seaton herself, had a calming influence on the ill-mannered Nimbus.

"How long ago did Lord Killerby ride out?" she asked as they waited on the front steps for her mount to arrive.

"According to his groom, he left about noon—which means he's been gone more than four hours." Anthony's anxiety, momentarily muted by other thoughts—and her presence—returned full force. "He would have returned by now if he were able."

She put a comforting hand on his sleeve. "No doubt, but we needn't assume the worst. He could have been thrown, far from home, and is having to make his way back on foot. He could be perfectly well, but that would still take some time."

"I suppose so," he admitted, realizing he had indeed assumed the worst from the moment he learned what Killer had done. Her explanation seemed no more rational, however, and he was suddenly irritated by her soothing tone—so similar to the one he'd heard her use on horses. He would not let her uncanny gift—magic, or whatever it was—divert him from his purpose or his responsibility to his friend.

"He should never have gone out on that brute in the first place," he said sharply, moving a step away from her distracting nearness. "He wouldn't have, if you hadn't misled him about Nimbus's tractability."

Her hand dropped to her side, and he saw shock and hurt in her eyes, but only for an instant, for anger quickly took their place. "Lord Killerby is a grown man," she snapped, "and, one might *assume*, able to draw his own conclusions and make his own decisions. I said nothing to him about Nimbus, as I recall, good or bad."

"You didn't have to," he retorted. "But did you honestly think—" He broke off as a stable lad approached, leading the roan mare Cinnamon.

"Mr. Emery thought there might be some mistake," the boy said when he reached them, his gaze frankly curious. "Didn't you just come back from riding that new chestnut gelding, Miss Seaton?"

She nodded. "Yes, Billy, but I need to go out again. I don't suppose Nimbus has shown up at the stables?"

The lad shook his head, eyes wide. "Should he have?"

"No, never mind," she said. "You may tell Mr. Emery that I've been invited to dinner at a neighbor's, if he demands some sort of explanation of you."

"Aye, miss," the lad responded, handing her the reins.

"I told Father I was invited to dine with the Hilltops," she said to Anthony once the stable lad was out of earshot. "I didn't want him to worry."

"And young Mr. Emery? Does he keep track of your movements as well?" He wasn't sure how he felt about that.

She shrugged. "It seemed prudent to give him the same explanation I gave Papa, to lessen the chance he might let slip the truth—which would surely upset him. Besides—" She broke off.

"He might try to stop you, if he knew you were going out alone with me?"

"He might," she confessed. "He and Uncle Mercer seem to think it their place to protect me, though I've told them time and again that I can look out for myself perfectly well."

Anthony suspected there was more to it than simple concern for her welfare, but didn't say so. "Shall we go, then?" he asked, recalled to the urgency of their mission.

With a quick nod, she used the step as a mounting block to leap into the sidesaddle, then deftly arranged her worn brown skirts. "It's as well Papa didn't get a good look at me when I went upstairs," she commented, "or he'd never have believed I was going out socially. I suspect he was so delighted to think one of the neighbors might extend such an invitation that he didn't ask for details."

Anthony waited until they were cantering down the drive to ask, with studied casualness, "Do you often deceive your father, Miss Seaton?"

"Of course not!" she exclaimed. Then, after a moment's silence, "At least, not without good cause, to spare him anxiety, which could undermine his health."

Partly to himself, to mitigate his growing attraction to her, he commented, "It would appear that honesty is not one of your more prominent, ah, virtues." Honesty was a quality he'd always regarded highly. He'd be wise to remember that.

"What an ungallant thing to say." Her voice was prim, but lacked conviction. "You scarcely know me, after all."

A light mist began to fall as they turned down the road toward Ivy Lodge. "I know that you ride out in breeches and don't want your father to know it. I know that you and your uncle have conspired to sell at least one horse, and very probably more, at inflated prices. And I suspect that you are keeping Sir George ignorant of the true state of Wheatstone by keeping up only those portions he can reach in his chair."

She slowed her mare to a walk to stare at him, obviously stricken. "You haven't said any of this to my father, have you?"

"Of course not," he said, matching her pace. "In fact, I have only now puzzled it all out."

"And . . . and you won't tell him? It really would upset him dreadfully to know that the estate—and the Seaton name—is not what it once was."

Against his will, he felt a stab of sympathy for her, for the trials she must have endured and must still be enduring in her efforts to preserve her father's sense of pride. Slowly, he shook his head. "No, I won't tell him. But I think you should."

"But—"

"Let's continue this later, shall we? Killer—Lord Killerby—is still out there somewhere." He kicked Cinder back into a canter, and she followed suit, though from what he could see of her averted face, she was still upset.

They rode in silence until they reached the stables at Ivy Lodge, Anthony busy with his thoughts, and Miss Seaton no doubt busy with her own. Thinking over what he'd said? He hoped so.

"No word yet?" Anthony asked Carter, Killer's groom, who was waiting outside the stables.

The man shook his head. "I did try to stop 'im, m'lord, I told you. But—"

Anthony reached down to put a hand on the man's shoulder. "I know you did, Carter. It's not your fault. Lord Killerby has always been stubborn. Miss Seaton here has agreed to help me find him, as she knows that horse well."

The groom squinted up at her. "Does she, then? You must be the lady my master spoke of, what rode Nimbus so well in the hunt. What's your secret, miss?"

She shifted uncomfortably in her sidesaddle. "I'm just good with horses," she told him, as she'd told Anthony that first night they'd met. "I understand them, and seem able to get them to understand me. I . . . I wish I could explain it better."

Carter nodded sagely. "I've heard tell of such a thing. My grandpa told me about a lady could do summat like that, ride horses no one else could. Back in Ireland, that was."

Miss Seaton started, seemed about to say something, but then apparently changed her mind. "We'd best start looking, hadn't we?" she said to Anthony instead.

He nodded. "Carter said Killer took this path." He nudged Cinder toward the track. "It goes straight for almost a mile, then forks. The right fork links up with the main road, while the left heads into a wooded area. I followed the left fork for some way, and Lord Rushford followed the right, but neither of us saw any sign of man or horse."

"Where did you go from there?"

"We came back here—then I thought to seek you out." Telling her his original reason for doing so wouldn't help matters now, so he kept that to himself.

"Let's hurry on to the fork, then," she suggested.

Again they cantered, which brought them to the fork in just a few minutes. Once there, Miss Seaton pulled to a halt to look first to the right, then the left, through the gathering twilight.

"We'll have three-quarters of a moon tonight, if the clouds break," he commented as she hesitated. "We can't very well wait for that, though."

"No," she agreed. "Not if there's a chance Lord Killerby or Nimbus may be hurt." Instead of choosing a direction, however, she leaned forward to stroke her mare's neck and whisper into her ear. Anthony tried to catch her murmured words, but only heard the name "Nimbus." Then, she let the mare's reins go slack and waited.

"What are you—?" he started to ask, but she held up a hand to silence him.

"I just want to try something," she said softly. "Give her a moment."

The mare put her head down, and at first Anthony thought she was grazing on the withered grass at the edge of the path, but then she swung her head the other way, as though searching for something on the ground. He tensed, waiting. Surely Miss Seaton couldn't think—

Suddenly Cinnamon gave a soft whicker, then raised her head and took a few steps down the right-hand path.

"This way," Miss Seaton said to him, an edge of

excitement in her voice. "Come, Cinnamon, let's hurry."

Torn between hope and disbelief, Anthony urged Cinder to match the mare's trot. "Do you really think they went this way?" he couldn't help asking.

"Cinnamon seems to think so," she replied with a delicate shrug, her eyes on the path ahead.

"She's a horse. How can you know what she thinks?"

She spared him a sidelong look. "Horses are capable of more than most people give them credit for."

"Yes, yes, I agree—to a point. Certainly, I have great respect for horses, for I rode cavalry in the army, but I also know their limitations. How can you trust this mare to track Killer? You said you haven't even owned her for very long."

"No, but I've come to know her fairly well. And she knows Nimbus." The quiet confidence in her voice was oddly compelling—and seductive.

An instinct for self-preservation prompted him to say, "You knew Nimbus, too. You had to know no one else would be able to ride him the way you did on Monday."

She was silent for a long moment, then said, "My uncle tells me many breeders hire excellent riders to show their horses to best advantage before auctioning them for sale."

"That's true," Anthony admitted, trying to put his finger on why this bothered him more. "But your skill with horses seems to go beyond that of even the best riders I've seen—myself included. And because you are a woman, some men will be easily fooled into believing they can do as well, or better."

"So now I am to apologize for my gender? Or perhaps my uncle should tell potential buyers to disregard it before he will consider their bids?" she asked archly. "*Caveat emptor.*"

He had no ready argument for that. Perhaps she was right. Perhaps it was simply the fact that she was female that made this seem different from what so many others did.

Still, he tried one more time to articulate his objection. "It seems disingenuous to use one's natural skills to that sort of advantage, I suppose."

"You use your own skill at riding to be first in at the kill," she pointed out. "Most of the others on the field have not had the advantage of years in the cavalry. Is that so different?"

Before he could answer, she abruptly stopped. "What is it, Cinnamon?" she asked the mare. "Oh! Lord Anthony, did you know that there is another path here? Look."

He did look, and was just able to see that there was indeed another, narrower track branching off to the left. He'd never noticed it before, and he was willing to bet Rush had missed it earlier, even though it had been full light then.

"Let's check it out," he suggested, but Miss Seaton had already headed that way.

They followed the faint path for almost two miles through the mist and gloom, passing a dilapidated cottage at one point. Finally the mare stopped again. Miss Seaton pointed at a clump of trees just off to the side. "Those lower branches are damaged. Do you suppose—?"

Anthony passed her to inspect the branches. "Yes, I'd say they left the path here and crashed through these trees. Something large caused this—and quite recently." He looked more closely and saw a scrap of cloth caught on one of the broken branches. It looked like the same spotted cloth Killer had been wearing as a cravat this morning.

In the dim light, he could find no other sign of his friend, however. "Bring Cinnamon up," he said, unconsciously putting a ring of command, unused since the end of the war, into his voice. "Let her nose around and see if she can lead us to them."

Though startled by the sudden authority in his tone, Tessa complied at once, fully aware of the urgency of the situation. As before, she gave Cinnamon her head so that she could nose about in the brush. "Find them," she whispered to the horse. "Find Nimbus."

Despite her protests, she couldn't help feeling responsible for whatever might have happened to Lord Killerby. Lord Anthony had put voice to her doubts in a way she had avoided doing herself, even in her protests to her uncle and cousin. She'd been given a special gift, and she had been using it for profit.

Cinnamon gave an anxious whinny and turned her head to look at her rider. Peering down at the area directly in front of her, Tessa saw the jaggedly broken branch of a thorn tree with something dark on the end. Blood? Her heart beat faster.

"This way," she said, when Cinnamon faced forward again and took a couple of trembling steps past the battered tree. "Let's hurry." *And please don't let them be badly hurt*, she prayed silently.

After a narrow band of gorse, they headed into a stand of trees and undergrowth that was doubtless used as a covert by some hunt or other. Now their path was easy to pick out, for bushes and small trees had been trampled and broken. Clearly, Nimbus had bolted, too frightened to worry about scrapes along the way.

"Keep an eye to either side, in case Lord Killerby was thrown," she called back as Cinnamon quickened her pace. It seemed almost impossible that he hadn't been, given Nimbus's strength and Lord Killerby's merely competent riding skills. Hadn't he said something during the last hunt about being good at falling? She hoped it was true.

"What's that, up ahead?" Lord Anthony asked sharply from behind her.

She'd been focusing on the brush to either side, but now she looked over Cinnamon's head and saw a barrier of some sort—a ramshackle fence of wood and wire, some of its timbers fallen at awkward angles. Just beyond it, something large lay on the ground.

Cinnamon gave a loud neigh before Tessa could call out, and at once the shape on the ground moved and answered with the call of a hurt and frightened horse.

"It's them," Lord Anthony exclaimed, moving past her. "Killer, are you all right?"

His words were answered by a moan, and Tessa breathed a tiny bit easier. At least he was alive. Had he been killed, she doubted Lord Anthony would ever have forgiven her—nor would she have been able to forgive herself.

Lord Anthony stopped at the tumbledown fence and dismounted, rather than risk leaping it in the dark. At his approach, however, Nimbus began to thrash about, clearly struggling to regain his feet.

"Wait!" Tessa cried. "Let me get to him first, so I can calm him." She hoped it would be possible. Slipping from the sidesaddle without the help of a block or assistant, she hit the ground with a thump, then hurried to the fence.

When she reached it, she saw that it was not so much a fence as a tangle of wood and wire, sprawling for three or four feet along the ground. No wonder Nimbus had fallen. Hiking up her skirts, heedless of what Lord Anthony might think—or see—she began picking her way through the mess.

"Nimbus, Nimbus, be still," she called in her soothing lilt as she approached the downed horse. "Everything will be fine."

Was it her imagination, or did Nimbus's answering whinny hold a note of relief? A moment later she reached his head and ran gentle hands along his neck, murmuring hushing sounds. He stilled, and she called softly to Lord Anthony that he could come up now.

She heard him scrambling over to his friend, who still lay moaning on the ground a few feet away, while she examined, mostly by feel, Nimbus's situation. He lay partly on his side, and she feared from his inability to rise that one of his legs must be broken. When she gently felt down his length, however, she discovered that his right hind leg was caught in some sort of snare. At once she set to work to free him.

"Talk to me, Killer," Lord Anthony was saying urgently to his friend. "Can you talk to me?"

"Anthony? Is it you?" came a weak reply. "I . . . I think my ankle is broken. You may say, 'I told you so,' if you wish."

"I'll save that for later. Right now, we need to figure a way to get you back to the lodge so that a surgeon can have a look at you. Is anything else hurt?"

There was a pause, then Lord Killerby said, "No,

just bruised, I think. Except for poor Nimbus. He won't have to be put down, will he? This was as much my fault as his, you know."

When Lord Anthony didn't respond, Tessa said, "It's too soon to tell, but I don't think his leg is broken. I can't seem to undo this snare, however."

"Will he let me approach?" Lord Anthony asked.

"Yes, he's calm now." She put a hand on Nimbus's neck, just to be sure.

His shape loomed up in the dark, then he knelt beside her. She reached out with her other hand and caught his, so that she could guide it to the offending snare. It was somehow an intimate act in the concealing darkness, and she had to steel herself against the thrill that went through her at the contact.

"Ah, it's a rabbit snare." The tremor in his voice told her that he must still be fearful for his friend. "I just need to twist this bit this way, and there—it's off. We should move away before you let him try to stand."

"Thank you," she said. "Get back to Lord Killerby, and I'll handle Nimbus now."

He rose and moved away, leaving her feeling oddly bereft. Shaking off such a foolish notion, she focused her attention on the horse. "Come, then, Nimbus, let's see what you can do," she said encouragingly. Half rising, she tugged gently on his reins.

Nimbus rolled onto his chest and then, with a convulsive effort, heaved himself to his feet. "Good boy!" she exclaimed. "Now, stand still while I see how you've fared."

The horse stood obedient as an old nag as she ran her hands along his neck, withers, sides, and legs. There was a long cut on his left flank that made him flinch when she touched it, but at least none of his legs was broken. She breathed a sigh of relief, then guiltily remembered Lord Killerby.

"How is he?" she asked.

"He won't be walking back," Lord Anthony replied, "but I'm pretty sure he'll live—won't you, Killer?"

"Yes, I'll be fine." His voice was a little stronger than it had been when they arrived. "How is my horse?"

Tessa couldn't help smiling at his concern for the beast that had injured him—but was just as glad Lord Anthony couldn't see her smile. "No breaks, but a nasty gash that will probably have to be stitched."

"Can he walk?" Lord Anthony asked.

She led Nimbus forward for a few steps, and though he favored his right foreleg, he seemed able to move fairly well. "Yes, I believe so, if we take it slowly."

"Then our first task will be to get all of us to the other side of that damnable thing that used to be a fence. Killer, you'll have to use me as a crutch. Up with you, then." The authority was back in his voice.

With a last, whispered command to Nimbus to stay still, Tessa hurried over to the two men. "Let me help," she said. It was the least she could do.

"I've got him," Lord Anthony replied brusquely, but then Lord Killerby stumbled as the taller man, stooping, tried to move him forward.

Tessa stepped up in time to keep him from falling, then inserted herself under his other arm. "I'm a better height to be a proper crutch anyway."

Anthony grunted but didn't protest, and together they were able to help Lord Killerby through the tangle of the fallen fence to the horses waiting on the other side.

"I don't suppose we dare let anyone but you ride Cinnamon." There was no mistaking the cynicism in Lord Anthony's tone.

"That's not true at all," Tessa said, stung. "In fact, I was going to suggest that Lord Killerby ride her, while I lead Nimbus. Cinnamon is perfectly good-tempered—and not just with me. You saw my uncle on her, remember?"

Lord Anthony nodded. "My apologies, Miss Seaton. If Mercer Emery could ride her, I've no doubt anyone can."

She couldn't resist a chuckle at her uncle's expense. "My point exactly. Let's get this sidesaddle off of Cinnamon, then I'll remove Nimbus's saddle so Lord Killerby can use it. I hope it wasn't damaged—I didn't think to check."

The operation of changing saddles took some time in the dark, but at last the mare was fitted with Nimbus's—thankfully operational—saddle, and the sidesaddle was set atop the injured horse, though of course Tessa wouldn't be riding him. Then they had to get Lord Killerby to his feet again.

"You're both being far more patient with me than I deserve after my idiocy today," he said as he slowly hobbled toward Cinnamon with their help. "I'm terribly sorry to put you to such trouble."

"As Lord Anthony has pointed out, I hold a share of the blame as well," Tessa said, another pang of guilt assailing her. Lord Killerby really was a nice man, and didn't deserve a brute like Nimbus. "You'll have to mount from the right, to spare your left ankle."

Mounting from the wrong side was awkward, of course, but with Tessa and Anthony pushing from below, he was finally able to throw his left leg over Cinnamon's back and settle himself in the saddle. "There! I'd have sworn ten minutes ago I couldn't have done that. You're better than a tonic, Miss Seaton."

She knew he was only trying to make her feel better, but it helped a little, all the same. Then Lord Anthony put a hand on her shoulder and she looked up at him in sudden alarm, sure he was about to lambast her for her part in this crisis. To her surprise, however, she could see his teeth flash in a smile.

"You really are a most capable—and kind—young lady, Miss Seaton," he said. "Thank you."

Confused and suddenly breathless, she could only nod. "I'll . . . I'll go get Nimbus," she said when she found her voice.

The big bay was still standing quietly where she'd left him. Carefully, she led him through the tricky remains of the fence, made more difficult by his limp. Lord Anthony mounted his gray, and they slowly headed back the way they'd come.

After just a few minutes, however, it became obvious that Nimbus could by no means match even the walking pace of the other two horses.

"You two had better go on," Tessa said. "Lord Killerby needs a surgeon for that ankle, and the sooner the better."

"Don't be absurd, Miss Seaton," Lord Killerby protested, though his voice was weak again. "We can't leave you out here alone in the dark and mist. Suppose it turns to rain?"

Tessa looked up at Lord Anthony imploringly. "Please. I refuse to be the cause of any more pain tonight. If the weather worsens, I can take shelter in that cottage we passed earlier. I'll be fine there."

He frowned down at her for a long moment, then nodded curtly. "Very well. I'll get him back to the lodge as quickly as possible, then I'll come back for you. Come on, Killer. Gallantry demands celerity."

With a last worried glance at Tessa, Lord Killerby nodded, and the two men headed back to the path at a fast walk. Tessa watched them go with relief, feeling that she'd done what she could to alleviate the trouble she'd caused. And now she wouldn't have to push Nimbus faster than he could comfortably go, either.

"Come on, then, lad," she said to the bay, leading him forward one trembling step at a time. Their progress was painfully slow, for every few yards Nimbus insisted on stopping to rest his leg, and she thought it best to allow it, if he were not to be permanently lamed.

The mist turned into a drizzle. It would be at least an hour before Lord Anthony could return, for Lord Killerby would be unable to trot, as that would jar his ankle beyond endurance. She only hoped he would not faint before they reached the lodge, for she hadn't liked the sound of his voice when last he spoke.

The sound of Lord Anthony's last words to her before they'd started off, however, had been immensely comforting. Over and over, she replayed them in her mind. Capable and kind, he'd called her. There was nothing loverlike in the words, of course, but his tone had indicated honest approval. It meant far more to her than she would have expected.

Before she could reach the cottage, the drizzle increased to a small but steady rain. Though she tried to distract her thoughts by concentrating on Nimbus, she could not help wondering what she and Lord Anthony would talk about when he returned.

If he returned.

She had just sighted the cottage ahead when she heard the sound of hooves coming toward her along the path, and a moment later Lord Anthony came into view, carrying a shielded lantern. He was riding Cinnamon rather than his gray, but dismounted as soon as he reached her. "Slow going, I see."

"Yes, I'm afraid it is going to take half the night to get him back to the stables, for he needs to stop every few steps. I've decided to stay here and let him rest for a while. Please don't feel you have to remain out here with me, though I would appreciate it if you could send a note to my father to keep him from worrying."

"I've already done so," he said, to her surprise. "It purported to be from the Hilltops, saying that they had invited you to stay the night because of the weather, and that you had accepted, and would return home in the morning. I trust they have at least one daughter?"

She nodded. "Cynthia—though she would no more ask me to spend the night, even if it were blizzarding. She doesn't exactly . . . consider me her equal."

"But does Sir George know that?"

"No, of course not." She stopped, for he could not know how she shielded her father from the opinions of their neighbors—nor did she particularly want him to, after what he'd said earlier.

"All is well, then. Let's check out the cottage. If it is as empty as it appears, we can remain there at least until the rain stops, and allow Nimbus to rest for a bit."

Tessa felt a wild thrill go through her at the prospect of spending what could be hours alone—most improperly alone!—with Lord Anthony. She knew she should protest, but she also knew that an opportunity like this was unlikely to ever come her way again.

And it *would* be the best thing for poor Nimbus, she belatedly realized.

"If . . . if you think it best," she managed to stammer, hoping he could not hear any trace of eagerness in her voice.

"I do. Come. I'm sure you wish to get out of this rain as much as I do."

Chapter 8

Anthony knocked at the door of the darkened cottage, telling himself that they really had no choice if Nimbus was to escape permanent injury— and Killer had been quite insistent that he do all he could for the horse. Quite simply, he owed it to his friend. His feelings for Miss Seaton had nothing to do with it.

"No answer," he said. The latch was broken, and the door yielded easily to his push. "Hello?"

The cottage had the musty smell of a place that had been vacant for some time. "Definitely empty— which helps to explain the state of that fence back there. When I find out who owns this land, I'll give him a piece of my mind for allowing it to fall into such a state."

Holding the lantern high, he surveyed the cottage's single room. The furnishings consisted of a table, two rickety chairs, and a rough bedstead in one corner. The stone fireplace opposite the door still had a black pot hanging on a hook, and a few sticks of firewood were stacked on the hearth. The mantel held nothing but a half-burned candle in a holder. Throughout, the dust was thick and undisturbed.

"It seems safe enough," Anthony said over his shoulder. "Come in and see."

She peered past him, but didn't come inside. "We need to take care of the horses first. I don't suppose you thought to bring any grain with you?"

"Actually, I did." Anthony felt a bit foolish to have forgotten. Something about this girl seemed to addle his thinking. Of course she couldn't follow him inside while holding the reins of both horses.

He came outside to remove the saddlebags he'd slung over Cimmamon's back. "I also thought to bring something for the two of us to eat, since I didn't get dinner and I assume you didn't, either. First the horses, though."

They led the animals around to the rear of the cottage and found a rough lean-to against the back wall that had clearly been used as a makeshift stable and storage area.

"I believe they can both fit in here," she said. "It's a mercy you brought Cinnamon back rather than Cinder, as Nimbus likely wouldn't tolerate sharing such a small space with him."

Anthony nodded. "I was thinking more of your convenience when I brought her, but you're right. It's lucky that she is the one horse Nimbus won't attempt to savage."

She bit her lip and glanced away, and he realized belatedly that she had taken his words as another criticism of the bay's temperament—not that it was undeserved. Still, he had no desire to distress her further just now.

"There," he said when both horses were tied out of the rain and munching on the grain he'd brought. "They'll need water, too. I saw a cistern near the door."

Anthony went into the cottage, took the pot from the fireplace, then came out and dipped it into the half-full cistern. The water was brackish and full of fallen leaves, but it was better than nothing. He was glad he'd brought other drink for Miss Seaton and himself, however.

"Here," he said, handing her the pot. "I let the mare have a good drink back at the lodge."

The horses fed, watered, and bedded down, they returned to the cottage. This time she ventured inside. "Are you—how long do you think we should stay?" She nervously eyed the narrow bed. "It could rain all night."

All night would be fine by him. "At least an hour or two, for Nimbus's sake," he said. He closed the door behind them, lit the candle on the mantelpiece from the lantern, then set the lantern on the table. "I'll see if I can get a fire going." Glancing back at her, he realized he meant that in more ways than one.

Taking off her sodden hat, she moved to sit in one of the rough chairs by the table while he stacked kindling and lit tinder from the candle. It took him a few minutes, but eventually he had a small blaze going. He stood and dusted off his hands.

"Did you say you'd brought food of some sort?" she asked, looking everywhere but at him.

"Not much, I'm afraid, but it'll be better than nothing." He picked up the other satchel, which he'd left by the door, and pulled out half a cheese, a loaf that had been fresh that morning, and a bottle of wine.

He spread his handkerchief on the table for the bread and cheese. "No glasses, I'm afraid," he apologized, setting the bottle beside them, "but I did think to bring a knife." He deftly opened the wine bottle, then began slicing bread and cheese.

Glancing up, he found her looking at him strangely. "You couldn't have known when you left me before that Nimbus was so badly hurt, yet you clearly planned on staying here. Why?"

"It was raining. My army training taught me to prepare for any eventuality." He lifted a shoulder in a half shrug, hoping it sounded convincing. Her look told him otherwise, however.

When she didn't reply, he met her gaze squarely. "Very well, I confess I hoped to convince you to stop here for a bit, even if Nimbus was walking perfectly well by the time I returned. You intrigue me, Miss Seaton, and I thought this might be a splendid chance to get to know you better."

Her brown eyes widened before she dropped her gaze. "I . . . I see."

"Besides, as I said, it was raining," he continued in a casual tone that he hoped would put her at her ease. "If you prefer, you can take Cinnamon and ride home now and leave me here to lead Nimbus back to Ivy Lodge once he's rested a bit."

She shook her head. "No, I won't risk him hurting you, too. I'll stay until he's ready to go on."

He wanted to assure her that he'd be in no danger from the horse, but he wanted even more for her to stay. "Besides," he said instead, "I was hungry and certain that you were, too. You wouldn't want to go home and ask for dinner after telling your father you were dining out, would you?"

"No, I suppose not. It's bad enough young Billy knows I rode out with you. He may tell Harold, but I'd rather not do anything else to raise suspicion," she said wryly. "And you're right—I'm famished." She picked up a slab of bread and cheese and proved her words by taking a big bite.

Anthony hid a grin by doing the same, then held out the wine bottle. "As we'll have to share, you should have the first sip."

She regarded the bottle dubiously for a moment, then gave a small shrug and took it, tilting it to her lips for a swallow. Handing it back to him, she smiled. "I've never drunk directly from a wine bottle before."

"I expect you've never been in any such situation before," he replied, now grinning openly, trying unsuccessfully to ignore the effect her smile had on him. "This is a night of firsts for you, is it not?"

Tessa swallowed again before nodding, for her thoughts flew unbidden to other "firsts" she had yet to experience—a first kiss, a first—but no, that wasn't what he'd meant at all. Confused, she took another bite of her bread and cheese while he took a long pull from the wine bottle.

"You said that you've been hunting in the Shires since you were a youngster," she commented, mainly to break the awkward silence. "Has that been a tradition in your family?" She realized that she had no idea who his family was. His father must be at least an earl for him to be a lord, but she had never studied the family names of the peerage.

"Only on my mother's side," he replied. "The uncle I mentioned to your father, Alden Trowbridge, was brother to her father, and mad for hunting. I used to visit him when I was a lad, and he taught me all the finer points of riding and hunting. My own father has never hunted, to my knowledge, and only one of my brothers has done much of it."

"How many brothers do you have?" She much preferred learning about him to talking of herself.

"Four. Two older, two younger." That made his father at least a marquess, then. "My next older brother, Edward, used to hunt, but gave it up after he married three years ago. Robert, the eldest, was never much of a rider, and my younger brothers, Peter and Marcus, hunted a bit early on, but didn't stick with it."

"Any sisters?" she asked.

He shook his head. "All boys—a source of pride for my father." His smile was cynical. "I take it you have no siblings?"

"No." She longed to ask who his father was, but perhaps it would come out later. "There's my cousin Harold, of course, but he's six years older than I, and didn't live on the estate until my uncle came back to manage it, after my father's accident."

Lord Anthony nodded. "Is that when he began working as horse trainer?"

"No, not until his—our—grandfather died, two years ago, though he did work with Grandfather a bit before that." She took the proferred wine bottle for another drink. He didn't seem startled by her information, so she added, "I assume you have already heard that my mother's father was a horse trainer, though you've been too much a gentleman to ask outright."

"Someone did mention it during the first meeting of the Quorn," he admitted, "but I don't see it as anything to be ashamed of. After all, there are members of the nobility who train their own horses."

She supposed that was true, though it didn't apply in her case. Grandfather had been of merchant and yeoman stock. "Thank you," she said. "So, where do you make your home when it isn't hunting season?"

"London," he said with a grin that told her he knew she'd wanted to change the subject. "Or, occasionally, at Marland, though I can only take my parents in small doses."

"I see," she said mechanically, trying to conceal her sudden shock. His father was the Duke of Marland, one of the richest and most powerful men in all England. And she, daughter to a country baronet and granddaughter to a horse trainer, had been on the verge of developing a *tendre* for this man!

She took another swallow of wine.

"What of you?" he said when she remained silent, trying to wrap her mind around this unwelcome revelation. "Have you always lived here in Leicestershire?"

"Me? Yes. I've never been more than twenty miles from home, in fact." How rustic and provincial he must think her.

"A pity to have deprived London of your presence—though I can't help but be glad of it."

At the teasing note in his voice, she blinked. "Because I would undoubtedly have made a fool of myself in Town?"

He shook his head, his expression now gentle—almost tender. "Because no one's had a chance to snap you up. And because I might one day have the pleasure of showing you all that you have missed."

For a brief moment, she allowed a bright fantasy to weave itself in the air between them—a fantasy of balls and laughter and love—but then she shook her head.

"Most unlikely, my lord. I could scarcely leave my father to go gadding about London." *Even if we had the money for such a trip*, she added silently, the glittering images dissolving into far drearier ones of a spinster's life spent nursing her father, until she grew too old and proper to so much as sit a horse.

He reached across the table and took her hand in his, startling in its size and warmth. "Someday it will be your turn, Tessa Seaton," he said, as though he'd read her thoughts. "Perhaps sooner than you think."

Her gaze flew to his, and her breath caught in her throat at the intensity she saw there. A sudden longing surged through her that had nothing to do with balls or visits to London or even her beloved horses. Surely it would not be so wicked to snatch one moment of pleasure that she could remember through all the dull years ahead?

"Anthony—my lord—" she whispered.

"Anthony. And please let me call you Tessa. I've longed to do so from the time we first met."

"Of course," she said, then a small laugh escaped her. "Not quite from the moment we met, as you did not then know me at all," she reminded him.

"But I wished to," he said, his answering smile holding a promise that both thrilled and frightened her. "I spent the rest of that night wondering who my mysterious rescuer was and scheming to find out somehow. Imagine my delight to find her again the very next day." He squeezed her fingers in his own.

"Delight?" she breathed.

He nodded. "Definitely delight." He rose, pulling

her to her feet as well—pulling her close to him. "You're something special, Tessa. Never doubt that." Lowering his head, he brushed her lips with his. "Never doubt that," he repeated, then truly kissed her—her very first kiss.

Tessa's eyes drifted closed and she clutched at his shoulders, swept away by the sensation of his lips on hers, the intense intimacy and urgency of his kiss. As all girls must, she'd imagined this moment for years, but the reality was far more exciting. Tilting her head back, she gave herself up to the moment.

His hands, first resting lightly at her waist, now slid up her back, one pressing her more tightly to him, the other threading through her hair at the nape of her neck. Instinctively she parted her lips, and he teased the tip of her tongue with his.

Now her hands began to move, almost without volition. She found herself stroking the broad planes of his back through the thick, damp fabric of his coat, wondering what it would feel like without that barrier. He deepened the kiss until she felt that he was devouring her—that they were devouring each other—but their hunger was only growing.

With one thumb, he traced the line of her jaw, smoothed the curve of her cheek. His other hand moved from her back to her side, kept moving, until he brushed against her breast through the thickness of her cloak and habit.

Though the physical pleasure at this new contact was intense, she suddenly felt a thread of doubt snaking through, spreading a subtle poison. This was a practiced man of the world. What could he possibly want with her beyond a bit of dalliance to enliven the hunting season? A moment ago she'd thought that would be enough, but now she wavered.

He seemed to sense the change in her, for he drew back to look down at her questioningly. "It's all right," he said, his voice a bit ragged. "I won't press you to do anything you don't wish to do—no matter how much I might want to."

His impish grin reassured her even more than his words—and made her want to fling herself back into his arms.

"Th-thank you. It's not that I don't wish—that is, it's—" she stammered, trying frantically to remember why it would be unwise to keep kissing him. "My . . . my father—"

"I understand. I do."

But she knew he didn't, not really. How could he possibly understand the struggle within her right now—knowing that this would likely be the last chance she'd ever have for this sort of intimacy, knowing that no other man would ever make her feel the way this one did. Knowing that if she gave in to her desires, she would wound her father, perhaps beyond healing.

"We . . . we should rest," she said shakily after a moment, then immediately worried that he might misconstrue her words.

His mind, however, apparently traveled a purer plane than hers. "You're right. Here, let's get out of these wet cloaks. You can throw yours over the bed, and I'll take a spot on the floor, near the fire." He stripped off his own coat and tossed it down. "Unless you'd rather be closer to the fire?"

She shook her head, grateful that he couldn't read her thoughts. "I'll be fine on the bed. This habit is of wool, so I should be warm enough."

Suiting action to words, she forced herself to move away from him, to untie her cloak and spread it on the cot—only to hear something rustle underneath it. She sprang back up with a small cry.

"What is it?" he asked, coming toward her in obvious concern.

Already she felt foolish. "A . . . a mouse, most likely. It startled me, that is all." Still, she had no desire now to climb onto the bed. There were plenty of mice in the stables, of course, but that was not quite the same as sleeping with them. Or—what if it was a rat?

"I'm really not all that tired," she lied. "I believe I'll just sit by the fire for a bit. You're welcome to the bed."

One corner of his mouth quirked up, but he did not contradict her. "If that's what you'd prefer, though I'm not especially partial to mice myself. What say you we spread both cloaks on the floor here, and both of us rest by the fire—and away from the vermin?"

Again she fought a battle between propriety and desire, and this time desire won—though she would keep to propriety as much as possible, she promised herself. "Very well. That will help to dry the cloaks faster, and those chairs are not particularly comfortable."

He turned away, ostensibly to spread out the cloaks, but she suspected also to hide a grin at her transparency. No doubt he thought her completely lost to decency, but she couldn't quite make herself care.

"There. Join me? Oh, and bring along the rest of the wine, won't you?"

Feeling utterly wicked, she picked up the bottle, still almost half full, and lowered herself onto the makeshift bed beside him. Conversation was absolutely essential now.

"You were telling me before about when you started hunting. I assume you had to give it up for a while when you joined the army?"

"Not entirely," he said. "I was cavalry, so when the action was slow, many of us were given leave during the season, so that we could hunt. It was considered good training—or so they said. It helped to have a commander who was also an avid sportsman."

She did recall hearing something about that from her father. "Does your former commander still hunt?"

"He does indeed," he replied with a grin that made her heart race. "You've met him, in fact—Lord Rushford."

"He was your commander? Is that when you met, during the war?" Again she felt foolish, though she wasn't sure why.

"We were acquainted before that, as we'd ridden some of the same hunts in our younger days, but war has a way of strengthening bonds." For a moment his eyes were shadowed, but then he smiled. "That was the genesis of the Odd Sock Club, you see, for Stormy and Thor were also members of Rush's regiment."

"But not Lord Killerby?" she asked, feeling somehow privileged that he'd used the nicknames to her without even noticing. As though she were intimate enough with him to understand without explanation—which, of course, she did.

For someone who'd never had any close friends, it was a heady feeling.

"No, Killer's father refused to buy him a commission, and by the time he inherited, the war was nearly over—it was during the Hundred Days, as I recall. We knew him from the hunt. His estate is in southern Nottinghamshire, not so far from here."

Tessa smiled. "Poor Killer. It sounds as though he's been coddled all his life."

Anthony nodded, though his eyes were thoughtful. "Yes, I suppose so. We've taken over, now his father is gone. He somehow seems to bring out our protective natures, perhaps because his enthusiasm outstrips his abilities—and stature."

"Yet you feel I do wrong to protect my own father, who is hampered by an actual infirmity?" she couldn't help asking.

"Touché," he said with a rueful smile. "Perhaps we do Killer no favors with our hovering. Indeed, it's what likely led to his ill-advised adventure today."

But Tessa preferred not to follow that line of reasoning. Surely her protectiveness would not spur her father into similar foolishness? It hadn't so far. Still, it was a lesson to remember.

"It sounds as though the rain is getting worse," she said when the silence again threatened to become awkward.

He shifted and his shoulder brushed hers, making her acutely aware of his nearness and their isolation from the world. "No matter. Nimbus has barely had time to rest his leg yet. I suggest we both get some rest as well."

Suiting action to words, he pulled off his boots, then stretched out atop his cloak, his feet toward the fire. Tessa sat where she was for a long moment, her heart pounding. Did she dare to follow his example?

Steeling her nerve, she unlaced her riding boots, keeping her face averted so that he would not see her blushing. Her stockings were wet and her feet cold, so she extended her legs to warm them by the fire, as he was doing.

"There. Isn't that better?" he asked as she gingerly lowered herself onto her own cloak.

"I, ah, yes," she admitted, her voice unnaturally breathless. She could actually feel the warmth from his body, he was so close, though she'd been careful not to touch him.

He shifted, making her tense, then gently—very gently—stroked her hair. "Relax, Tessa. I promised not to press you to do anything you don't wish to do, and I'm a man of my word—inconvenient as that might be at a time like this."

"I trust you," she said, with perfect honesty. It was herself she did not trust, for in truth she wished him to do far more than was proper—far more than she could ever admit aloud.

"Then sleep." Withdrawing his hand, he rolled onto his back again and closed his eyes.

Tessa watched as his breathing slowed and his face relaxed, fighting a ridiculous sense of disappointment. Now she heartily regretted stopping him when he'd been kissing her earlier, for spoiling her one chance at pleasure, at a memory she could keep forever. It was wrong, but she regretted it all the same.

She lay back on her cloak, forcing herself to stare at the rough-timbered ceiling instead of at him. One thing was certain: she would never sleep a wink with him so close beside her.

Chapter 9

"Tessa? Tessa, wake up." With sunlight filtering through the cottage's one grimy window, Anthony gently shook her shoulder. She stretched, opened her lovely brown eyes, then sat up in sudden alarm to glance at the window.

"What time is it?"

He consulted his pocket watch. "Nearly seven. I've checked on the horses and they seem fine, though I didn't risk trying to touch Nimbus. I thought you'd want to look him over yourself, now that it's light."

"Yes. Yes, of course." Clearly embarrassed, she pulled on her boots and fumblingly laced them. "I must look a fright," she mumbled, trying to smooth her hair with her fingers.

"Not at all," Anthony assured her. Indeed, he thought she looked quite adorably tousled, her cheeks still flushed from sleep and her honey-colored hair in curly wisps around her face. "Would you care to borrow a comb, however?" He held his out to her.

"Thank you." Taking the comb, she undid her hair and began working on the tangles.

It was all he could do not to touch the shining golden-brown mass that tumbled past her shoulders, but he knew where such a caress might lead. Sternly he told himself that if he'd managed to play the gentleman all night, he would not disappoint her now.

"There's fresh water in the cistern now, after last night's rain. I'll bring some in so that you can freshen up." Snatching up the dilapidated ewer by the bed, he stepped outside, removing himself from temptation.

He paused by the cistern at the corner of the cottage to splash his own face with water before filling the ewer. Last night had been as difficult as any he'd spent during the war. He hadn't slept a wink, though he'd pretended to, so that she could relax enough to get some much-needed rest. Once her breathing told him she was asleep, he'd spent the next few hours watching the play of firelight over her face—and thinking.

Tessa had wanted him last night, nearly as much as he'd wanted her. He hadn't missed the eagerness in her touch when he'd kissed and caressed her, or the disappointment in her eyes when he'd stopped. Stopping had been one of the hardest things he'd ever done, but he'd known instinctively that she wasn't ready for more. Not yet. Even if she wished she were.

Nor was he. That was even stranger, but it was

true, for he had realized during the long watches of the night that if once he made Tessa his, he would never be able to let her go. And that thought scared him to his very soul.

He dipped the ewer into the cistern and strode quickly back to the cottage door. "Here. It's cold, so should wake you up nicely."

She took the ewer with a shy smile that went straight to his heart. "Thank you. I . . . I must have been more tired than I realized, for I never thought to sleep so late—or at all."

"You did have rather a trying evening," he reminded her. "I'll go saddle your mare and leave you to wash." He would far rather stay and attempt to rekindle what they'd begun last night, but once the words were spoken he was committed—which was just as well.

Cinnamon was restive and doubtless hungry, but stilled on his command so that he could tighten the girth of the sidesaddle. Tessa had been right that there was nothing wrong with her temperament. Nimbus, however, eyed him nervously.

He was tempted to see whether he could calm the big bay himself, using the methods he'd watched Tessa employ, but decided not to risk it, as she'd be out here herself in a moment. Perhaps later, once the horse was back at Ivy Lodge.

"He hasn't tried to kick or bite, has he?" came Tessa's voice from behind him just then.

"No, he's been a perfect gentleman—though I've not ventured too close." He strove to subdue the surge of desire that shot through him at her unexpected nearness.

She slipped past him, inflaming his errant body further. "What a good boy you are, Nimbus," she said to the horse in her lovely soft lilt. "Come, then, let's get you out into the light and see how you're doing this morning."

She led the bay out of the lean-to, then ran gentle hands along his body and down his legs, examining every inch of him. Anthony found himself quite envying Nimbus.

"He seems to be walking better today," she said at length. "Beyond his sore leg and that cut on his flank, I don't see anything else wrong with him. We'd best get him back so his flank can be stitched, if necessary."

Anthony nodded. "I'm sure Killer has notified the veterinary surgeon, who may already be waiting at Ivy Lodge."

Sudden worry flared in her eyes. "I hope he can be trusted to hold his tongue, should he see me. I know neither you nor Lord Killerby will say anything."

"Of course not. But there's no reason for him to see you. I can lead Nimbus back to Ivy Lodge myself."

She shrugged, drawing Anthony's attention back to her body. "Perhaps, but if Nimbus were to resist, he might end up worse off than before." She pinkened slightly and added, "Nor would I have you hurt."

Anthony grinned down at her. "I appreciate your concern, though I must tell you that I really am quite good with horses, despite what you saw that first night we met."

"Oh, I didn't mean—" She broke off, perceiving that he was teasing her. "Rogue! I'm well aware of that, for I've observed you in the hunt, you know. You're one of the best riders I've ever seen, in fact."

He held up a hand. "Please, please, no flattery. I have far too good an opinion of myself already, I assure you."

As he'd hoped, she burst into laughter—a delightful sound that he'd very much wanted to hear again. "You really are absurd, Lord Anthony," she finally said. "Here, then, why do you not lead Nimbus, and I will lead Cinnamon."

"Ah, the lady wishes to test me. Very well, I accept your challenge." With a mock bow, he extended his hand and she placed Nimbus's reins in it. "Come, lad," he said soothingly to the horse. "Help me to impress my lady, won't you?"

Tessa made a business of untangling Cinnamon's reins so that Anthony could not see her face. *My lady*? A thrill went through her at the thought of being his lady. But he was teasing again, of course. She mustn't let him see how those two little words affected her.

"Shall we go?" she asked in a tolerably disinterested voice.

To her surprise, Nimbus seemed not at all upset by the change. She resisted the temptation to speak to the horse, to continue to soothe him. Though Anthony had spoken teasingly, she suspected that he really did wish to prove, to himself, if not to her, that he could handle the difficult beast.

"I hope my father will not send any message to me at the Hilltops'," she said after a moment. "That would be rather awkward."

"Is he likely to?"

She thought for a moment. "No, I think not, as long as I'm home before noon. He often sleeps that late himself." Though the past few days Sir George had been rising earlier, she remembered.

"We'll have you back well before then," Anthony assured her. "Shall we walk a bit faster?" Nimbus still followed him docilely, but of course that could be because she was still nearby. He scarcely limped at all now.

"Yes, I believe Nimbus could manage a quicker pace, if you can convince him to attempt it."

Flashing her a grin, Anthony glanced back at the horse, then lengthened his stride so that Tessa had to trot a bit to keep up. Nimbus quickened his gait without protest.

"You may ride, if you prefer," he said.

For a moment she was tempted, as that would indeed get them back sooner, but then she shook her head. "I can more quickly get to Nimbus from the ground, should he suddenly become difficult."

"Good point," he agreed, and slowed his pace somewhat, so that she could more easily match it.

They had nearly an hour's walk ahead of them, so she cast about for a suitable topic for conversation.

"You said you have always enjoyed riding," she said. "Did you always wish to go into the army, as well?"

"From the time I was old enough to understand the war," he replied. "My father wasn't keen on the idea, mind you. But with five sons, the succession was in no real danger, so I was finally able to convince him to buy me a commission—as he did for my next younger brother, Peter."

"Did he go into the cavalry as well?" She wanted to learn everything she could about Anthony, to include his family. This might well be her only chance.

"No, he was never as horse-mad as I was. Peter's a prudent sort, focused, observant—incredible memory. Probably why he rose to the rank of colonel and I but to major." His grin showed only pride and affection for his brother, not bitterness.

She gazed at him for a moment, drinking in the

perfection of his handsome profile. "Somehow, I suspect you enjoyed your service more than he."

He glanced at her in surprise, then chuckled. "I won't say war was enjoyable, exactly, but you're probably right. I do have a knack for finding the fun in most any situation, if there's any fun to find."

"Like being caught in the rain with an injured horse and a damsel in distress?" Why had she said that?

"I didn't have to seek far for the enjoyment in *that* scenario," he assured her with twinkling eyes. "Or were you merely fishing for a compliment?"

Confused, she looked away. That wasn't what she was doing, was it? She wasn't sure. "I'm sure you'd have been far more comfortable in your own bed than on that floor," she said, only to realize that that, too, could be misinterpreted.

"There's more to life than comfort," he said. Something in his voice made her glance at him, but then his expression made her look away just as quickly.

This is the son of a duke, she reminded herself sternly. However much he might enjoy bantering— flirting—with her to pass the time, it could ulti- mately come to nothing. She must remember that.

"What of you, Tessa Seaton," he said when she made no response. "Have you always had a gift with horses?"

She flashed him a startled glance at his use of the same word she always used to herself for her ability. "Since my early teens, anyway. My mother had the same gift, the same affinity with horses, so was will- ing to let me spend more time with them than I might otherwise have been allowed to do."

"And her father?"

"Yes, though not to the same extent. He had enough to make him an exceptional trainer, however. It seems to run more strongly in the female line, for my mother told me once that her grandmother also had the gift."

He regarded her thoughtfully. "And was her grandmother Irish, perhaps?"

Tessa stared at him. "How did you know that?"

"I was remembering what Carter, Lord Killerby's groom, said last night—and how you reacted. I simply put the pieces together."

"Clearly, your brother Peter is not the only one with remarkable powers of observation," she exclaimed. "Yes, I wondered if the woman his grandfather remembered might not have been my great-grandmother. Or perhaps this gift is simply more common in Ireland."

"Perhaps. But tell me more about your abilities," he said, carefully leading Nimbus around a fallen tree branch. "Is there any horse you can't tame?"

She shrugged. "I'm sure there must be. I've never been tested against a truly wild one, of course. Even Nimbus here had received some training before we bought him."

"Bad training, I'd wager, and it appears your cousin did little to counteract it. I take it he does not possess your gift?"

"Alas, no. In fact, Harold seems to have quite the opposite effect on horses. I wish Papa could find some other employment for him than trainer, for he is remarkably ill-suited to that task." She knew she should not be telling him such things, but it was such a relief to put her worries into words.

"Perhaps we can think of something," he suggested. "From what I've seen of your cousin, however, I doubt he'll be amenable to anything he perceives as a demotion."

That was true enough, for Harold's ambitions far exceeded his abilities. She suspected that what he really wanted was ownership of Wheatstone itself—through her.

"We're nearly there," she commented, pointing ahead, rather than speak her thoughts.

While part of her wanted to tell Anthony all her problems and allow him to solve them for her, she knew it was not his responsibility. She mustn't come to depend on him, for he would be gone as soon as hunting season ended.

"You stay here," he said when they came within sight of the stables. "I'll lead Nimbus in, then return to help you into the saddle. We don't want to risk you being seen."

She nodded, trying to ignore the sudden knot in her throat. It wasn't as though she had expected him to make an offer rather than put her reputation at risk. That would be absurd, when they could so easily hide the truth. Nor would she accept him if he did. He must know that.

And it wasn't as though they'd done anything truly *wrong*, after all.

Speaking soothingly, he put a hand on Nimbus's withers, then, without Tessa's help, removed the saddle perched atop him. She watched in amazement as the big bay stood quietly during the process. Anthony might not possess her gift, but he really was extremely good with horses. If only . . .

By the time he returned, she had her emotions under control. To her surprise, he was leading Cinder.

"I thought I would escort you at least part of the way," he said in response to her questioning look. "Don't worry—I'll take care that no one sees us."

Though she knew she should protest the additional risk, she found she couldn't forgo the opportunity to spend a bit more time in his company. "If . . . if you insist," she said. Then, as she could not climb into a sidesaddle unassisted, she glanced over at him, only to find him watching her with a bemused expression.

"What?" she asked.

He shook his head. "Nothing. Here, let me help you." Instead of offering her a boost, however, he seized her by the waist and bodily lifted her into the saddle.

The feel of his hands spanning her middle stole her breath. Why had she not noticed before how strong he was?

"Thank you." Her voice sounded high and unnatural.

He vaulted into Cinder's saddle. "It was my pleasure, Tessa—believe me."

She smiled uncertainly, afraid her voice would betray her further. Turning the mare's head, she started in the direction of Wheatstone with him at her side. Though she knew it was impossible, she couldn't help thinking how nice it would be to always have him there.

"You're suddenly very quiet," he commented when they had trotted half the distance without a word.

"I'm sorry. I . . . I was merely working out the story I will give to my father when I get home." Belatedly, realized that she needed to do exactly that.

"It's barely ten o'clock. Can't you keep to the

story you gave last night? It's perfectly plausible that you'd have stayed the night, given the weather."

"Yes, of course, but he's likely to ask for details—topics discussed, dishes served, that sort of thing. I don't wish to sound as though I'm making them up on the spot. As you so astutely pointed out, my father is an intelligent man."

He nodded and changed the subject. "Your uncle said something about selling Cinnamon at auction tonight. Had he intended you to ride her in the Cottesmore today?"

"The Cottesmore!" Tessa gasped. "It has already begun! Uncle Mercer will be furious. Were you not intending to ride with it as well?"

"It's no matter," he said with a shrug. "I've hunted the last three days running, so should probably give Faro a rest anyway. What will your uncle do?" His voice was casual, but he was watching her closely.

Tessa urged Cinnamon to a canter before replying. "He really cannot *do* anything, I suppose, but he will be angry."

Occasionally Uncle Mercer, like Harold, threatened to tell her father about her evening rides, or the state of their finances, but she doubted he would really do it. He would not risk Papa's health that way. Besides, should her father actually learn the truth, her uncle would have little hold on her.

"He can't do a thing," she repeated with a growing sense of relief. "Either he can try to sell Cinnamon tonight anyway, or he can wait until I ride her in a meet next week. Sorry, girl," she added to the horse, patting her neck.

"I know it's business, but it seems a shame you

can't keep her," Anthony commented. "There is clearly affection on both sides."

But Tessa refused to discuss her family's financial straits, as it would only underscore the differences between them. "I will miss her," she admitted, "but we bought her with an eye to resale, so I've known from the first that she couldn't stay."

"Have you ever been allowed to keep a horse you cared about?" His voice was gentle, sympathetic—and almost moved her to tears.

Resolutely, she stiffened her spine. "Of course. When I was a child I had a pony, Bluebell, that I quite doted on. She died but two years since, and I kept her till the end." It was not quite the same thing, though, and she knew it.

"We're nearly in sight of Wheatstone, so I'll leave you now," he said after a long pause during which she wondered desperately what he was thinking. "Did I not promise we wouldn't be seen?"

She reined Cinnamon to a walk, wondering whether he was more concerned with preserving her reputation or his own freedom. Quickly, she thrust away such an ungrateful thought. "Thank you, my lord. You've been very kind—particularly since I bear some of the blame for what happened to your friend."

"Anthony," he reminded her with a smile that went straight to her heart. "And you've made me realize that I'm not free of blame myself. Good day, Tessa." He touched his hat to her, a look in his eyes that was almost as intimate as a kiss.

"Good day . . . Anthony," she said. Then, fearing that he might read in her expression what she felt in her heart, she turned away and set Cinnamon into a canter toward the house.

Anthony watched her ride away, various feelings battling for ascendancy—admiration, trepidation, and something stronger, stronger even than lust. With a muffled curse, he wheeled Cinder around and headed back to Ivy Lodge at a gallop, as though he could somehow leave all his conflicting emotions behind him.

Chapter 10

Bypassing the stables to postpone a meeting with her uncle or cousin, Tessa went straight to the front door, where she handed Cinnamon over to Jonas. Indeed, she was quite anxious to use the necessary and change before facing anyone. And to think.

Sir George called a greeting as Tessa hurried up the stairs toward her room. Anxious that he not see how she was attired, she responded without entering his study, saying she would return shortly. As Sally helped her out of her crumpled habit and into her rose-colored morning gown, she pondered the night just past.

Should the truth become known, her reputation would be ruined, but somehow she could not bring herself to care. Instead, her thoughts were filled with Anthony's face, his voice, the gentle way he'd spoken to her, the generous way he'd forgiven her for what she'd done to his friend. When would she see him again?

She gave her head a quick shake to dispel such thoughts, earning her a puzzled glance from the maid. The more she knew of Anthony, the more it seemed she had found her perfect match in him—in a man who liked her as she was, with her odd talents and many faults. But it didn't matter. He wasn't about to offer, and she couldn't leave her father even if he did—which made her fantasies just that.

"Thank you, Sally," she said when her hair had been brushed out and simply arranged for a day at home. With a nod at her reflection to remind her of her duty, she rose and headed downstairs.

"Here you are at last, Tessa," her father greeted her. "I see you must have slept well at the Hilltops', your eyes are so bright. I assume you have breakfasted?"

"Actually, no," she confessed, suddenly aware of her empty belly. "The Hilltops rise late, and I wished to get home to you. I'll ring for more tea and another plate." She did so, then seated herself at the small table across from her father.

"It was most kind of them to let you stay the night when the weather turned to rain," he commented as a maid brought in a fresh pot of tea and a plate of pastries. "As we now owe them an invitation, I'd thought to have them here to dine next week. What say you?"

Tessa nearly choked on the bun she was eating and had to take a long sip of tea before she could answer. "Surely there is no need of that, Papa? I'm certain they do not expect it, for they know you do not entertain."

"Nonsense. Have you already forgotten how well I did two nights since? It will be the neighborly thing to do. We could even invite two or three other families and make a party of it."

Why had she not foreseen this? It would be disastrous for her father to speak with any of the Hilltops now. Lying certainly had its pitfalls, but now she was obliged to do so again.

"I fear they would not be able to come anyway, Papa, for Mrs. Hilltop told me they leave for London in a few days, and mean to stay the whole winter in Town."

"Indeed? Then it was doubly kind of them to have you to dinner last night, when they must be busy with preparations for their journey."

Tessa glanced sharply at her father but saw no sign of suspicion in his expression. "Yes, I thought so," she said carefully. "I was quite profuse in my thanks."

"And how does Miss Hilltop? She is to make her come-out, is she?"

As Tessa had not seen Cynthia Hilltop in more than a year, she had no idea, but she murmured a vague assent, then changed the subject before she was forced into more falsehoods. "I hope Uncle Mercer was not put out that I was not here to ride in the Cottesmore today."

This successfully diverted her father. "He was, rather, but I told him it was no matter—that you could ride that mare he wishes to sell in the next hunt just as well. He was quite insistent, however, that you speak with him on your return. After you finish your breakfast, of course."

"Of course." She'd known that confrontation couldn't be put off for long. Finishing her pastry and tea, she stood. "Is he in his office, or at the stables?"

"The stables, I believe. Wear a cloak, my dear, for it has grown quite windy, I see."

"I will, Papa, thank you." Dropping a kiss on his head, she ran upstairs for her cloak before heading out to the stables.

"Here you are at last," Uncle Mercer greeted her. "Too late for the Cottesmore, of course. Now it will be Monday at the soonest before we can sell that mare, and you know how the estate needs the money."

"Two days will make little difference," Tessa replied, irritated by his manner. "Is that the only reason you wished to see me—to scold me for missing the hunt?"

He glared at her, then shook his head. "I want you to start working with Vulcan. I've discussed it with Harold, and we think you can have him ready to hunt by the end of the season. With his bloodlines, he'll fetch even more than Nimbus did, for he has breeding potential."

"Don't be absurd!" she exclaimed. Vulcan was the wildest horse they owned, an uncut stallion, far more vicious than Nimbus had been, even at his worst. He was kept in the far paddock, well away from the other horses, and even Tessa had never been allowed near him.

"You said it was absurd to expect Nimbus to behave well enough to hunt, and see how well that turned out?"

"But it didn't turn out well at all," she protested. "Did you not hear? Lord Killerby rode out on him yesterday and was injured, as was Nimbus."

Clearly this was news to him. "When did you hear this?" he demanded.

Belatedly, she realized she could not tell the truth—at least, not all of it. "Ah, Lord Anthony told me, when he escorted me to the Hilltops' last night."

Billy would likely have mentioned her riding out with Anthony, so there was little point in denying that much.

Her uncle cursed. "That's the same lordling who began the prying, is it not?"

"Yes, it is. I fear this incident may cast yet more suspicion on us—and on me. Indeed, he seemed quite angry when he told me." That much was true, even if he had forgiven her later. The memory brought a warm glow. "We'd best stick to properly trained horses for the remainder of the season, Uncle Mercer."

"We have few of those left," he replied sourly.

Tessa was tempted to point out that that was due to Harold's poor techniques, but knew that would only anger her uncle further. "We have Cinnamon. I'll ride her in Monday's meet, unless you wish to sell her tonight."

"No, she'll fetch a better price if your riding is fresh in the gentlemen's minds, and the Quorn is the biggest hunt. As you say, two extra days matter little. When Harold returns from the village, we can consider—ah, here he is now."

Tessa turned to see her cousin riding up on Thunder, their old brown gelding. "So, you are back, I see," Harold greeted her unpleasantly. "Have a good time at the Hilltops', did you?"

Had he spoken to someone in the village who had given the lie to her story? But she could do nothing but brazen it out. "Cynthia was rude to me, as usual, but the dinner was very fine."

"And what of that popinjay you rode out with last night—alone? Did your dear papa know about that?"

"Lord Anthony?" Her surprise was only partly

feigned. She was glad now she hadn't tried to conceal his presence here. "He merely escorted me there—he didn't stay for dinner." Again, fear that he'd discovered the truth gripped her.

"If he wasn't invited to dinner, what was he doing here?" Harold demanded then.

Tessa decided to take the offensive. "He came to tell me about Lord Killerby's accident on Nimbus. Perhaps you heard of it in the village?"

Harold nodded. "Aye, I heard, though it appears both man and horse are like to recover. It's not our fault, you know. Accidents do happen, after all."

Though her relief muted her anger for the moment, Tessa felt obliged to say, "They are less likely when a horse is properly trained beforehand. I won't be party to such a deception again."

"What?" Harold looked to his father. "Did you not tell her what we'd decided about Vulcan?"

Uncle Mercer nodded. "But she has a point. We'll make no profit if men start demanding their money back, for you know Sir George won't hesitate to comply. It might be wisest to sell a few of the better beasts first. Still, I'd like to see how she handles a brute like Vulcan—see what her limits are."

Though irritated at the way they discussed her as though she were not present, Tessa couldn't help feeling a degree of eagerness to take on such a challenge. "I'm quite willing to work with him," she said, "so long as you don't plan to sell him anytime soon."

The three of them walked out to Vulcan's paddock, picking their way carefully through the mud left by last night's rain. Along the way, they passed other horses being exercised by the stable hands, including the chestnut gelding Tessa had worked with yesterday.

"Here, now!" Harold called out to the lad longeing the horse. "Tighten up that line, and don't be afraid to ply the whip if he stops." He entered the paddock to demonstrate, and at once the gelding flattened his ears and veered away. Harold snatched the whip from the stable lad and sent it whistling toward the chestnut's hindquarters.

"Harold!" Tessa exclaimed. "Stop that. I made excellent progress with this horse yesterday, and I'll not have you undo it all by making a perfectly good-tempered horse fearful."

Her cousin whipped the horse again, apparently for mere spite, then rejoined them after a parting word with the stable hand. "I've warned you before, Tessa, don't tell me how to do my job," he growled. "Especially in front of the hands."

"If you did your job properly, I wouldn't have to say a thing," she snapped back. "You do more harm than good with such methods, as I've told you numerous times." She looked to her uncle for support.

Uncle Mercer, however, only shrugged. "There are many schools of thought on horse training," he said. "And Harold is right that it's bad for discipline when you criticize him in front of his underlings. But do try not to take your temper out on the horses, son, eh?"

Tessa bit back a retort, knowing it would do no good. Uncle Mercer always took Harold's part in such disputes, no matter how clearly in the wrong he was. She was glad Nimbus was no longer in Harold's power, however unready to hunt he might be. Soon Cinnamon would be away from him as well.

Most of their horses had the potential to be superb hunters or hacks, if they could only be removed from Harold's inept training. If only—

They reached Vulcan's paddock and were greeted by a scream of fury as the stallion spotted them and charged the tall fence. He was as intimidating as Tessa remembered—coal black, a full seventeen hands high, and completely unbroken. She stepped back, along with the others, when he stopped a hairsbreadth shy of crashing into the fence, only to stretch his long neck toward them, teeth snapping.

Harold nudged her. "Go on, go on, see if your magic works on him," he said with an unpleasant grin. Clearly he expected her to fail, and Tessa honestly expected the same. This horse was a monster.

She took a tentative step forward, staying well out of reach of those enormous teeth, which Vulcan instantly directed her way. "Now, then, lad, what are you so angry about?" she asked in her lilting sing-song.

The stallion snapped at her again, then gave another scream, this time of frustration.

Tessa tried again. "Vulcan, Vulcan, calm down. Everything will be fine, I assure you." She moved a tiny bit closer, though not close enough to be bitten.

Now Vulcan's ears twitched and a shudder ran across his skin, as though he were trying to twitch off a biting fly. He swung his head back and forth, teeth still bared, though he did not snap again. The wild look had not left his eyes, however.

"That's better," she cooed. "Not much better, but better." The words, of course, were unimportant. It was the tone that mattered—and he seemed to be attending, at least a little.

Half an hour later, the horse was standing quietly,

only an occasional stamp of a rear hoof showing any sign of agitation. Tessa had not attempted to touch him, of course, but she was gratified that she'd been able to soothe him to this point with her voice alone.

Backing away from the fence, she turned to her uncle and cousin, who had been watching in open-mouthed silence. "I believe that is enough for today. Trust takes time to build, but I seem to have made a first step. I'll visit him again tomorrow."

"I'd not have believed it," Harold exclaimed. At the sound of his voice, Vulcan reared, neighed fiercely, and galloped away.

Tessa sighed. "Perhaps it would be best if I came alone next time. I promise to be extremely careful."

Neither man thought this wise. "How can I gauge your progress with him if I do not watch?" Harold asked, and his father agreed.

"And what if the brute were to injure you?" Uncle Mercer added. "There would be no one around to know, or to go for help."

In vain she argued that one of the stable lads could watch from a distance. Finally she gave up, hoping that they would eventually realize that she was right, at which point their greed would likely win out over any concern for her safety.

Walking back to the house, she felt that her life had become much happier of late. Not only was she riding to the hunt, a wonderful, exhilarating experience, but she was able to spend more time with the horses. She also had the first real friend she'd had in years in Lord Anthony—and it appeared that last night's indiscretion had gone undiscovered.

Her shoes were muddy from the fields, so she went in by the kitchens and upstairs to change her footwear before coming down to speak with her father. Perhaps between them they could come up with some other task for Harold, one that would keep him from spending so much time with the horses.

As she approached his study, the sound of voices told her that her father was not alone. This was surprising, as Griffith had been in the kitchens eating when she'd passed through. Had he finished so quickly? But when she entered, it was to see Lord Anthony sitting in the chair next to her father.

At her entrance, he rose and bowed. "Ah, Miss Seaton, I'm delighted that you have returned. I understand you were forced to stay the night at the Hilltops'?"

She curtsied, hoping her father would not notice the color she felt rushing to her face. "I, ah, yes, my lord. They were kind enough to invite me so that I would not have to ride back in the rain. How does Lord Killerby today?"

Her father's startled glance reminded her belatedly that he did not know about the accident. She would trip herself up with her web of lies yet! But Anthony covered her blunder smoothly.

"He is doing much better, though he won't be walking for some time yet. I presume Mr. Emery told you about his fall?" He directed the question to both of them.

Tessa nodded, while her father shook his head. "Harold heard about it in the village," she improvised. "I was quite sorry to hear of it. What of the horse he was riding?" She tried to communicate with a look that she preferred her father not learn it was Nimbus.

"A strain and a bad scratch, but the vet assures us it will recover." He turned back to Sir George before he could ask questions and said, "I'm sure, immobilized as he is, Lord Killerby will be delighted that you have accepted my invitation."

"Invitation?" Tessa echoed. "What do you mean? Papa?"

Sir George beamed at her. "Lord Anthony has been kind enough to invite me to dinner tomorrow night at Ivy Lodge. He has promised to send a carriage for me, and to wrestle me into it, one way or another."

"I have indeed," Anthony agreed, smiling first at his host and then at Tessa. He held her eyes for a long moment, and she smoothed her instinctive frown before her father could see it.

Still, she could not quell her misgivings. "And you're certain you wish to do this, Papa?"

"I wish to try," he replied with a determined nod. "If I can't manage it, best to know it at once, eh? And if I can, why then, who knows what I may attempt next?" He winked at her.

Tessa blinked, unaccustomed to her father in such a mood. Recalling her conversation with Anthony that morning, however, she restrained herself from voicing her concerns.

"Very well, Papa." She would have to speak privately to Anthony before he left. He needed to understand the risks, not only to her father's health, but to his peace of mind, should he discover himself unable to travel after all. She would prefer to spare Sir George the potential blow to his pride, but he seemed set on this course.

The conversation turned to the hunt then, with her father expressing regret that neither she nor Anthony had been able to ride in the Cottesmore meet today. Tessa found herself blushing as she remembered the reason, even though her father had no inkling.

Last night, even this morning, seemed almost like a dream now, with Anthony sitting there so formally, paying her no special attention. Had she read too much into the intimacy they had briefly shared? His demeanor now would suggest so.

"—won't you, Tessa?" her father was saying.

She turned to him with a start. "My apologies, Papa, I was woolgathering. What did you ask of me?"

"I was suggesting that you see Lord Anthony out, as I'm well aware you'll want to give him advice on how he should deal with me tomorrow, out of my hearing." Her father's eyes twinkled.

"Oh, but I—" she started to protest, startled, then shook her head. "You know me far too well, Papa, for I'd planned to do just that. I'll try not to fuss, however. Lord Anthony?"

He stood, and she accompanied him from the room and down to the front door. "I suppose I need not tell you to be careful of him tomorrow night?" she said with a self-conscious smile. "I'm trying to take your advice to heart, as you see."

"And doing an admirable job," he assured her, his answering smile making her heart flutter. "I wish you could come as well, but of course it would not be proper."

"No. I understand. I'll trust you not to tire my father." Much as she was trying to avoid coddling, she needed that reassurance.

He gave it. "I'll be as watchful of his health as ever you could be, Tessa, I promise."

She knew he meant it and smiled her relief. Just as she relaxed, however, he glanced up the stairs behind her, then bent down to give her a swift kiss. "Until tomorrow," he whispered, and then he was gone.

Tessa stood by the front door for a long moment, her fingers at her lips. Smiling to herself, she turned—only to notice the shabbiness of the front hall. If Papa was going to be carried through here tomorrow, she had work to do!

Over the next few hours, she set their few servants to polishing and rearranging, moving out those things that were worn or obviously repaired and replacing them with anything she could find that could be cleaned up to look elegant. The silver sconces were stripped of tarnish, an ornament or two was fetched from storage, the carpet was taken out and beaten to within an inch of its life. By dinnertime, the hall was presentable, making her wonder why she'd never done this before.

"Thank you, Mrs. Bealls," she said to the matronly woman who acted as both housekeeper and cook—not that Sir George knew that. "You really are a treasure."

"Thankee, miss, but if we're to convince your father of that, I'd best go check on Sally in the kitchen. I left her to watch the soup, but she's no cook, I fear. I'll send her up to you once I've taken over."

Tessa nodded and sent her off, then headed upstairs herself to put off the mobcap she'd donned for her share in the work. She really must speak with Uncle Mercer about hiring more staff, if Papa persisted in his plan to entertain more. The servants they had now were by no means sufficient to a house of this size.

She came down to dinner early, again hoping to have a private word with her father about Harold, but discovered Uncle Mercer already in the parlor with him. Sir George was talking animatedly about his outing the next day, but Uncle Mercer was frowning.

"Really, sir, you should have consulted with me before agreeing, for I cannot think this wise. At least let me send for your physician, that we may hear his opinion on the matter."

"Nonsense," Sir George exclaimed. "That old charlatan is far too conservative for my tastes. The two of you would have me keep to my bed continually, and there's clearly no need of that. Eh, Tessa?" He turned to her for confirmation as she entered the parlor and took a seat.

"No need at all." For all that she'd not been in favor of this outing herself, she would not take Uncle Mercer's side now. Not when her father was so eager to go.

Her uncle shrugged. "I must hope that you'll prove me wrong then," he said somewhat sourly.

Harold came in then, and a few moments later dinner was announced. Tessa realized with a sigh that her talk with her father would have to wait until tomorrow, for by the time dinner was over, he would certainly have had too much wine to be trusted to carry on a discreet conversation.

After breakfast the next morning, the rector came, as he always did on Sundays, to conduct a private service for the family in the little chapel at the rear of the first floor. Tessa took the opportunity to pray for guidance in the matter of her cousin's training—and in the matter of Lord Anthony—but couldn't say that she received any sort of answers.

The afternoon was spent out at the stables, where

she again worked with Vulcan, finally progressing to the point where she could place a hand on his shoulder without him snapping at her.

"You've got him good and calm now," Harold said softly from behind her. "Here, let's see if I can touch him while he's quiet."

Before Harold could get within two feet of him, however, the stallion reached out his long neck and snapped, narrowly missing Harold's shoulder. Harold jumped back and Vulcan reared, screaming, before galloping away to the far corner of the paddock.

Tessa sighed. "Really, Harold, I'll make much better headway with him if you stay well away."

"We had this all out yesterday. You've been out alone a deal more than is wise lately, in my opinion. People are beginning to talk."

She stared at him. "People? What people?"

He shrugged. "Those hereabouts," he said evasively.

"I've been riding out alone for years," she reminded him. "I've never cared about any talk before, and neither have you, as it's made your job easier."

Now he scowled at her. "That was before—I just think I need to keep a closer eye on you, that's all, and Father agrees."

She suspected this had something to do with her riding out alone with Anthony Friday night, but thought it wiser not to ask. The less she seemed to make of that, the better. It would not do at all for Harold to suspect her feelings there. At best, he'd taunt her for entertaining foolish hopes. At worst, he might see Anthony as a threat, and do or say something to warn him off.

Such thoughts led inevitably to Anthony's impending visit to take her father to Ivy Lodge. With that in mind, she bathed and dressed with unusual care, even though she knew she would see him for only a few moments. When she came downstairs shortly before he was due to arrive, she felt confident that she looked her best.

Again she hoped to have time to talk to her father about Harold's training, and again her hopes were dashed, for both Harold and his father were in the parlor with Sir George. All three stared at her in some surprise when she entered, and suddenly she wished she hadn't taken such pains with her appearance.

"My, you look lovely, Tessa," her father exclaimed. "Does she not, gentlemen?"

They both murmured agreement, Harold frowning at her suspiciously. She thanked them, though her heart sank at the thought of an evening spent hearing her cousin's barbed comments and clumsy attempts at gallantry. She tried to think of something to say that would turn their attention elsewhere, but before she could do so, a knock came at the front door, and a moment later Lord Anthony and his friend Mr. Turpin were announced.

As she'd hoped, Anthony's eyes lit up when he saw her. "You are lovelier every time I see you, Miss Seaton," he declared.

Taking her hand, he bent over it, his eyes holding hers in a way that made her stomach start to flutter. Harold cleared his throat loudly, and Anthony's smile widened a fraction. He dropped a lingering kiss on the back of her gloved hand, then straightened and turned toward her father.

"Sir George, with your permission, I should like to extend my dinner invitation to your daughter as well."

Tessa stared. "But—" she began, even as her father spoke her thoughts, with evident surprise.

"That's very kind of you, Lord Anthony, but as you yourself pointed out, Ivy Lodge is a bachelor establishment."

"Aye," Harold chimed in belligerently. "What do you mean by insulting her with such an invitation?"

Though Anthony's smile did not falter, there was something in his eyes as he glanced Harold's way that made Harold step back a pace.

"I would never insult Miss Seaton," Anthony said, his voice reminding her somehow of a drawn sword. "As it happens, Lord Killerby's mother has come to stay with her son during his convalescence. Lady Killerby's presence at Ivy Lodge makes it perfectly eligible for Miss Seaton to visit."

"In that case," said Sir George, "I'm sure my daughter will be delighted to accept. Will you not, Tessa?"

She smiled, her spirits suddenly soaring at the prospect of an evening in Anthony's company instead of Harold's. "I will indeed," she said.

Chapter 11

Anthony couldn't help enjoying the impotent fury on Harold Emery's face as he returned Tessa's smile. "I am delighted," he said with perfect sincerity. "Shall we go, then?"

"Will you not at least have a glass of sherry first?" asked Sir George.

Anthony shook his head, still smiling. "It is our turn to play host, Sir George, and I am eager to hear your opinion of Ivy Lodge—nor do I wish to be scolded by Lady Killerby, should we delay. The carriage is at the door, so let us get you into it."

Sir George glanced at Tessa, the merest flicker of nervousness passing over his face, but then he nodded. "Very well, gentlemen, I put myself in your hands—literally."

As they had planned it between themselves, Thor stepped forward to grasp the back of Sir George's

Merlin Chair, while Anthony bent down to take hold of the front. Between them, they were easily able to lift man and chair, carrying him through the study door and down the stairs.

Anthony glanced about the hall as they paused there, noting the changes that had taken place since yesterday. Catching Tessa's eye, he winked and nodded to show that he understood. She colored slightly, smiling self-consciously in reply.

Lifting the chair again, Anthony and Thor carried Sir George out the front door and down the broad steps to the waiting carriage. There they carefully helped Sir George from his chair, Thor lifting him under the arms and Anthony catching him about the knees. Though Tessa hovered anxiously, they were able to get him into the carriage with little difficulty.

"There. Did I not tell you it would be quite easy?" Anthony asked. He placed pillows under Sir George's feet while Thor helped the coachman to tie his chair securely on top of the carriage.

"You did indeed, though I confess I didn't quite believe you," Sir George replied. "If I'd any idea it would be so simple as this, I'd have left the house years ago. I am indebted to you, Lord Anthony."

Anthony glanced back at Tessa, still standing outside the carriage, to find her frowning. With a glance at the others, he quickly moved to her side. "Are you still worried?" he asked softly. "You need not be, I assure you."

She looked up at him, her brown eyes troubled. "No, not worried, precisely. It is only, well, I begin to realize how much I have sheltered him, and to wonder whether it was truly for the best."

Looking down at her, he had to resist a strong urge to pull her close, to erase the unhappiness from her eyes with a kiss. "I have not the smallest doubt that you have always acted in what you believed to be your father's best interests. He is very lucky to have you for a daughter, Tessa."

"Thank you," she whispered.

"Anthony!" Thor called from the carriage. "Are we going or not?"

Looking up, he saw Harold Emery watching from the open front door, his eyes narrowed. "Coming!" he called back, holding out his arm to Tessa, as much to tweak young Emery as out of politeness. "Shall we?"

She nodded, thanking him again with her eyes. He escorted her to the carriage and helped her into the seat beside her father, and a moment later they were off, Anthony taking care to distract Sir George with conversation, so that he would not look too closely at the exterior of Wheatstone and notice the still-sagging roof of the west wing. Luckily it would be dark when they returned.

Sir George himself was quite animated during the drive, commenting along the way about landmarks he remembered and a few small changes he noticed in the landscape.

In only about twenty minutes, they reached Ivy Lodge. Using the same process in reverse, Thor and Anthony extricated Sir George from the carriage, seated him in his chair, and carried him up to the main drawing room. Accepting the glass of sherry Stormy offered him, Sir George looked around happily.

"How pleasant this is," he exclaimed. "Really, I must make a habit of this sort of thing."

"I hope that you can do so, Papa," Tessa said, and Anthony thought she sounded sincere—though there was still a trace of worry in her eyes. She then turned to Killer, who was ensconced on a sofa, his bound foot elevated on a pillow.

"You will excuse me for not rising, will you not, Miss Seaton?" he asked with a grin, his exuberance dampened not at all by his injury.

"Of course, Lord Killerby," she replied warmly. "Are you in much pain?"

He shook his head cheerfully. "Devil a bit, so long as I stay like this. Even if I were, it would be a small price to pay for your concern."

Anthony felt obliged to step forward. "The surgeon says he is mending nicely, though of course he won't be up to any more foolish antics anytime soon."

"Foolish antics? My William?" came a voice from the doorway. Everyone turned to see Lady Killerby make her entrance, resplendent in magenta satin, an enormous green feather sprouting from her bright yellow turban. "Surely he hasn't managed any yet this evening? I should hate to have missed them."

Nearer fifty than forty, Lady Killerby was still a handsome woman with a fine figure, though her fading beauty was rather overshadowed by her flamboyant choice of attire. Tessa blinked at this unlikely vision before stepping forward to curtsy.

"Lady Killerby," said Lord Anthony, "may I present Miss Tessa Seaton and her father, Sir George Seaton."

The dowager pierced Tessa with a searching gaze, then gave a slight nod before turning to her father. "I'm delighted, of course, but we need no introduction, do we, Sir George? I'm certain you won't have forgotten Lily Gilthwaite."

Tessa glanced at her father in surprise, to find him

grinning widely. "No indeed! What a delight to see you again, Lily—or, should I say, my lady. It has been what, twenty-five years? I was devastated along with all of the other young men in the country when Lord Killerby snatched you up."

"Flatterer." Lady Killerby swept out a pink feathered fan and fluttered it flirtatiously.

While Tessa watched the playful banter between her father and Lady Killerby with astonishment, Lord Anthony moved to her side. "I begin to think this visit will be even better for Sir George than I had predicted. Lady Killerby said nothing beforehand about being previously acquainted with him."

"I suspect she is a woman who prefers to preserve the element of surprise," Tessa replied in an undertone. "Thus she ensures that all attention is hers."

"Now, Tessa, don't begrudge your father this bit of enjoyment," Anthony chided her softly. "It will do him more good than harm, I'm certain."

Tessa glanced up at him uncertainly. Was that what she was doing? Perhaps so, for she couldn't deny a spark of resentment toward the lady for winning smiles from her papa so easily. "You're right, and I'm sorry," she said, determined not to be so selfish in the future.

He patted her shoulder. "There's my girl. Now, come meet the other members of the Odd Sock Club." He led her across the room and introduced her to Roger Littleton and Lord Uppingwood. Lord Rushford and Sir Charles Storm she already knew, of course, and they expressed their delight at seeing her again.

It was a genial group that went in to dinner a few minutes later. Tessa found herself seated in the middle of the table, with Lord Anthony on her right and Lord Uppingwood on her left. Directly across from her sat Lady Killerby, flanked by her son, his injured foot propped on a low stool, and Tessa's father.

"What is this I hear of you riding to hunt, Miss Seaton?" Lady Killerby asked as the soup was served, showing not the least reticence about speaking across the table. "That's sure to have raised some eyebrows, eh?"

Tessa glanced at her father in alarm. "Not . . . not that I've noticed, my lady."

"Pish. People are so prudish these days, I'd be amazed if it hasn't caused talk. When I was your age, girls had a bit more freedom, but nowadays it pays to be more circumspect—or so I hear."

"No, Mother, really," Lord Killerby protested. "Miss Seaton's done nothing improper. Just a bit unconventional, is all."

"Indeed, ma'am," Sir George put in, "I made certain the huntmasters were amenable before allowing her to ride, and her uncle always accompanies her, to preserve propriety."

"Her uncle?" Lady Killerby echoed. "And who—?"

"Mercer Emery, my Grace's brother," Sir George clarified.

She sniffed, making her turban quiver. "Oh, yes, I remember Mercer Emery. Married some local tradesman's daughter, didn't he?"

"I believe she was a solicitor's daughter," he replied uncertainly. "She died some twenty years ago."

"Well, that's neither here nor there," she said, waving a hand dismissively. "The point—"

"The point," Lord Anthony interrupted her, "is that Miss Seaton is by no means dependent only on her uncle's chaperonage. Sir George can trust me, and the rest of the Odd Sock Club, to take care of her safety in the hunt."

Lady Killerby stared. "A lusty group of single young gentlemen? What earthly good are they? As soon set a fox to take care of the henhouse and thereby declare it safe."

Tessa felt herself blushing at such plain speaking, vividly remembering her night alone with Lord Anthony. Heaven preserve them if Lady Killerby learned of that.

"Indeed, Miss Seaton needs no one to keep her safe in the hunt," Lord Killerby declared then. "She rides better than the rest of us put together, so should any man attempt the least thing, she could simply leave him in her dust."

Those around him chuckled and voiced their agreement. Tessa felt her cheeks warm even more, but at least her father seemed pleased by the praise.

Lady Killerby, however, seemed unimpressed. "Is that so? No, no more of your assurances, gentlemen. I will form my own opinion tomorrow."

"Then you mean to join the Quorn yourself, my lady?" Lord Anthony asked in evident surprise.

"Tut. I was never much of a horsewoman, even in my heyday. I'll follow in my phaeton, as I'm wont to do at home—and as I did here once or twice in my youth. It will be a fine thing to watch the Quorn again, I declare! And with me there," she added, "there can be no question of proper chaperonage of Miss Seaton. That will put paid to any wagging tongues, I'll be bound."

Tessa noted that her father still looked uncomfortable. "Really, Lily, I must protest," he said. "I've heard nothing of any wagging tongues at my Tessa's expense."

The look Lady Killerby turned on him was almost pitying. "But then you wouldn't, George, dear. Indeed, you'd be the last to hear—the father always is."

"Then I suppose I must be grateful that you will be there to lend her added respectability." He shrugged slightly in response to Tessa's frown.

Lady Killerby appeared not to notice. "You young men should be thanking me as well, you know," she declared, evidently enjoying their somewhat scandalized attention. "I know you all consider yourselves confirmed bachelors, though one or two of you will have to marry eventually, for your successions." She glanced at her son, who grimaced.

"However," she continued, "you would all do well to beware of situations that can thwart your intentions—which, I assure you, clever young ladies are all too adept at creating. None of you, I'm sure, would care to be *trapped* into marriage. Not, of course, that I am implying Miss Seaton would attempt such a thing."

Tessa felt her insides contract. She dared not glance at Lord Anthony, though she was acutely aware of him by her side. That situation had not been of her devising, of course. Still, it was quite true that if it became public, he would be obliged to marry her, willing or no. Thank heaven no one knew of it!

Anthony stirred. "Believe me, my lady, we need no such caution. We're all well aware of how precarious our enviable bachelorhood is, are we not, gentlemen?"

A chorus of agreement went around the table, followed by laughter, and then the conversation moved on to other matters, much to Tessa's relief. She tried to appear interested and to take her part in the ensuing discussion of tomorrow's meet, but in truth she still stung from Anthony's words.

So he saw his freedom as both precarious and enviable? She was determined, then, that he should never see *her* as any sort of threat to it. No longer would she harbor foolish hopes that he'd made it more than clear were beyond his power to realize.

The carriage ride home was a trial for Tessa, for Lord Anthony persisted in complimenting her on how she'd handled Lady Killerby's interference, which was a constant reminder of that part of the conversation that now preyed on Tessa's mind.

"Most young ladies would have given her a right set-down," he was saying, "or at least have felt the need to defend themselves against her insinuations. You did neither and won her respect thereby. I congratulate you, for that's a rare prize, believe me."

Tessa hoped the dimness of the coach hid the effort it cost her to smile. "I am gratified, my lord, that you should say so."

He reached across to place his hand on hers, heedless of Sir George at her side. "I have reason to thank you as well, Miss Seaton."

She glanced up in surprise. He must mean her silence about the night they'd spent together.

"Aye, you added greatly to the enjoyment of the evening," Mr. Turpin said. "As did you, Sir George. I hope you will both visit again—particularly while Lady Killerby is in residence."

They all chuckled at that, and Tessa forced herself to do so as well, trying desperately to ignore the fresh pain Lord Anthony's gratitude gave her.

A few moments later they reached Wheatstone,

and the gentlemen soon had Sir George safely returned to his study.

"There, see what a bit of practice has done for our efficiency?" Lord Anthony exclaimed. "Anytime you wish to go out, Sir George, don't hesitate to call upon us. We'll be happy to oblige, eh, Thor?"

Mr. Turpin agreed, then they took their leave. As before, Tessa walked down to the front door with them, though the presence of Mr. Turpin precluded any sort of private conversation with Anthony. She realized that was probably just as well.

"We look forward to seeing you at tomorrow's meet, Miss Seaton," he said, smiling down into her eyes, his expression reflecting none of the turmoil she'd been feeling all evening.

"I hope Cinnamon and I will acquit ourselves well," she replied, her voice sounding stiff to her own ears. If only she could ask him . . . But ask him what? Whether he'd meant what he said about being a confirmed bachelor? Foolishness!

He sent her a searching look, but she turned away before he could decipher her expression. "Thank you, my lord, and you, Mr. Turpin, for your help in getting my father to and from Ivy Lodge. It meant more to him than you can imagine—and to me, as well."

Again they expressed their willingness to be of service at any time in the future, and then they took their leave. Tessa returned to her father, putting on a determinedly cheerful expression as she entered his study.

"What a pleasant evening that was," she said. "I had no idea that you'd known Lord Killerby's mother in your youth, Papa."

Sir George's grin was almost boyish. "I confess, I

hadn't made the connection before seeing her to-night. Stewart, her late husband, was still plain Mr. Verge when he married her all those years ago."

Griffith entered then, so Tessa retreated, glad to hear the happiness in her father's voice as he regaled his manservant with stories of his first outing in six years. Despite her earlier misgivings, the visit had been good for him. She would do nothing to oppose future excursions—though Uncle Mercer might.

That thought reminded her that she had yet to talk with her father about replacing Harold as horse trainer. It was as well she had that problem to distract her, for she had a difficult time sleeping, her emotions were in such a jumble. When she finally did fall asleep, it was to dream of Anthony—first tender, as he'd been that night in the cottage, then pushing her away with a laugh. It was a relief when Sally woke her at daybreak.

"Papa, I've been meaning to talk with you about Harold," she said without preamble as soon as she joined her father in his study before leaving for the Quorn. He had risen early as well, to see her off. "I'm not entirely certain that horse training is the best career for him."

Sir George blinked, clearly startled. "But Mercer says he is doing quite well. Look at the fabulous sum he got for that new horse, Nimbus, last week. Surely Harold's training had something to do with that?"

Tessa bit her lip, uncertain how much of the truth to disclose. Memory of Harold's cruelty to that new chestnut yesterday spurred her on, however. "Actually, Papa, I believe I had more influence on Nimbus than Harold did. In fact, he frequently needs my help with the more . . . difficult horses."

"Indeed?" Sir George frowned. "I knew you were riding more than you used to, to train for the hunt, but you know I don't care to have you spending too much time at the stables, Tessa. It's not proper. You heard what Lady Killerby said last night."

She didn't care to be reminded of that. "I know, Papa, but truly, I don't mind. I like spending time with the horses, as I've always told you, and I'm careful that no one outside our family and servants ever sees me there. To be honest, I rather doubt Harold would be able to do his job there without my help."

"Are you suggesting I hire another trainer? Mercer would never allow me to turn him off."

"No, not turn him off, of course, but I thought that perhaps we could find some other job on the estate that he could do, something better suited to his, ah, temperament. Meanwhile, I would be more than happy to take over the bulk of his training duties, with the help of the stable hands."

But Sir George shook his head. "That won't do at all, Tessa. Why, you are just beginning to go out socially, dining at the Hilltops' and at Ivy Lodge. There will be hunt balls later, as well. You won't have time to train all of our horses, as well."

"But Harold—"

"Harold what?" Harold and his father walked into the study, Harold's eyes narrowed suspiciously.

Sir George turned to them with a smile. "Tessa feels that horse training may not be the best utilization of Harold's talents," he said, surprising her with his diplomacy. "We were simply discussing other options."

Harold turned an angry glance on Tessa. "Criticizing my training again, were you? I told you—"

He broke off when his father laid a restraining hand on his shoulder.

"Miss Seaton has a tender heart," Uncle Mercer said. "It is small wonder her feminine sensitivity recoils from some of the methods necessary to get the most out of the horses. Perhaps it would be better if she not watch Harold at his work quite so often, much as she seems to enjoy spending time with him—and the horses, of course."

Tessa gaped at his implication, even as her father nodded his agreement. She, enjoy spending time with Harold? Not bloody likely.

"I quite concur, Mercer," Sir George was saying. "She was suggesting the opposite, that she spend more time at the stables.

"I can't say I'm surprised," Uncle Mercer said, "but under the circumstances—"

Her father blinked, then frowned slightly, shooting a glance Tessa's way. "Yes, yes, it is quite out of the question—particularly given what you have just said."

Tessa noticed with irritation that Harold was smirking. "Very well," she said, trying to keep the frustration from her voice. "I'll not work with the horses at all, then." So much for taming Vulcan for them.

Though Harold's smirk disappeared at this threat, her uncle actually smiled. "That might be best. Except for those horses you will be riding for sale, of course. I myself can oversee your time spent familiarizing yourself with them. After all, a reputation is a fragile thing—don't you agree, Sir George?"

"I'm certain I can leave such matters entirely in your hands, Mercer," her father said quickly. "There, Tessa, all is well."

She couldn't bring herself to speak. It was clear that if he chose, Uncle Mercer could convince her father to forbid her riding at all—something she didn't wish to provoke him to.

Tessa found herself unable to eat much breakfast, so upset was she by the conversation just past. Harold kept smirking at her, making her want to slap him. Meanwhile, Uncle Mercer discussed estate business with her father, though most of what he said Tessa knew to be false.

More and more, she found herself regretting her original decision six years ago to keep the truth about the estate from her father. If he discovered it now, as much worse as things had become over the years, the shock might well kill him—which left her trapped in her own web of lies.

Surely there must be some way to extricate herself without shattering her father's pride or destroying his health?

"Come, Tessa, we must go if we are to be in at the start of today's meet," her uncle said, breaking into her thoughts.

"Give Lady Killerby my regards," said Sir George as she rose. "I'll look forward to hearing everything upon your return."

Tessa nodded mechanically and followed Uncle Mercer from the room. Harold followed them downstairs and out the front door.

"What game are you playing at, Cousin?" he demanded as soon as they were out of the house. "I told you Sir George would never turn me off, didn't I?"

She glared at him. "I only asked him to consider a position better suited to you than that of trainer. Anyone else—anyone who could see you at work, that is—would have turned you off long ago."

His face darkened and he took a step toward her, but as before, Uncle Mercer intervened. "There was no harm done, Harold," he said to his son. Then, to Tessa, "I'd advise you not to try anything of the sort again, missy. Unless you want your father to learn the true state of his finances—not to mention the truth about your own behavior?"

She was sorely tempted to tell him to do his worst, but the thought of her father's weak heart stopped her. "I felt obliged to do something, for the sake of the horses," she said, forcing an apology she didn't feel into her tone. "I never intended to harm Harold in any way."

"If you don't want the horses out of your reach for good, you'd be wise to leave such concerns to me," her uncle told her. "Now, we'd best be on our way."

Harold made a point of boosting her into Cinnamon's sidesaddle. Though his touch made Tessa cringe, she was careful not to show it, for Harold could be trusted to make the most of any weakness she revealed. Touching her heel to Cinnamon's side, she left him behind, wishing it could be forever. After tonight, Cinnamon, at least, would never have to face Harold again. Tessa took what comfort she could from that thought.

Upon reaching the meet at Quorndon Hall, however, she at once saw Lord Anthony in conversation with Lady Killerby, and all traces of comfort fled.

Chapter 12

"**I**f you'll excuse me, my lady?" Anthony couldn't help being amused at Lady Killerby's wicked assessments of each sportsman as he arrived at the meet, but the moment he saw Tessa, he felt an intense need to be at her side.

Lady Killerby followed his gaze. "Ah, that's where the wind sets, does it? I suspected as much last night. Run along then, lad—but be cautious. Your father would scarcely approve, you know." She waved him away from the side of her pink and green phaeton with her orange parasol.

Anthony merely tipped his hat to her, determined not to give her any more ammunition for gossip or advice. In vain did he remind himself that she was right, as he approached Tessa. His father *wouldn't* approve. But the more time he spent with Tessa—and the more time he spent away from her—the more he felt that he would never be happy without her.

"I began to fear you wouldn't make it today, Miss Seaton," he said, riding up to her and executing a bow from the saddle, sweeping his top hat before him with a flourish.

"We were a bit late starting," she replied with a glance at her uncle, on the same brown gelding he'd ridden before.

Mercer Emery nodded. "No chance we'd miss today—not after missing the Cottesmore meet on Saturday. Feel free to tell your friends that this mare will be up for sale tonight."

Mention of the Cottesmore brought the reason for Tessa's missing it vividly to Anthony's mind—and to other parts of his body. That Tessa avoided his eye made him hope that her memory was similarly—and as pleasantly—engaged. She did not look precisely happy, however. He made a guess at the reason.

"I know you're not as eager to sell, Miss Seaton, but I trust you won't let that hamper your riding today." He leaned down as he spoke, trying to get a better glimpse of her face.

"She won't," her uncle said curtly. "Business is business. She knows that as well as I."

Tessa nodded, though Anthony thought he detected a small sigh before she spoke. "Yes, I know it well. We'll have a fine last run, won't we, Cinnamon?" She stroked the mare's neck with a small, gloved hand. The motion did something profound to Anthony's nether regions, and he found himself quite envying the horse.

The signal was given to start for the covert, so with a nod—and another unsuccessful attempt to catch

Tessa's eye—Anthony turned Cinder and headed over to where the Odd Sock was assembled.

"Something wrong?" Rush asked as he reached them.

"What? No, not at all." He quickly schooled his expression to one of anticipation for the hunt. "Mr. Emery bade me spread the word that Miss Seaton's mare will be sold tonight. I'm half minded to buy her myself."

"The mare, you mean?" Stormy teased him.

Anthony, however, was not amused. "Don't let Lady Killerby hear you implying such things," he admonished his friend. "Nor anyone else, for that matter."

"A joke, Anthony, just a joke," Stormy protested with a chuckle, putting up a hand as if to ward off a blow. "Come, the field is leaving us behind."

True to her word, Tessa rode her mare extremely well. Though Anthony knew it would drive up the price to his detriment, he couldn't help feeling proud of her. At the third check, Anthony managed to get her a bit apart from the others long enough to tell her so.

"You and Cinnamon are putting us all to shame," he said cheerfully. "Well done."

She gave him the first smile he'd seen on her face that day. "Thank you. Really, though, neither of us would be happy doing less than our best, whatever the inducement."

He nodded his understanding. "I see that now— and how that would be true no matter what horse you rode." His intent was to let her know he no longer blamed her for Nimbus, but she frowned at his words.

"I . . . I suppose," she said.

Drawing closer, he lowered his voice so that none of those milling nearby could hear him. "I presume there is still no reason to believe our, ah, evening together has been discovered?"

She shook her head. "You need not worry, my lord. Your reputation seems quite safe."

Startled, he laughed. "My reputation? That's scarcely what I was worrying about. I should not care to see you made uncomfortable on my account, however."

"That's very kind of you—" she began, but was interrupted by a cheery "Halloo."

Turning, they saw Lady Killerby wheeling toward them, her burly coachman expertly guiding her low phaeton over the rough field. "I see they did not exaggerate about you, Miss Seaton," she called as she drew near. "Indeed, you are the best rider out here today, bar none. Sorry if that offends your male pride, Lord Anthony." She winked at him playfully.

"Not at all, my lady," he replied with a mock bow. "Indeed, I must agree with you."

She regarded him narrowly for a moment before turning back to Tessa. "Your mother rode much as you do, my dear, but I suppose you've been told that before. You, like she, are a credit to our sex."

"Thank you, my lady." Tessa seemed vaguely uncomfortable with the praise, though Anthony couldn't think why.

"Good of the farmers to place their gates for my convenience," Lady Killerby continued. "That way I'm never too far behind the action. Also good of the fox to lose himself periodically so that I can catch up, eh, Henry?" she said to her coachman.

"Aye, m'lady," he agreed blandly, though Anthony noticed a faint twitch of his lips. "There, the hounds have found 'im again. We'd best be off." He flicked the pair of bays into a trot, and Lady Killerby waved a teal-gloved hand.

"I'll see you at the next check," she called.

"It would appear she did not only come to Leicestershire to care for her son," Tessa commented as she and Anthony urged their horses in the same direction. "I'd no idea before today that someone could follow the hunt thus."

"It's not common, but I've seen it done before—though some courses will not allow it, naturally. Perhaps your father would enjoy doing the same sometimes?"

The look she gave him was fraught with alarm, though she quickly concealed it. "Perhaps," was all she said, before setting her mare into a canter to again take the lead in the chase.

It was with definite regret that Tessa saw the hunt end, even though the fox escaped the hounds, which would normally have been a source of relief to her. Riding back to Quorndon Hall, she tried to eke every bit of enjoyment possible from her last moments on Cinnamon's back, but doubts and worries kept getting in the way.

"Perhaps she'll sell to someone you know, so that you'll still be able to visit her," Anthony suggested kindly, riding up next to her.

She tried to force a smile. "Perhaps. In any case, I'm sure I'll become just as attached to another horse soon enough." She did not believe it, however. She had formed a special bond with Cinnamon, and that was something rare, even for her. Especially for her.

"What horse do you plan to ride next?"

"You mean, what horse does my uncle intend me to ride?" she asked, only realizing when he frowned that she should not have spoken so clearly. Why was it that she could not seem to guard her tongue around this man?

"Probably the gelding my uncle bought last week," she said before he could comment. "Though he won't be ready for sale for some weeks. He does need experience in the hunt, however."

She tried not to think about Vulcan, afraid Anthony would somehow divine her thoughts—or that she'd end up telling him everything. He'd forgiven her for the business with Nimbus, but Vulcan was far worse. The very fact that he was in her father's stables was damning, to her mind, for no reputable dealer would ever have purchased such an animal.

Glancing ahead, she saw Lady Killerby in her phaeton, waiting for the returning field. She'd been forced to stop an hour or so ago, when they'd leaped a ditch with no convenient way around.

"So, Miss Seaton, were you first in at the kill?" she demanded as they drew close.

Tessa shook her head. "There was no kill today, my lady. But I confess that if there had been, I'd not have been there to watch it. I fear I'm too squeamish to be a truly competitive foxhunter."

"That's hardly a failing in a lady," said Lord Rushford, riding in from their left just then. "It's the riding that's the thing, in any event. Which reminds me, Anthony, did you hear? Harleston is talking of organizing a steeplechase."

Lady Killerby actually clapped her hands. "Lovely! I adore a steeplechase. We have one or two per season in Nottinghamshire, and I make it a point never to miss watching them. What is the purse to be?"

"It will depend on the number of entrants, I presume," Anthony said.

"Aye, and the wagering—which is like to be brisk," Lord Rushford agreed. "I'll be surprised if the winner walks away with less than ten thousand pounds."

Tessa's attention was caught, along with her breath. Ten thousand pounds? Such a sum would pay for all the repairs needed at Wheatstone, with a substantial amount left over.

"How many gentlemen are likely to enter?" she asked with studied casualness, ignoring the look Anthony gave her.

Lord Rushford shrugged. "I'd guess twenty at the least, though it will depend on the weather and the course, which hasn't been decided yet."

When they got back to Quorndon Hall, she would ask Uncle Mercer to discover the details. If there was any way she could compete, she would do so, for with ten thousand pounds she'd never have need to ride a questionable horse for sale again. Surely even her uncle would see the wisdom in that?

She was still mulling the possibilities with growing excitement when Sir Charles Storm joined the group around Lady Killerby's phaeton. "Miss Seaton, I've had a thought," he said. "Well, it was someone else's thought, but I'm not averse to stealing a good idea."

"I fear I don't understand," she said, though when he beckoned her to move a bit apart from the others, she followed—as did Anthony, she noticed.

"No, no, of course not. Never seem able to come

right to the point, do I?" He shook his head, grinning. "Thing is, I overheard a couple of men talking, saying they meant to approach you about riding their mounts in upcoming meets so that they might sell them for more—rather as Mr. Mercer had you do today, with this mare."

"Don't be absurd," said Anthony before she could respond. "Tessa—Miss Seaton—isn't for hire."

Sir Charles looked shocked. "Of course not. Never meant to imply she was. I was thinking more along the lines of a favor—though of course I'd be willing to share a percentage of the profits, if I get a good price for this fellow." He tapped his gelding between the ears.

"Still," Anthony began, but Tessa reached out to touch his arm.

"It's all right, my lord, I'm not offended."

Suddenly it seemed that all manner of opportunities to raise revenue were coming her way. Opportunities that wouldn't compromise her ethics—though they might compromise her reputation. But as long as her father never got wind of it . . .

She turned to Sir Charles with a smile. "In fact," she said, "I'm quite flattered by your request. I promise to give it some consideration, and to discuss it with my uncle."

Lord Anthony seemed less pleased than she at this development, though she couldn't think why. To her, it seemed an admirable answer to her problems, for she could not be assured of winning a steeplechase, even if she were allowed to enter.

When the members of the Quorn met for dinner that evening, Anthony discovered that Stormy was only one among many who were eager to convince Tessa to ride for them. Her performance that day—and the price her mare was likely to fetch as a result—was second only to the proposed steeple-chase among the topics discussed over the meal.

"I hear Wheatstone isn't what it used to be," said Sir Brian Olney in response to another comment. "Seems as though the Seatons might be amenable to a bit of extra blunt, if that's true."

Tom Billingsley nodded vigorously. "That's what I'm hoping. Mean to offer her a fair sum to ride my Striker. Hoped to sell him this season anyway, and there's no question he'll fetch more with such a rider to show him."

"But is he broken to sidesaddle?" Sir Brian asked. "Ah, thought as much," he crowed when the crest-fallen Billingsley shook his head. "Conqueror is— m'sister insisted on riding him last summer. Guess that gives me the advantage, eh?"

Anthony felt obliged to speak up. "You all speak of this as a certainty, but I rather doubt Sir George will be sanguine about his daughter riding other men's horses for money. I'd advise against counting your chickens—or pounds—just yet."

"Perhaps, perhaps," Stormy agreed from across the table. "But that doesn't mean we can't talk about it—and plan our own strategies." His smile showed that he clearly thought his talk with Tessa that after-noon gave him the edge.

The others agreed, and Anthony resisted the urge to speak again on the subject. He hadn't missed the eagerness in Tessa's eyes when the steeplechase had been mentioned, or her apparent willingness to do as Stormy suggested and ride for hire. He was deter-mined to prevent her from involving herself in ei-ther enterprise.

Still, it wouldn't do to display an obvious interest in Tessa before the other sportsmen, not yet—particularly as he would be bidding on her mare after dinner.

He was glad of that restraint later, when John Bingle said to him, during the auction for Cinnamon, "You seem determined to come away with that mare, Lord Anthony. Does that mean you've found a companion for the remainder of the season?"

In seasons past, Anthony had gifted more than one mistress with a mount, though he hadn't realized it was common knowledge. Considering his plans for Cinnamon, he wasn't particularly pleased to discover that.

"Not at all," he said dampeningly. "I've been wanting to add some depth to my stable for some time. This mare seems a good start."

"Ah. Good luck to you, then." And Bingle turned to top Anthony's last bid.

In the end, Anthony had to pay just over eight hundred pounds for Cinnamon, but he was content. He could scarcely wait to see the expression on Tessa's face when he gifted her with the mare. Not that he could do so immediately, of course—that would give rise to unwelcome talk, given what Bingle had said. He wouldn't do anything that would pose the slightest risk to Tessa's reputation.

No, he would wait for . . . Yes, of course. The vague plans that had been circling in his brain for the past few days suddenly crystalized.

He would give her the horse as a wedding gift.

Startled by his own thoughts, he stared into space for a moment, waiting for his usual, instinctive revulsion to the idea of matrimony to assert itself. Instead he felt a sense of rightness, even inevitability.

Mesmerized by this sudden shift in his thinking, he at first did not hear Thor speaking to him.

"—hurry to leave," he was saying.

Anthony shook his head sharply, bringing his friend into focus. "What? Who?"

Thor grinned. "You seemed miles away—and at some pleasant place, judging by that smile on your face."

"Yes, a most pleasant place," Anthony agreed. "But you were saying?"

"I was just observing that Emery seemed in a hurry to leave once he had your money in hand. Stopped to talk to that gent there, then headed straight for the door. Bad form, if you ask me." The big man shook his head with a frown.

Anthony followed his gaze. "That gent, you say? Who is he?"

Thor shrugged. "He wasn't at the meet today, nor at dinner. Didn't arrive until the auctions were nearly over, in fact. Local fellow, I think. Saw him last year at a meet or two. Hightop? Something like that."

"Hilltop?" Anthony asked with a sense of foreboding.

"Aye, that's it. At least, I think that's it. I see Rush has ordered another bottle. Let's go help him drink it, shall we?"

"Of course," Anthony said mechanically. Mr. Hilltop would hardly have made a point of telling Mr. Mercer that his niece hadn't been to dine at his house, he reminded himself. No reason to think either one of them would have mentioned Tessa, in fact.

He sat down with his friends, who toasted his acquisition of the new mare, joining in their talk about the next meet they planned to attend. Not until they were leaving for Ivy Lodge an hour or two later did he think of Mr. Hilltop again.

For a moment he frowned, but then shrugged. If the worst occurred and it was discovered Tessa had not been at the Hilltops' Friday night, it would only speed the decision he'd made tonight. And perhaps that would be no bad thing, he thought, remembering again the softness of Tessa's lips beneath his own.

He would make her an offer this very week, he decided, gripped by a sudden eagerness to taste those lips again—and more. Then discovery, if it came, would not matter. Nor would she need to put herself at risk in a steeplechase or take other men's money for her riding. Yes, it was an admirable solution.

Tessa and her father had just finished breakfast in the parlor the next morning when a knock came at the front door. Startled, Tessa rose and went out, reaching the top of the stairs just as Griffith opened the door to reveal Lord Anthony—alone.

"Good morning," he called out, spotting her at the same moment. "I have a favor to ask of you and your father, if I might come up?"

She nodded to Griffith, who preceded Lord Anthony up the stairs so that he could properly introduce the visitor before he entered the parlor.

"Lord Anthony," Sir George exclaimed. "What a pleasant surprise this is. I assumed you would be at the Cottesmore meet this morning."

Anthony bowed, first to Sir George and then to Tessa, holding her gaze with his until she felt herself beginning to color. "I will ride with the Belvoir tomorrow, but today I thought to do something a bit more productive—and I have come to beg Miss Seaton's assistance, if you will allow it, sir."

"Assistance?" Sir George echoed Tessa's thoughts. "What sort of assistance, my lord?"

"As you may recall, I recently acquired a gelding that once resided in your stables—the horse I originally came here to ask about. I am attempting to improve his manners, but I feel sure I would make more headway with Miss Seaton's help, as she already knows the horse."

"He means Zephyr, Papa," Tessa said. "Please—"

But Sir George was frowning. "Yes, yes, I know what horse he means. A chestnut, sold to a fellow named Ballard. Though at the time you pretended to be interested in purchasing another beast from us, as I recall," he said with a sharp glance at Anthony.

Tessa blinked at her father's easy recollection of the details of that earlier conversation. She hadn't thought he'd paid such close attention.

"I was not precisely pretending," Anthony said with a grin, "though that was not the primary motive for that visit." He slid a glance at Tessa, and she remembered how worried she'd been at the time that he would reveal her secret. She felt no such worry now.

"Papa, I would very much like to assist Lord Anthony in this." She turned her most beseeching gaze upon her father. "He was most forbearing, you know, given that the horse was not fully trained when Uncle Mercer sold it. I feel we owe it to Lord Anthony to ensure as far as possible that he does not suffer from his generosity in buying Zephyr from Mr. Ballard."

Though he still frowned, Sir George nodded slowly. "I do see your point, Tessa, but I cannot feel it is proper for you to go to this gentleman's stables, to work with horses there, when—"

"I assure you that propriety will be preserved, sir," Lord Anthony broke in. "Lady Killerby is at the house, and there are any number of grooms and stable lads about the stables. Indeed, Lady Killerby insisted that Miss Seaton take tea with her during the course of the morning, could I prevail upon her to come."

Sir George's brow cleared. "Did she indeed? Dear Lily, how kind she is. In that case, Tessa, I suppose it will be all right, provided you do not spend *too* much time at the stables."

"She need not spend any time there, Sir George, now I think on it, for I can have the horse brought round to the front lawn and we can work with him there—in full view of the house. Really, all I seek is Miss Seaton's advice and presence," he added with another glance at Tessa. "I would never expect her to do any of the dirty work of training."

She opened her mouth and then closed it, realizing that to protest that she enjoyed the "dirty work," as he put it, would do her case no good with her father.

"Very well," said Sir George, making her glad she'd held her tongue. "That will serve nicely, I believe. Pray thank Lady Killerby for her hospitality, as I know Tessa will do as well. Really, we must return it, and soon."

"Thank you, Papa," Tessa said, giving her father a quick hug and a kiss on the cheek. "I will run upstairs and change into something suitable for a few hours outdoors, and be ready to go in a few moments."

"No hurry," said Anthony equably, dropping into an armchair near the fire. "Your father and I can talk hunting until you return."

Tessa did hurry, nonetheless, for she was more than eager to show Lord Anthony that she could be of help—more help than he expected, in fact. Of course, she also wanted to see Zephyr again, she reminded herself as Sally buttoned her into a peach wool day dress that was loose enough in the skirt to allow for riding, but demure enough for a tea indoors as well. Snatching up her brown pelisse and matching bonnet, she ran back down to the parlor.

"My, that was quick, Tessa," her father said as she entered. "Why, Lord Anthony had barely begun telling me his version of yesterday's hunt."

"I'm sure it would not have varied substantially from what I told you last night," she assured him. "But perhaps you will have a chance later to continue your talk?" She glanced at Anthony, who had already risen.

"Of course," he said. "I will be happy to pick up where we left off when I bring Miss Seaton home this afternoon."

"Very well, very well, off with you both," said Sir George with a chuckle and a wave of his hand. "I'll also be eager to hear what sort of progress you make with the chestnut."

Tessa waited until they were out of the house to say, "You handle him very well, you know. Thank you."

Anthony smiled down into her eyes, making her breath quicken. "Your thanks make every little effort worthwhile—though in truth I find it no real effort at all. I quite like Sir George."

"I believe the feeling is mutual, my lord," she said primly, though her lips twitched with what she really wished to say. He handed her into the waiting carriage with a smile that told her he understood.

After a few moments, she commented, "It feels odd to ride in a carriage rather than on horseback."

"Does it? I thought your father might find it more,

ah, proper. Do you always go on horseback when visiting or shopping?"

She nodded. "We sold our carriage four or five years ago, as Papa could no longer use it. On the rare occasions I go into the village, or to Melton-Mowbray to shop, I generally have my purchases delivered or send Griffith with the farm cart."

"Was it your uncle's idea to sell the carriage?" he asked, glancing out at the passing countryside.

"Yes, but I agreed." She stopped herself short of admitting that they'd needed the money and could not justify the expense of keeping a carriage and coachman when there was barely enough to pay the few servants they had retained.

He turned to look at her. "I see," he said, and she had the uncomfortable feeling that he saw much more than she would like. "Perhaps, now that Sir George has shown he is capable of visiting, you may wish for one again. I'll keep an eye out for something suitable."

"Thank you," she said, knowing they could never afford one. How limiting it was to have money problems. She really must discuss the idea of riding other gentlemen's horses with her uncle.

He put a hand over hers. "Tessa, please don't worry. If you'll let me, I'd like to solve all of your problems."

She stared at him, her heart thudding in her chest at his nearness, the masculine scent of him in the enclosed carriage. "I . . . I don't see how you can do that," she stammered. What, exactly, was he suggesting?

As if in answer, he leaned closer and covered her lips with his own. She felt as if she'd been waiting for this forever—certainly she'd been wanting his kiss again since the last, brief one they'd shared three days ago, when she'd walked him to the door. Now she melted into him, losing herself in the illusion that this was right, natural, and something she deserved always.

His lips moved over hers, coaxing more from her. She slid her hands up his shoulders, clinging to him for support—not from the swaying carriage, but from the storm of her own feelings. Obligingly, his arms went around her, pulling her securely to him, enfolding her with a welcome sense that she was cherished, protected. At that moment, she believed he really could solve her problems, that she could lean on him for anything.

The carriage slowed and he released her, with obvious reluctance. "I suppose I shouldn't have done that," he said, "but I can't say I'm sorry I did."

Tessa felt herself flushing crimson. What must he think of her, giving in to his caresses without hesitation, responding so eagerly to his kiss? "I'm . . . I . . ."

"Didn't I tell you not to worry?" he said gently as the carriage came to a stop in front of Ivy Lodge. "Let me take care of you, Tessa, please."

Still confused, she took a shaky breath. She didn't want to ask, but she had to. "Are . . . are you asking me to be your mistress?" She was shocked to realize it was a tempting prospect.

He stared at her, suddenly pale. "God, no, Tessa. Of course not! How can you think it? I'm asking you to be my wife."

Chapter 13

Anthony cursed his inept timing as the coachman opened the carriage door. Tessa was
clearly still trying to absorb what he'd just said.
"Thank you, John," he said curtly. "I'll help Miss
Seaton out myself."

At his tone, the coachman hastily bowed and
backed away to busy himself with the horses.

"Tessa?" Anthony asked tenderly, hopefully.

She met his gaze, her expression dazed. "I—I
don't know. I must think. I . . . I suppose we'd best
go in. Lady Killerby will be wondering what is keeping us out here."

"Of course." He stepped out of the carriage and
offered her his hand. In silence, she took it and went
down the two steps to the ground, and in silence, she
accompanied him to the house.

He wished he knew what she was thinking. What

a blockhead he was to make such a clumsy offer, without preamble. So clumsy that she had completely mistaken his meaning—and no wonder, he thought, remembering his phrasing. A man of his reputation, who had given her no indication of his intentions, why should she not think the worst of him? Surely, though, now that he'd plainly stated his wishes—

"Ah, Miss Seaton, how nice to see you again," exclaimed Lady Killerby, standing just behind the butler as the door opened. "Could you not prevail upon your father to accompany you?"

Tessa glanced questioningly up at Anthony, who cleared his throat. "Ah, Sir George was not prepared to go out just yet, my lady, nor was he certain that his manservant was up to the task of helping me carry him down the stairs."

He'd completely forgotten that Lady Killerby had suggested Sir George come as well, so anxious was he to have some time alone with Tessa. After all his lecturing to her on honesty, what must she be thinking of him now?

"No matter," Lady Killerby said with a toss of her head. "Perhaps I shall call on him later. But now, do come in and have some tea, Miss Seaton, before you begin this, ah, curious task Lord Anthony has set for you."

Her gaze was frankly questioning, and Anthony was relieved when Tessa summoned a smile. "Not so curious, my lady, for Zephyr came from my father's stable and I had a small hand in his early training. I merely came to offer some advice."

"I see," Lady Killerby responded in a tone that implied she did not see at all. They entered the parlor then, where Killer was again propped on the sofa. "Look, William, Miss Seaton has come to visit," his mother said with a fond smile at the invalid.

"Give you good day, Miss Seaton," Killer exclaimed, inclining his head. "Kind of you to stop by to amuse me while the others are all gone hunting."

Tessa stepped forward, concern making her even more beautiful, in Anthony's opinion. "Have you been very bored then, my lord?"

"Bored! How can he be bored when I am here?" his mother replied indignantly. "I simply thought some other diversion might be beneficial."

Killer glanced from his mother to Tessa, doing a poor job of hiding a grin. "Very beneficial. I feel better already."

"I'm delighted, Killer, but you can't have her for long, I'm afraid," Anthony said then. "Once she's had her tea, she's going to help me with that chestnut I bought off Ballard. You're welcome to watch from the window, if we can maneuver you into a chair."

"That might be amusing, I suppose," Killer said, his smile dimming slightly.

"The tea is ready," announced Lady Killerby, pouring out. She then took charge of the conversation while everyone sipped.

Anthony decided it was just as well, as neither he nor Tessa was likely to be good company until they had finished their aborted conversation. Draining his cup, he stood. "Now, what say we reintroduce you to Zephyr, Miss Seaton?"

She nodded and stood as well, though her gaze slid away from his, as it had done since they entered the house. "Yes, I'm quite looking forward to seeing him again."

Thanking Lady Killerby, she followed him out to the front steps, where he sent a footman to the stables to have Zephyr brought around. The moment the man was gone, he turned to Tessa.

"You didn't give me an answer," he reminded her, ducking his head to peer into her face.

"I know."

The moment he had clarified his intentions, Tessa had thought her heart would burst for joy. Surely, this was the answer to all her prayers! But as soon as shock subsided, doubts had crept in, and during the brief interlude in the parlor of Ivy Lodge, common sense had reasserted itself. Now she was glad she had not instantly accepted him, as every instinct had prompted her to do.

"I . . . I think you cannot have thought this through, Anthony," she said carefully. "Kind as your impulse was, I fear a match between us is impossible."

He looked startled but not angry, as she'd feared he might. "Might I ask why?" he asked stiffly, guardedly.

At once she sought to reassure him. "Not because I do not care for you, please believe me. But your world and mine are so different, and . . . and I cannot leave Papa. He needs me."

Anthony put a hand on her shoulder, and she could feel him quivering with suppressed emotion. "I need you, too, Tessa. I've wanted you almost from the moment we met, and now—" He broke off, for a groom was approaching with Zephyr on a lead.

"We'll finish this later," he promised.

She nodded, but doubted her decision would change, much as she wished it could. He clearly desired her . . . and pitied her. But he had said nothing of love, which surely meant he would take no lasting harm from her refusal. Once he was gone from the Shires and she was no longer immediately before him, he would forget her.

After all, Anthony was the son of a duke, a member of one of the most exalted families in all England. His parents must surely have higher hopes for him than the daughter of an impoverished country squire, granddaughter of a yeoman horse trainer. Marrying her might make him a laughingstock, from what she had heard of Society.

And then, of course, there was Papa. Losing her mother had nearly killed him, making him so reckless of his life that he'd ended up permanently maimed. What would losing *her* cause him to do? He might pretend to be happy, for her sake, but once she was gone? No, she dared not risk it.

Anthony took Zephyr's lead from the groom, speaking softly to the horse. "There, then, fellow. Let's show Miss Seaton how much better you're doing, eh?" He placed a hand on the gelding's neck, and, to Tessa's surprise, Zephyr didn't even flinch.

"Bring me his saddle and bridle," Anthony said to the groom, who nodded and headed back to the stables. Then, to the horse, "Let's warm you up a bit, shall we?"

Holding the lead firmly, he led the chestnut around the lawn, first at a walk, then at a trot. By then the groom had returned with the tack. Tessa stepped forward, ready to help saddle the horse, but Anthony shook his head. "Not yet. I want you to see how much progress we've made already."

She watched skeptically as Anthony threw pad and saddle over Zephyr's back, for she recalled that he always shied when the girth was tightened—at least, if it was tightened by anyone but her. To her surprise, however, he stood quietly as Anthony performed that operation, not even protesting when Anthony gently punched him in the side to make him let out his breath for the final cinching.

"You certainly have made progress," she exclaimed. At the sound of her voice, Zephyr's ears pricked forward, and he half turned his head toward her.

"Not yet, lad," Anthony said. "You can visit with her soon enough." He fastened on the bridle, then vaulted into the saddle. Again, the horse made no protest whatsoever.

Tessa stared. "I begin to wonder what you needed me for."

"He still startles much too easily," Anthony said. "A definite failing, if he's ever to make a good hunter. I've been gradually getting him used to various objects and people, but the sudden appearance of, say, a dog will still make him shy badly. I'd like to get him past that, and thought your presence might help there."

"Of course." She was amazed, and a bit embarrassed at her own conceit. Anthony had made as much progress with Zephyr in two weeks as she'd managed in two months. Had she come to rely too heavily on her special gift, neglecting more conventional training methods? It was a chastening thought.

After trotting Zephyr up to a few trees and a pump in the side yard—objects that certainly would have made him shy under any rider but Tessa a month ago—he sent the groom for a dog.

"Now will come the real test," he said.

Tessa moved closer, ready to calm Zephyr if

necessary—though in truth she was beginning to think Anthony had nearly as exceptional a touch with horses as she did. She'd never seen any man except her grandfather handle a difficult horse so well.

The groom came around the corner with a foxhound on a lead.

"One of Thor's hounds," Anthony told her. "He's begun building his own pack since the war ended. Steady, Zephyr," he added as the horse took a nervous step backward.

He motioned the groom to move closer, keeping the chestnut on a tightened rein. "All right, Tessa," he said softly. "Talk to him."

Wanting to allow Anthony to do as much of the calming as possible, she waited until Zephyr looked ready to bolt. "Come now, Zephyr, it's not so bad," she called then, in her lilt. "Listen to Lord Anthony, your new master."

At the same time, Anthony stroked the horse's neck, murmuring words of comfort himself. The gelding stopped trembling and prancing, though he still eyed the approaching dog askance. Tessa wasn't sure how much was due to her influence and how much to Anthony's. Perhaps Zephyr wasn't, either, which was all to the good.

With Anthony continually soothing the horse but Tessa speaking only once or twice more, the groom was able to bring the dog to within a few feet of the chestnut, lead it in a circle around the horse, then away. Tessa had not touched Zephyr even once. "Amazing," she breathed.

"You see? I do have talents of my own," Anthony said with a grin as the groom moved out of earshot. "Perhaps I can convince you to let me—"

Just then, a shrill voice came from above them.

"What on earth were you doing with that dog, Anthony?" called Lady Killerby from the parlor window, which she'd apparently opened just for that purpose, as the November air was chill.

Tessa jumped, and so did Zephyr, though Anthony calmed him again at once. "Training this horse, my lady, as you see," he called back. "We are finished for now, however."

"Good. I'm having luncheon brought up, so you have just time to wash and join us." With a nod that made the chartreuse feather in her turban bounce, she slammed the window shut.

Anthony rolled his eyes, then said, "Why don't you go on inside while I return Zephyr to his stall. I'll be with you directly."

Part of her was glad that their discussion had again been postponed, but another part of her was as frustrated as Anthony looked. Was she secretly hoping he *could* convince her to change her mind? Folly, if so, for it would be most unwise—for both of them.

Conversation was general but lively during the elegant luncheon Lady Killerby had ordered, allowing Tessa little time for contemplation. Every time her thoughts strayed to Anthony's remarkable declaration, Lady Killerby demanded her response to some trivial question or other. It was some small comfort that Anthony seemed similarly preoccupied.

The meal at an end, Tessa thanked her hostess as well as the others, saying that it was time she returned to Wheatstone and her father. Anthony rose with her, and she tried to marshal her thoughts for the inevitable argument during the carriage ride back, when they would finally be alone again.

"A moment," said Lady Killerby. "I believe I will come with you and pay a call on Sir George myself, as he was unable to come here. It cannot be good for him to spend so much time alone."

Tessa glanced at Anthony in time to see him smooth a sudden frown. "Of course, my lady," he said blandly. "I will have the carriage brought round while you get your wrap."

Ten minutes later all three of them were trundling along the road to Wheatstone, Lady Killerby dominating the conversation much as Sir George had done during his drive to Ivy Lodge on Sunday.

"I know that your father does not go out as a rule, Miss Seaton," she was saying, "but do none of his neighbors visit him? He was such a sociable man in his youth, I can't imagine him living so isolated now."

"He has been weak since the accident that crippled him six years ago, my lady," Tessa replied. "As he tires so easily, he has rarely been at home to visitors, and they eventually stopped coming."

She did not mention that it was she herself who had generally sent any callers away, usually without notifying her father.

"Hmph. He didn't appear particularly weak or tired Sunday night. More society will do him good, I'll be bound," said Lady Killerby decidedly. "Once it's known I have called upon him, the neighbors will follow suit, mark my words. And it will be known by nightfall, country gossip being what it is." She chuckled.

Tessa smiled uncertainly. "Perhaps you are right, my lady."

Sir George certainly seemed pleased to see Lady Killerby when they arrived at Wheatstone. "What a delightful surprise!" he exclaimed, welcoming her into the parlor. "Tessa, see if Cook can arrange for a little something extra on the tea tray, won't you?

Come in, my lady, come in, do, and make yourself comfortable."

While Tessa rang the bell, then consulted with Mrs. Bealls, Lady Killerby settled herself into the chair by the parlor fire that Sir George indicated. Soon the two of them were deep in conversation, reminiscing about the days of their youth in Leicestershire.

"Perhaps I've done wrong to shield him from callers all these years," Tessa admitted in an undertone to Anthony, observing the animation in her father's face. "I really thought—"

"I know. You thought you were acting for the best. Perfectly understandable, as I said before. Now you see him doing so well, though, might you be persuaded that he is not, perhaps, quite so dependent upon you as you have believed?"

She looked at him to find him regarding her tenderly—persuasively. Her very eagerness to believe him, however, warned her that her motives were by no means pure. "Perhaps in time that will be true, my lord, but I dare not put my own wishes above his health. Not when I am all he has."

His frustration was evident in his sigh. "I've realized I can't ask—" he began, when Lady Killerby interrupted them.

"Don't you agree, Miss Seaton?" she was saying.

"I beg your pardon, my lady?" Tessa asked. What had Anthony been about to say? That he could not ask her to marry him after all? Had he wisely reconsidered? Her heart twisted within her, though she told herself that was what she wanted.

Lady Killerby explained, "I have just invited your father to accompany me in my phaeton to the Belvoir meet tomorrow. The Duke of Rutland was quite an admirer of mine once upon a time, you know." She tittered. "But that is neither here nor there," she said quickly when Sir George frowned.

"We can all stop here before leaving for the meet in the morning," she continued. "It should be an easy enough matter for Anthony and his hulking friends to help Sir George into my phaeton. What a jolly time we will have!"

Tessa glanced at her father in alarm. Spend all day outdoors, riding across rough country in an open carriage, in November? That could not be good for his heart. Surely he would never—

"I believe I would quite enjoy it, truth to tell," he said before she could express her reservations. "The fresh air will surely do me good, so long as it doesn't rain."

Tessa seized upon that. "But suppose it does rain, Papa? It often does this time of year, you know."

"Pish!" exclaimed Lady Killerby. "It's clear as a bell outside right now, and like to stay that way for a day or two more. If it looks like rain in the morning, I won't be going myself, so there's no need to worry on that head."

"There, Tessa." Sir George seemed pleased. "Lily has no more desire to get wet than I do, of course. We shall be fine."

Though she still had grave misgivings, it was not Tessa's place to give or withhold permission, though long habit had made it seem so. "I hope so," was all she said. Perhaps later, when they were alone, she would be able to dissuade him.

Once everything was settled, Lady Killerby rose. "Come, Anthony, I promised my son I'd not be too long away. He gets so restless, confined to his couch. I don't want him to attempt rising, or anything else foolish."

Tessa accompanied them out to the carriage, trying to sound sincere in her thanks for Lady Killerby's kindness. Anthony handed the older woman into the conveyance, then turned to Tessa. "I have much more to say to you, but I suppose it must wait for a better opportunity—perhaps during tomorrow's meet."

She nodded, trying to read the expression in his eyes. "Anthony, I—" she began, then broke off. There seemed nothing she could say that would not provoke another argument, and that was out of the question with Lady Killerby waiting in the carriage. "Tomorrow, then," she finally said.

He looked as though he wanted to kiss her—or perhaps that was just her imagination?—but then he turned suddenly on his heel and jumped into the carriage. "Tomorrow," he said as the door was closed, making it sound almost like a threat.

Tessa watched the carriage drive away and sighed. Surely a night of reflection would convince Anthony how ill-advised a union between them would be. Or perhaps he already realized it, and planned tomorrow to retract his offer as gently as possible? Either way, it would be for the best, for both of them.

Wouldn't it?

Sir George was still in high spirits when Tessa returned to the parlor, and seemed more inclined to talk about tomorrow's outing than to return to his study and his memoirs—which he'd been neglecting of late.

"Would you like me to help you get your notes in better order, Papa?" Tessa asked after a while, trying to steer the conversation away from a topic she couldn't help finding distressing.

"No need," he replied cheerfully. "Take a peep into my study and see what I've done already."

Curious, she stepped across the hall. To her astonishment, her father's study was the cleanest she'd ever seen it, with papers—far fewer than before—neatly stacked, and every book in its proper place on the shelves. "Did you have Griffith do that while I was gone this morning?" she asked, returning to the parlor.

Sir George shook his head. "He put away a few of the books for me, but I did the rest myself. Amazing how little time it took, once I set my mind to it and simply started. I disposed of all of my out-of-date notes and duplicates, and filed and organized the rest."

"That's . . . wonderful. I'm proud of you, Papa," said Tessa, still amazed. It seemed today was her day to be surprised by men—first Lord Anthony, and now her father.

"I'm rather proud of myself, actually," he said, beaming. "Now it will be much easier to write—should I find the time to do so," he added, an unfamiliar twinkle in his eye.

Tessa wasn't sure what to make of the transformation in her father over the past two weeks, but she was reluctantly coming to the conclusion that it was a good thing for him. He was drinking far less, for one thing, and—

A knock at the front door interrupted her bemused thoughts.

She rose, smoothing her hair with her fingers. Had Anthony returned to speak privately with her—or perhaps with her father? she wondered with a flutter. No, he wouldn't have had time to take

Lady Killerby to Ivy Lodge and ride back to Wheatstone yet.

Griffith appeared in the parlor doorway. "Mrs. Hilltop and Miss Hilltop, sir," he announced. "Shall I send them up?"

Tessa, caught wholly off-guard, could only gasp. She began shaking her head, groping for a plausible excuse to deny them, when her father said, "Of course, man. Don't leave them standing below. And have Cook send up a fresh tea tray."

"But Papa," she protested weakly, then subsided, unable to think of a single thing that might dissuade him. She would simply have to do her best to brazen out this visit, and hope against hope that somehow her secret would not come out.

A moment later, stout Mrs. Hilltop came puffing into the room, the single flight of stairs apparently having taxed her. Behind her came Cynthia Hilltop, whom Tessa had once described to herself as ferret-faced. Alas, the description still fit the girl's thin face and narrow, rapidly shifting eyes that looked as though they meant to discover every possible discreditable detail.

"Welcome, Mrs. Hilltop, Miss Hilltop," said Sir George before Mrs. Hilltop regained her breath. "We are most honored to have you come visit us."

The matron dropped into the nearest chair and fanned herself with a handkerchief. "I was delighted to find you at home, Sir George, and you, too, of course, dear Miss Seaton!" She motioned to her daughter to sit next to her.

Cynthia complied, glancing quickly from Tessa to Sir George to the ornaments on the mantelpiece, then back to her mother.

"I confess, sir, I did not know what to think at first when I read your note thanking us for our kindness," Mrs. Hilltop continued, her breath no longer coming in gasps. "But at last I realized that it must be a sort of irony, and a good joke it was, too, for we have been dreadfully neglectful neighbors of late."

Tessa pinned a bright smile on her face. "Not at all, ma'am! I haven't found you neglectful in the slightest, nor Miss Hilltop, either."

Sir George nodded. "Indeed no, madam. Why, your calling today is quite a kindness in itself, for you must be fairly on your way to London."

"Oh, did I not tell you, Papa?" Tessa interjected rather loudly before Mrs. Hilltop could give voice to her surprise. "It turns out I was quite mistaken on that point. I completely misunderstood what I heard."

Mrs. Hilltop gave a jarringly artificial laugh. "Yes, rumor does have a way of becoming distorted, does it not? Which reminds me—is it true, as my husband says, that you have actually ridden to hunt this season, Miss Seaton?"

Grateful for the change of topic, hoping that Papa would not think it odd that the Hilltops wouldn't know this after an evening supposedly spent in their company, Tessa nodded.

"Yes, quite true. Papa agreed to allow it, so long as Uncle Mercer rides with me to preserve propriety. I rather hope other ladies might follow my example eventually." She glanced at Cynthia, who looked as though she'd eaten something nasty.

"You see, Mama?" she began, but her mother gave a quick shake of her head before continuing.

"Yes, it was Mr. Emery my husband spoke to last

night, at the Swan. He was sur—er, pleased to see him hobnobbing with some of the young aristocrats who come here to hunt. I understand you've dined with some of them?"

Suddenly Tessa understood the real reason for this visit: Mrs. Hilltop was hoping that by cultivating a friendship, she might throw Cynthia in the way of some of those gentlemen. It appeared that Lady Killerby had been right, she thought with a small smile. But, she remembered abruptly, that motive did not make her own danger any less.

"Yes," Sir George replied with obvious pride, "we had several members of the Odd Sock Club to dine here, and they returned the favor on Sunday. Lady Killerby, Lord Killerby's mother, is staying at Ivy Lodge, you see, which made Tessa's visit there perfectly proper. She was invited again for tea this morning, in fact."

Tessa prayed that her father's fond illusions about her would not be shattered before this visit ended. "Yes, Lady Killerby and all of the gentlemen have been most kind," she said, noticing that Cynthia was now regarding her with surprise, and something like respect. "Lord Rushford and Lord Anthony Northrup, among others, have expressed a desire to spend more time with Papa in future."

At mention of those illustrious names, Mrs. Hilltop's eyes widened, as did her daughter's. Smiling more broadly than ever, she exclaimed, "Well, that is lovely, I must say! We must have you to dine soon, and I will be certain to extend an invitation to those gentlemen as well, as they are particular friends of yours."

Suddenly they were back on dangerous ground, which became even more treacherous when Sir

George responded, "Oh, but we should first have you here, as we are quite a dinner in your debt."

Mrs. Hilltop blinked. "In our debt? Oh! From when we had Miss Seaton to dine three years since, do you mean? Nonsense. But now, we really must be going." She and her daughter rose, to Tessa's intense relief.

Papa would certainly question her after they left, but she was now confident that she could manufacture some sort of plausible explanation for Mrs. Hilltop's odd-seeming comments.

"Thank you so much for coming," she said, rising to see them out, her relief giving her words added warmth.

The ladies smiled upon her, then Mrs. Hilltop said, "Not at all, my dear. Indeed, we would have called earlier, but we only returned from London yesterday afternoon, after spending all of September and October there. Much as I adore Town, it is nice to be back in the country—and among friends."

With a nod to Sir George, who, after an alarmed glance at Tessa, nodded back mechanically, she and her daughter swept from the room. Tessa followed only to the top of the stairs before turning reluctantly back to the parlor. As she'd feared, her father greeted her with a scandalized frown.

"Tessa, perhaps you can explain to me how you were able to dine with the Hilltops Friday night—to stay overnight at their house—when they were not even in the country?" he asked ominously.

Her heart sank. She knew how important propriety was to Papa, what store he set on her being accepted by the neighborhood. The truth would devastate him. Perhaps, if she made no mention of Lord Anthony . . .

"I, ah—" she began, only to be interrupted by the entrance of Uncle Mercer, with Harold close behind.

"Sir George, a matter of some concern has just come to my attention," he said, with a sidelong look at Tessa.

"I'm afraid I can't discuss estate matters right now, Mercer," her father replied impatiently. "Tessa and I have something rather important to deal with."

Uncle Mercer nodded. "Yes, I saw Mrs. Hilltop leaving just now. I presume you have discovered, as I have, that they were not at home on Friday, when your daughter claims to have dined there. I believe my son has something to say that will clarify things."

Tessa and Sir George both turned toward Harold in surprise as his father nudged him forward. The younger man nodded with apparent reluctance, but Tessa caught a triumphant gleam in his eye. She bit back an unladylike curse, certain that Harold was about to make things even worse. How much worse, however, she hadn't even imagined.

Standing in front of Sir George and hanging his head, Harold said, "I must beg your forgiveness, Sir George, particularly after your kindness to me." His words had a rehearsed quality. "The truth is, Tessa spent Friday night with me."

"With you!" Sir George exclaimed, as startled as Tessa was. "But where—how—?"

Harold glanced at Tessa with a sheepish smile. "I know it was wrong of us, but we've grown quite fond of each other and Friday night, well, our passions got the better of us."

Tessa stared, openmouthed, at her cousin. What on earth was he saying—and why?

"I'm prepared to do the right thing, of course," Harold continued. "With your permission, Sir George, I am willing to make Tessa my wife—at once."

Chapter 14

Tessa gasped. "Papa, it is not true!" she exclaimed as soon as she could speak. "You must know I would never—"

"Unfortunately, they were seen," Uncle Mercer broke in. "She rode out with Harold Friday night, and returned with him Saturday morning, bold as you please."

"With Harold?" Tessa echoed. "You know perfectly well—" But then she stopped. To mention Lord Anthony would be tantamount to admitting she'd spent the night with him, instead. "That nothing happened," she finished lamely.

Her father looked up at her, his eyes shadowed and sad, which nearly broke her heart. "I'm sorry, Tessa. Even if that's true—yes, yes, of course I believe you—it matters not a whit. Word is bound to get around, if you were seen. The only solution is the one Harold has so generously offered."

"Generously!" she spat, glaring at her cousin. "Papa, do you not see—"

"Generously," Sir George repeated heavily. "Particularly if, as you say, nothing truly improper occurred. I admit I had rather hoped—but that is neither here nor there. I will send to the bishop and make arrangements for a license. If all goes smoothly, you should be able to wed sometime next week."

Tessa stared, first at her father, then at Harold and Uncle Mercer, who both looked insufferably smug. They had planned this, clearly—probably right after Uncle Mercer spoke with Mr. Hilltop last night. Her choices now were to marry Harold or to drag Lord Anthony's name through the dirt so that she could marry him instead. Or to run away, abandoning her father to her scheming uncle and cousin.

Bursting into tears of frustration and anger, she fled the room and ran up the stairs to her own chamber to rail against the unfairness of it all to her unsympathetic pillow.

Anthony reined Cinder to a stop in front of Wheatstone the next morning, gazing up at the solid main block of golden stone with new appreciation. Yes, he would be more than willing to live here, if that's what it would take to make Tessa happy.

Perhaps Rush or Killer would be interested in renting Ivy Lodge—which would also provide Anthony with an income independent of his father.

"The phaeton will be here in a moment," Thor said, stopping next to him on his big smoky black.

"Shall we get Sir George ready before they arrive, do you think?"

"Yes, let's go ahead and knock," Anthony said, dismounting.

When he'd first considered the idea of offering to live at Wheatstone, his pride had rebelled, particularly since he had relatively little to offer of his own. Ivy Lodge was his only real asset, for as third son, he was unlikely to inherit an estate from his father. His army stipend and his allowance—which his father might well cut off if he married Tessa—would scarcely support her in the sort of style she deserved.

Thinking of that again, he wondered whether Tessa would be foolish to marry him. As long as he had enough income to be independent, he'd never worried much about the future, as he'd never intended to wed. But now—

No, she cared for him, he was certain. And he loved her to distraction. He could live here, help to make the estate profitable again and so earn his keep—and in time become a man she could be proud of.

Not that they *had* to live here, of course. On a hunch, he had spoken with the surgeon when he'd come to check on Killer's progress last night. Though he was not the same man who attended Sir George, he knew that physician well. He'd been reluctant to answer Anthony's questions, but finally admitted that there was nothing wrong with Sir George's heart—but that Mercer Emery had persuaded the physician to tell Tessa otherwise.

The front door opened, and Anthony stepped forward, eager to see her again. At the first opportunity, perhaps even during the ride to Belvoir, if he could draw her away from the others, he would present her with his plan, and the good news about her father. He smiled, imagining her delight—and acceptance.

"Good morning, gentlemen," Sir George greeted them when they reached the parlor. Tessa was not present, to Anthony's disappointment.

"Lady Killerby should be here with her phaeton in a moment," Anthony said, thinking Sir George looked a trifle more tired than usual. "Shall we take you downstairs to wait?"

The older man nodded. "Very well." He definitely didn't seem to be in spirits today.

Anthony wondered whether he had dismissed Tessa's concerns for her father's health too lightly, even if his heart was not the problem. Frowning, he lifted the back of the Merlin Chair while Thor took the front. They all reached the front step just as Lady Killerby's phaeton came wheeling up the drive, flanked by Rush and Stormy on horseback. Tessa was still nowhere in sight.

"You are quite the early bird I see, Sir George," Lady Killerby called out as her driver pulled the phaeton to a halt. "I believe I will choose to be flattered—though in truth you are probably just anxious to witness the hunt again."

Sir George murmured something complimentary, but looked rather embarrassed as Anthony and Thor carried him into the phaeton and settled him. Lady Killerby must have perceived it, for she at once began chattering about the beautiful day they were likely to have, and to relate her plans for an impromptu tea party at Ivy Lodge after the day's run ended.

They were preparing to leave when Anthony

could restrain himself no longer. "Is Miss Seaton not to accompany us?" he asked, as casually as he could.

Her father shook his head, a trace of sadness in his eyes. "No, she has already left, with her uncle. They will meet us at Belvoir Castle."

"I see." His hopes temporarily dashed, Anthony strove to put on a cheerful front. Until he had Tessa secure, it would be wisest not to advertise his feelings for her. "Let us go, then."

Designed as it was to follow the hunt, the phaeton was able to travel quickly along the road. Still, it was all Anthony could do to keep from dashing on ahead so that he could see Tessa sooner. At length, however, they came in sight of the rounded turrets and towers of the newly built Belvoir Castle.

Perhaps half the field was already assembled on the front lawn, and Anthony gazed around eagerly for the flash of purple that would be Tessa's habit. Ah, there she was, at the foot of the rise leading to the imposing mock-medieval castle, atop the gelding Mr. Mercer had bought last week. Excusing himself from the others, Anthony spurred Cinder forward at a quick trot.

Tessa looked up as he approached but did not smile, rather to his surprise. Then, just before he reached her, Mr. Mercer moved his brown gelding to block Anthony's path.

"I'm sorry, my lord," he said blandly, "but I fear it is no longer appropriate for you to speak privately with my niece. I must ask you to keep your distance from her today, and in the future."

Anthony blinked. Had their night alone been discovered? Why had Sir George not confronted him, then? Certainly, he was more than eager to do the right thing. Wouldn't Tessa have told him that?

"Might I ask why?" he finally asked, when no other explanation seemed forthcoming. Tessa's eyes were downcast, which also seemed odd.

"I am merely looking out for my son's interests, as he is not here to do so himself," Mr. Mercer replied, increasing Anthony's confusion. "You see, Miss Seaton is very shortly to become his wife."

"What?" Anthony demanded, staring at Tessa, who still refused to meet his eyes. "How—? When did this . . . this betrothal take place?"

Mr. Mercer positively smirked. "Last night. You are welcome to speak with Sir George if you doubt my word, my lord."

"I believe I'll do that," Anthony snapped, wheeling Cinder about to return to the phaeton.

Rush glanced at his face in surprise as he approached, which warned him to school his expression somewhat before confronting Sir George. Still, he could not keep all traces of outrage from his voice as he asked, without preamble, "Is it true, sir, that your daughter is engaged to marry Harold Emery?"

"What?" Lady Killerby exclaimed, much as Anthony had just done. "Surely not."

But Sir George nodded, the corners of his mouth drooping. "Yes, it is quite true," he said with surprising firmness. "Tessa and her cousin have always been fond of each other, so I saw no reason to withhold my consent."

"Fond—!" Anthony remembered the scene he had interrupted after dinner at Wheatstone last week. There had been strong emotion between Tessa and Harold Emery certainly, but he would swear it had not been fondness.

"I . . . I see," he finally managed to say. "Then I suppose I must offer my congratulations to both of them."

But Lady Killerby was still frowning. "Congratulations. Hmph. Really, George, you cannot have thought this through. Your daughter is quite lovely, not to mention talented and intelligent. She can aspire—"

"Nevertheless, it is done," Sir George interrupted her sharply. "I won't go back on my word."

It was clear he did not wish to discuss it further, so Anthony executed a curt bow from the saddle and retreated. Rush followed him.

"Now there's a stunner," Rush said as soon as they were out of earshot. "I could have sworn she only had eyes for you. How are you holding up, old man?"

Anthony shot him an angry glance. "Was my partiality so obvious, then? Not that it matters now, I suppose, except to add to my humiliation."

But Rush shook his head. "Nothing for you to be embarrassed about, old chap. But did you notice something odd in Sir George's manner just now? If he's happy about this match, then I'm a codfish."

"Yes, I thought the same," Anthony said, a glimmer of hope reviving in his breast. "Nor did Tessa look happy when I tried to speak with her. Her uncle warned me off before I could say a word to her, however."

"Or before she could say a word to you." Rush looked across the field to where Tessa still waited by Mercer Emery. "If you ask me, there's something deuced havey-cavey about this sudden betrothal."

"Do you know, I believe you may be right." Making a swift decision, Anthony quickly told his friend about the innocent but damning night he'd spent with Tessa, his certainty that she cared for him, and finally that he had made an offer to her only yesterday.

"I can't help thinking that somehow precipitated this sudden betrothal," he finished, "for I'm convinced the Emerys have their claws deep in Wheatstone's affairs—and income—and aren't eager to give that up. Will you help me get to the bottom of it, Rush?"

The earl grinned. "What are friends for? You try and see if you can manage a few words alone with Miss Seaton, and I'll do a bit of digging about our two Mr. Emerys and what sort of hold they might have over Sir George."

"As always, I'm at your command," Anthony said with a mock salute. In truth, though, it was reassuring to have Rush take charge as he had during the war. And Anthony was more than willing to carry out his assignment.

One way or another, he'd get Tessa to admit the truth about this preposterous betrothal—and about her feelings for him.

Tessa watched Anthony turn and ride away, her heart dying within her. She should have said something—anything—to him, despite her uncle's command that she stay silent. He had looked so stunned—much as she'd felt last night when her father had accepted Harold's lie.

What, though, could she have said? She could scarcely have denied the betrothal, since her father had insisted upon it.

And that was something she still did not understand. This morning she had told Sir George that she had not so much as seen Harold Friday night, that she'd spent the night with an injured horse, alone, but he had merely shaken his head.

"It doesn't matter now, Tessa," he'd said. "I've given Mercer and Harold my word."

"And that matters more than my future? My happiness?" she had demanded.

Her father had looked at her sadly. "It is your future I am thinking of, my dear. Trust me in this."

"But Harold lied to you to coerce this promise," she had protested. Still, incredibly, her father would not relent. It almost seemed as though he was afraid of what Uncle Mercer or Harold might do if he changed his mind. She simply didn't understand it.

Helplessly, she watched as Anthony approached her father, saw Lady Killerby's surprise, then her father's confirmation of the terrible truth. The sag of Anthony's shoulders as he turned away nearly undid her. What was the worst that could happen if she told the truth—the whole truth? Perhaps there was still a chance that she could be happy, be Anthony's wife, as he'd proposed.

Uncle Mercer, also watching the exchange, chuckled, infuriating her.

"I always knew you put your own interests ahead of mine or Papa's," she exclaimed, "but I never thought you would take actual pleasure in the unhappiness of another."

He snorted. "That young popinjay thought he'd have everything he wanted—you, Wheatstone, your father's stables. All he had to do was snap his fingers. A lesson in humility will do him good."

"Is it to do me good as well?" she asked. "You know I don't want to marry Harold, nor do I imagine that he really wants to marry me. Why are you so bent on this course, Uncle?"

But she knew the answer already, for he had just

revealed it: Wheatstone. The stables. They were to come to her, and therefore to whomever she married.

Why had she not realized it before, been more on her guard against Harold, against both of them? Because they were family, she had told herself they must have her best interests at heart, but it was not so—it had never been so.

"Don't think to persuade your father to change his mind," her uncle said now. "He won't want word of your indiscretion to get about, any more than you do. Nor will your young gallant come to the rescue once the world knows the truth about you."

Tessa stared at him. "What do you mean? You know I wasn't with Harold that night."

"Maybe not, but I'll lay odds you weren't alone, either. You're ruined, missy, and if the man responsible—the man you rode out with—was going to step forward and make it right, he'd have done so already. You should be grateful to my son for his willingness to take you, secondhand goods that you are now."

"Grateful—!" She turned her back on her uncle, unwilling to trust herself not to assault him physically if he continued to smirk at her.

To her relief, the master of the hunt, the Duke of Rutland, sounded his horn just then, and the field began moving toward the covert. Should she attempt a word with Anthony during the day's run? Her uncle would be left behind once the hunt began in earnest, so it should be easy enough to manage—though she had no idea of what to say.

She had refused his offer already, and could scarcely ask him to offer again, now that she was betrothed to her cousin—or ask him to admit openly that he was the one who had spent Friday night with her. Her father had seemed to believe her when she said she'd been alone, but that news would devastate him afresh.

Her uncle's spiteful words came back to haunt her. Did Anthony's hesitation mean that he had doubts? Had he spoken to her father before Harold had made his "admission"—but no. How could he have done so, when she had refused him? Still, if he learned of the circumstances behind this hasty betrothal, would he step forward with the truth . . . or not?

Even if he did, his family—nay, all of Society—would despise and reject her if word got out that Anthony married her only because he had to. And her cousin and uncle would make certain word got out, she had no doubt of that. No, she could not tell Anthony the truth and so risk both his happiness and her father's health.

On the way to the covert, Tessa kept her distance from everyone else on the field, Anthony included, deliberately riding off to the side. When they all stopped to wait for the hounds to draw the fox, her uncle moved to her side again.

"We're not looking to sell this horse just yet, so there's no need for you to ride him all-out today. Stay near the back while I look over the rest of the field with an eye to our next purchase."

She glanced over to where Anthony and his friends were changing from their hacks to their hunters. For an instant she caught his eye, but then he turned away, his expression unreadable.

"Very well," she said with a sigh.

Though the run so far had been excellent, this was proving to be a most unsatisfying meet for Anthony. Instead of riding near the front of the field, as she'd done in the past, Tessa was hanging back with the stragglers, staying close to her uncle. She must have been told to do so, for Anthony knew she loved speed, and the thrill of the hunt, as much as he did.

For himself, he felt torn between warring instincts—to be first in the field, and to be with Tessa. Poor Faro couldn't understand why Anthony kept reining him in, and Anthony himself was nearly as frustrated as his hunter. No matter how slowly he went, Tessa couldn't—or wouldn't—catch up to him. He even considered a deliberate fall, and pretending an injury, but feared that he might inadvertently hurt Faro if he tried it.

It must have been past noon when they came to the first serious check, when the hounds lost the fox at the border of a stream. While the hunstman urged them across the water to cast for the scent on the other side, the strung-out field finally had time to coalesce into a single group again.

At once, Anthony seized his opportunity. Tessa was still shadowed by her uncle, but she was also close to Lady Killerby's phaeton, which he should be able to use to his advantage. He rode over to the group, smiling broadly.

"What say you, my lady, Sir George? Quite a run so far, eh? The best we've seen this season, I believe."

Sir George nodded, his earlier melancholy apparently forgotten in the excitement of the hunt. "Aye, I'm enjoying it immensely. Don't know why I never thought to do this before."

"You needed a push—and I'm quite pushy, I've been told," Lady Killerby said with a wink. "But Anthony, what ails you? On Monday, you were right at the forefront, as was Miss Seaton. I must say that neither of you are acquitting yourselves nearly so well today." She glanced from him to Tessa, who gave a small shrug.

"Indeed, Tessa, there's no need for you to hang back with Mercer," Sir George said. "I know this is the first time you've ridden to hunt on that horse, but I'm sure you can do better than this. Make me proud, won't you?"

Tessa blinked, clearly startled. With a quick glance at her uncle, she nodded. "Very well, Papa, if you wish. When the hounds find the scent again, we shall see what this gelding can do."

"And what of you, Anthony?" Lady Killerby prompted. "Is your horse lame, or are you grown fainthearted?"

"Neither, my lady," he replied with a grin. "I, too, promise to show Sir George what I'm capable of."

"Excellent," Lady Killerby exclaimed. "Then we'll all enjoy the hunt as we ought. But now, if you'll excuse us, we must seek for a place where we can ford this stream, or we'll see nothing at all when the hunt continues."

Bowing from the saddle to them both, Anthony shot a glance under his brows at Emery to see the man looking both angry and frustrated. Tessa, however, sent him a grateful look when her uncle wasn't watching her.

Satisfied, Anthony did not attempt to speak to Tessa yet, confident that he'd have a chance to do so once they were again on the move. Still, he could not resist giving her a small, reassuring smile in response to her look, and was rewarded by seeing her blink and smile tentatively in return.

Emery, who had been watching the retreating

phaeton with a scowl, turned back to his niece. "Don't think this means—" he began, but just then the hounds gave tongue and the huntsman's horn sounded the resumption of the hunt.

"Let's go," Anthony cried to both of them, knowing that only Tessa was capable of complying. "We've given our word, after all."

He spurred Faro toward the confusion of the reanimated field and was conscious of Tessa just behind him. The leaders began splashing across the stream, some with more difficulty than others, for the water was better than hock-high.

Glancing back, he saw to his surprise that Mercer Emery was cantering alongside Tessa, though clearly with some difficulty. Really, the man was an execrable horseman. The three of them reached the stream along with the middle of the field. The water, up to the bellies of the shorter hunters, was flowing fast.

Anthony slowed Faro to a walk so that he could better find footing, raising his feet to keep his boots dry. Tessa, now beside him, did likewise. Emery, however, rode into the water at a canter, apparently determined not to let the two of them get away. Predictably, his horse slipped, then lunged to the side to regain its feet.

With a yell, Emery landed in the stream, face-first. Sputtering, he scrambled to his feet, glaring about as though his tumble had been someone else's fault instead of his own.

"Uncle! Are you hurt?" called Tessa, though Anthony thought he could hear a hint of laughter in her voice.

It was all he could do not to laugh himself, for Emery looked quite comical, wringing water from his tricorn hat. Others around them were not so restrained, and guffaws broke out on all sides. Emery was not particularly well liked.

The sodden man's face turned dark red, but he shook his head. "I'm fine," he growled. "Get on with you—all of you!"

Anthony needed no further urging. "Come on," he said to Tessa. "Your father and Lady Killerby are already across." He pointed upstream to where the phaeton had just reached the other side. "We did promise."

With one last glance at her glowering uncle, she gave a quick nod and nudged her mount the rest of the way across. They both spurred their horses to a trot, then a canter, and finally a gallop. There were still too many people about to attempt a shouted conversation, but Anthony felt a welcome sense of rightness pervade his being.

Though there was no chance now of Emery catching them up, Anthony and Tessa both increased their speed, passing more and more of the field until they had taken their accustomed place in the lead. "That's more like it," he finally shouted across to her.

Smiling, she nodded but did not reply.

Soon they had to slow to a canter, so as not to override the hounds. That made conversation easier, but also allowed the rest of the field to draw closer. "That gelding seems to be shaping up nicely," Anthony commented.

"Yes, I think he'll make a fine hunter with some work," she replied, keeping her eyes resolutely forward.

So she didn't wish for real conversation? Too bad.

Subtly, by repeatedly angling Faro barely within a comfortable distance for her mount, he guided her off to the right, out of the direct path of the rest of the field. When the hounds checked again a few minutes later, they were both well out of earshot of the others.

The moment they halted, he got right to the point. "All right, Tessa, suppose you tell me what's really going on?"

She tried to evade him, both physically and verbally, sidling her horse back toward the field as she said, "I don't know what you mean."

He was having none of it, however. "You know exactly what I mean. What is this nonsense about a betrothal to Harold Emery?"

She stopped sidling, but still did not meet his eye. "It's not nonsense," she said in a voice he had to strain to hear. "As my uncle told you and my father doubtless confirmed, I am to marry my cousin . . . as soon as is reasonably possible."

"But why?" he demanded, aware that the hounds might find the scent again at any moment. "It's obvious you don't even like the fellow. Is it something to do with my making you an offer yesterday?"

Though she glanced up for an instant, allowing him to see the pain in her eyes, she did not answer.

"Tessa?" he prompted. "Are you somehow being forced to this?"

Still she said nothing, responding only with a quick shake of her head.

Frustrated, he said, with deliberate sarcasm, "So, is this your way of ensuring that no one can ever take you away from your precious papa? Is it because he needs you so much, or because you need him? I thought you more courageous than that, Tessa."

Her head came up and she glared at him, anger replacing pain—as he'd intended. "Courage has nothing to do with it! And you're a fine one to talk, when it's as much your fault as—" She broke off, clearly having said more than she'd intended.

"So it does have something to do with our night out together," he said. "I take it we were somehow discovered? Are the Emerys threatening to tell your father unless you marry your cousin?"

"Not . . . not exactly." She averted her eyes again. "Papa did find out I wasn't at the Hilltops' that night, but not that I was with you. He is convinced that I'll be ruined if I do not marry quickly, so when Harold, ah, offered, he insisted I accept."

"You did not see fit to tell them that you'd already received an offer of marriage—from me?" Anthony wasn't sure whether he was more hurt or angry. Had he completely misinterpreted her feelings for him?

But when she faced him again, her brown eyes swam with sadness—and a longing that gave him hope again. "I couldn't! Don't you see? That would be tantamount to admitting—"

At that most inopportune moment, the hounds gave tongue again, and at once she spurred her mount forward to get in position for the continuation of the hunt. Anthony cursed under his breath, but only at the delay.

His path now seemed clear. As soon as he could arrange a private audience with Sir George, he would admit the truth. Surely then he would insist that Tessa marry Anthony, rather than her opportunistic cousin. Anthony would inform her of his plan at the next check.

Chapter 15

Tessa was determined to keep her distance from Lord Anthony for the remainder of the day's ride. He had already tricked her into admitting more than she'd intended, but if she told him the rest, he would feel obliged to do something he'd regret for the rest of his life. She couldn't allow him to do that.

Her efforts were helped by the fact that the hounds cornered the fox only half an hour later, without another check. Using the excuse that she didn't want to watch the kill, she at once rode back to meet her father and Lady Killerby, coming up at the rear of the field in the phaeton.

"Let's go home, Papa, shall we?" she suggested as soon as she reached them. "You must be cold—and tired."

"Nonsense," said Lady Killerby. "You're neither, are you, George?"

He shook his head. "I appreciate your concern, Tessa, but this has been the most enjoyable day I've spent in years."

"And you certainly don't want to miss my little party," the dowager added. "Not to worry, Miss Seaton, we can sit him near the fire at Ivy Lodge, just as you would at Wheatstone."

Tessa nodded, but her heart sank. How would she avoid more conversation with Anthony if they all went to Ivy Lodge?

"I'll just go home to change, then," she said, thinking that perhaps she could take long enough about it that the party would be over before she arrived.

But Lady Killerby would have none of it. "No, no, my dear! That's the point, don't you see? Everyone is to come in their hunting attire—though I suppose those who managed to get muddy or wet, like your poor Mr. Emery, will insist on changing into something dry."

"Then Uncle Emery is coming?" she asked her father.

Sir George nodded. "And Harold, too. It seemed only proper, considering you two are now betrothed." Some of the sparkle left his eyes.

Lady Killerby sniffed, but only said, "Yes, I told Emery to bring his son along, at Sir George's behest. But now we'd best be on our way, if I'm to be there to welcome my guests. Let's take the road back, Henry," she said to her driver.

Tessa rode alongside, glancing nervously behind from time to time to make certain Anthony wasn't catching them up. Surely with both Uncle Mercer and Harold at Ivy Lodge, she needn't worry about his resuming their earlier conversation?

Unfortunately, he was already at his hunting box

when they arrived, having apparently taken a quicker route back. "Ah, there you are," he greeted them from the front steps. "Killer has been directing the preparations in our absence, and everything is ready. Did you enjoy the meet, Sir George?"

"Very much indeed," Tessa's father replied. "Lily insists I accompany her to every hunt she attends while she is in the country, and I plan to do just that."

That was news to Tessa, and not particularly welcome. "Papa, are you sure—" she began, but Anthony was already talking again.

"Excellent! Glad to hear it. Clearly, you're a tonic for more than your son, Lady Killerby." He gave Tessa a meaning look, which she ignored.

"Is there a room where I might freshen up, my lady?" she asked, dismounting and handing her reins to a waiting groom just as Mr. Turpin, Lord Rushford, and Sir Charles came around the corner from the stables.

Lady Killerby jumped lightly down from the phaeton. "Of course. I'll take you up while Anthony and one of these others help your father into the house."

Tessa followed Lady Killerby inside and up two flights of stairs to the bedchamber she indicated. Inside, she found a washstand with hot and cold water, a comb, a looking glass, and a necessary.

Ten minutes later, feeling much refreshed, she reemerged—to find Anthony waiting in the hallway.

"What say we finish our talk?" he suggested, smiling down at her in an intimate manner—far too intimate a manner, considering that she was technically betrothed to another man.

Her heart quickened its beat. "I . . . I don't believe I

have anything more to say," she stammered, cursing her tongue for not giving him the scathing set-down he deserved.

He moved closer, which did not help at all. "But I have many questions to ask," he said softly. "Tessa, do you really wish to marry Harold Emery?"

She looked up at him, and he seemed to fill her senses. Clutching at the shreds of reason, of what she knew was right, she nodded. "I must," she whispered.

"That's not what I asked. Do you *want* to?"

Now he was only inches away, his hazel eyes boring into hers. He smelled of horses and the clean outdoors and something else, a masculine scent uniquely his. She knew that her response to this question would seal her fate—and his.

Steeling her resolve, for his sake and for her father's, she looked into his eyes and lied. "Yes."

There. She'd done it. Now—

He gripped her by the shoulders and pulled her against him, then pressed his lips to hers—roughly, demandingly, not at all like the tender caresses she remembered from the abandoned cottage.

She froze, stunned, but only for an instant, before something equally demanding awoke within her. With a moan, she pressed herself against him, not caring how wrong this was, how foolish, how . . . anything. Only that she needed this, and needed it now.

He released her shoulders and gathered her to him, his lips gentling as she responded. Scarcely knowing what she did, she opened her mouth to him, and he plundered it with his tongue, stroking, possessing—knowing. They were fused. One.

It was as though she'd been waiting for this since they'd left the cottage, as though her body, her mind, had been craving exactly this, and she was now complete—or more nearly complete. His lips moved over hers, and parts of her body far distant responded, from the tips of her breasts to the place below her belly, to her very toes. She never wanted this kiss to end, never wanted to return to cold reality.

Even as a shadow of that thought passed through her fevered brain, a slight sound from downstairs intruded, breaking the spell of madness that had her in its grip. With a gasp, she pulled back, panting, to stare up at him.

Though he was still flushed with passion, he smiled, humor glinting in his eyes. "Now. Tell me again that you wish to marry Harold Emery."

"Why—? How could—?"

"I know how adept you are at deception, Tessa," he said. "You've hidden things from your father for years. But while you may be able to lie convincingly with words, your body has not yet learned to do so. I wanted to know the truth—and now I do."

She swallowed painfully. "But . . . it really doesn't change anything, except to make me regret what I must do even more."

"Why?" he demanded fiercely. "Why can't you marry me instead? Because of your father?"

"That's only a part of it," she confessed, finally admitting her deepest worry. "I could never fit into your world, Anthony. You must know that. Your family would despise me, and I would be a constant embarrassment. I may be able to acquit myself well on the hunting field, but in a ballroom, or in London Society, I would be as out of place as a horse or a hound would be."

"I don't believe that," he said with a certainty that

tempted her to trust him, though she knew she dared not. "Tessa, please, let me—"

At the sound of footsteps on the stairs, he broke off and hastily released her. Tessa took two quick steps backward, frantically smoothing her hair with her fingers.

"Here you are, still," exclaimed Lady Killerby from halfway up the stairs. "Come along down, both of you. Our guests are beginning to arrive."

Wordlessly, they followed her down, Tessa completely unsure whether she felt more relief or vexation at the interruption. She *should* feel relief—she knew that. Nothing Anthony could say would change the facts. A match between them would be unsuitable in the extreme, and Society would be only too eager to point that out.

A hum of voices greeted them as they approached the parlor and Tessa found upon entering that nearly a dozen people were already present—including her uncle and cousin.

"Ah, there's my bride-to-be," said Harold loudly, coming toward her. She was almost certain his father had prodded him from behind, and the joviality of his tone sounded decidedly forced. "I wondered where you were, my dear."

Turning up the corners of her mouth in something she hoped approximated a smile, she said, "I merely went to freshen up after the hunt. My hair was quite a disaster, I assure you."

She suspected it was not much better now, after her passionate encounter in the hallway. Her lips felt bruised and swollen. Surely the whole room must suspect the truth? But no one seemed to be staring, and Harold merely put a possessive hand on her elbow and led her to a chair between him and his father.

Lady Killerby was greeting a pair of newcomers, two men Tessa remembered from the hunt, though she did not recall their names. Once Lady Killerby had them supplied with sherry and biscuits, she moved about the room to be certain all her guests were comfortable. Tessa thought she took particular trouble over Sir George, who looked delighted at the attention.

"Thank you again, my lady, for inviting my son and myself to your little gathering," Uncle Mercer said when she passed them.

Tessa thought Lady Killerby's smile looked very slightly strained. "Not at all, sir. As connections of Sir George's, you are quite welcome, I assure you. But pray don't monopolize Miss Seaton. As the only other lady here, she must help me to entertain our guests. You two see her all the time, after all."

Out of the corner of her eye, Tessa saw Harold frown. "But—" he began, but his father nudged him.

"Not here, Harold." Tessa barely caught his whispered words. "If we want to be accepted by people like these, we must play by their rules." Then, to Tessa, "Go on, then, girl. Help Her Ladyship pour tea, or whatever it is she needs you to do."

"Perhaps you can speak with Mr. Thornton, there in the corner, and draw him into conversation with some others," Lady Killerby suggested.

Hoping that she could keep her thoughts focused enough for such a task, Tessa moved to comply.

Anthony, watching from across the room, noticed young Emery's deepening scowl with some amusement. So the fellow didn't care to have Tessa speaking to other men, did he? Small wonder, since Tessa had not entered into this betrothal of her free will. Both Emerys must worry she'd find some way to get out of it.

None of the other men was taking any notice of the pair, apparently realizing instinctively that they were not really a part of this circle. Smiling, Anthony walked over to them and sketched a bow that was so slight as to be a mockery.

"Welcome to Ivy Lodge, gentlemen," he said. "I trust you will not catch a chill from your dunking today, Mr. Emery?"

One or two gentlemen within earshot chuckled, and the older man frowned. "I imagine not, my lord. Our family is known for possessing excellent health in general."

"Glad to hear it. I'm sorry you were not able to join us in today's meet," Anthony then said to the younger Mr. Emery. "Why have we not had the pleasure of seeing you ride this Season?"

Harold Emery's face darkened, but after darting a glance at his father, he managed a brief smile. "I've been too busy." His abrupt reply bordered on rudeness.

"Ah. I should think spending so much time with horses would make you an excellent rider, sir."

"I do all right."

"I'm glad to hear it," Anthony said cheerfully, "for you wouldn't want your bride to show you up, I'm sure. Never good for a man's ego, that—or so I hear. Which reminds me, I have not yet congratulated you on your . . . conquest."

Now young Emery was scowling again, heedless of his father's nudging. "Thank you," he grated.

"I must say, you don't seem nearly as happy as I

would expect of a man who is to take the lovely Miss Seaton to wife. Why, if I were in your place—"

"You're not," Emery snapped. "She'll make me happy enough once we're wed—if she knows what's good for her." He did smile then, but it was far from a pleasant expression.

Mercer Emery leaped to his feet. "Really, you are most kind, my lord, and my son is more grateful than he can properly express for your attention. Come, Harold, I believe Sir George wishes to speak with us." So saying, he fairly dragged the younger man over to the fireplace, where Sir George was chatting animatedly with several of the sportsmen, oblivious to the exchange which had just taken place.

Anthony watched them go, a grim smile playing about his mouth. Perhaps it was uncharitable of him to goad a man he was so certain of defeating, but young Emery seemed such an uncouth, bullying fellow that he really couldn't resist it.

Still, he didn't want to make things more unpleasant for Tessa before he had an opportunity to extricate her from Emery's clutches. He glanced over to where she was urging Mr. Thornton to try a canapé. Several other men had gathered around her and seemed to be vying for her attention—not that Anthony could blame them.

As though feeling his eyes on her, she looked up, and for a long moment their gazes locked across the room. Faint color stole into her cheeks, and a shy smile curved her lips before she turned back to the group of gentlemen.

Tessa was the loveliest, liveliest, most generous, and most intelligent woman Anthony had ever known. The very idea of her bound to a boor like

Harold Emery was outrageous—a crime against nature itself. How could Sir George even consider such a thing?

He moved over to Rush, who had just returned to the room. "Have you discovered anything?" he asked in a low voice.

"I haven't had time for much," Rush replied softly, "but it seems the decline of Wheatstone's productivity has coincided precisely with Mr. Mercer's stewardship of the estate. Invalid or not, Sir George can't be entirely blind to it. Emery must have some sort of hold over him, and I suspect it is more than his relationship to the late Lady Seaton."

Anthony nodded. "And the son?"

"I watched him ride up to the house," Rush said, "and he makes his father look a right Meltonian. Worst seat I've ever seen. I'd guess he's as poor a horse trainer as his father is a steward. We'd be doing Sir George a real favor to rid him of those two, apart from the threat they pose to Miss Seaton."

"I agree—and the sooner the better." He wouldn't put it past young Emery to compromise Tessa in some way to make it that much harder for her to cry off. The fellow might not even be above rape, if he thought it would serve his interests.

"Will you come along when we take Sir George home after the party?" he asked.

Rush nodded. "Of course. What do you have in mind?"

Briefly, Anthony outlined his plan.

Afternoon was creeping toward dusk when the party began to break up, the gentlemen heading out to their lodgings to change for dinner. Tessa was relieved, for the past hour had been one of the most difficult of her life.

For her father's sake, she had continued to accept congratulations on her upcoming marriage, though she felt sure it would never take place. If her father would not release her from the betrothal, she would run away rather than marry Harold.

Then there was Anthony's disturbing presence—though he had not so much as spoken to her for the duration of the party. The occasional glances they exchanged, however, had heated her blood and turned her thoughts into most improper channels.

Even when he was not looking at her, just knowing he was in the room was so distracting that it was all she could do to attend to whatever conversation she was a part of. She'd had to ask various gentlemen to repeat themselves so many times that by now they probably all thought her hard of hearing.

"Oh, are we not returning in the phaeton?" Sir George asked when they reached the front door.

"I've asked Lady Killerby to let us use the closed carriage, Papa, as it is turning colder," Tessa explained. Also, as it was still light, she was hoping the enclosed vehicle might impede her father's view of Wheatstone somewhat as they approached.

To her surprise, Lord Anthony, Lord Rushford, and Mr. Turpin all insisted on accompanying them home.

"Yes, I'm sure you and your father are quite capable of taking Sir George into the house," said Lord Rushford when Harold protested, "but Lady Killerby has shooed us all away while she has the detritus of her party cleared up. Stormy is only staying behind to keep Killer amused. Besides, Anthony and Thor here are become quite adept at his transfer, haven't they, Sir George?"

"Indeed they have," Sir George agreed. "And once we reach Wheatstone, I insist you all come in for some brandy, for your trouble."

They all declared that they would be quite honored to do so, and Sir George was content. Tessa, however, was not. Now she would have to ride home with both Anthony and Harold as escorts, which had the potential to become most awkward.

On sudden inspiration, she turned to her uncle. "I find myself a bit stiff. I believe I would prefer to ride in the carriage with Papa. Will you lead my horse, Uncle Mercer?"

He agreed, but rather reluctantly.

"Not to worry, Emery," said Anthony. "If you have difficulties, one of us can easily take Miss Seaton's mount off of your hands."

Tessa hid a smile, knowing how that would chafe her uncle—even though it was entirely possible that he really couldn't ride and lead at the same time. Resolving to ignore any further byplay between the men, she climbed into the carriage beside her father.

"It's good of you to keep me company, Tessa, when I've no doubt you'd prefer to be on horseback," Sir George said once they'd all started off. "Particularly after . . . Well, I'll just say that perhaps I haven't treated you quite fairly over this matter with Harold. I did mean it for the best, but—"

"I know you did, Papa, but really, we won't suit at all. You must know that." She held her breath. Ending this betrothal would not make a match with Anthony possible, but at least she wouldn't be obliged to run away, abandoning her father.

He sighed deeply. "Lily—Lady Killerby, that is—

says the same. But I don't see that we have a choice. Harold and Mercer will make things most unpleasant for you if we renege now—unpleasant for us both."

"But how, Papa? Do you really think they will go to the trouble of telling people that I was away from home Friday night, simply for spite?"

"They might. And there are other things . . . I dare not risk it, my dear. For your sake."

Tessa wanted to ask what other things he meant, but it was clear from his expression that he would not tell her. Instead, she turned the conversation to the party just past, hoping she'd be able to wear him down before being forced to a terrible decision.

Soon, however, she lapsed into silence, reliving those stolen moments in the upstairs hallway of Ivy Lodge. If only—

Not until her father gasped did she remember why she should have continued to distract his attention.

"Tessa!" he exclaimed, staring out the window of the carriage at Wheatstone as they drove up the long drive. "What is wrong with the roof of the west wing? And that chimney—is it leaning?"

"It is all under repair already, Papa," she quickly assured him. "Uncle Mercer has engaged workers to—"

"Mercer should never have allowed the house to reach such a state in the first place," Sir George said severely. "Why did he not tell me it was in need of such extensive repair? I know we haven't quite the funds we used to, but—"

Tessa stared at her father. "You know—? What do you mean?"

He turned from the window to gaze at her sadly. "Despite Mercer's assurances, I can see that things at Wheatstone are not what they once were. How many servants do we have now? Less than a dozen,

I'll warrant. Though I knew he was not telling me all, I fear I believed more than I should have."

Knowing that her uncle was bound to throw the blame her way if her father confronted him, Tessa said, "I confess it is not all Uncle Mercer's fault, Papa. I knew there were some problems, but I asked him not to burden you with them."

"I appreciate your care and concern for me all of these years, Tessa, but it was not for you to decide what I should know about my own estate. As my steward, Mercer should answer to me, not to you, a mere girl. He knows that."

"But you've been ill. Your heart—"

"Not so ill as that. I've been negligent, however, and clearly that must stop—at once."

Tessa let the matter drop, for Uncle Mercer had said that the doctor thought it best that Sir George not be told about the state of his health. They pulled to a halt before the house, and the carriage door was opened. Anthony handed her down, then he and Mr. Turpin efficiently whisked her father back into his chair and through the front door, which the waiting Griffith held wide.

Following them up the stairs, flanked by Harold, Uncle Mercer, and Lord Rushford, Tessa could not help feeling that control of her life was slipping inexorably away from her. A month ago, her life had been routine, predictable, if not precisely happy, and had seemed likely to remain so. Now she could not see her future at all, which frightened her. She must find a way to regain her perspective, her control—her freedom.

Upon reaching the parlor, Tessa rang for tea while her father told Griffith to pour brandy for all the gentlemen. Harold and Uncle Mercer stood to one side of the fireplace while Lord Anthony and his friends stood on the other. Tessa thought it looked rather like a standoff—though surely that was absurd.

She took the chair next to her father, in the middle of the room. With a possessive air, Harold immediately moved to take the chair on her other side. She couldn't resist a quick glance at Anthony, and found him watching Harold, a small, enigmatic smile playing about his lips.

"It was very kind of Lady Killerby to have a party on such short notice," Tessa said brightly, mostly to break the silence.

"Indeed," her father agreed, so heartily that she thought he must have noticed the growing awkwardness as well. "And following the hunt in her phaeton went off far better than I anticipated, I must say. I'd thought we'd be left behind at once, remembering the breakneck pace of the rides of my youth, but there were gates in every hedge and fence, and the checks and changes of direction allowed us to remain in sight of the bulk of the field. I quite enjoyed myself."

"I am glad to hear it," said Lord Anthony, coming suddenly to life. He glanced at each of his friends, who responded with almost imperceptible nods, then stepped forward. "Sir George, I must ask you a question."

Tessa tensed, but her father only looked up at him with mild curiosity. "Of course, my boy, er, my lord. What is it?"

Anthony flashed Tessa a quick look that only increased her trepidation before saying, "What is the true reason for this sudden betrothal between your daughter and Mr. Emery?"

Clearly startled, Sir George hesitated, while on her other side, Harold jumped to his feet. "What kind of question is that?" he demanded. "I offered, Tessa accepted, Sir George gave his consent. That's all you need know."

Coolly, Anthony looked Harold up and down before returning his attention to Sir George. Tessa could only watch in stunned silence, wondering, fearing where this might lead.

"My question was for Sir George," he said. "Well, sir?"

"It . . . it is as Harold says," her father answered unconvincingly. "Why do you ask?"

Again Anthony looked at Tessa, and this time she saw a determination in his eyes that somehow both chilled and warmed her. "I have reason to believe this betrothal stems from Miss Seaton's absence from home Friday night. Is this true?"

Tessa gasped. Surely he was not going to—?

Her father slowly nodded, his face anguished and pale. "I don't know how you learned of it, but yes. It appears my daughter was . . . less than wise, though no doubt she told me what she did to spare me worry. Under the circumstances—"

"Tell me," Anthony interrupted, "did Mr. Emery claim to know where she was, after informing you she was not at the Hilltops' as you had believed?"

"He said that she was with him," replied Sir George, frowning, "though Tessa swears that nothing improper occurred. Mercer said that they were seen, however—which must be true, as you gentlemen seem to know of it. So marriage is clearly the only possible option."

Harold, still standing, began to look smug, but then Anthony turned his steely gaze on him. "In that case, Mr. Emery, I presume you can tell Sir George exactly *where* you and Miss Seaton spent the night?"

"That's none of your business," Harold blustered.

Anthony's mouth curved in a smile that did not reach his eyes. "Oh, but I believe it is."

When Harold only glowered, Anthony turned back to Sir George. "He will not say, sir, because he does not know. I believe your nephew—persuaded, perhaps, by your brother-in-law—merely seized opportunity in both hands when he learned of your daughter's truancy, using it as a lever to force her into marriage. She did not spend Friday night with him at all, though it was to his advantage to say she did."

Now Tessa was thoroughly alarmed, but Sir George simply looked thoroughly confused. "To his advantage?" he echoed.

"Of course," Anthony said. "If—"

Harold stepped forward menacingly. "Now see here, Northrup," he began, but Anthony's sudden glare made him hesitate.

"Sit down, Harold," Sir George advised. "You were saying, my lord?"

Anthony waited until Harold had resumed his seat before continuing. "If I'm not mistaken, your daughter stands to inherit Wheatstone. As her husband, Mr. Emery would have control of the estate after your death—though of course we all hope that will be many, many years delayed."

"Yes, I suppose that is true," Sir George confessed, "though I hadn't thought of it in quite that way. Not that Wheatstone—that is—but where was Tessa Friday night, if not with Harold?" he asked, looking to Tessa herself for an answer.

An answer she refused to give. Folding her lips tightly together, she glared at Anthony. All her arguments against marriage with him were still valid. He could not force her to implicate him.

"She was with me," Anthony said.

Chapter 16

"What?" Harold was again on his feet, and Uncle Mercer came forward as well, his face nearly as angry as his son's. Curiously, neither Mr. Turpin nor Lord Rushford looked surprised.

"I think you'd better explain yourself, Lord Anthony," Mercer said menacingly. "How dare you come here, pretending to be a friend to Sir George, when all the time—"

"Silence!" shouted Sir George with an authority that startled Tessa exceedingly. "Lord Anthony, explain yourself."

Anthony flicked a glance at the two livid Emerys before turning back to Sir George with a respectful nod. "Of course, sir. It all stemmed from Lord Killerby's foolishness and Miss Seaton's generosity." Quickly, he described the events that had led to Tessa's being trapped at the abandoned cottage overnight.

"I was unwilling to allow her to stay there alone, for there was no guarantee that the gamekeeper or poacher who lived there would not return, or that some other untrustworthy person might not happen by during the night. Therefore, I returned to the cottage and spent the night there as well."

Slowly, Sir George nodded. "I can appreciate your dilemma, my lord, and I certainly can't fault you for your concern for my daughter's safety. However, it would have been wiser to have come here, so that someone else could be sent to stay with the horse while Tessa came home to spend the night in her own bed."

"In retrospect, I must agree," Anthony said, "but Miss Seaton insisted that the horse would suffer more if she herself did not stay with him."

She couldn't help feeling grateful that he had not revealed the full truth—about Nimbus, about her role in helping to sell such an ill-tempered horse . . . about what had occurred between the two of them.

"Yes, well, my Tessa does have a special way with horses," her father admitted with visible pride. "And I suppose what's done is done. The question, my lord, is what are we to do now?"

Suddenly seeing her way clear to regaining control of her life, Tessa spoke up. "Papa, surely we need do nothing, now that you know the truth? No one outside this room is aware I was even gone, and I'm sure we can trust everyone here to say nothing of the matter."

Her uncle and cousin would not wish to facilitate her marriage to Anthony, she was fairly certain, so would hold their tongues. "I needn't marry Harold or . . . anyone else," she concluded.

"If we could be certain, perhaps," said her father with a worried frown. "But—"

"But there is no guarantee that we were not seen by anyone else, such as a servant," Anthony said. Abruptly, Tessa remembered Billy, the stable lad.

"Are you offering to do the honorable thing, then, my lord?" Sir George asked.

"Honorable!" Harold exclaimed. "He's simply scheming to have Wheatstone for himself. What makes his offer more honorable than mine?"

"For one thing, mine would be based on truth rather than a deception," Anthony said mildly.

Again Tessa felt obliged to intervene. "Stop it, all of you. There has been no offer—nor is there any necessity for one. Nothing untoward happened, after all."

They all turned to look at her. Suddenly, vividly remembering what *had* occurred that night—and again this very afternoon—Tessa fought desperately not to blush, knowing that would give the lie to her words. After a moment, her father turned to Anthony.

"Is that true, my lord?"

Tessa blinked, startled that her father should require his word in addition to hers, but she was far more surprised by Anthony's response.

"As a man of honor, I find myself in rather a delicate position," he said, glancing at Tessa and then away—but not before she caught the glint of humor in his eyes. "I pride myself on my honesty, yet a gentleman would never say anything to impugn a lady's reputation. Therefore, I am unable to answer your question, Sir George."

Her father turned shocked, saddened eyes on Tessa, making her long to fling herself into his arms and beg his forgiveness. How could Anthony do this to him—to her?

"As I tried to say before, I am more than willing to marry Miss Seaton," he said then.

Again, Harold began to protest, but Sir George held up a hand. "Under the circumstances, my lord, I fear that is the only course open to you—to you both."

"But—" Tessa began, but her father shook his head.

"I'm sorry, Tessa, but this puts an entirely different light on things—as I'm sure you must realize."

"It does indeed," said Uncle Mercer from across the room. "However, I wonder if Lord Anthony would be so, ah, eager to do the right thing if he knew—"

"Mercer!" Sir George all but barked the name, startling him to silence. "Tessa, I believe it might be best if you left us for a time . . . so that we can discuss the particulars."

For a moment, Tessa sat motionless, unable to believe that her brief glimpse of freedom had been so suddenly snatched away, and even more stunned that Anthony, whom she had trusted, had done this to her. She would not let him—let any of them—see her cry, however. She'd done far too much of that of late. With one withering glance at Anthony, she stalked out of the room.

Anthony watched her go with more than a little regret. He'd carried his main point, but he had lost Tessa's trust—and perhaps her regard—in the process. He hoped it was not gone past rebuilding. Meanwhile, he had other matters to resolve.

"You were saying, Emery?" he prompted the elder of his antagonists.

Ignoring a pleading glance from Sir George, Mr.

Emery smiled unpleasantly. "I can't say I'm terribly surprised to learn that my niece has landed herself in such trouble, though I'm pained, of course. Doubly so, because it brings old wounds to the surface. But blood will out, they say—isn't that true, Sir George?"

"Don't, Mercer. Please." There was real anguish in Sir George's voice, but his brother-in-law appeared unmoved.

"It seems only fair that Lord Anthony know the truth," he said. "About your daughter's birth."

Anthony started, though his resolve never wavered. He knew already that his parents would not approve his choice. But even if they cut him off entirely, it scarcely mattered, as he spent so little time with his family anyway. He was more concerned about Sir George—and Tessa.

"Sir, if this truth, whatever it is, upsets you, rest assured that I will not insist upon hearing it," Anthony said now.

The older man gave him a sad smile. "No, Mercer is right. You should know—but I will ask you not to tell Tessa. I'd not have her memory of her mother tainted in any way, particularly for something that was entirely my own fault."

"Your fault, sir?" Anthony asked in surprise. "I'm afraid I don't understand."

Sir George stared into the fire, his eyes misty with reminiscence. "Grace was the most beautiful woman I'd ever known. I loved her to distraction and, in time, won her love in return. It mattered nothing to me that her father was our horse trainer, but my own father was incensed. He was the first baronet, you see, and considered the honor hard-won. It made him acutely conscious of our position in Society, of what people thought of us—of him. He was determined that I should make a brilliant match, to further elevate our social standing."

He sighed, shaking his head. "He never understood that the match I made was the most brilliant one imaginable. My father forbade our marriage. Grace refused to come between me and my father, or risk her own father's position here, so she ran away. Alas, we had already been rather . . . imprudent, though I had no idea, when she left, of the result of our indiscretion."

"I take it she was already with child—with Tessa?" Anthony prompted when Sir George paused again.

With a sigh, he nodded. "Aye. By the time I found her, she was near her time. As soon as she could travel after the birth, I convinced her to accompany me to Ireland so that we could be married—for the sake of the child. My father died just a few months later, and we were able to return to Wheatstone."

"Where you told everyone you'd married right after Grace ran away," said Mercer Emery sourly. "Luckily for my sister, no one here in Leicestershire knew when the marriage took place."

Anthony regarded Tessa's uncle through narrowed eyes. "But you discovered it?"

"Aye. She confessed the truth to me once, when I was grieved over the death of my wife, nigh on twenty years ago."

"And you've held it over Sir George's head ever since."

It was a statement, not a question, and it made the steward flush an ugly shade of red. "What are you implying?" he demanded.

Anthony looked from him to his son and back.

"It's clear that Sir George feels strongly about preserving his late wife's memory—quite understandably. It's also clear that neither of you are particularly well-suited to your occupations here, which tells me that you've had to exert some hold over Sir George to retain them. Family loyalty only goes so far, after all."

"I've had about enough of your insults," Harold Emery exclaimed, stepping forward belligerently. "It's one thing for Tessa to criticize my work, but I don't have to take that from the likes of you."

Anthony faced him, a slight smile playing about his lips. "Is that a challenge, Mr. Emery?"

Rather to his disappointment, Harold backed down immediately. "I, er, not exactly. But—"

"Sit down, Harold," his father said impatiently. "Even if what you say is true, Lord Anthony, what do you propose to do about it? Convince Sir George to turn us off?"

Anthony looked at Sir George, who was still staring into the fire, looking troubled. "Sir?" he asked gently.

Finally he raised his head, meeting Anthony's gaze. "You're right, my lord—but so is Mercer. I'll risk my estate before I'll risk Grace's name, or Tessa's. Incompetence is no crime, in any event."

Rush, who, with Thor, had remained motionless and silent throughout all of this remarkable exchange, suddenly spoke. "No, but embezzlement is."

"Embezzlement?" Sir George echoed in surprise.

Now the elder Mr. Emery looked as pugnacious as his hot-tempered son. "I doubt you can prove such an accusation, my lord."

"I rather suspect I can," said Rush, coming forward and pulling a card from inside his coat. "Sir

George, I have here the name of my own man of business, whom I am willing to have spend a few days going over your account books. He is known for both his thoroughness and his integrity."

Mercer Emery blanched visibly, then, realizing that all eyes were on him, fell back on bluster. "There's no need to bring in outsiders, Sir George, for what is a family matter. Besides, it was your daughter who insisted—"

"Yes, Tessa told me that she'd enlisted your help to keep me ignorant of the estate's true condition. That must have been extremely convenient, allowing you to play on her sympathies even as you plundered her inheritance." There was no vagueness in Sir George's expression now.

Mercer shook his head, his eyes darting about at the others in the room. "No! It . . . it wasn't like that."

"Suppose we let Mr. Frobish determine that," Rush suggested. "Or, in the alternative, perhaps we can give Mr. Emery the opportunity to leave his post voluntarily instead?"

"Mercer?" Sir George said.

Emery's face went from white to red. "Very well, then. If family means so little to you, I will be gone by morning—and Harold, too. We'll see how well Wheatstone does with no steward at all—and no trainer for your stables."

He stalked to the door. "Come, Harold," he snapped, and his son, who had been standing open-mouthed listening to the exchange, jerked to life and followed him from the room. The others could hear them arguing as they went upstairs to pack their belongings.

Sir George still looked worried. "I fear that they

are more than capable of dragging my name—and worse, Tessa's—through the dirt, out of revenge. But if they were truly stealing from her—"

"You had no choice, sir," Anthony assured him. "Already, they were getting greedier—thus their plot to force Tessa into marriage with her cousin. They had to be stopped."

"Aye," said Sir George with a heavy sigh. "I just hope the price will not be too high—for Tessa."

"Leave the Emerys to us, Sir George," said Thor, speaking for the first time. "We are not without influence in this area, you know. If they try to spread their poison, we will be ready to counteract it, I promise you."

For the first time since the uncomfortable interview began, their host smiled. "Thank you. Thank you all . . . for everything. But now, I find myself quite tired. Still, I believe I shall sleep better tonight than I have in an age."

Less than a week later, Tessa found herself exchanging marriage vows in the village church. While she was exceedingly grateful that it was Anthony and not Harold at her side, she had not completely forgiven him for the shock he'd occasioned her father, or for taking her destiny out of her hands.

Still, she could not deny that most of the revelations over the past few days had been welcome ones. Though her father had been evasive about why Uncle Mercer and Harold had left Wheatstone so precipitately, he confirmed her suspicion that Mercer had been diverting some of the estate funds into his own pocket.

He was interviewing for a new steward, while a man recommended by Lord Rushford combed through the estate books. Already Mr. Frobish had discovered revenues that could now benefit Wheatstone instead of Uncle Mercer's gaming habit—something Tessa had known nothing about.

Then there was the matter of the horses, which were far better off without Harold around, even if they were now without a trainer. When Tessa had hinted again to her father that she would like to play a role there, he had at least listened carefully before repeating that it would not be proper, giving her hope that in time she might wear down his resistance to the idea. At any rate, there would now be no question of attempting to sell Vulcan before the stallion was properly broken and trained.

But by far the most wonderful news was that Anthony had discovered that Uncle Mercer had been lying to her about her father's heart all these years. She had hugged Anthony when he'd told her, the day after their betrothal, almost forgiving him on the spot for everything else. Almost. But there was still the matter of her father's disappointment in her, her lost freedom—and the ordeal Anthony was about to put her through.

For it had been agreed between Anthony and her father that the new couple would leave on the morrow for London, to meet Anthony's family. Tessa could not recall ever dreading anything so much. First, however, there was the ceremony to get through.

"—so long as you both shall live?" the vicar asked Anthony.

"I will," he replied without the slightest quaver in his voice.

Tessa's voice was not so steady, her emotions were

in such turmoil. A few moments later, however, it was done—she and Anthony were married. And she still didn't know if that meant that her fondest dreams were to be fulfilled—or her worst nightmares.

Or perhaps both.

"Congratulations, my dear," said her father, the first to greet her after the ceremony. "I believe the two of you will be extremely happy together."

Tessa leaned down to give him a hug. "Thank you, Papa. You've been so good to me this week past, particularly considering—"

"Water under the bridge, sweetheart," he said, and his smile really did look genuine. "Look forward, not back. It's what I mean to do."

She nodded, realizing what that meant to a man who'd spent years doing just the opposite. Her father then turned to Anthony.

"I'm trusting you with my greatest treasure, lad. See you take proper care of her."

Anthony smiled, and Tessa couldn't help noticing again, dazedly, that he was by far the handsomest man she'd ever seen. "If I don't, you will be able to bring me to heel for it, sir, as you'll be seeing her daily once we return from London."

That had been yet another pleasant surprise for Tessa: that Anthony was willing to live at Wheatstone after their marriage, that he'd already made arrangements for Lord Rushford to rent Ivy Lodge from him. It meant that she wouldn't have to leave her father after all.

Except for her trip to London, she remembered with renewed dread.

The rest of the small crowd came forward to offer their congratulations: Lord Rushford, Sir Charles,

Mr. Turpin, Lady Killerby, and even Lord Killerby, who was now able to get about a little with the help of crutches.

"Brides are always lovely, of course, but you are the loveliest I've ever seen," Lady Killerby declared, coming up to kiss Tessa's cheek before wiping her eyes. "It makes me wish I had a daughter of my own."

"Perhaps Killer will oblige and bring you one someday, my lady," Sir Charles suggested.

"I can only hope," she replied with a despairing shake of her head. "I'd thought being off the hunting field might throw him more in the way of the local girls, at least, but I see I'll have to insist he go to London in the spring if he's ever to catch himself a wife."

The others chuckled. "Perhaps we'll all go, and urge him along," said Lord Rushford. "There's little else to do in the spring, after all."

"Or this next week or so," complained Sir Charles. "At least you won't miss much while you're gone, Anthony."

An early frost had put a temporary stop to fox-hunting, though the ground was sure to thaw before Tessa and Anthony returned.

"And you can trust me to see that your father is well looked-after and never bored, Lady Anthony," said Lady Killerby.

Tessa started at this first use of her married name. It sounded so odd—and so very unlikely.

Anthony apparently noticed her reaction. "Lady Anthony Northrup," he said. "I rather like the sound of that. Think you can live with it, Tessa?"

"I suppose I must," she said, then realized how ungracious that sounded. "That is, I'm sure I'll grow accustomed to it in time." That wasn't much better. What was wrong with her?

Lady Killerby had insisted on holding the wedding breakfast at Ivy Lodge, claiming that her hostessing skills would get rusty otherwise. Tessa suspected the dilapidated condition of most of Wheatstone had something to do with the plan, and that Anthony had had a hand in it. In any case, it was perfectly true that Ivy Lodge was better suited to a large gathering—for now.

They all repaired, therefore, to Ivy Lodge, and soon Tessa was surrounded by members of the Quorn, Belvoir, Cottesmore, and Pytchley hunts, as well as many of their wives. Even the Hilltops were there to offer their well-wishes, completely oblivious to the fact that they'd unwittingly helped to bring the match about.

Many of those present remembered Sir George from his hunting days and made a point of seeking him out to talk over old times. Tessa couldn't help smiling to see him in such glory, managing to ignore for the moment the trials that still lay ahead of her.

"Penny for your thoughts," Anthony whispered in her ear, making her jump. "I'd guess they are agreeable, judging by your expression—though perhaps not so agreeable as mine." He placed a hand at her waist and gave her a gentle squeeze.

Abruptly, Tessa could think of nothing but the coming night. She swallowed. "I, ah, was just thinking that my father looks very happy—and healthy—today."

"I'm glad," said Anthony, following her gaze. "I would not want our marriage to be a source of pain to him. However, if you are happy, I believe he will be as well. And I mean to make sure that you are happy, Tessa."

She turned to look up at him. "I only hope you

won't discover we are so mismatched that *you* cannot be happy. Right now you seem to regard marriage as a new sport to master, but in time the novelty will fade."

"I have no fear that my interest will fade, Tessa," he said with a grin. "If you'd seen some of the debutantes my mother used to throw at my head—! Any of those girls would have bored me inside of a fortnight."

"As you've not known me much longer than that, I'd say I have yet to be put to that test," she said lightly, trying not to imagine the lovely, polished daughters of Society with whom he must be mentally comparing her.

He gazed down at her, and the expression in his eyes made her heart turn over. "You've more than passed that test, my sweet, believe me. Time is not what matters, though time will prove the truth of my words. You'll see."

She could only pray he was right.

Two hours later, people finally began to leave. Tessa was just as glad, for her face was beginning to ache from smiling so much. She was exchanging farewells with the Hilltops when she became aware of a slight commotion near the doorway. Turning, she was surprised to see her uncle and cousin, declaring—rather loudly—that they'd come to pay their respects to the newlyweds.

It was the first time Tessa had seen them in a week, and habit, if nothing else, prompted a reluctant concern for their welfare. They were, after all, family.

"Uncle Mercer! Harold! I trust you are both well?" she exclaimed, meeting them halfway across the room. "Wheatstone is not the same without you." That was true enough, though most of the changes so far seemed to be for the better.

"I'll wager it's not," Uncle Mercer said, a trace of bitterness in his smile. "I hope taking over the management of the estate is not taxing your father's health." He glanced over to where Sir George sat near the fireplace, talking with another gentleman and watching the newcomers warily.

"Not at all—though it turns out his health is not so fragile as I had been led to believe," Tessa replied with a significant look that made her uncle frown suddenly.

Harold's expression was more sneer than smile. "But then, you're not noticing much at home these days, I'll warrant, eh?" He nodded in Anthony's direction. "I imagine your poor papa is feeling rather neglected."

Tessa followed his gaze in time to see Anthony excuse himself from the small group about him and head in their direction. She smiled at him, trying to ignore Harold's spiteful words. That was a demon she'd already wrestled—and vanquished, she reminded herself.

"Ah, Mr. Emery." Anthony's voice was cool. "I am delighted you could both stop by."

He laid a protective hand on Tessa's shoulder as he spoke, and she was abruptly irritated. Did he think her unequal to holding her own against her kinsmen? Suddenly, chillingly, she wondered if that was the real reason he had married her.

"They merely came to offer their congratulations," she said quickly, trying not to let that insidious doubt take hold.

Anthony's smile did not reach his eyes. "How nice."

"It seemed the least we could do," Uncle Mercer said, again a bit more loudly than necessary. "Other than Sir George, we are the nearest family Lady Anthony has, after all." He sent a quick glance around the room.

"Meaning that her good fortune is yours?" said Anthony cynically. "How very, ah, enterprising of you."

Uncle Mercer's smile dimmed. "Not at all, not at all," he blustered. "Remember, I've shared in Tessa's care for years, and she and Harold used to be quite . . . close. It's natural we should take an interest in her future."

Tessa was surprised to see Anthony's jaw clench. "Of course," he said shortly. Then, with a stilted nod of his head, he turned away—almost as though he didn't trust himself to remain.

"Your bridegroom looks less happy than I would expect, considering the prize he has just won," Harold commented.

Startled again, Tessa glanced up at her cousin. "Prize—? I presume you mean Wheatstone."

He raised a thick eyebrow. "What else? You're a fetching enough thing, of course, but I doubt that alone would have induced a man like Lord Anthony to marry you, particulary once he learned the truth about your birth. Mind you don't let him throw it in your face, since it's really not *your* fault, after all."

"What on earth are you talking about?" She glanced from her cousin to her uncle, who only shrugged.

"Harold should not have said anything, for it

would upset your father greatly if he knew you were aware of it. I recommend you not mention it to him, for his health is hardly robust, whatever Lord Anthony may have told you to the contrary."

"But—" She was still confused.

"Come, Harold. We will pay our respects to Lady Killerby, then be on our way. I wish you very happy, Tessa," Uncle Mercer said, his tone implying the opposite. "Very happy indeed."

Frowning, Tessa watched them go. What could Harold have meant about her birth? She had never heard a hint that there had been the slightest irregularity there . . . though if there was, Papa would not have told her, or anyone else, with his concern for the good opinion of the neighborhood.

It was possible, of course, that Harold had simply made it up. She would not put it past him, though she wouldn't have thought Uncle Mercer so petty, particularly as it would cast her mother—his sister—in a negative light. He had implied that Anthony knew about it, whatever it was. She would simply ask him, she decided.

Anthony was relieved to see the Emerys leaving, along with the rest of the guests. Not only did her uncle and cousin push him perilously close to losing his temper with their veiled insults, but he was eager to have Tessa to himself.

His wife—he loved thinking of her that way!—gave her father a parting hug before Rush and Thor loaded him into the carriage for his return to Wheatstone. Anthony helped the coachman to secure his new father-in-law's Merlin Chair to the top of the vehicle.

"I will write as soon as I reach London, Papa, and

will return as quickly as I may," he heard Tessa saying. "Neither Anthony nor I wish to miss any more of the foxhunting season than we must, after all."

That comment made Sir George smile, as Tessa had surely intended. Anthony had not missed the anxiety in the older man's eyes. "I'm sure that's true enough. Don't worry, Tessa, I shall be fine—and I'll answer every letter you send, to assure you of it."

Tessa watched the carriage as it retreated down the drive, her expression a bittersweet mixture of regret and relief.

As they climbed the front steps of Ivy Lodge together, Anthony realized with a sweet stab of anticipation that nothing now prevented him from taking Tessa upstairs. The sun would not set for another hour or more, but he refused to wait until nightfall— not when he had waited so long already.

He had to smile at that thought, for in reality it had been only a few weeks since he'd first met Tessa. But it felt as though he'd wanted her for an eternity.

"Come," he said softly, guiding her back into the house. "It is our time now."

Chapter 17

Tessa felt a thrill go through her at his words—at the touch of his hand at her waist, intimate, even though they were still surrounded by people.

"Let's go upstairs," he suggested in her ear as they reentered Ivy Lodge.

"Now?" she whispered back, glancing around at Lady Killerby, the remaining members of the Odd Sock Club, and the servants cleaning up after the departed guests. Though she was nervous, she was not unwilling—quite the contrary, in fact.

"They won't mind," he promised her. Then, to Lady Killerby, "I'm going to show my wife to our chamber so that she can rest a bit before dinner."

My wife. He actually sounded proud when he said those words! Tessa felt a delicious warmth spread through her midsection.

Lady Killerby nodded, commenting tactfully that

Tessa was bound to be tired after such a hectic day. There was a twinkle in her eye, however, that made Tessa blush. She knew—they all must know—what they were really going upstairs to do.

Tucking her hand into the crook of his arm, Anthony led her from the room and up the stairs. "See?" he murmured. "No censure whatsoever."

"Not censure, but . . . they'll be expecting you to come back down, will they not?"

He chuckled. "I rather doubt it."

She knew she was turning even pinker, but said nothing.

A moment later, he opened the door to his chamber and stepped back to let her enter first. She looked around with interest at the masculine but cozy room with its hangings of green and gold at bed and windows and a comfortable-looking chaise by the fire, upholstered in a cheerful floral print in the same colors.

He was watching her face for her reaction, and looked relieved when she smiled.

"What a pleasant room," she said, and his smile broadened. "It's just how I'd have imagined your chamber to be—except for that chaise. I presume it was added for me?"

He nodded. "I did a bit of refurbishing over the past week, with you in mind, so I'm glad you approve. Lady Killerby feared my tastes were rather too somber for a lady."

"Somber? Not at all. I find it soothing—even cheerful. Like you." To cover her sudden embarrassment, she glanced at the large hunting scene hanging opposite the window.

"Does that picture bother you?" he asked. "It used to hang in my bedchamber in the London house I shared with two of my brothers, and has only lately been removed here. I'll have it taken down if you prefer."

Tessa understood his concern, for though it was not bloody, the painting was rather energetic for a bedroom, with the hounds and horsemen in full pursuit of a fleeing fox. She could understand why he'd have liked having it in London, when he had to be away from his favorite pursuit.

"Not at all," she said warmly, "for it captures this part of the world beautifully. If . . . if we should ever have to live any length of time elsewhere, I'd rather like to bring it along."

He grinned with apparent delight, then kicked the door shut and swept her into his arms. "I think I must be the luckiest man on earth," he told her. "You are unique, Tessa."

She gazed up at him, heart pounding, her lips only a few inches from his own. "Is that a good thing, my lord?"

"It is indeed, my lady," he replied, and closed the small gap between them, his lips warm and firm upon hers. He tightened his arms around her, pulling her against him from chest to knee. She reveled in the feel of his body so close to hers, wanting to be closer yet.

For a long moment he deepened his kiss, then drew back, but only far enough to trail his lips along her cheek to her earlobe, then down her throat. Her hair had been pinned up for the wedding, which now gave him easy access to the row of tiny pearl buttons down her back.

Nuzzling the hollow of her throat, he released them, one by one, working his way from the nape of her neck to her waist. When his fingers touched the bare skin above her shift and corset, she tilted her head back and sucked in a quick breath at the contact, which sent a frisson of excitement through her body. He glanced up at her and smiled, but his hands did not pause in their work.

Her buttons undone, he slowly, gently slid his hands up her back to her shoulders and tugged the dress toward him. Bringing his lips back to hers, he pulled the gown open and down until it finally lay in a shimmering pool of ivory satin and velvet at her feet. Then, still with deliberate care, he went to work on the lacing of her corset.

As he undid the corset, it occurred to her that he was amazingly adept at undoing buttons and lacings that he could not see. It spoke of much practice. The thought cost her a pang, but then his lips were against her flesh again, and all she could think of was the present.

Soon, her corset lay on the floor atop her dress, leaving her clad only in her shift. She swallowed, tentatively placing one hand on his broad chest, rising and falling beneath his blue superfine coat and snowy linen shirt, wondering what was to come next.

"You're welcome to help me out of my things as well, you know," he murmured, nuzzling the sensitive spot below her ear. "I won't mind."

She swallowed again, then, with a shy glance up at him, began to undo his cravat with trembling fingers while he ran his hands up and down her bare arms, warming them—and stoking the growing fire within her. It took her a few minutes, for unlike him, she had no experience with such things.

When she finally managed to undo the intricately tied cravat, she unfastened the three buttons of his shirt, then paused, feeling rather foolish. "I, ah, I think I'll need your help here." Her voice quivered between nervousness and laughter.

With a grin, he pulled his shirttails from his breeches and in one fluid motion swept the shirt over his head and off, adding it to the growing pile on the floor. Her eyes widened slightly, and she put out a tentative hand to touch the crip, curling hairs on his chest. She'd been right—he was a magnificent creature.

At her touch, she heard him catch his breath, then he again pulled her against him, her breasts now separated from his bare chest by only the thin cotton of her shift. She could feel his arousal straining against his breeches.

He kissed her with growing urgency, then began untying the ribbons at the neckline of her shift, his lips still moving over hers. After only the slightest hesitation, she slid her hands down his warm, naked sides, then around to his front to fumble clumsily at the fastening of his breeches. A low moan escaped him.

"I—I understand, I think," she whispered against his lips. "It's like the excitement of the hunt—the breathless waiting for the fox to be sighted, then—" She finally undid his breeches, and his rampant manhood sprang free.

He chuckled. "And then?" he prompted, and then she was laughing, too, though she felt herself thrumming with desire—and curiosity.

"Every hunt is different, is it not?" she said after a moment. "This is like none I've ever experienced, so I don't know what comes next."

"I'll show you," he said, suddenly serious. He led

her to the bed, and she noticed with another prickle of embarrassment that someone had already obligingly turned down the counterpane.

Seating her on the edge of the bed, he knelt down to remove her slippers and stockings. It was a heady yet humbling experience, having him on his knees before her like a servant. Rolling down the first stocking, he paused to kiss her knee, and smiled when she drew in her breath at the sensation.

"That's nothing compared to what is to come, my sweet," he said, removing the other stocking, then sitting beside her to divest himself of his own shoes and stockings. His eagerness showed in his haste, for he accidentally knotted one of his shoelaces while trying to untie it.

"First check," he said with a grin as he undid the knot. "There, now." He kicked off the offending shoe and ripped off the stocking. "We're on the scent again—wouldn't you say?" he asked with a wink.

Mutely, she nodded. She could hear her heart pounding.

Standing again, he stripped his breeches the rest of the way off, then tugged her to her feet so that he could pull her loosened shift off over her head. Suddenly they were both completely naked.

It was all Tessa could do not to stare. She had never quite realized that a man's body would be so different, so exciting, so . . . large. She had seen horses mating, of course, and sheep, but somehow she'd imagined that a human bonding would be more spiritual, less earthy. Now, however, she felt like a mare in heat, as desperate for her stallion, and as lost to reason.

"Come to me, Tessa."

Her last shred of hesitation disappeared, and she went willingly into his arms, hungry for the feel of his skin against hers, his lips, his . . . everything.

For a long, breathless moment he kissed her, deeply and passionately, a kiss that was a promise of unguessed delights to come. Then, so gently that she wasn't sure whether he moved her or she him, he drew her back down onto the bed. "I want this to be perfect for you," he whispered.

How could it not be? she wondered. Though she didn't know exactly what to expect, she had no doubt that what she was about to share with Anthony would be both profound and exciting.

He pulled her down beside him until they lay side by side, then he pushed himself up on his forearms to gaze down at her. Suddenly embarrassed, she made a move as if to cover herself, but he shook his head.

"No, don't. I want to look at you, Tessa. You are so beautiful. Even more beautiful than I'd imagined— and I've done rather a lot of imagining these past weeks."

She smiled shyly up at him. "You, too?"

Especially since knowing they were to wed, her thoughts, her dreams, had been filled with Anthony: what he might say, what he might do, what this particular moment might be like. All had fallen far short of the reality—so far.

A tiny thread of uncertainty threatened her enjoyment, but he seemed to sense it, for he lowered himself onto her until he was kissing her again, this time with his body pressing against hers along their whole lengths. Then, rolling onto his side, he caressed her, beginning with her shoulder, her collarbone, then gradually working his way lower.

Tessa felt as though her whole body were licked with flames as heat washed over her, spreading outward from his touch. He splayed his hand against her chest, then slid it around to cup one breast. "So beautiful," he whispered again.

She could have said the same, for the strong planes of his chest, the defined muscling of his arms, made her think of a painting or sculpture—a work of art. She'd always appreciated the lines of a fine horse, but this was so much more . . . personal. *Mine*, she thought, with sudden exultation.

His hand was moving again, making circles on her belly, spanning her waist from thumb to smallest finger, sliding lower.

"I think the hounds must be closing on their quarry," she breathed, afraid of what might come next, but even more afraid that he might stop.

"Soon," he murmured, "but there is still much excitement to come." He captured her lips again for a long, sweet moment, and even as he did so, his hand slipped into the tangle of curls at the juncture of her thighs.

She gasped, but he took her gasp into his mouth and deepened the kiss as, with one finger, he found the spot that hungered most for his touch. Gently, so, so gently, he stroked, and she felt her body tense.

More. She needed more! Arching against him, she tried to intensify the contact, but still he was maddeningly gentle, taking his time while she was ready to rush her fences, to meet whatever was on the other side. She heard a small whimpering noise and realized it was coming from her own throat.

Clutching at his shoulders, she tried to pull him against her, to force him to . . . to what, she wasn't sure. But to do something more. For a moment he resisted her, still stroking, still driving her to the brink of some crisis, then he slowly rolled until he was again atop her.

Still kissing her, he began to move, rubbing his length against hers. She felt his arousal, so near to the place that demanded more and more of his touch, and shifted slightly beneath him, to give him better access.

Gently, still more gently than she wanted, he guided himself to her, massaging her sensitive nubbin with the tip of his manhood. She groaned with delight at this new sensation, the excitement of having him so close, then she opened fully to him, using her legs and arms to draw him into herself.

Releasing her lips, he nuzzled her ear and whispered, "Now, my love, we finally reach the climax of the hunt."

Rhythmically, he moved in and out, each time delving just a little deeper. At the same time, he slipped a hand between them so that he could continue stroking that tiny bit of flesh that was the heart of her desire.

Tessa began to tremble, teetering on the edge of an exquisite precipice. Tumbling over might kill her, but she didn't care, for surely heaven lay on the other side. He moved quicker, deeper, stroked more firmly, then suddenly she fell, gasping, into a chasm of ecstasy beyond anything she'd ever imagined.

The world disappeared and only she and Anthony remained, bonded together as one. Above her, she heard him groan, then he drove himself deep, deep inside her, vaulting her back to the heights as he found his own release.

Slowly, very slowly, the world reassembled itself around them as her senses gradually recovered from the overwhelming experience. Opening her eyes, she gazed up at Anthony in wonder, unwilling to speak, for no words could be worthy of what had just occurred.

Gazing down at her, he smiled—a slow, lazy smile that reflected the languor she felt stealing through her own body, now that the most amazing experience of her life was over. "Poor little fox," he said, caressing her face with his eyes.

She smiled up at him. "Poor? Only because the hunt is over."

"For the moment," he said. "I promise you many more."

Surely no one could experience anything like that more than once in a lifetime? "Is . . . is it always like this?"

Slowly, he shook his head. "I've never experienced anything like this before—but I have no doubt I will again, now that we're together. And so will you. This is only the beginning."

Anthony meant what he said. Though he was by no means inexperienced, what he'd just shared with Tessa was astounding, with no parallel from his past. Was this the difference love made? He thought it must be.

For a moment he wondered whether he should have dissembled his expertise in such things as removing feminine attire. But no, he never wanted to be dishonest with Tessa. He was who he was—past, present, and future. And somehow he felt sure that with her, the future would be best of all.

Leaning down, he kissed her again, a sweet, lingering kiss. "Does this mean you forgive me for insisting that we marry?" he asked teasingly, though a part of him tensed for her answer.

"Certainly you've proved that there is much more of good in marriage than I'd ever suspected," she responded with a shy smile.

"I'm glad—but that's not what I asked."

For a long moment she didn't answer, then she said, "I believe I've come to understand why you did what you did. What Harold did was dishonest, while what you did was . . . more honest than I'd have liked. But more and more, I'm learning that honesty is best, whatever I believed in the past."

"I'm glad to hear it. I hope we will never have occasion to lie to each other, Tessa."

"I hope so, too," she said, then she frowned. "That reminds me—Harold said something before he left that I didn't understand. I'm hoping you can explain it to me."

Anthony rolled so that they were side by side, though still facing each other. With one finger, he stroked the side of her face, wondering what young Emery was up to now. "I will if I can," he told her.

She hesitated, biting her lip, then gave a little shrug and met his eyes. "He said you were marrying me for Wheatstone," she began.

He frowned, but before he could deny it, she continued. "I didn't believe that, and still don't. I wouldn't have mentioned it at all, except that we've just said we'll be honest with each other."

"Thank you for telling me, then," he said, cupping her cheek. "Was there something else he said? You said you didn't understand."

"Yes. He said something about my birth. That . . . that you had learned the truth of it, whatever it is. My uncle seemed to confirm it, and said my father didn't want me to know. Do you know what they were talking about?"

Anthony tried not to let his sudden fury at the Emerys show in his expression. So that's why they had come to Ivy Lodge today—to try to poison this marriage at its very inception! He should have had them thrown out the moment they arrived.

But no, that would only have postponed the inevitable.

"Anthony?" She looked worried now. He had hesitated too long. "There is something, isn't there?"

"It's nothing so ominous as your cousin doubtless made it sound," he said quickly, determined to wipe the worry from her brow. "You knew, did you not, that your parents eloped?"

She nodded. "Father mentioned it once. I, of course, wanted all of the details, for it sounded terribly romantic," she said with a smile, "but he would say nothing more about it, seeming to feel it was not a fit subject for my ears." Her smile dimmed. "Were they . . . not actually married before I was born?"

There was no denying his Tessa was quick on the uptake. "Not until just after," he told her gently. "No one here knows that, however, as the wedding took place in Ireland."

"No one except my uncle and cousin," she said hollowly, feeling as though the bottom had just dropped out of her world. She was illegitimate, and her father had hidden it from her all these years— hidden it from everyone.

"Yes, that was the hold they had over your father. Emery convinced him that if the truth were known, even after so many years, it would create a scandal— a far greater scandal than most would be likely to consider it."

"Most?" she asked doubtfully, thinking of his family. Surely this news could not have been welcome to Anthony, however much he chose to downplay it now.

"Oh, there will always be those willing to blow any little thing out of proportion for gossip," he said lightly. "But there's no reason anyone else should ever know of this."

Given her uncle's parting comment, she didn't necessarily agree, but she refused to worry Anthony with what was only speculation.

"Poor Papa," she said. "I suppose his excessive concern with the opinions of others worked against him in this case." She managed a small smile, and he hugged her to him.

"That's my girl. Sir George spent years worrying about such things, but you have no need to do so. Not now."

But Tessa wasn't at all certain that her father's concerns had been misplaced. More than ever, she was conscious that she had married above her station. She only hoped that Anthony would not suffer too much for his compassion for her and her father.

Anthony quite enjoyed dinner that evening. Not only was Tessa at his side where she belonged, but he felt far more relaxed than he had in weeks—and he was fully aware of the reason. As the soup was served, then again over the fish, he shared intimate smiles with his new bride, delighting in her blushes—which everyone else at the table pretended not to notice.

Really, he must be the luckiest man alive, he thought. Not particularly wealthy, perhaps, but with great riches in good friends and a wife he knew would be a constant source of pleasure to him—on many levels.

Not until the sweetmeats were brought in did he

notice how quiet Tessa had been throughout the meal. He hoped it was no more than mild embarrassment in front of his friends, but he feared it was more. Learning the truth about her birth couldn't have been easy for her. Then there was the trip to London. She hadn't said so, but he knew she was worried about his family's reception.

To be truthful, so was he. He'd waited until today to send word of their marriage, partly from a superstitious worry that something might happen to prevent it, and partly from a hope that his father might not have time to discover everything there was to know about Tessa before they arrived in London. The Duke of Marland prided himself on knowing everything about everyone.

He'd considered not sending word at all, simply arriving at Marland House and introducing Tessa as his bride, but he'd rejected that plan as too risky. This way, if his parents greeted the news with horror or anger, the storm would have time to abate before Tessa could see it.

She was insecure enough about fitting into his world without that. If they were rude to her, he would whisk her back here before they could so much as catch their breath. As far as it was in his power, he intended to keep her safe and happy— always. On that thought, he remembered the surprise he still had in store for her and smiled.

"In light of today's events, I hope you won't mind if my wife and I break with tradition somewhat and leave you all to your port," he said when the ladies rose to remove to the parlor. "Lady Killerby, I know you will excuse Tessa this evening. There is something in the stables I wish to show her."

Tessa took his proffered arm, her eyes frankly curious. "Is it Nimbus?" she asked as they left the dining room. "Or Zephyr?"

Instead of answering, he just smiled and said, "Run upstairs and get a wrap, and I'll show you."

With a last, puzzled frown, she complied, and a minute or two later was back, a warm blue cape clasped about her shoulders. "I'm ready. Now, what is this mystery?"

Tucking her hand into the crook of his elbow, he led her down the front steps and around the side of the house to the stables. The horses had been fed and were quiet for the most part, though Nimbus shied at the sound of approaching footsteps when they neared his stall.

"It's just me," Tessa called to him, and at once he quieted.

Anthony didn't think he'd ever get tired of watching her effect on horses. Then, as it had once before, a thread of doubt assailed him. Had she somehow affected him with her "magic," making him disregard his own desire for independence as well as his family's expectations for her sake? Or was this simply love?

Would he ever really know?

"Here we are," he said, pushing the traitorous doubt from his mind. "Someone I think you may have missed." He was speaking as much to the horse as to Tessa.

"Cinnamon!" she exclaimed in delight. "Why didn't you tell me you'd bought her, Anthony?" She threw her arms around him and kissed him before turning back to the mare, who was whickering excitedly at the sound of Tessa's voice.

He grinned at Tessa's response, as effusive as he'd hoped. "I feared you might have already discovered it from your uncle. I'm glad I was able to make her a surprise."

"I never asked," she said, stroking the mare's outstretched neck. "Everything last week was so . . . chaotic."

"I understand, believe me. I'd intended to give her to you last Tuesday, but then you refused me—and then, on Wednesday—"

"On Wednesday, you were told I was engaged to marry my cousin, the very day after you had offered for me," she finished quietly. "Oh, Anthony, I am so sorry for the pain I must have caused you. I still cannot believe you can forgive me for that."

He caressed her shoulder through the fabric of her cape. "I never blamed you, Tessa. Or, at least, not for more than a few minutes," honesty compelled him to admit, remembering his emotions on that day. "But even during the brief time that I believed you would really marry Emery, I still intended to give Cinnamon to you as a wedding gift."

Her eyes grew misty, then she turned back to the horse. "Perhaps it's as well you didn't tell me about Cinnamon before. I'd have felt so much worse . . ."

Abruptly, Tessa remembered what Harold had told her about Anthony buying a horse for his mistresses each year. He'd bought Cinnamon before making his initial offer—the one she had misinterpreted. Had his original intention been—? No! She would not doubt him, not now.

Even if, in light of what she'd learned about her birth, she was more suited to that role.

"Thank you, Anthony," she said then, meaning far more than just his gift of the mare.

* * *

For Tessa, the journey to London was both exciting and dreamlike, two days out of time—two special days of getting to know Anthony better, both physically, during their one night on the road, and through their long conversations in the coach. Two days of imagining that her life could always be like this, free of the judgment, the censure, of others.

Dusk was falling—a very foggy dusk—when they rolled into the streets of London. Tessa peered through the carriage windows, wonder at the sights and sounds dampened by a growing dread. They were to drive straight to Marland House, in the very heart of fashionable London, and there she was to be introduced to the Duke and Duchess of Marland—Anthony's parents.

The fog turned the gas streetlights into fuzzy yellow globes and muted the sounds of more traffic than she'd even imagined. As they slowly worked their way into Mayfair along the thronged streets, she caught glimpses of gracious squares filled with trees and tall, elegant town houses, with liveried servants and sumptuously dressed people passing in and out of them.

"This is Grosvenor Square," Anthony told her as they turned into the largest square she'd yet seen, surrounded by the grandest of houses. "And this," he continued as the carriage pulled to a halt, "is Marland House."

Tessa knew the hand she placed into Anthony's as he helped her from the carriage was trembling. She had never felt so unequal to anything in her life. What good was her one talent now? she wondered. None at all.

Desperately, she tried to remember the proper way to curtsy to a duke. Why had she not found a private moment to practice it before they left Leicestershire?

"You'll be fine."

Anthony's whispered assurance told her that her panic must be evident on her face. Quickly she tried to smooth her features into some semblance of calm and dignity, though she doubted her success. Her heart in her throat, she accompanied her new husband up the broad marble steps and through the double front doors, held wide by a pair of satin-liveried footmen.

The elegance of the front hall surpassed Tessa's wildest imaginings, with its floor of intricately patterned black and white marble, mahogany paneling, and undoubtedly priceless works of art displayed on walls and in alcoves. She barely had time to take it in before Anthony ushered her through another pair of tall doors, this one leading into a parlor sumptuously hung with gold.

Several people rose at their entrance, and an imposing man with silvering hair and penetrating, pale gray eyes came forward to peer down his hawk-like nose at her. "This, I presume, is the newest addition to our family?" he asked in icy tones.

Tessa released Anthony's arm to sink into her lowest curtsy, barely hearing Anthony's response. One leg began to shake, unused to such a position, so she glanced up, expecting either Anthony or the duke to take her hand to help her to rise. Instead, she saw them all but glaring at each other, apparently engaged in some contest of wills, while she quivered below, in her absurd pose.

Afraid her leg would give out on her, she tried to rise on her own, only to overbalance and end up ignominiously sprawled on the floor of the elegant Marland House parlor.

Chapter 18

Anthony broke free of his father's censorious stare to kneel in guilty concern. "Tessa! Are you all right?" he asked. How could he have forgotten her, even for a moment, knowing how nervous she was?

Already Tessa was scrambling to her feet, her face bright red with embarrassment. "I'm so sorry," she said to him in an anguished whisper. Then, to his father, "I do apologize, Your Grace. I . . . I am most honored to meet you."

The duke quirked one eyebrow, but his mouth remained in a grim line. "Perhaps you would like to compose yourself before dinner, Lady Anthony. My son will show you to your chamber."

"Of course," Anthony said, fighting a wild urge to knock his own father down for treating Tessa so dismissively.

A glance showed his mother, his brother Robert, Lord Bagstead, and Lady Bagstead all looking shocked and disapproving. Best to get Tessa out of this poisonous atmosphere as quickly as possible, he decided, wondering where Edward, Peter, and Marcus were.

"I'm sorry," he told her as soon as they were out of the room. "I should have—"

"Pray don't apologize," she interrupted him. "It only makes me feel worse. How can I be so accomplished a rider and so very clumsy doing something as simple as a curtsy? I've doubtless confirmed their worst fears about me." She looked ready to cry.

Anthony paused on the landing to put an arm around her shoulders. "Tessa, please don't distress yourself so. My parents are enough to frighten royalty into momentary clumsiness. They may be obnoxiously high in the instep, but I'm sure they don't think poorly of you for losing your balance— particularly when I left you down there so long. Much of the blame is indeed mine, for letting my father distract me from my duty to you."

She took a long, shuddering breath. "You are very good to me, Anthony—far better than I deserve. Perhaps if I'd paid more attention to my lessons in deportment, instead of always being so wild to go riding—"

"Then you might have become like those simpering misses I've made it a point to avoid," he said, guiding her up the next flight of stairs. He hoped to make her smile, but she did not.

"Or perhaps I would not now be such an embarrassment to you."

There were two footmen stationed along the hallway, so he ushered her into the room he occupied during his infrequent stays at Marland House and closed the door before taking her face between his hands.

"You are in no way an embarrassment to me, Tessa. Quite the reverse, in fact, for I am sure to be the envy of everyone for securing such a lovely wife." Her eyes still doubted him, so he gathered her to him for a kiss that started as mere reassurance, but soon became passionate.

He slid his hands down her back to cup her bottom, pulling her more tightly against him, against his rising arousal. "Can you doubt that you make me happy?" he murmured against her lips.

Her lips curved against his in a smile—finally. "At least when we are alone," she said, laying her cheek against his chest so that he could not see her expression. "Can we perhaps stay here and have our dinner sent up?"

"What, and admit defeat? I thought you more courageous than that, Tessa," he said, only half teasing.

"I don't think I can face your family again—not yet. Not after making such a fool of myself just now." She looked up at him, pleadingly.

Had he made a terrible mistake in bringing her to London? He'd thought to prove to her that she could handle herself as well here as in the country, to overcome her doubts about herself. Was he instead only reinforcing them?

"Of course you can face them, Tessa," he said with more confidence than he felt. "They are only people, after all, flesh, blood, and bone like every other creature. What is the worst thing you can do when a horse displays a bad temper toward you?"

"Show fear," she answered promptly. "Oh. But . . . this is not the same."

"Isn't it? Think of my parents as particularly obstreperous horses whose trust and confidence you have to win. They may be skittish and aloof at first, but I've no doubt that you will win them over in time."

Though she still looked skeptical, she finally nodded. "Very well. I'll try—for your sake."

Would she never do anything for her own sake? He almost asked it aloud, but then realized that might undercut her determination. "Thank you. Just remember, you've tamed more frightening beasts than those waiting below."

Twenty minutes later, clad in her best gown of pale blue satin, Tessa accompanied Anthony back downstairs with considerably more trepidation than she'd felt when approaching the wild black stallion Vulcan. On reentering the parlor, she saw that two more couples had arrived.

"Ah, Peter, Marcus," Anthony exclaimed. "I'm delighted to see you both, and to present you to my bride. Tessa, my two younger brothers and their wives, Lady Peter and Lady Marcus."

Luckily the newcomers required only the shallowest of curtsies, which Tessa was able to perform without mishap, though she couldn't bring herself to look at those who had witnessed her earlier disaster. Instead, she forced a smile to her lips and focused on the new couples.

To her surprise, all four of them were smiling, making her worry for a moment that she'd done something wrong after all. But then the short, dark-haired lady—Lady Marcus?—came toward her with hands outstretched.

"I'm delighted to meet you, Lady Anthony—or

may I call you Tessa?" Her accent was decidedly American. "And you must call me Quinn. I'm sorry we were not here to greet you when you first arrived." A sidelong glance toward the original four occupants of the room told Tessa that she had heard an account of that meeting.

Though she felt herself blushing again at the reminder, she forced herself to speak, not wanting to appear ungrateful for such a friendly overture. "I thank you . . . Quinn. And yes, please do call me Tessa. I . . . am unused to formality."

"Informality is becoming quite the epidemic in this family, I perceive," said Lady Bagstead sourly from across the room. "I believe I speak for the duke and duchess, as well as Lord Bagstead, when I say that it is important to preserve the dignity of the position that the name of Northrup holds."

The duchess nodded. "I quite agree. Therefore, I trust that those of you who feel compelled to refer to each other so familiarly will confine your use of Christian names to private gatherings such as this one."

Now Quinn colored, and Tessa sent her an apologetic glance for involving her new sister-in-law in her own disgrace. However, the dark-haired girl lifted her chin to regard the duchess with a touch of defiance.

"Of course, Your Grace. Sarah and I have always been careful to observe the proprieties when in public, as I'm sure Tessa here will do as well. If you prefer, we can refrain from behaving in a friendly manner while in your presence, as well."

Lady Bagstead's eyes widened in horror, but the duchess only lifted a brow. "That will not be necessary, of course. Propriety and family affection are not mutually exclusive. Have a mind for the servants, however."

Quinn nodded demurely, then glanced at Tessa, her eyes now twinkling. "Now you know why we didn't get here earlier," she whispered, leading her over to Lords Peter and Marcus, whom Anthony had already joined.

He took her hand as she reached him, drawing her into the group. "I'll say again how glad I am that you all came, especially on such short notice. I really didn't want Tessa to think our whole family was like that."

"I assure you, we are not," Lord Peter said, sweeping her an exaggerated bow, though he kept his voice as low as Anthony's. His coat was of deep turquoise and his waistcoat of sky blue, in marked contrast to the attire of the other gentlemen present. "It is a constant source of chagrin to our father that only one of his sons is properly stuffy."

Lord Marcus nodded his agreement. "Edward, our eldest brother save Robert, is a good sort as well. His wife is approaching her confinement, however, so they have retired to the country early this year."

"I am very pleased to make your acquaintance, as well as Anthony's," said Lord Peter's wife, a dazzlingly lovely blond. "We were both delighted when we got word this morning of your marriage. You must call me Sarah—at least when the duchess is not about." Her smile was as genuinely friendly as Quinn's.

Tessa smiled in return, though between Quinn's petite stature and Sarah's ethereal beauty she felt like a sturdy peasant woman. She learned that both were also recent brides, Quinn since the summer and Sarah only a month married, and that both marriages had been as hasty as her own, to the disapproval of the four eldest members of the family.

"So you see," concluded Quinn after a brief explanation, "your match is quite in keeping with the new family tradition."

The others all chuckled, and Tessa began to relax. Perhaps she was not quite so dreadfully out of place in this family as she had feared. Certainly, it was pleasant to suddenly have two sisters-in-law who seemed eager to become friends as well. It occurred to her that she'd never really had a close girlfriend.

By the time they all went in to dinner, she was chatting with Quinn and Sarah as though they'd known one another for years.

"You and Quinn must go riding together," Sarah was saying, "for it sounds as though it's a passion you share."

"Perhaps we can all go," Tessa said, delighted at the idea of spending more time with her new sisters-in-law, but Sarah shook her head.

"I'm no horsewoman, I fear, for I've had little practice, though Peter is teaching me. I would love to watch, however."

It was agreed among them that if the weather accommodated, they would ride in the Park the next day. Anthony promised to procure a mount for Tessa from his father's stables, or from one of his brothers, as Cinnamon was still in Leicestershire.

Once they were all seated in the austerely opulent dining room, the group became more subdued under the watchful eyes of the duchess and her eldest daughter-in-law. Tessa, seated at the duke's right hand, hardly dared speak at all, managing only brief responses if someone directed a query to her.

Anthony and his younger brothers were more animated, occasionally poking subtle fun at their eldest brother. Lord Bagstead seemed largely oblivious, though Tessa noticed that the duke sent more than one disapproving frown their way.

In this household, not surprisingly, strict formality was observed in the matter of the ladies removing to the parlor as soon as the meal ended, leaving the gentlemen to whatever it was gentlemen did when alone. The duchess led the way, followed by Lady Bagstead.

Tessa was distressed to discover she was to go next, as Anthony was the next eldest son present, followed by Sarah and then Quinn. No such ceremony was observed in the country—at least, not among any of the families she knew—so this extra bit of pomp took her by surprise and struck her as both unnecessary and a tiny bit ridiculous.

"Now, Augusta," said the duchess to Lady Bagstead once they were all seated in the parlor, "do tell me how dear little William does. I spoke with his nurse yesterday, but she told me only that he is in fine health."

"He is indeed, Your Grace," replied Lady Bagstead in the pleasantest tones Tessa had yet heard her use. "I'm sure you will agree that he is exceptionally large for only five years old, and promises to grow into a tall and handsome young man. His speech is quite advanced for his age, as well."

The two continued to discuss the boy, whom Quinn informed Tessa was next in line for the dukedom after Lord Bagstead and therefore of particular importance. "I rather doubt that dear Rosalie, Edward's wife, will receive so much attention when her child makes its appearance," she said in an undertone.

"Though, to be fair, the duchess really does seem to dote on little William as any fond grandmother might," Sarah put in. "Perhaps she will show similar affection for Edward's child, even if it should have the misfortune to be a girl." They all chuckled quietly.

All too soon for Tessa's comfort, however, the duchess turned her attention back to her newest daughter-in-law, asking her about Wheatstone and her parents. As at dinner, Tessa gave the briefest answers possible without rudeness, unwilling to volunteer any information that would give her autocratic mother-in-law yet more reason to despise her.

"I presume that gown is representative of your wardrobe?" the duchess asked then.

Tessa glanced down at her very best gown, which she had already realized looked hopelessly dowdy next to the fashionable ensembles of the other ladies. "Yes, Your Grace."

"I feared as much. I should like to think my son would have made certain—but no. Anthony never did pay proper attention to such things. Still, you must have something better if you are to attend Lady Twyford's ball with us, two nights hence."

A ball? A London ball? Tessa fought down the panic that rose in her throat at the very thought. "I . . . I don't see how—" she began, vaguely hoping that her inferior wardrobe might prevent her from attending. Why had she ever agreed to come here?

"We can take her shopping tomorrow, Your Grace," Quinn offered. "Can't we, Sarah? You are welcome to come as well, Lady Bagstead. And Your Grace, too, if you should wish to offer your advice."

But those two ladies evinced identical expressions of distaste. "Tomorrow is one of my at-home days," the duchess informed them. "I presume you will wish to be here to receive callers with me, Augusta?"

Lady Bagstead nodded. "Of course, Your Grace. Indeed, like yourself, I never go into the shops myself. It is far more convenient to have the modistes come to me, I find."

"But not half so fun," Quinn whispered to Tessa with a pert grin. Then, aloud, "We will call directly after breakfast, then, Tessa. Lord Anthony is welcome to come along, of course, but if he is like most men, you can count on him to find a plausible reason to decline."

The duchess then took control of the conversation again, offering advice on fashion, deportment, and which people it was important for Tessa to meet while in Town, until the gentlemen joined them.

Anthony was soon apprised of the proposed shopping expedition and, as Quinn had predicted, excused himself on the grounds that he needed to find a suitable mount for Tessa's use during their stay in Town.

"You'll all do much better without me, at any rate," he concluded. "Peter may be up on all the latest fashions, but I, like most of us ignorant males, haven't the least clue which colors or sleeves or frills are in or out this season."

Even Lord Peter showed no inclination to join them, however, offering, along with Lord Marcus, to help Anthony with his task, instead. "With any luck, we'll have a hack for you by the time you return," Lord Peter said with an encouraging smile.

Though the evening itself had been rather an ordeal, when Tessa accompanied Anthony upstairs at the conclusion of it, she was able to look forward to the morrow with a fair degree of eagerness.

"Perhaps you were right," she told him as he escorted her up to her bedchamber, which adjoined his own. "Perhaps, with Quinn's and Sarah's help, I can do this after all. They are both showing me uncommon kindness, and I confess I like them very much."

With a motion of his head, he dismissed her waiting maid so that they could be private. When the girl had gone, Tessa looked around the sumptuous room that had been set aside for her use, so grand that she couldn't quite feel she belonged in it.

"I . . . I don't suppose it would be possible for us to stay with one of your brothers, instead of here?"

Regretfully, he shook his head. "Not on this visit, at least not without offending my parents. But we will not be here long, you know—only a few days. When next we come to London, we'll arrange to stay elsewhere, I promise you."

Though she knew that was meant to be encouraging, Tessa's heart sank at this intimation that they would be making longer visits to Town in the future. She had seen but little of London as yet, but already she felt stifled here—and not only because of the dirty fog. She simply wasn't suited to city life.

"Besides," he said when she did not reply, "anywhere we can be together can be home, can it not?" Smiling intimately down at her, he gathered her into his arms.

She nodded, feeling oddly shy—perhaps because she now had a clearer idea of the position in Society her husband occupied. He was even further above her than she'd realized—but she knew that if she said so, he would only laugh and try to soothe her.

"I hope I can always make you feel at home, Anthony," she said instead, tentatively stroking his sleeve.

He lowered his lips to hers. "With you here, I feel more at home in this house than I ever have before," he assured her. Then he was kissing her, and the pressure of his lips drove her doubts from her mind, leaving no room for anything but him, for the feelings he aroused in her.

With an urgency she didn't fully understand, she helped him to remove her clothing and then his, stopping only for frequent kisses, until they faced each other completely unclad. Tessa devoured his perfect body with her eyes, even as she saw him doing the same to hers. Certainly, he didn't seem to find her inferior in any way to other women—not here, not now.

After one long moment of mutual appreciation, they were in each other's arms again, flesh against flesh, lips against lips. With a low growl, Anthony moved backward, dragging her with him, to collapse on the bed with her atop him.

For an instant Tessa felt a passing worry for the satin-covered counterpane that doubtless cost more than her entire bedroom at Wheatstone, but then Anthony's hands were stroking her back, her sides, the nape of her neck, and such trivial matters were forgotten in another wild rush of desire.

Anthony had not been oblivious to the byplay between his mother, sisters-in-law, and Tessa that evening. He knew that she still felt out of her element, but he had told the simple truth when he said that when she was with him, he was home—no matter where he was. Now, with her above him, her beautiful, athletic, voluptuous body pressed against his, he knew beyond doubt that without her he would never feel complete again.

With one knee, he nudged her legs apart, and then

she took the initiative, straddling him, rubbing her secret, shadowed cleft against his straining arousal so that he had to forcibly control himself, to wait until she could match him in pleasure. Spanning her narrow waist with both hands, he lifted her slightly, then impaled her with his shaft, finding her slick and ready for him.

She gave a gasp, then a moan, and began rocking atop him, driving him closer and closer to the edge. This position gave him easy access to her sensitive nubbin, and he gently massaged her there, bringing her along with him to the very brink of climax.

Finally, with her head thrown back, panting in rhythm with his thrusts, she cried aloud and convulsed about him. Driving upward, he buried himself deep within her and released his control, emptying himself into her in an ecstatic rush.

After a long, trembling moment, they relaxed as one, Tessa lowering herself atop him again to nestle her face confidingly in the hollow of his throat. He cradled her to him in silent wonderment, amazed anew that such a woman could be his. Surely he'd done nothing in his life to deserve such a rich reward?

"Never let anyone make you feel you are less than you are, Tessa," he whispered as they both drifted off to sleep, still entwined. "To me, you rank above every woman in the world."

Anthony's last words still had the power to warm Tessa as she dressed the next morning. He had risen early, waking her only slightly as he kissed her before returning to his own room. She remembered that he and his brothers had planned an early visit to the mews on her behalf.

For a moment, she considered following them,

then realized that was impossible, here in London. The sorts of activities she took for granted in the country would raise eyebrows and more, here in Town. She reminded herself that this was to be a short stay, that she would be back at her beloved Wheatstone soon.

"Thank you, Sally. That looks very nice," she told her maid as she put the finishing touches to Tessa's hair.

Today's gown, a yellow walking dress, was even more countrified than the one she'd worn to dinner, but she tried not to dwell on it, as that was the point of her shopping trip today. She trusted Quinn and Sarah to bring her in line with current fashions. She only hoped they could do it without spending more than she and Anthony could afford.

Over breakfast, which she took alone in the dining room, as the duchess and Lady Bagstead had not yet risen, she began to worry about what this expedition might cost. Should she have asked Anthony how much she could reasonably spend? Too late now.

She was just finishing a second cup of tea when a footman led Quinn and Sarah into the room.

"Ah, I see you are an early riser," Quinn exclaimed. "I told Sarah you would be, used as you are to country hours. This will give us a chance to have Madame Fanchot to ourselves, while most other ladies in Town are still sitting in their boudoirs sipping chocolate."

"How luxurious that sounds," Tessa said, greeting her sisters-in-law with a smile. "I confess such a plan never occurred to me. At home, I would have been up for hours by now."

Sarah nodded. "I was the same when I first came to London, for I'd spent several years at school, where we were required to rise before the sun did. And Quinn, of course, came here from America, where they do things rather differently."

"Better, in other words," said Quinn loftily, then grinned. "I don't seem able to convince any of my English family of that, however. But now, if you are finished eating, let us go. We have a great deal to accomplish this morning."

Tessa soon discovered that she was right. Their first stop was the modiste's shop. Madame Fanchot was clearly well acquainted with both Quinn and Sarah, and seemed delighted at the chance to outfit Tessa as well.

"*Oui*, I can have a ball gown for her by tomorrow night," she said in response to Quinn's explanation of their needs. "And a day dress or two by the following day. Now, let us consider fabrics, shall we?"

With a flick of her fingers, she directed her assistants to bring out bolts of silks, satins, and velvets of every imaginable hue and pattern, spreading them across sofas and tables for consideration.

"Lady Anthony has a richer complexion than some," she said, which Tessa thought a very discreet way of saying that she was far more tanned than was fashionable, owing to the time she spent outdoors at home.

"This gives us more leeway in the matter of color than some ladies might enjoy," the modiste continued. "Here, hold up that amethyst velvet." Her assistant hastened to comply. "Yes, that will do nicely for a winter walking dress."

Over the next hour, Madame Fanchot recommended various day dresses, evening gowns and riding habits, showing Tessa fashion plates of the styles she meant to match with the various fabrics.

In addition, she triumphantly produced a ball gown in rich cream and gold brocade with rust-colored trim that needed only a little work to be fitted to Tessa's measurements.

At one point, when the modiste had accompanied her assistants to the back room to find a particular length of lace, the dazzled Tessa whispered urgently to Quinn, "How much will all of this cost? Neither Anthony nor my father—"

But Sarah smiled and shook her head. "Pray, don't worry about that. Peter spoke with the duke and duchess last night on just that concern, and they both agreed that we must not stint. They have set aside an allowance that you will find it difficult to exceed."

Tessa stared. "That rather smacks of charity, does it not? I cannot think that Anthony would care to be so indebted to his parents for my wardrobe."

"I imagine they regard it in the light of ensuring you are a credit to their son—and to them," Quinn said.

Sarah nodded her agreement. "Believe me, I understand exactly how you feel, for I brought nothing at all to my marriage."

Considering Sarah's exceptional beauty, Tessa could not agree, but she did understand what both ladies were saying. Appearances were of supreme importance to the Duke and Duchess of Marland, and they had more than enough money to ensure that Tessa would not embarrass them—at least in the matter of her clothing.

She therefore tried to relax and enjoy herself, which was not difficult to do. Madame Fanchot's taste was exquisite, and she could not help imagining Anthony's face when he saw her properly attired, as stylish as any London lady.

On leaving the modiste's shop, the three ladies proceeded to a milliner's shop for a selection of bonnets, on to a boot and shoe retailer's, then to a dry goods store to complete Tessa's ensembles with appropriate ribbons, parasols, gloves, and other accessories. Tessa was near the back of the store sorting through some artificial flowers while the others examined a display of stockings, when a strident feminine voice cut through the shop.

"Lady Marcus, upon my word," the newcomer exclaimed. "Just the lady I was hoping to see."

Tessa glanced up to see a lovely, voluptuous brunette, her full lips redder than nature had likely tinted them.

"How nice to see you, Lady Adelaide," Quinn responded. Tessa thought she perceived a coolness in her tone she had not heard before. "Have you but recently arrived in Town?"

The brunette nodded. "Last week. Is it true your brother-in-law, Lord Anthony, has just come to Town as well? I hear he is staying at Marland House. I scarcely dared believe it, as I know he is always in the Shires at this season."

"Yes, it's true," Quinn told her. "But I don't believe you have met my sister-in-law, Lady Peter Northrup, nor—"

"Delighted, delighted," Lady Adelaide interrupted with a distracted smile at Sarah. "Tell me, Lady Marcus, will Lord Anthony be at Lady Twyford's ball tomorrow night? He all but offered for me last spring, you know, so I am determined that when he first sees me, he will be completely smitten again."

Quinn's laugh sounded forced, ringing harshly in Tessa's stunned ears. "I fear you may have overestimated his interest, Lady Adelaide," she said. "As it happens—"

But now Lady Adelaide laughed in her turn. "Oh, I think not." Then, lowering her voice to a carrying whisper that Tessa had no difficulty hearing, "We became rather, ah, intimate, if truth be told. Had my father known, he would have insisted on marriage before now, but of course I preferred to wait for a proper declaration from dear Anthony."

Tessa swallowed painfully. This beauty, this titled lady, had been on the point of marrying Anthony last spring? Had been . . . intimate with him? Mistresses were one thing, but—

"I have someone else to introduce to you, Lady Adelaide," Quinn said firmly, turning. "This is my newest sister-in-law, Lady Anthony Northrup."

Chapter 19

I f the floor had opened to swallow her at that moment, Tessa would have been eternally grateful, but as it did not, she had no choice but to come forward, a smile pinned painfully to her face.

"I am pleased to make your acquaintance, Lady Adelaide," she forced herself to say.

Lady Adelaide looked no more pleased than Tessa felt, turning pale, then flushing red. Tessa hoped she was hiding her feelings better than the newcomer was able to do.

"Lady . . . Anthony," Lady Adelaide said flatly, her eyes narrowing as they swept Tessa from head to toe. "What a . . . surprise, to be sure."

With an effort, Tessa clung to her smile. "I suppose it would be, as our marriage was quite recent. I don't believe there has yet been an announcement in the London papers."

"No. No, there hasn't." Lady Adelaide's eyes flicked from Tessa to Quinn and back. She looked confused and hurt, as well she might, Tessa thought. Despite herself, she felt a flicker of sympathy for the woman, imagining how she herself would feel in Lady Adelaide's place. But surely Anthony hadn't really—

"I believe the duchess chose to wait until Lord and Lady Anthony were in Town to make the announcement," Quinn said then, interrupting Tessa's unsettling line of thought. "They were married quietly in the country, as Lady Anthony's father is an invalid and therefore unable to travel."

"I see." Lady Adelaide's eyes swiveled back to Tessa. "Lord Anthony always did have a soft spot for hard-luck cases. You are to be congratulated."

Then, without another word, she turned and swept out of the shop, leaving the shopkeeper and other customers openmouthed.

"What cheek!" Quinn exclaimed as soon as the door closed behind her. "I'm certain that when I saw her and Lord Anthony at the same gathering last summer, he paid her no special attention. Clearly, her expectations were all on one side."

Tessa burned to ask about the "intimacy" Lady Adelaide had mentioned, but of course could not do so in front of strangers—not that Quinn would necessarily know the truth, anyway.

"I . . . I've decided on these flowers, I think," she said instead, desperate to divert her thoughts for fear she might cry in public, disgracing herself yet again.

Taking her cue, Quinn and Sarah fell to discussing the various items she needed to purchase, and a few minutes later the trio left the shop, rather more subdued than when they went in.

"Pray take no notice of what Lady Adelaide said," Quinn implored her as they settled themselves in the carriage to return to their homes. "Whenever someone like Anthony marries, some ladies are bound to be disappointed. They weave fantasies about handsome and eligible gentlemen, and some manage to convince themselves that their fancies are truth."

Sarah nodded vigorously. "She's right. I've heard numerous stories of women making complete cakes of themselves, simply because they had convinced themselves that some man felt more than he truly did."

"Thank you. Thank you both," Tessa said, managing a shaky smile. Certainly she had been guilty of weaving fantasies about Anthony after meeting him—but her dreams had come true.

Hadn't they?

"You must be joking." Marcus eyed the tall, red-and-white skewbald gelding with obvious misgiving. "Not only is he foul-tempered, he's too big for a lady—and ugly, as well. Why would you want to put your wife on such an animal?"

Anthony grinned. "I might ask why you have such an animal in your stables, if he has nothing to recommend him."

His youngest brother grimaced. "Quinn saw him being mistreated by some tinker and insisted on rescuing him—by buying him. I believe even she has come to regret the impulse, however."

"I have to agree with Marcus," Peter put in. "We've looked at half a dozen horses that would make better mounts for Tessa than this monstrosity."

But Anthony was firm. "I want her to try this one first."

"As far as I know, he's not even broken to sidesaddle," Marcus cautioned him. "Certainly we haven't attempted to put one on him. In truth, he'd be better suited for a cart horse—or the knacker."

Peter shook his head. "He'd overturn a cart, I've no doubt. I still don't understand, Anthony—but I presume you have some method to your madness?"

"I do, indeed. Let's see if we can find a sidesaddle to fit him, shall we?"

He wasn't about to tell his brothers about Tessa's crisis of confidence last night, but he thought a difficult horse might be the very thing to restore it, reminding her that she was indeed special. While he'd have preferred a prettier animal, that really wasn't the point. She needed something to distract her from her worries about being accepted by his parents and Society, and he was pretty sure this fellow would do just that.

Tessa arrived back at Marland House only a few minutes after Anthony, two footmen following her from the carriage, laden with purchases.

"You appear to have made quite a haul, my dear," he greeted her cheerfully. "Shall we go upstairs so that you can show me all of your new fripperies?"

"If . . . if you'd like." Though he'd have expected such a shopping expedition to lighten any feminine heart, Tessa's expression was subdued, even guarded.

He waited until they were alone in Tessa's chamber to ask, "What's wrong? Is it the money? I know it must seem excessive, when you've had to pinch pennies in recent years, but—"

"No. Well, that is part of it, I suppose. Quinn told me that the duke and duchess had agreed to bear the cost, if necessary." He noticed that she did not face him as she spoke.

Anthony felt a spurt of irritation. "Kind of them," he said, knowing full well that such an offer was rooted in self-interest, "but it won't be necessary. I've a bit laid by. No fortune, of course, but more than enough to dress my wife properly."

"That . . . that is good to know." Still she did not meet his eye. "I would prefer not to be indebted to your parents."

He put a gentle hand on her shoulder. "There's something else, isn't there?"

She hesitated so long that he thought she wasn't going to answer at all, but then she said, in an expressionless voice, "We, ah, met an acquaintance of yours while shopping today. A Lady Adelaide."

"Lady Adelaide?" It took him a moment to place the name, but then he remembered the forward brunette who had been one of several reasons he'd left Town early last summer. "Oh, yes. But—what did she say? Was she rude to you?"

"Quinn thought so, but I imagine she was simply too surprised to think before she spoke. She seemed quite . . . taken aback when she learned of our marriage."

Anthony grimaced, remembering Lady Adelaide's triumphant smugness when she'd inveigled him into a most unwise kiss at the Creamcroft ball last Season. They hadn't been seen, thank heaven, and he'd been careful not to be alone with her again, but she'd made it clear she considered his moment of weakness tantamount to a declaration.

She'd begun accosting him at every gathering, even going so far as to write his name on her dance card herself on one occasion. He'd been pursued by other ladies—or their mamas on their behalf—but Lady Adelaide had been the most importunate.

He'd felt like a fox on the run from a very determined hound.

Between her pursuit and that of two or three other
determined young ladies, he'd decided to go north
immediately after Marcus's wedding to shoot before
cub hunting and then foxhunting began. Now he
wondered if that had been wise, for there was no
knowing what stories Lady Adelaide might have put
about in his absence.

"Lady Adelaide formed, ah, expectations based
on the slightest of attentions and refused to be discouraged, though I did try, believe me," he finally
told Tessa. "I promise you she was nothing to me."

"I see," Tessa said quietly, though he wasn't sure
she really did. "Quinn said the same, though of
course she was not in London until summer." She
turned away again. "Lady Adelaide is very beautiful."

Anthony took two quick steps to grasp Tessa by
the shoulders, then turned her to face him.

"Lady Adelaide is pretty, yes, like a hundred other
simpering London misses, but she holds not one-
tenth the attraction for me that you do, Tessa. Not
only are you far more beautiful than you realize, but
you have a strength of character that is exceedingly
rare—and that appeals to me far more than mere
beauty ever could."

Finally, she brought her gaze to his, her lovely
brown eyes sparkling with unshed tears. "Truly?"
she breathed.

"Truly," he replied firmly. "You are the only
woman I care for, Tessa. The only woman I've ever
really cared for. Why do you think I insisted upon
marrying you?"

For a long moment she stared at him, as though trying to divine his true thoughts from his expression. Then, to his relief, she smiled—not a happy smile, but a smile, nonetheless. "Thank you, Anthony. I'm sorry I doubted you."

Bending down, he kissed her lingeringly on the lips. "I can't help feeling it is yourself you have doubted, more than me, Tessa. But come, show me what you've bought. After that we'll have a spot of tea, and then I have a surprise for you."

He was doubly glad now that he hadn't listened to his brothers' advice in the matter of that horse. That snappish skewbald was just the thing to restore Tessa's confidence.

Tessa was feeling much more herself after a light luncheon accompanied by light conversation about London and Society, which allowed her to momentarily forget her worries. The duchess and Lady Bagstead largely ignored her, but she didn't mind that. Quite the contrary, in fact.

They had just finished eating, and the other two ladies had gone upstairs to dress for an afternoon engagement, when Quinn, Sarah, and their husbands arrived.

"Marcus tells me you've found a mount for Tessa, but he refuses to tell me which horse it is," Quinn said.

Tessa glanced at Anthony. "Is this the surprise you spoke of?"

He nodded. "Let's all walk round to the mews, and you can tell me what you think. Then, if everyone is amenable, we can take a ride in the Park, as the fog has lifted for the moment."

They waited while Tessa went up to change into her best riding attire—the fashionable new habit she'd ordered wouldn't be ready for two or three days—then they all walked down Grosvenor Square and around the corner to the mews that ran between Brook and Grosvenor streets.

"I hope you don't mind the walk," Quinn commented as they approached Lord Marcus's stables. "I suppose most people would drive, even though it would doubtless take longer."

"Goodness, no." Tessa tried to hide her amusement. "Why, it's three or four times as far from the house to the stables at Wheatstone, and I walk it several times a day." Were people in London really so lazy—or so bound by propriety? If so, she really would never fit in.

"Here we are," Anthony announced then. "What think you of this fellow, Tessa?"

She looked up at the rangy red-and-white blotched gelding he indicated and blinked. He was perhaps the least attractive horse she'd ever seen, and the angle of his ears implied that his disposition by no means made up for his appearance.

"Anthony!" Quinn exclaimed before she could speak. "This is a joke, is it not? Which horse have you really chosen for Tessa?"

Sarah, carefully keeping her distance from the gelding, looked to Lord Peter, who shrugged. "This is the one he insisted upon, is it not, Marcus?"

Lord Marcus nodded. "We both tried to dissuade him, believe me. But he was quite insistent. Perhaps now you can tell us why?"

Tessa glanced up at Anthony, who was grinning. "I thought Tessa might enjoy the challenge. Though of course, my dear, if you think he will be beyond you, we can find another mount—one of your choosing."

"I should think so," Quinn said. "This brute isn't—"

"I'll try him," Tessa interrupted her, glancing back at the gelding, whose ears pricked forward at the sound of her voice. "He is already saddled, after all."

Quinn stared at her, openmouthed, then turned on her husband. "And how did you even manage to get that sidesaddle on him?" she demanded. "I know just how bad-tempered that horse is, Marcus—not that it's his fault. He was badly mistreated by his previous owner," she explained to Tessa.

"It did take two grooms and a stable lad to saddle him," Lord Marcus confessed. "Really, Anthony, I must insist—"

But Anthony shook his head. "It's Tessa's decision."

"Tessa, you mustn't," Quinn pleaded. "His mouth is like leather and he's a biter, as well as a kicker. I know Anthony says you're a remarkable rider, but this horse could do you serious injury—and I'd never forgive myself if that happened."

"You can trust Quinn," Marcus said, "for she's an exceptional rider herself—but even she wouldn't try to sit this brute."

Tessa kept her eyes on the gelding, gauging his mood, examining his lines. He would be fast, she thought, though probably not smooth-gaited. "I appreciate your concern," she said. "Truly. But I'd like to try my hand at him."

Quinn tried to protest again, but Marcus shook

his head and she stopped, though she still looked extremely worried. "Let's get mounted ourselves," he suggested. "Anthony, you're riding Mephisto, I presume. Peter, Sarah, a groom has your horses down there, at the end."

While the others were occupied mounting their own horses, Tessa moved toward the skewbald gelding. "There, now, you funny-looking beast, you're not so bad as all that, are you?" she asked in her special singsong lilt. "You'd enjoy a bit of exercise in the Park, wouldn't you?"

He was nowhere as testy as Nimbus had been, much less Vulcan, and in under a minute was willing to let her place a hand on the side of his long neck. She stroked him, still talking, and he nodded his head, his ears now in a relaxed, forward position.

"There," she said to the openmouthed groom. "You can lead him out now."

Still gaping, the man complied, and Tessa walked alongside the gelding, one hand on his flank. They joined the others, who were already mounted. Quinn's mare, Tessa noted with approval, was both pretty and spirited, while Sarah sat on the most placid little gelding Tessa had ever seen—and still looked rather nervous.

They turned to watch as the groom tossed Tessa into the sidesaddle, all but Anthony staring in amazement. The gelding sidestepped, but quieted at once with a soft word from Tessa.

"I don't believe it," Quinn breathed. "How on earth—?"

Lord Peter shook his head. "It appears you weren't bamming us, Anthony. She really does have the touch."

Though gratified by their evident admiration,

Tessa felt suddenly embarrassed. "Shall we go?" she suggested.

With lingering, disbelieving glances from the others, they set out for Hyde Park. Tessa was careful to keep her mount well away from Sarah's so as not to make her inexperienced sister-in-law any more nervous, but Quinn had no qualms about bringing her mare alongside the skewbald.

"Anthony told Marcus you had an almost magical touch with difficult horses, but I confess I credited it to the besottedness of a new husband," she said. "I see now that I was mistaken. But how did you become so skilled?"

As they rode through the crowded streets of Mayfair, Tessa explained about her mother and her own gift with horses. "So I can't exactly take credit for it," she concluded, "any more than I can take credit for my eye color."

"But you can take credit for the use to which you've put that gift," Quinn said. "Someone blessed with a head for numbers can use it to make a business successful, or to falsify account books for his own profit. I can see that this horse is happier already with you riding him."

Tessa smiled, but Quinn's analogy troubled her, for she *had* used her gift for profit—and not necessarily in the most honest way possible. She would never do so again, of course, but other than making dumb beasts more comfortable, what real good had ever come from her ability?

They found Hyde Park nearly as congested as the London streets, so many people were taking advantage of the rare good weather. Anthony explained to Tessa that during the Season one could scarcely move along the paths, particularly at the fashionable hour of five o'clock. Now, of course, people tended to congregate earlier, as the days were shorter—and colder.

It was frustrating to keep to a decorous hand canter when her mount so clearly needed a good gallop, but Tessa realized that she was drawing enough attention already from the fashionable throng. Heads turned as she passed, and she heard snatches of conversation.

Some comments were complimentary. "Excellent seat," was a phrase she heard more than once, mainly from gentlemen.

But more than one feminine titter of laughter followed her progress, along with comments like "ugly horse" and "hopelessly outmoded habit."

She hoped Anthony wasn't noticing, for he'd been both kind and perceptive to realize she needed the challenge of this mount to snap her out of the doldrums. Still, she couldn't help worrying that her appearance—in her old habit, on this odd-looking horse—would reflect poorly on him in the eyes of Society.

They had completed two circuits of the Park—or, more accurately, Tessa, Quinn, and their husbands had, while Peter and Sarah had completed one, much slower circuit—and were preparing to head back to Grosvenor Square when Tessa saw Lady Adelaide driving toward them in a smart yellow phaeton.

"Why, Lord Anthony," she exclaimed. "What a surprise to see you in Town at this Season. Was the hunting so poor this year?" Her eyes flicked toward Tessa and then away.

He bowed from the saddle, a certain tightness about his lips. "Not at all, Lady Adelaide. I merely wished to bring my wife to London for a few days. I believe you have already met?"

She looked startled for a moment, as though surprised Tessa would have told him of their earlier meeting, but then flashed a brilliant smile. "Of course. I already expressed my congratulations to Lady Anthony, and now I can convey the same to you. Your new bride appears to be quite an . . . original."

Tessa could not help flushing at the woman's tone, which was anything but complimentary, as her haughty eye swept over Tessa's mount and attire. Anthony, however, responded without hesitation.

"She is indeed, Lady Adelaide. Not only original, but quite superior to any other lady of my acquaintance, I assure you. No doubt you—and the rest of Society—will agree, once you come to know her."

His words warmed Tessa, but there was a dangerous glitter in the other woman's eye. "Indeed?" Her voice was now rather shrill. "Well, we shall see, shall we not? Good day, Lord Anthony." With a sharp word to her driver, she continued on her way.

"Poisonous woman!" Quinn exclaimed. "Honestly, Anthony, I can't imagine what you ever saw in her."

"Nor can I," he said with a grimace, but Tessa felt chilled again. Clearly there *had* been something between Anthony and Lady Adelaide at one time, despite his earlier assurances.

"You won't let her jealousy bother you, will you, Tessa?" Lord Peter asked, riding up then. "For that's all it is, you know. Both Quinn and Sarah have had to endure backbiting from the London tabbies, but they've both survived it—and come out the stronger for it. I'm convinced you'll do the same."

Tessa couldn't help smiling at her perceptive

brother-in-law's comforting words. "Thank you, Lord Peter. I will try to prove you right."

"Now, suppose we head back," Lord Marcus suggested. "It's growing late, and those clouds in the west look rather ominous."

"Oh, my lady." Sally sighed when she finished weaving a strand of artificial autumn leaves through Tessa's hair. "You look like a fairy princess, indeed you do. You'll put them other fine ladies to shame, just see if you don't."

"I don't know about that, but thank you, Sally." Tessa eyed her reflection with mingled awe and relief.

The brocade ball gown became her well, in its autumn shades of rust, cream, and gold, accented by the red and gold leaves in her hair. It was lower in the bosom than anything she'd ever worn before and, with the support of her new corset, made her look quite buxom. Her shoulders and décolletage, at least, were creamy, and Sally had applied a dusting of powder that minimized the tan on her cheeks.

She *did* look far better than she'd have believed possible. Perhaps she would not disgrace Anthony at the ball tonight after all.

The past two days had been so busy, she'd had little time to worry, but now she couldn't help remembering how important tonight would be. The duchess had made it abundantly clear that Tessa's acceptance would depend on her reception at this ball, which would be attended by the very cream of Society.

"As the newest addition to our family, you will be examined most minutely," the duchess had told her that afternoon. "I trust that by now you've been instructed in everything that will be expected of you at such a function."

The family had certainly tried, Tessa had to admit. Anthony had brought in a pianist so that he could help her to practice the more fashionable dances. Lady Bagstead had drilled her on which people to befriend and which to avoid. And Quinn and Sarah had offered her all manner of advice and, more importantly, their unwavering support and friendship.

Still, she felt far from ready for the coming ordeal, becoming new gown or no.

Anthony and his eldest brother stood in the main hall, near the foot of the grand staircase, waiting for their wives. Conversation had been stilted and awkward, as the two had so little in common. Robert had no interest whatsoever in foxhunting or any other sports, while Anthony had little to offer on the topics of political influence or the latest scandals.

He was just giving thanks, yet again, that he was blessedly safe from inheriting a dukedom, when a stir on the stairs made him look up—and catch his breath. Beside him, Robert stopped his droning, apparently speechless for a rare moment.

Tessa was descending the staircase, resplendent in gold-shot cream brocade, her honey-colored hair upswept and wreathed in leaves that matched her unusual gown. Anthony was sure he had never seen anything more beautiful in his life. As she reached the bottom, however, he could see the uncertainty in her eyes, and hurried forward to take her hand.

"You are exquisite, my dear," he assured her. "Like a beautiful wood nymph."

Robert surprised him by saying, "Aye, you'll do very well, Lady Anthony. Very well, indeed."

Lady Bagstead and the duchess reached the landing just then, and swept down the last flight of stairs together, heads held high. "What's that, Lord Bagstead?" said his wife. "Oh. Yes. Quite nice, Lady Anthony. What say you, Your Grace?"

The duchess brought her lorgnette to her eye to examine Tessa from head to toe. "Passable, certainly. The leaves are a nice touch. Was that your maid's idea?"

"Lady Peter's, actually, Your Grace," Tessa replied, drawing closer to Anthony, as if for support. He placed a hand at her waist and gave her a small squeeze of reassurance.

A footman announced that the carriage was at the door, and the duke emerged from the library, where he'd been tending to some business. His eyebrows went up when he saw Tessa, and he nodded approvingly, though he did not deign to give her an actual compliment. Still, Anthony thought, it was something, after all the private criticisms he'd had from his parents since his arrival in Town.

Keeping a protective hand over the one Tessa tucked through his arm, Anthony escorted her out to the carriage, determined to make this one of the most memorable nights of her life. He couldn't help recalling the conversation they'd had in that gamekeeper's cottage—it seemed so long ago now—or her wistfulness when she'd spoken of visiting London. This would be her night to shine.

The carriage drew up in front of the assembly rooms in St. James's, where Lord and Lady Twyford were holding their ball, and Anthony felt Tessa tense beside him as she stared out the window at the arriving guests, all dressed in the absolute height of elegance.

"You outshine them all," he whispered encouragingly into her ear. He saw her swallow, but then she squeezed his hand and lifted her chin, showing him that she was prepared to go forward.

The coachman opened the carriage door and handed down the ladies in order of precedence, the duchess first, then Lady Bagstead, and finally Tessa. When the couples were reassembled at the foot of the steps, they proceeded up to the doors of the assembly rooms in the same order.

Lord and Lady Twyford waited at the top of the grand staircase to greet their guests. This time, when Tessa sank into her deepest curtsy, Anthony made certain to help her up at the precise right instant. Her grateful smile cost him a pang of guilt for his earlier lapse, the night of their arrival in Town.

"And now, the worst is over," he murmured to her as they proceeded into the brilliantly lit ballroom. "We have only to mingle and dance and respond to the compliments that are certain to come your way."

She looked up at him doubtfully. "You make that sound easy, but I've never done any of those things—at least, not in a setting such as this. It really is beautiful, though," she added, gazing around her in awe. "I never would have imagined there could be so many hothouse flowers available in November. And the candles—there must be thousands upon thousands of them."

"I'm glad you like it," he said, drawing her farther into the room. As he'd predicted, numerous people came forward for introductions, though most already knew who Tessa was, from the announcement that had appeared in that morning's papers.

"Charming," murmured Lady Jersey, after Tessa responded to her greeting. Other influential ladies and gentlemen also expressed their approval and admiration, complimenting Anthony on his good fortune in acquiring such a wife.

"You see?" he whispered. "You are a success."

The orchestra began tuning its instruments in preparation for the first dance, so he led her toward the center of the floor. "The first will be a minuet," he told her, probably unnecessarily. "You did beautifully with that one when we practiced."

She nodded, looking only slightly nervous, as they took their places in one of the lines forming.

Suddenly they were accosted by a voice he'd hoped not to hear tonight. "Ah, Lady Anthony," exclaimed Lady Adelaide, coming up just then with another lady who looked vaguely familiar, both of them trailed by the gentlemen partnering them in the opening dance. "I wanted you to meet a friend of mine, Miss Porrington."

Anthony bit back a curse at the name even as Tessa turned with a wary smile.

"I wished to meet you, Lady Anthony," Miss Porrington said, "for my brother mentioned a Miss Seaton in his letters. That was your name until your marriage, was it not?"

"It was," Tessa replied. Anthony was proud to see that her chin was still high.

The two ladies tittered together. "Then everything Penelope tells me must be true." Lady Adelaide's eyes glittered with malicious glee as she continued in a carrying voice. "That your father's estate is in shambles and that your mother"—she punctuated her words with a delicate shudder—"was a commoner. In fact, the daughter of . . . of a horse trainer!"

"Indeed," added Miss Porrington, "according to

my brother, you have even been in the habit of fox-hunting with the gentlemen, among those wild 'Meltonians' we hear so much about. Tell me, Lady Anthony, what is it like to flout convention so? Or do you even know the difference between proper and improper behavior?"

The two did not wait for a reply, but with a high burst of laughter moved down the line to find places well away from Tessa and Anthony. He was glad to see them go, but the damage had been done, for the lady to Tessa's left was looking at her askance while the gentleman to Anthony's left reached across the line to take his wife's hand and lead her to an entirely different set.

Heads began to turn all up and down their line and the next as the gossip about the new Lady Anthony spread through the room like wildfire.

Chapter 20

Tessa felt the color draining from her face at the unexpected attack. If the truth caused raised eyebrows in the Shires, how much more scandalous must it seem in the highest social circles of London? She looked bleakly across at Anthony, who was staring after Lady Adelaide and Miss Porrington with a face like thunder. She tried to mouth an apology as the music began.

His eyes snapped back to her face, his expression still hard. "Dance," he commanded her.

Confused, not sure whether he was angry with her or only at what had just happened, Tessa automatically complied.

Luckily, the minuet had been drilled into her when she was quite young, so that she did not have to think about her steps. Even so, toward the end of the dance, when a turbaned matron sent her an outraged glare, she stumbled, barely recovering her balance in time to avert a fall. She felt sure that every eye in the room was on her—judging her, condemning her.

The dance ended, and a moment later the Duchess of Marland and Lady Bagstead descended upon her, both fairly quivering with fury.

"What is this nonsense Lady Adelaide is spreading?" the duchess demanded, glaring at Tessa and then Anthony. "I know it must be false, but she must have based it upon something."

"What story did you hear, Mother?" Anthony asked with what Tessa thought was commendable coolness, given the magnitude of the disaster.

The duchess blinked at his tone. "Some faradiddle about Lady Anthony's mother being daughter to a horse trainer. I assume he was a gentleman farmer or some such, but Lady Adelaide is making him sound like the veriest commoner."

"It's true, Your Grace," Tessa forced herself to say. The truth could scarcely be concealed, as it was common knowledge in Leicestershire. "My maternal grandfather was employed as horse trainer by my paternal grandfather. He owned no lands of his own."

Both ladies gasped.

"And what of her other tale?" asked Lady Bagstead urgently. "Surely you have not actually ridden after hounds in a foxhunt?"

"She has indeed," Anthony said before Tessa could answer. "And extremely well, I might add. I don't see why—"

"Quiet, Anthony," snapped the duchess. "Of course you wouldn't see, as seldom as you are in Town, but I assure you that such behavior is the stuff of scandals here, however lax things may be in the country." Lady Bagstead nodded vigorously.

"The next set is forming," the duchess said then. "We must try to brazen it out for the remainder of the evening, and then we will determine what is to be done. I am most disappointed in you, Anthony—in both of you. See you do not disgrace us further tonight." With that, she turned on her heel, Lady Bagstead in tow.

Tessa swallowed hard, feeling tears prickling beneath her eyelids. "Anthony, I—" she began, but he shook his head.

"It's not your fault, Tessa. I should have known, should have warned you, should have . . . I'm sorry." He looked both angry and unhappy, and there was no doubt that she was the cause, whatever he said. "Come, we must do as Mother said and dance, pretending nothing is wrong. It's the only possible response."

Taking her by the hand, he led her into the country dance just beginning, resolutely ignoring the curious or outraged stares they received. Tessa followed his lead, keeping her expression carefully blank, though inside her heart was breaking—not for herself, but for the agonies Anthony must be enduring.

This was not her world, she reminded herself as she concentrated on her steps, determined not to stumble again. It had never been her world, and in a few days they would be back in the country. Surely, after this, Anthony would agree that they must never come to London again, she thought, striving to find a positive amid so many negatives.

Or, came the chilling thought, perhaps Anthony would simply resolve not to bring *her* to London again, when he came here himself. It would be a reasonable compromise, she realized bleakly.

The next dance was more complicated, requiring all her attention as she moved down the line from gentleman to lady and back to gentleman. Some of them seemed vaguely sympathetic, nodding politely as they turned about her, but others—mainly ladies—refused even to link arms with her when the dance demanded it, instead keeping their distance as they simulated the motions.

A waltz allowed Tessa a brief respite from censure, as for this dance she need not face anyone but Anthony. The strain of the evening was evident on his face, however.

"Perhaps we should leave early," Tessa suggested, too miserable to thrill at his touch, as she had during their practice session yesterday.

"We can't," he replied, his voice expressionless. "The Prince Regent has arrived, which means no one can leave until he does."

Tessa glanced about, excited in spite of herself at being in the same room with the Regent. "Oh, I . . . I did not know. Which one is he?"

Anthony motioned to the right with his head. "The heavyset gentleman in the regimentals."

She followed his glance and regarded the portly monarch with awe. That she, Tessa, simple country girl, should be in the same room with royalty seemed impossible. No wonder everyone here was offended by her presence. She truly didn't belong.

She opened her mouth to apologize again to Anthony, but stopped herself, knowing he would brush it aside again, that her apologies only made him feel worse. But what else could she do?

When they adjourned to the supper tables, it became evident that the rest of the family had been discussing that very question. Quinn, Sarah, and their husbands all greeted her warmly, but the other four faces were grave.

"I can't imagine what you were thinking, Anthony," Lord Bagstead began as they reached the group. "At the very least, you could have warned us, so that we could have prepared some sort of defense."

Anthony glared at his brother. "Do you mean to say that Father doesn't already know everything there was to know about Tessa's background? I'm stunned." He looked at the duke, as did everyone else.

"I knew about her parentage," the duke conceded, in no way apologetic, "though I did not expect it to become common knowledge in so explosive a manner. I had not had time to discover the financial status of Wheatstone or that your wife had done something so unwise as join the hunting field—as you no doubt intended, by waiting until the last possible moment to inform me of your marriage."

Tessa glanced at Anthony, who merely shrugged, his jaw clenched.

"And now I learn that Lady Anthony was apparently betrothed to her cousin mere days before you married her," the duke continued, "which also smacks of some sort of irregularity."

Lady Bagstead clicked her tongue and turned scandalized eyes on Tessa again, as though expecting her to do something outrageous on the spot. "So what are we to do, Your Grace?"

"I will take Tessa back to the country tomorrow," Anthony said with sudden decision. "I won't have her subjected to any more insult—particularly not from my own family."

"Yes, I think that would be best," the duchess agreed. "Give this thing a chance to blow over. By spring, or perhaps the Season after that, people will have moved on to other gossip."

Tessa's embarrassment and guilt over the grief she'd brought to her husband was assuaged for a moment by a surge of relief at this plan, but then Lord Peter shook his head.

"No, that's the last thing you can do," he said firmly.

Lord Bagstead frowned. "But—"

"Don't you see?" Lord Peter continued. "To run away is to admit that the gossips are right and we are wrong—that we are ashamed of Tessa's background. Are we not Northrups? *We* should set the standards, not allow others to dictate their standards to us."

The duke nodded slowly. "There is something in what you say. I could wish these facts had not surfaced in such a setting, but now they are out, we cannot allow certain people to use them as ammunition. The political situation—"

"Exactly," Lord Peter said, looking to the others for agreement.

Sarah spoke up in support of her husband. "My lineage is little better than Tessa's, after all."

"And I'm an American," Quinn put in. "Yet I am accepted."

Anthony still looked stubborn. "I won't have Tessa hurt by any more snubs. It is my responsibility as her husband to protect her, and I mean to do just that." He took her hand in a firm grip that felt more determined than affectionate.

"Nevertheless, I believe Peter is right," the duke said, in a tone that brooked no argument. "Anthony and his wife will stay—at Marland House—until we deem that Society has accepted her."

Tessa's spirits fell. Such a thing could take weeks—or months—assuming it ever happened at all. Was she never to be allowed to return to Wheatstone, to her father? She looked pleadingly at Anthony, but though he frowned, he said nothing.

"The Regent will likely leave soon after supper," Peter said then, "at which point we should probably make a strategic retreat. Tomorrow is Sunday, which will give us a respite to plan how to turn this setback into a triumph for Tessa and the family."

"I'm sorry, Tessa. I know I promised that we would only stay in Town a few days."

It was a few minutes past two, and Anthony had just joined Tessa in her bedchamber after her maid and his valet had completed their tasks of divesting them of their evening attire. She had put on a brave front during the final hour of the ball and the ride home, but Anthony suspected that she was near a breaking point.

Now she managed a smile, but her eyes were shadowed with weariness and strain. "It's not your fault, Anthony. If Peter is right, it would be folly to leave now, much as I long to return home. I only wish you had believed me when I told you I would not fit in here."

Anthony felt a fist of guilt squeezing his vitals. He had failed Tessa at every turn, it seemed, and now she would suffer yet more because of his arrogant assumption that he could shape the world to his liking.

"It is my fault." He placed his hands on her shoulders, soft but firm through the thin satin of her peignoir. "I should never have brought you here, torn you away from the place where you were happy. I have complicated your life terribly, Tessa, and I apologize for that."

She reached up to caress his jaw with gentle fingers. "Perhaps you'd have done better to simply make me your mistress after all. Maybe both of us would have been happier that way."

"No." He released her as though her skin burned him. "I've been happier since marrying you than I've ever been in my life."

But still her smile was sad. "Thank you for saying so, Anthony. But even if it's true, I'm not sure it will be enough. Already I am forcing you to miss the remainder of the foxhunting season. How many other inconveniences—even hardships—will I cause you? And how long will it be before you resent me for them?"

"Do you think any of that matters to me?" But even as he asked it, he knew that it did, at least a little bit. Foxhunting had been his passion for most of his life. Still, he would give it up in a heartbeat if it would make Tessa happy—not that it would.

"I'm far more concerned about you—and about your father. I know you are worried about leaving him for longer than you'd planned. I'll write tomorrow, let Rush and Lady Killerby know—"

"I'm . . . I'm sure Papa will be fine," she said with obvious effort. "He would not want me to run away before I can establish myself in Society."

He reached out to stroke her unbound hair, rippling in sensuous waves past her shoulders. "I just don't want to see you hurt anymore."

"Weren't you the one who warned me not to show

fear?" she asked, lifting her chin to meet his eyes squarely. "Surely that applies here as well. I simply have a whole herd of horses to win over now, instead of a few."

"Have I told you that you are a remarkable woman, Tessa?" His heart swelled with pride as well as love. "You will win them over, I have no doubt whatsoever. As you've won me." He pulled her to him for a kiss.

She responded eagerly at first, but as he led her to the bed, she swayed, understandably worn out by her evening's ordeal. Unwilling to tire her further, he ceased his caresses, instead drawing back the coverlet for her. With a sleepy, confused glance, she crawled beneath it.

Tenderly, he tucked her in, then kissed her brow. "Sleep, Tessa. Everything will look brighter in the morning." Then he returned to his own chamber, hoping fervently that his words would prove true.

When Tessa awoke the next morning, the sun was already streaming across the bed, reflecting in the dressing table mirror to cast a bright oval on the opposite wall. Confused, she looked around, trying to guess the hour. Where was Anthony?

Abrubtly, memory returned: the glittering ballroom, the evening that had started so well and ended so disastrously, her bedtime conversation with her husband . . . his sudden loss of interest in her kisses. Or had she dreamed that part?

But no, a glance at the other side of the bed showed that she had been the only occupant, her pillow the only one dented by use. Sitting up, she bit her lip, fighting down her disappointment. It was the first night since their wedding that they hadn't—

Quickly she rose, banishing that thought, trying not to blow it out of proportion. She had been tired. So had he. Still, it seemed a depressing harbinger of how last night's events would affect their marriage.

A tap at the door was immediately followed by Sally, bearing a tray of toast and chocolate—the very luxury she had imagined, but which today seemed a lonely way to breakfast.

"I thought you might be wanting a bit of something, my lady," the maid said, setting the tray on a low table. "Or would you like to dress first?"

Tessa took a sip of chocolate, but found its sweetness cloying. "What time is it, Sally?"

"Close on eleven o'clock, my lady, but Lord Anthony said I wasn't to wake you. Lady Marcus just arrived to see if you wanted to go riding, so I brought up a tray, in case you were up. She says it is quite the thing to walk or ride in the Park after services on Sunday—though of course you slept through them."

Though amazed that she could have slept so late, Tessa realized she must have needed the sleep. Quickly, she made a decision.

"Run and tell Lady Marcus I will be down directly, then come back and help me into my new habit." A ride would be just the thing to clear the cobwebs from her brain and make her feel like herself again.

"I still can't get over how well you manage that horse," Quinn said as she and Tessa entered the Park gates. "It was all I could do to lead him from the mews to Marland House without him biting my Tempest." She patted her mare's neck.

Tessa smiled, determined not to mind that Anthony had not offered to come along. She told herself that he had doubtless believed that she and

Quinn wanted time alone to discuss feminine matters, unlikely as that might seem for one as little accustomed to feminine pursuits as herself.

"I believe he is calmer today than he was before,
don't you?" she asked, mainly to divert her thoughts.

"Oh, yes. I wouldn't have dared lead him before.
Which also amazes me—that in scarcely more than
an hour on his back, you have already effected a permanent change in him. Have you considered training horses yourself?"

Tessa sent her a sharp look, but she appeared to be
quite serious. "Actually, that has been my dream for
years, though of course my father would never allow it. Think how that would scandalize Society, after the way they reacted to learning about my
grandfather."

"Oh, pooh," said Quinn dismissively. "Society
places far too much store on such things, in my
opinion—but then, that is my American upbringing
speaking, I suppose. My own father was as insistent
that I observe the proprieties as yours has been—not
that I always obeyed," she added with a wink.

"Nor have I," Tessa confessed. "In fact—" But she
stopped short of admitting that her poor judgment
had ultimately resulted in her marriage. It would be
to admit that Anthony likely would not have wed
her under normal circumstances, and she could not
bear to voice that thought aloud.

Luckily, a diversion occurred to distract Quinn
from her unfinished sentence. Lady Bagstead was
entering the Park gates just then in a dark green
high-perch phaeton, handling the ribbons herself. A
small boy sat at her side.

"Good day, my lady," Quinn greeted her cheerfully. "And good day to you, too, William. Out for

your Sunday drive with your mother? How grown up you look today!"

The little boy beamed, but the marchioness looked less than pleased. "Lord Northing, if you please. I did not know you and Lady Anthony meant to ride today." She glanced about. "Perhaps it would be best if you did not spend too much time speaking with me—or my son—until we know whether Lord Peter's plan will work."

"Afraid of contagion, my lady?" Quinn asked sarcastically, with a sidelong glance at Tessa.

But Tessa had been watching Lady Bagstead's horses, a beautifully matched pair of chestnuts. The one on the left kept trying to throw up his head, his ears flicking backward in evident irritation, rolling his eyes at every sound. The other, virtually identical in appearance, was calmer, but still skittish.

The temperaments of both horses seemed remarkably ill-suited for a lady's carriage.

"Have you often driven this pair together, my lady?" Tessa asked, interrupting Lady Bagstead's rambling explanation of how proximity to Tessa could damage her standing in Society.

She blinked. "Why, no. I just purchased them this week past. Are they not a handsome pair?" she asked with a critical glance at Tessa's unattractive mount.

"They are lovely, yes. Did they give you no trouble on your drive to the Park?" Perhaps her concern was misplaced.

"A groom drove here," she replied, and Tessa noticed a man in Marland livery hovering just outside the gates. "Then I took the ribbons, as I always do in the Park. It's quite fashionable, you know. But then, I suppose you *wouldn't* know."

Tessa sent a questioning glance at the groom, who was looking rather worried, but he only shook his head and shrugged. "Forgive me, my lady, but I can't help thinking this pair may be rather difficult to handle, particularly for a lady. Consider William—"

"Lord Northing," Lady Bagstead snapped. "I wish him to grow accustomed to his title and position as heir. And how dare you attempt to advise *me* on any matter whatsoever?"

Though her cheeks burned at the rebuke, Tessa felt conscience bound to make one more effort. "I was thinking only of your son's safety, my lady—and your own. If the horses should—"

"And now you criticize my driving, as well?" the marchioness huffed, glancing about again. The Park was growing quite crowded, and several people were now watching them with interest. "Good day, Lady Anthony."

With a flick of her fashionable whip, she set the pair into a brisk trot, heedless of the way the phaeton swayed when one started off more quickly than the other. Tessa frowned after them.

"Foolish woman," she muttered. "But perhaps I should have—"

"You did try, Tessa," Quinn assured her. "I don't know what else you could have—Oh! Oh, look!"

Tessa turned back to watch with horror. As the phaeton neared the Serpentine, a pair of swans took flight only a few yards away. The chestnut on the left shied violently and tried to rear, causing his mate to pull in the opposite direction. The phaeton, a precarious enough vehicle under the best of circumstances, lurched and swayed.

"Hurry, Tessa," Quinn exclaimed. "Perhaps you can—"

The rest of her sentence was lost, as Tessa was already kicking her mount into a canter. Before she could reach the phaeton, however, Lady Bagstead foolishly brought her whip into play, and with that extra goad the pair bolted.

With an unladylike curse, Tessa urged the rangy skewbald into a full gallop. Surely the Park rules did not apply in an emergency? People and horses were leaping out of the way of the careening phaeton as it sped along the path, first on one wheel and then the other. It could be only a matter of moments before it went over.

"Come on, fellow, we can do it," Tessa called to her horse, and he increased his speed until he fairly flew down the path, closing the gap with the runaway phaeton. She guided him alongside it, so that she could draw level with the panicked horse on the left. "Closer, closer," she chanted, both to herself and to her mount.

Responding to reins and the angle of her body, the skewbald drew within a foot or two of the chestnut. Wishing desperately that she were riding astride, Tessa leaned as far as the sidesaddle would allow and managed to get a hand on the chestnut's bridle. He tried to jerk away, but she held on grimly while her mount obediently matched speed.

"Calm down, calm down, it's all right," she called to the chestnut, putting every bit of her soothing lilt into her voice, despite her own fear. If only she could get a hand on the horse—

Though the phaeton still rocked wildly from side to side, the chestnuts slowed to a canter.

"That's better, that's better, you're doing fine," Tessa sang out, above the thundering of all three sets of hooves. With an extra stretch that nearly unseated her, she managed to touch the chestnut's jaw and stroked with quick fingers. "Slow down, now, slow down," she chanted.

The wild look left the chestnut's eyes and he slowed to a trot, his partner matching his pace. The phaeton steadied back on both wheels, swaying only slightly now. Though the main danger was past, Tessa did not take her hand away or stop cooing to the horses until they came to a complete stop.

Only then did she realize that she had come more than halfway out of her own saddle and was hanging off the skewbald at a precarious angle. Still, she waited until someone—some gentleman on a black horse—took control of the chestnuts before attempting to right herself.

"Steady, boy," she murmured to the skewbald as she awkwardly heaved herself back into position on the sidesaddle. "You may be ugly, but you're a noble fellow," she told the horse, gratefully patting his neck.

She was heaving a sigh of relief when the sound of cheering made her finally look around. A large crowd had come up to surround them and they were all smiling and applauding. Startled, she looked toward the phaeton. Lady Bagstead was clutching William to her, sobbing hysterically. The man holding the chestnuts' heads shrugged slightly, then relinquished the reins to Her Ladyship's groom, who came panting up just then.

"Three cheers for the heroine!" the man called out to the crowd. Immediately they took up the cheer, much to Tessa's embarrassment. At least they didn't know her name.

Quinn came up beside her, her face still pale with

her recent fright. "Three cheers for Lady Anthony!" she cried.

"Lady Anthony," roared the crowd. "Hurrah for Lady Anthony! Hip, hip, hurrah!"

Tessa's face was burning now, and she scarcely knew which way to turn. Then, behind her, she heard little William take up the cheer. Another surge of relief washed over her that she had stopped the phaeton in time. Glancing back to smile at the boy, she saw Lady Bagstead wiping her eyes.

With a shuddering sigh, the plump marchioness gave Tessa a shaky smile. "Hip, hip, hurrah," she said with the crowd.

Chapter 21

The news reached Marland House even before Tessa, Quinn, and Lady Bagstead returned from the Park. A breathless footman, completely heedless of protocol, burst into the library, where Anthony and his brothers were all closeted with the duke, taking the opportunity to discuss various family and estate business.

"Beggin' your pardon, Your Grace, but I thought you'd want to hear right away," the footman panted to their astonished faces. "I was runnin' an errand over by Park Lane and heard the hubbub at Grosvenor Gate. It'll be all over London in an hour, I'm thinking."

"What will? Out with it, man," commanded the duke.

"Why, how Lady Anthony saved Lady Bagstead's life, Your Grace—and little Lord Northing's, as well.

Stopped a runaway carriage single-handedly, the way I heard it. But no doubt they'll all be home soon and you can hear the story direct."

Even as he spoke, Anthony heard a commotion in the hall. He leaped up and hurried out of the library, his brothers and father on his heels, heedless of dignity.

"Tessa! Are you all right?" he exclaimed as his very disheveled wife entered on Quinn's arm.

She looked up at him rather dazedly, but Quinn was grinning. "All right? Lord Anthony, your wife is the bravest woman—nay, the bravest person—I've ever seen!"

Before he could do more than stare confusedly, Robert pushed past him. "Never mind that. Where is Augusta? And William? Is William safe?"

"What is going on?" demanded the duchess, descending the staircase just then to add to the confusion in the hall. "Why on earth is everyone shouting? This is most—"

"Augusta!" Robert exclaimed, interrupting his mother as his wife came in, supported by a groom. He hugged his wife and then his son, in the most indecorous—and human—show of affection Anthony had ever witnessed in his eldest brother. "Are you all right? Are you both all right?"

Lady Bagstead nodded, the evidence of recent tears on her strained face. "Yes, yes, we are both safe . . . thanks to Lady Anthony. Oh, Robert, I was so frightened." She threw herself back into her husband's arms.

"It was terribly exciting, Father," little William piped up. "The horses ran away with us and we were bouncing all over the place and Mother was screaming like anything! Then Lady Anthony rode up on her big spotted horse and just grabbed the reins and the horses calmed down—like magic! All of the people cheered and cheered. And then we came home."

Everyone turned to regard Tessa, who still stood rather awkwardly in the doorway. "I, er, could think of nothing else to do," she stammered, blushing deeply. "I know it was terribly unladylike of me, but—"

The duke came forward to take her hands in both of his and she stopped, gazing up at him fearfully.

"It seems we owe you a great debt of gratitude, my dear," he said in the kindest tone Anthony had ever heard him use. "Had you not been so quick-witted—and so skilled—Augusta and my grandson could easily have been killed. I, for one, am exceedingly glad that you were there . . . and that you are a member of this family."

Robert nodded. "As am I."

"And I," echoed the duchess and Lady Bagstead, both smiling at Tessa for the first time since Anthony had brought her to London.

Anthony moved to put an arm around Tessa's shoulders, pulling her against his side. She was trembling. "I can't say I'm surprised, but I'm very, very proud. Thank you, Tessa," he said.

Then, to the others, "If you don't mind, I'd like to take my wife up to her chamber. I imagine Robert would like to do the same with his wife. Both ladies have had a rather . . . full morning."

Everyone chuckled at this understatement, their laughter a release of tension.

"An excellent proposal," said the duke, while the duchess gave directions for hot baths to be prepared. "Lady Marcus, suppose you give us a complete account while our heroine and poor Lady Bagstead freshen and compose themselves. And then, my dear," he said to the duchess, "I suggest you see how quickly you can throw together a ball. I should say this event calls for a celebration."

It was truly remarkable what money, power, and determination could achieve, Tessa thought, gazing about at the glittering ballroom of Marland House the next evening. In only four-and-twenty hours, extra servants had been hired, all manner of delicacies prepared, and the cream of Society assembled for the Duchess of Marland's impromptu ball.

After her bath yesterday afternoon, Anthony had insisted on treating Tessa almost like an invalid, bringing her tea and dainties in bed and regaling her with every amusing story he could bring to mind. When she had insisted that she felt fine, he had only smiled and shaken his head.

"Quinn told us exactly what you did," he'd said. "You risked your life, Tessa, to save someone who has treated you most shabbily. In my opinion, there is no pampering, no reward, you do not deserve for such a selfless act."

"I only did it because no one else could," she told him, bemused by the pride and love shining in his eyes as he gazed at her. "You'd have done the same, had you been there."

He kissed her tenderly on the cheek. "Perhaps. But I doubt I'd have had the same success. You have a special gift, Tessa. Today you have proved it once again."

He had kissed her on the lips then, and further discussion was abandoned as they reaffirmed their joy at being alive—at being together—in the most satisfying way possible. Now, though, Tessa recalled his words thoughtfully.

Perhaps it was true that no one else could have done what she had yesterday. Always, she had felt certain she'd been given her ability with horses for a reason. Not for profit, not for pride, but for some higher purpose. Looking at little William, who had been given special dispensation to attend the first hour of the ball, she suddenly felt profoundly grateful for that gift.

"May I have this dance?" Anthony asked in her ear as the orchestra struck up the opening minuet.

Turning, she smiled up at him, feeling that her heart might overflow. "Of course."

That evening was everything Tessa had ever imagined in all her fantasies about a London debut—and more. It turned out that the gentleman who had taken the reins of the phaeton had been the Duke of Wellington himself—and that he had spread the story far and wide among the highest tiers of Society.

Now, gentlemen clamored to dance with Tessa, while ladies and gentlemen alike went out of their way to speak to her, to tell her how much they admired her courage and skill with horses.

Anthony, at her side, beamed with pride, which brought her more pleasure still, after all her worries about embarrassing him. Lady Bagstead had apologized repeatedly for her earlier coldness, and the duke and duchess had made a point of presenting her to the Prince Regent, who had put in an appearance at the ball just to meet the new heroine.

"I should say your success is assured," Anthony

told her as they concluded the waltz before supper. "Every door in England will be open to you now."

"Do you really think so?" Tessa asked, remembering how everyone had acted toward her only two nights earlier. "Society seems so fickle."

"Not when true heroism is involved. Indeed, hostesses will vie for your attendance at their entertainments, to give them added cachet. If you'd like, we can spend the winter in Town so that you may bask in your new popularity."

Though the idea had a certain appeal, she shook her head. "No, what I should really like to do is go home—to Wheatstone. Do you think your parents will mind, now that I am no longer a liability to your family?"

"I don't care whether they mind or not." He gave her a quick, scandalous kiss. "If that is what you wish, that is what we will do," he promised. "In fact, if you like, we can leave for Leicestershire the day after tomorrow."

Tessa smiled up at him, her heart again full. "Thank you, Anthony. I'd like that very much."

As the coach rolled up Wheatstone's long drive, Tessa drank in the sights and smells of home. It seemed as though she'd been away for months, rather than barely more than a week. Much as she'd enjoyed the return journey, she was glad it was nearly over. Not only was she eager to see her father again, the long hours in the carriage had made her restless.

"The Quorn meets tomorrow," Anthony said suddenly, as though reading her thoughts. "What say you we ride with them?"

She turned from the window in pleased surprise. "I should like that very much. I was just thinking how I longed for a good, hard gallop across country. I imagine you are, too."

He nodded. "I am, indeed. That's the worst of London, in my mind—and the reason I spend as little time as possible there. I'm happiest when flying across the countryside on horseback. Well," he amended, "there is *one* thing that makes me happier." He winked, and she giggled.

"I must admit, that has surpassed riding as my favorite, ah, sport, as well."

Anthony pulled her to him for a quick kiss, and then they were pulling up before Wheatstone's front door. Tessa smiled, thinking how pleased and surprised Papa would be to have her home again so soon. When a startled Griffith opened the front door at Anthony's knock, she hurried past him and up the stairs to her father's study.

"Papa! I'm—Oh!" She stopped on the threshold, startled to see Lady Killerby sitting with her father. Papers were spread over the low table between them, and they had apparently been busy with them.

Sir George looked up and smiled. "Why, Tessa! I did not look to see you for another week at the earliest." Then, with a sudden frown, "Everything is all right, is it not?"

With a curious glance at Lady Killerby, she continued into the room to kiss her father on the cheek, just as Anthony came up behind her. "Yes, Papa, everything is perfectly fine. But I missed you, and was anxious—that is—I take it everything has gone smoothly in my absence?"

"Indeed it has," he assured her. "Lily here has devoted many hours to helping me organize my notes. She believes I may have enough material here to write an entire book on the subject of foxhunting, and perhaps another on horse breeding."

Lady Killerby rose then to greet Tessa and Anthony. "Really, Sir George has amassed an amazing amount of information over the past few years. I've been trying to convince him to preserve it through publication."

"What a good idea," Anthony said, coming up to drape an arm about Tessa's shoulders. "Thank you for taking such an interest, Lady Killerby."

To Tessa's amazement, the older lady actually pinkened slightly. "It has been my pleasure. That is to say . . . It seemed the least I could do. As a neighbor, you know." She was almost babbling, looking to Sir George for support.

He beamed at her. "Lily has been a comfort as well as a help, after all of the recent changes here. I don't know what I'd have done without her."

Tessa blinked. Had her father and Lady Killerby developed a *tendre* for each other? At their age? It seemed unlikely, but there was no denying that they found pleasure in each other's company.

"I should be going," Lady Killerby said then, before Tessa could decide how she felt about this development. "Anthony, I presume you'll wish me to tell your friends of your return?"

"Yes," he replied. "I have a few things to discuss with them, so had thought to call at Ivy Lodge tomorrow."

"Why not have them here for dinner tonight?" Sir George suggested.

Tessa glanced at her father with surprise, but reminded herself that there was no longer any cause for alarm at such a proposal. That there never had been, in truth.

She therefore did not protest when Anthony offered to escort Lady Killerby back to Ivy Lodge and extend the invitation. In fact, she was grateful for the chance of a private word with her father—as she suspected Anthony had known.

"You seem . . . happy, Papa," she said as soon as they were alone. "I'm glad."

"Yes, I believe I am," he said with something like surprise. "But what of you, Tessa? You look a trifle worried. Come, sit here next to me, tell me all about your time in London."

Moving to her accustomed chair, she proceeded to regale him with an account of her visit to the metropolis, making light of both her embarrassments and her heroism. His eyes shone, however, as she told about stopping the runaway carriage and the resulting gratitude of the duke and his family.

"I doubt not they'll make a legend of it," he said when she concluded. "I'm sorry you had to endure such censure beforehand, though. Perhaps I was wrong to allow you to ride to hunt after all."

"Pray do not say so, Papa," Tessa exclaimed. "Truly, once the tide of opinion turned, many ladies were saying they wished to do likewise. Soon it may be commonplace, who knows? But you need not worry about my reputation now, in any event."

Sir George smiled, though his eyes were still shadowed. "I hope—that is, you are right, of course."

For a moment, Tessa bit her lip, debating, but then decided that she was done keeping secrets from her father. "Papa," she said gently, "I know what is worrying you. Anthony told me the truth about my birth."

"What? But he promised me—"

"It wasn't his fault," she said quickly. "Harold said something to me on my wedding day, and then I insisted Anthony tell me the whole."

Her father covered his eyes with his hand. "I'm so sorry you had to learn of it, Tessa. What must you think of me, after all of my strictures about propriety?"

She laid a hand on his arm. "I think you were young, very much in love—and very human, Papa, and it all came right in the end. I'm only sorry that Uncle Mercer was able to use it against you, against us, all these years."

He clasped her hand in both of his own. "You're the best daughter anyone could have, Tessa. I've never been able to truly regret what happened, because it resulted in you."

"Oh, Papa." She pressed her cheek against his, with a happy sigh, then heard a stir downstairs. "It sounds as though Anthony has brought his friends back with him. I'll go speak with Cook."

Dinner was a festive, informal affair. Anthony took great delight in embarrassing Tessa by telling his friends of her heroism in London. They seemed suitably impressed, and Sir George commented that he was glad to hear the details that Tessa had modestly omitted from her own account.

"The Duke of Wellington himself," he said more than once, with a fond look at his daughter.

After the sweetmeats had been served, Tessa rose. "If you don't mind, I'd like to visit the stables while you gentlemen continue your discussion."

Anthony grinned across at her. "Before we elevate you to sainthood? Very well, my dear, go on. We'll no doubt be in the parlor when you return."

With a self-conscious smile at the others, she went to get her cloak. Anthony turned back to his friends as soon as she was gone. "You said you had some news for me and Sir George?"

"Indeed we do," said Rush. "It concerns our friend, Mercer Emery. I thought you both might like to hear how we solved that little problem."

Anthony glanced at Sir George, who looked as surprised as he himself felt. "We are all ears."

"Well, after the conversation the, ah, day of your betrothal, and then after watching his behavior on your wedding day, I realized he still posed a potential threat."

"That he might spread word about Tessa's birth, you mean?" Sir George said, frowning.

Rush nodded. "He was still hanging about Melton. Not hunting, precisely—he's an execrable horseman, after all—but gaming and trying to insinuate himself into the better circles in the evenings. That was my inspiration."

Thor and Stormy chuckled, and Anthony looked from one to the other curiously, then back to Rush. "Inspiration for what?"

"Choosing my moment and my witnesses carefully, a few nights ago at one of the aprés-hunt gatherings, I, ah, made a disparaging remark about his late sister."

"What?" exclaimed Sir George.

"*You* did?" Anthony echoed disbelievingly. "But—"

"Mr. Mercer has become quite jealous of his reputation as a would-be gentleman," Rush continued. "Given the company and the preceding conversation, he had no choice but to challenge me over my rather . . . rude remark."

Anthony began to understand, though Sir George was still frowning. "After defending his sister's honor, he could scarcely besmirch it himself," Anthony explained to his father-in-law.

Sir George's brow cleared. "How clever of you, my lord. But what of the challenge? You did not kill him?"

Stormy snorted derisively as Rush shook his head. "I intended to miss, after scaring him badly—to shoot into the air, in fact, by way of admitting my error—but I overestimated his courage."

"The bounder never showed," Stormy put in. "Hasn't been seen since, in fact. As far as we know, he's left the area for good."

"And what of his son?" Anthony asked. "Is he gone as well?" He looked forward to telling Tessa she need never worry about her uncle or cousin again.

But Sir George was shaking his head. "I suspect not. Only yesterday, one of the servants said something about seeing Harold near the stables."

"Did you not find out what he wanted?" Anthony asked in surprise.

"I assumed he had merely stopped by to retrieve something he had forgotten."

"Let's hope that was it," Rush said, "though I'm afraid I wouldn't put it past the young rascal to make off with one of the horses, out of simple spite."

But it wasn't the horses Anthony was thinking about. "If you'll excuse me, gentlemen?" he said, heading for the door.

"I missed you, too, Cinnamon," Tessa was saying as she stroked the roan mare's soft nose. "But now I'm back to stay, and tomorrow we'll ride together again—in the hunt. I believe Papa will let me spend more time with you and the other horses from now on, as well. Won't that be nice?"

The horse whickered enthusiastically, just as though she understood Tessa's words.

"A nice little plan," came a voice from behind her. "Shame it won't work out quite that way."

Whirling in alarm, she saw her cousin leaning against the doorway of the stables. No one else was in sight.

"Harold? What are you doing here?" she demanded. "Where—?"

Grinning unpleasantly in the dim light of a single hanging lantern, he heaved himself away from the door frame and sauntered toward her. "All the stable hands are abed by now—and like to sleep soundly, after the bottles I gave them."

Tessa kept one hand on Cinnamon's neck. "Why would you do that?" He couldn't have known she'd be home tonight.

"I'd thought to take that mare off your little lordship's hands before you returned. Figured he'd have a time explaining that to you, not to mention that I could sell her for a fair price up north. But now I can take something he'll miss a sight more."

"You're mad," she exclaimed. "You can't seriously think you could kidnap me? You'll never even get me out of the stables."

His grin twisted into something far uglier. "Probably not. But then, I won't have to—and I'll still have the mare." He pulled a pistol from his pocket and pointed it at her.

"Father bought this for his meeting with Rushford, but then he got cold feet after hearing tales of the fellow's military exploits. He left for the north two days ago—but lucky for me, he didn't take this."

"Harold, think what you're doing," Tessa said as persuasively as she could, using the voice she used on difficult horses, her eyes riveted on the pistol. "If you leave now, you'll have done nothing illegal. You can begin a new life in the north, or wherever you wish to go."

"Don't try your sorcery on me," he growled. "Why should you and your lordling have it all your own way while I have to start over with nothing? Wheatstone was to be mine—Father promised me. He convinced me to put up with all your jibes and airs, your oh-so-superior ways. You don't know how many times I wanted to put you in your place, Tessa."

She swallowed, her fear growing. Harold had always been a bully, but she'd never known he resented her so badly. Now, it seemed, he was completely mad. "Please, Harold," she whispered.

"No. If I can't have Wheatstone, then neither will you—or your arrogant lordling." He raised the pistol higher.

"Perhaps the arrogant lordling will have something to say about that," came Anthony's voice from behind him.

With a curse, Harold swung around, but before he could aim the pistol at this new threat, Tessa flung open Cinnamon's stall. Together, she and the mare charged. Harold looked back, his eyes widening just before Cinnamon struck him with both front hooves. The pistol fired and Tessa screamed.

Terrified by the noise, all the horses screamed as well, some of them kicking at their stalls. Cinnamon reared and backed away. Harold, shaken but still clutching the pistol, struggled to his knees, but before he could rise, Anthony knocked him back to the ground with a well-placed fist to his jaw.

"Are you all right?" he shouted to Tessa.

Numbly, she nodded. The pistol ball was embedded in the door of Cinnamon's stall, having passed only inches from her head. Gathering her courage and her breath, she called aloud to the panicked horses.

"Calm down, calm down, all of you. It's over. It's over. It's over." As she chanted, the kicking and whinnying stopped, and in a few moments the stables were quiet once again.

Tessa looked down at her cousin, groaning groggily from his position spread-eagle on the stable floor. "He—he was going to kill me," she said, her voice breaking. "He would have, if you had not come, Anthony."

With two quick steps, Anthony reached her and gathered her into his arms. "But I did, thank God! It's over, Tessa. You're safe." Then, releasing her with obvious reluctance, "Now, suppose you go to the house and get the others while I keep watch over this vermin. Then we'll send someone for the magistrate and see what's to be done with him."

Harold only groaned again.

Anthony watched Tessa flying over the fields on Cinnamon's back with a profound sense of gratitude. How close he had come last night to never seeing this sight again, never holding her in his arms again! Not until he'd come so close to losing her had he realized just how deeply he loved her—her spirit, her selflessness, the way she shared his passion for riding like this . . . everything about her.

They had not gone to bed until well after midnight, for it had taken some time to get through the business with the magistrate. Now, though, all was settled. Harold Emery had agreed to leave the country, and word had been sent to his father, to give him the option of joining his son. The Emerys would never bother Tessa again.

"Reynard is giving us a good run, eh?" he shouted across to Tessa as they cleared a hedge together at the front of the field.

"A wonderful run," she called back, her cheeks and eyes bright from the chilly breeze and her joyful exercise. "I hope he escapes as his reward."

As it happened, the fox did escape, but not until he'd run the hounds till well past one o'clock. Riding back, everyone agreed that it had been the best run of the Season. The weather was bright and fair, and horses, hounds, and sportsmen—and woman— were all tired but happy.

Back at Wheatstone a short time later, Tessa watched her father and Lady Killerby laughing together as they talked about the hunt, which they'd again followed in Lady Killerby's phaeton. Her father looked happier than she'd ever seen him—so why were her feelings so conflicted?

"Come upstairs with me?" Anthony suggested softly in her ear, snapping her out of her bemusement.

"What? Oh, ah, all right. Papa, if you'll excuse us?"

Her father nodded absently, his eyes still on Lady Killerby.

"I hope you don't begrudge your father a bit of companionship," Anthony said as they reached the upper landing. "I confess I suspected once or twice that things were tending that way, and I'm delighted to see I was right."

Tessa paused, realizing that Anthony was right—she *was* bothered that her father so obviously enjoyed Lady Killerby's company. And perhaps even more bothered that he clearly didn't need her, Tessa, nearly as much as she'd always believed.

Anthony opened the door to the chamber adjoining her own, which had previously been used for storage. Mrs. Bealls had worked a miracle over the past week, doubtless with the help of some of the staff from Ivy Lodge. Most of Anthony's furniture had been moved here, to include the hunting scene Tessa had admired. Anthony had said last night that he felt completely at home here.

"You're right," Tessa finally said. "How can I begrudge Papa any kind of happiness when I have found so much myself? It will just . . . take a bit of getting used to, I suppose."

He took her hand and drew her into the room. "Changes always do, but that does not mean change is a bad thing. Some changes are very much for the better."

"Do you really think so, Anthony?" she asked, looking up at him anxiously. "I have all but turned your life upside down, made you miss part of the hunting season, and now you have even left the home you had made in the Shires—all for my sake."

He folded her in his arms. "Perhaps it began for your sake, but I am finding the benefits to myself are too many to count. Here, I can finally accomplish something worthwhile by helping you and your father rebuild Wheatstone into what it once was."

"Even the stables?"

"Especially the stables," he replied. "Though I believe you should be in charge of that area, Tessa. You've more than proved your abilities there."

Feeling as though her last dream had come true, she threw her arms around his neck. "Oh, Anthony, thank you. I'll make both you and Papa proud, I promise. And I'll behave myself, you'll see. I can be a proper wife as well as a horse trainer."

"Don't change on my account," he said, kissing the tip of her nose. "Propriety is overrated, in my opinion. As long as you're happy, I'd rather you stay the same, wild Tessa that I fell in love with."

She stared up at him, her heart in her throat. "Fell in—?"

His eyes now were serious as they looked into hers. "I love you Tessa, more than life itself. Never doubt that."

"Oh, Anthony, I love you, too—so much."

He tightened his hold on her and lowered his lips to hers. "We have our whole lives to show each other just how much, my beautiful, untamed bride," he murmured, and proceeded to demonstrate exactly what he meant.